MAGIC CITY MAYHEM

MAGIC CITY MAYHEM

MARCUS X. FIGUEROLA

BANNERMEN
BOOKS

MAGIC CITY MAYHEM

Published by Bannermen Books, Incorporated.

Bannermen Books is a nonprofit 501(c) (3) publisher of fiction dedicated to the development of genre literature and the support of emerging writers of fantasy, horror, science fiction, and historical fiction. To support new writers and to discover great literature, visit https://bannermenbooks.org.

Cover illustration: Andreu Zaragoza
Text design: Peter Burgess

First Printing, 2026

ISBN: 978-1-971703-00-8
Library of Congress Control Number: 2026937829
Cataloging-in-Publication data available
from the Library of Congress

Printed by Lakeside Book Company in the United States of America

For Mom and Dad, with all my love.

Prologue

"Dead Sunday: A Retrospective"

By **EMILY HARMON**, senior contributing editor,
Miami New Times

THIS WEEKEND MARKS the twentieth anniversary of Dead Sunday, the day when the dead rose and sprinted through our streets. Not since the Mariel Boat Lift, the Arthur McDuffie riots, or Hurricane Andrew had the streets of the Magic City come to such a grinding halt.

We all have our stories from that day—larcenous corpses, armed forces on high alert, the construction of Emérico's Aerie. The world seems comfortable letting the day pass into history. A paradigm shifting event became yesterday's news, the masses content to turn a blind eye to history. Despite what the media and the government would have you believe, there are victims of that day, people who continue to pay for the harm inflicted by waking the dead.

Alex Bueno is one of them. He is forty-nine now and walks with a cane. His living room and kitchen are conspicuously free of electronics due to his pacemaker, although you can hear his children playing video games down the hall.

Everything inside the house is sturdy and made of wood, but the house itself dates back to the 1960s, when cinderblocks reinforced with concrete were the order of the day. He says he chose the house because it withstood not only Hurricane Andrew, but Donna, Carla, and Camille. The wrought-iron bolted-on bars on every window hint at what the owner truly fears.

He asked me to turn off my cellular phone when I came in. I did so. He wouldn't let me use my tape recorder, so these notes were transcribed by hand.

"I had the early shift that Sunday. Sunday mornings are the worst at the morgue. Everyone getting stupid on Saturday night. But I didn't mind. I remember the receptionist telling me it was going to hit 97 degrees, so I'd rather be in the cooler."

The cooler is what the technicians call the morgue.

"My shift started at 2:00 a.m. By six, I was sitting down to lunch, four fresh bodies on the slabs. There's this thing that can sometimes happen. They'll twitch or contort, and it isn't pretty, because there's a lot of popping and snapping. I had heard it a few times—an arm, a wrist, an ankle. It's ugly.

"The stories get around, too, that sometimes a body will just sit up. I'd never seen it before, but I had heard.

"So I'm having my sandwich in the cooler, because at the time all the nurses were female and very clique-ish. One of the bodies, under a white pall, sits right up. You're never ready for that, you know? I calm down long enough for my pulse to stop racing, and then the other three sit up. When the first dude stands, that's when I started having my heart attack. All four of them got up and started walking out of the cooler while I'm going down.

"The last one, a teenager who wrapped himself around a telephone pole, picks me up! He must have been one-forty [140 pounds] soaking wet, but he just lifts me right off my feet, like I was nothing, and drops me on the receptionist's desk. I was in too much pain to remember, but Arlyene [Rodriguez, the receptionist] tells me he tapped my chest then walked right out, naked as the day he was born, following the other three."

Bueno, now on disability because of his pacemaker, volunteers at the VA helping returning soldiers with PTSD.

The dead continued to rise at Mercy Hospital and all over the city. These workmen of the damned sought not the brains of the living, but brick and mortar and rebar and nails. At first, they rose sporadically from the hospitals, but then the curse spread to the smaller cemeteries: Pinewood Cemetery and Miami Memorial Park in South Miami, as well as Charlotte Jane Memorial in Coconut Grove. Even though it was early, the number of traffic accidents began mounting up.

Sergeant Sandro Jimenez was a deputy at the time for the City of Miami. He and other officers were stupefied by the number of incoming reports. He responded to a civil disturbance at George Washington Carver Middle School. At the time, the school was being remodeled, and there was construction equipment and material everywhere.

"I was on patrol at 6:30 in the morning when we got the call. Fourteen officers responded. When we arrived at the scene, there was no mistaking what we were looking at. Those were dead bodies running around, carrying bags of cement and two-by-fours.

"It was very tense. The locals were all standing around, watching, and every single one of them was armed—machetes, handguns, I even saw one guy with an AK-47. They were scared.

"A powder keg, that's the word, right? You only see this type of [expletive] in movies. I thought [expletive] was really over when a man ran up to one of them and chopped the head clean off. I'll never forget it; he dropped his machete when the body ran away carrying a cinderblock in each hand.

"By that point, my sergeant was on scene and telling us that we were supposed to give them a motorcade. A [expletive] motorcade. I didn't hear [then-Mayor] Manny Diaz on the radio because I was following the stiffs with my sirens on."

The victim, in this case, was the decapitator. Sgt. Jimenez explains: "The dude who cut off the corpse's head killed himself a few weeks later. His name was Randall Jackson. The person he decapitated turned out to be his brother. When the brother's corpse returned to the cemetery, he did so without a head. I don't think Mr. Jackson could live with the guilt."

Mayor Diaz declared a state of emergency by 8:00 a.m. During his broadcast, the bodies interred at Dade South Memorial Park and Woodlawn Park Cemetery emerged and made their way to—of all places—the nearest Home Depots.

Candace Williams was working at the Home Depot on Coral Reef Drive when her grandfather, laid to rest two months earlier, shambled in with about 1,300 other corpses. "I damn near had a heart attack!" she laughs now. "I always loved Grandfather Williams, but I didn't expect to see him again so soon! I thought, Lord, help me, Lord, help. This cannot be happening. Judgment Day can't be so soon.

"Then I saw all my coworkers. They start grabbing shovels and axes, and I tell them, 'You touch my grandfather, and I'll take that axe to you!'

And sure enough, they put down the tools and let the dead do their business."

These dead, and those at the Home Depot on Eighth Street, gathered every piece of hardware they could and waited patiently at the registers. "My coworkers were all just watching, and I pushed past them and grabbed my granddad by the arm, and I asked him what he was doing and he pushed a hammer into my hands. He didn't say nothing, and I didn't need him to. I took him to my register and rang him up."

I ask her how he paid. "Oh, *Lord*. You know. Everyone knows, I guess." Ms. Williams is referring to the Spanish galleon *Santa Inés* floating across the city. The *Santa Inés* was part of the Spanish Plate Fleet that disappeared in 1715, en route to Spain from Cuba, carrying a small nation's GDP in silver and gold coins. The ship emerged from Biscayne Bay and floated through the air like a dirigible. It followed Eighth Street before heading south. A crew of ambulatory skeletons disembarked and left a small chest full of gold coins at both Home Depot locations. "My manager didn't know what to do, so of course I had to call and ask the region supervisor if we accepted the coins," says Williams. "It was a whole to-do. But we did, and my grandfather tipped me a bag of coins before he left." Ms. Williams never divulged how many coins she received, but apparently three were enough to get her through a Bachelor's degree and M.B.A. She still works for Home Depot, but as Regional Vice President.

While Ms. Williams may have fared well, two men expired at the Home Depot on Eighth Street, one from a heart attack, the other from a stroke. Ambulances could not reach them in time, and they got up and joined the host of the dead.

The *Santa Inés* floated down the Turnpike, trailed by some 1,600 corpses carrying their legally-purchased sundries. It took them several hours to reach the Florida International University campus, but by then, the contingent from Eighth Street had already begun clearing the grounds and erecting scaffolding. The city watched as the *Santa Inés* was disassembled, her planks used to erect a Gothic spire. The tower of brick and concrete was built by bodies whose souls had long departed. Santa Inés Hall, or Emérico's Aerie, or the College of Practical Arts (whichever name you prefer) stood.

While stained glass now decorates every floor of the College of Practical Arts, on Dead Sunday the highest level was open to the elements, revealing the inner gothic columns and the black marble throne cobbled together while the rest of the concrete hardened.

Victor Preston was a low-level correspondent for Fox's Miami affiliate, WSVN 7, when the dead were shuffling back to their final resting places. He convinced Captain Michael Monoghan to get the station's helicopter in the air, violating military no-fly orders. "How do you ignore the story of a lifetime? I couldn't. No cameraman would come with us, so I stole the nearest shoulder cam and Mike got us in the air."

After a tense flight, with Southern Command yelling at Monoghan to land immediately, Preston trained his borrowed camera on the top floors of the tower. Monoghan circled, until Preston got the generation-defining shot: a robed skeleton with flaming blue eyes emerging from a sarcophagus. This was the city's first glimpse of Emérico de Menezes.

"You can hear me on the tape yelling 'Steady!' at Mike. We crept around to a hover, and between all those columns, you watch the lid open. Smoke and blue light pour out of the thing, and then Emérico stands up, this floating skeleton. They gave me a Pulitzer and a Peabody for those shots." Preston said this unapologetically. Captain Monoghan sits in prison to this day, serving out a twenty-five-year sentence for disobeying direct orders from the military.

According to sources, the future Chancellor of the College of Practical Arts, yelled down to the police below. He asked to meet with the Dean of FIU. Not the President of the United States or the Secretary-General of the United Nations. Dr. John Levin, Dean of Florida International University.

"I wasn't on campus, of course," Levin says. "The only audio on the camera was [Victor] Preston and the helicopter, so I had no idea he was calling for me. The police showed up around 5:00 a.m. on Monday, but I was awake. There was nothing that could have ripped me away from the television. I'm sure it was the same for everyone else.

"They drove me to campus and I couldn't believe what I was seeing. Right between the performing arts center and the football field was a building that hadn't been there on Friday, and standing in front of it was a shrouded, walking skeleton, smoke pouring off of him.

"'John, hello!' he said when I approached. The English accent was unexpected. 'I'm so sorry to bother you, but I was hoping to get started immediately. Don't worry, it won't kill you to shake my hand.' So I did, and here I am." He holds up his hand for me; there are four lines across his palm. "Frostbite. He did apologize. Everything else was business."

What business?

"Establishing the College of Practical Arts as a branch of the University. He told me potential candidates would begin showing up at dawn, so get the appropriate documentation to him immediately. Accepted applicants would then be directed to the admissions office."

And you just let it happen?

"Let it? How do you fight the sun rising?"

The sun did indeed rise. The dead returned to their graves, while the living clamored to get inside the College of Practical Arts. Meanwhile, the rest of the world woke up from a fugue, surrounded by chaos, clamoring for answers.

Those answers came directly from Emérico Abílio Ovidio de Menezes. He met with everyone who asked, including Mayor Manny Diaz and President George W. Bush. He answered their questions, was fast-tracked through naturalization, and even repaid all the damages that could be directly attributed to him and the legion of dead men that had run amok across Miami.

Twenty years later, the College of Practical Arts stands as an institution that draws students from all over the world. But that building came at a heavy cost that no one in the Magic City should ever forget.

1
Jobs Aplenty

I WISH I WAS the wizard that arrives precisely when he means to. My clients deserve punctuality, since I allow them to speak to the dead one last time. But Miami is a death sentence for timeliness.

Dade South Memorial Park is sandwiched between the Turnpike and a residential neighborhood. Chain-link fence separates the cemetery from the Turnpike and provides commuters with a glimpse of the inevitable. An archway stands at the entrance, bearing a tile mosaic of Saint Uriel the Archangel at its zenith. St. Uriel wears gray robes, holds scales in his left hand, and a lantern holding the sun in his right. He is only mentioned in apocryphal writings, which sometimes rubs Catholics the wrong way, but the choice has always seemed obvious to me—the Archangel of Death guarding a cemetery.

Late as usual, I feel judged as I pass under the archway. The burial is at eleven. A post-mortem interview usually doesn't take more than an hour but I know I'm going to have to deal with Benito Jimenez, the director. My tardiness gives him an excuse to treat me as a subordinate.

Opulent royal palms shade the central boulevard leading to the management office. Live oaks line the wide thoroughfares between the headstones. A yellow, single-story building serves as the management office. I park my run-down Civic between Jimenez's BMW and the groundskeeper's rusty pick-up.

I tug open the pane of glass that serves as a door. Large windows light the cramped office, turning the bone-white tiles and walls yellow. Six cushioned chairs crowd against the wall across from the open receptionist's sliding-glass window, making the place feel like a doctor's office.

Maggy peeps above the counter and smiles when she sees me. She's a large woman, well-tanned, motherly, and she's sweet on me. "*Buenos días, Doctor Díaz*," (Good morning, Doctor Diaz) she says.

"Good morning," I say back in Spanish. I lean in through the window and give her a kiss on the cheek. If I didn't, she would be offended.

"*Cafecito*?" (Coffee?) She holds up a tiny Styrofoam cup with a plastic cap. Let me be frank: I play with magic, with the unthinkable; I have pushed my hands through the ether and wiped away the essence of life and death itself; but what Maggy offers me is the most powerful concoction I have encountered. Cuban coffee is just espresso, but the foam is four tablespoons of sugar. I know how to make it, but I never have time in the mornings. The whole of Miami runs on Cuban coffee. If you ever want to decimate South Florida's productivity, just bomb the Bustelo plant.

Maggy makes the offer, even though she sees me carrying a thirty-ounce cup of iced coffee. She proffers a thimble-sized plastic cup out of genetic habit. I take it. "Thank you," I say.

"You're welcome, *papi*. You're late again."

I smile and throw back the shot. "Are they in there?"

"Talking. You're okay."

I take sweet relief from her beautiful, chubby face. "How many?"

"Just the widow."

They come in expecting a lot, and Jimenez is the front man who lets them down, grounds them, making sure they know the rules. I'm not working a miracle; I'm just accessing memories. They're not going to speak to the deceased, just to the storage system for memory. Information can be accessed, yes or no questions can be answered, but emotions, closure? Those things are beyond my reach.

"What are you reading?" I ask.

"The Russians are at it again." She sucks her teeth and flips *El Nuevo Herald*—the Spanish-language sister newspaper of the *Miami Herald*—around to face me.

Spanish was my first language, the language of my immigrant parents, but I stopped reading it after high school. I struggle with the headlines, but the picture of a police boat loaded with black body bags speaks louder than words.

Maggy taps the picture. "The bodies were missing their tongues, hands, and teeth! ¡*Que salvajada*!" (What savagery!)

Whoever did that was smart. They must know what I can do with a dead body.

Jimenez pokes his head out of the back office and grimaces. "Practitioner Diaz, would you mind joining us?" When he asks me into the room in English, I know what language to speak when I get inside.

The honorifics of being a wizard are tricky. Officially, I have a doctorate, so on paper I am Doctor Pablo Diaz. I serve as the Necromancy Department Head at the College of Practical Arts, so among wizards and other magical creatures my title is Archmagus. But practicality—that loathsome place between the officious and the magical—came up with the title 'practitioner' to imply someone who works with magic, an annoying catchall meant to pigeonhole me. Jimenez only ever uses the honorific when he is upset. I swallow this insult.

I chug the rest of the iced coffee and start looking for a garbage can. Maggy motions for the cup. "Thank you," I say.

"*A la orden, mi corazón*," (At your service, my heart) she says.

My breathing becomes choppy. My pulse quickens. I wring my hands. I have done what I am about to do hundreds of times. But the nerves always jump. The opportunity to do what we love, even when we have done it countless times—the unique and mundane nature of performance—may be at the heart of all human achievement.

I walk into the ritual room, the largest area in the office. Armless wooden chairs dominate the walls. Black-out curtains stymie all but one of the windows. The floor is empty, save for a casket. Jimenez and the bereaved flank the casket, but he stands while she sits.

"Good morning, Mr. Jimenez," I say.

"Good morning," he says, hands folded in front of him. Jimenez has always played the role of the mortician well. I can't imagine there's more than a foot of space between his bald head and the ceiling. He has dark bags under his eyes, a wide forehead, gaunt cheeks, and a pencil thin mustache. The Latino Lurch. He looks down his nose at me and motions to the other person in the room. "Mrs. Maria Batista, this is Practitioner Pablo Diaz."

"I am sorry for your loss." I extend a hand to her.

The Widow Batista takes it. "Thank you." Behind a black veil, I can see the wrinkles radiating from her lips—a smoker. Otherwise, her skin is still taut. Her lips are well-rouged. Mascara smudges the underside of her eyes. "René was a good man," she says.

She turns in her seat and lays a hand on the coffin behind her. The belly of the man inside of it rises above the lip of the casket. His jowls reach below his collar, his neck threatening to devour his chest. His hands are folded awkwardly over his stomach. Even in death, this man's body seems to find no comfort.

"This is not an easy procedure, Mrs. Batista. Are you sure you want to go through with it?" This is a lie. For me, it couldn't be easier. But hearing the voice of a deceased loved one is a volley of rocks against the glass of our souls.

She nods, so I begin to set up. "Remember, yes or no questions are easier, and don't be frightened. There is no soul in the body. Only motion." I jut my chin toward the curtain and Jimenez closes the remaining open window. I open my doctor's bag and pull out my occult accoutrements: a black silk pall, a candle made from the rendered fat of a yearling calf, an earthenware jar full of coarse sea salt. I drape the body. I light the candle at the head of the casket and wait for Jimenez to turn off the lights. I pour salt from the jar over the corpse. I speak a few syllables unfit to print. There is a hiss as the salt drags itself over the silk, taking the same pattern as veins. The granules begin to glow blue. I take a pinch under my tongue and place a hand on the deceased's forehead.

"You may ask your questions, Ms. Batista," I say.

She might be on the verge of sobbing. "René?"

The salt burns. "The questions, please," I say, trying my best to keep my voice level.

"Did you love me, René?" Mrs. Batista says. Nine times out of ten, this is the first question my clients ask. They might word it differently—*Did we live a good life together? Was our marriage worth the pain?*—but the sentiment is the same.

Under the pall, the muscles of the jaw creak and pop. "Yes." Barely a whisper, but unmistakable.

She sobs. "Did you cheat on me?"

"Yes." The words are René Batista's, but the life in the corpse is my own. The salt veins pulse to my heartbeat. I am sweating. Hot wax drips down my fingers.

"With who?"

"Margaret, Estrella, Lourdes..." The corpse rattles off a litany of indiscretions, robbing René Batista of the dignity death might have ensured. The corpse finishes its catalogue with, "And whores."

Maria Batista covers her mouth, trying to muffle her sobs.

I keep my mouth open as the salt sublimes. The wisps of white smoke dissipate quickly. The same happens on the corpse. I grab another handful from the jar and let it slide through my fingers onto the pall, then throw another pinch in my mouth.

"Mrs. Batista," I say, "please continue."

She gathers herself up. "Why cheat, René?"

"They did what I wanted," the corpse says.

Maria Batista jumps up and slaps the lip of the coffin. "Don't I mean anything to you?"

"You're my wife." Rene's thoughts distilled into inscrutable simplicity, sure to provide no comfort.

I watch her hands grip the edge of the casket. She stands a little taller. "That's enough," she says.

"Are you sure?" The ember in my mouth is horrific, but this is my job. Satisfaction guaranteed.

Maria Batista frowns. She glares at what was once her husband. "What happened to Bati?"

"I broke his neck."

She thumps on the casket. "I knew it!" She rests her chin against her own chest with a sigh. "You can stop," she says to me.

I snuff the candle with my fingers. The salt on the body goes up in a large puff while the salt in my mouth fizzles. I flick the lights back on. "Water, please." Jimenez goes out. "Mrs. Batista, I have to ask who Bati is, because if I have learned of a crime, I have to report it to the authorities. You understand."

"Bati was my parrot twenty years ago. No crime, except the ones against me. And it is *Ms*. Batista. Thank you very much, Practitioner Diaz. Pablo." She walks away.

Jimenez returns and hands me a water bottle. I chug the entire thing. He tries to talk to me, but I can't hear him. "What?" I say.

"Are you okay?"

"I'm fine. Do I not look okay?" I retrieve some hand sanitizer from my bag and apply it liberally.

Jimenez purses his lips. "A bit pale," he says.

"I don't get to the beach a lot." I begin gathering the magical paraphernalia.

Jimenez watches me from the doorway. "Such frivolous questions."

"Tell her that when she signs the check."

"She already has. I'm sure you'll want your *cut*, as well. Follow me." He doesn't wait to see if I follow.

I join him in his putrid green office. Black and white photographs in ostentatious gold frames hang on the left and right walls, showing the groundbreaking of the cemetery and Jimenez's ancestors. Jimenez sits at his formidable credenza writing out a check from a tome-sized ledger. Behind him, an austere display case filled with sample urns partially blocks the window on the back wall.

The charge is $5,000 for a post-mortem interview. After taxes, Jimenez takes fifteen-percent, leaving me with less than $3,000. "I will never understand you, practitioner," Jimenez says. "You could easily ask for double and people would still pay."

"Asking for any more would be predatory."

Jimenez rips out the check and holds it out to me. "Do you know the difference between you and I?"

I can still be classified as a mammal? "Tell me," I say instead and grab the check.

Jimenez doesn't release it. "I know what my expertise is worth. This is a business. These people would give us absolutely nothing if we didn't take it." He lets go of the check and straightens the front of his jacket. "You peddle a fantasy, but all you cause is pain. And you are never on time."

The word 'pain' conjures Maria Batista's face when the corpse of her husband listed off his dalliances. I purse my lips and stare at him. "Did you know that curses fall under the purview of necromancy?" I wait until he looks away. Only then do I fold the check in half and stow it in my breast pocket. "I will be conducting the senior-level Necromancy Laboratory on the grounds this evening."

"I am well aware," Jimenez says. He keeps his eyes down.

"My students and I will be sure to maintain the sanctity of your grounds through proper warding. Something, I think, that your *customers* appreciate." My cell phone chimes in my pocket. "Is there anything else?"

"No," he says.

"I apologize for my tardiness. It won't happen again," I say, knowing it to be a lie. I pick up my doctor's bag and leave.

There's nothing anyone can do about traffic in Miami. From sunrise to sunset, the streets are packed with the inconsiderate and hostile masses trying to force their way into your lane and then slowing down as soon as they get there. No amount of magic can influence them, and what should be a twenty minute drive takes me over an hour.

Tucked away behind a local bar and a cigar shop in South Miami is Smoke and Lace, a gentlemen's club. I've never seen gentlemen inside the club. But I haven't seen police tape outside the entrance before, either.

The text I got earlier was from Sergeant Sean Richards. I try to pull into the parking lot, but a deputy stops me. He radios Richards then waves me through. I bring my doctor's bag with me, because Richards only calls me for one reason.

The metal door to the bar is open. I have to explain who I am to another officer. Usually this place is a smoky neon hole. Even at 11:00 a.m., it still reeks of stale beer and cigarettes, but the fluorescent lights are on, and there is nary a stripper to be found.

"Diaz!" Richards calls to me from across the main stage—a two-foot high platform with brass poles at each end, flanked by two levels of small tables and large armchairs. He's wearing a suit, not a uniform. He's tall, steely-eyed, with a severe, clean-shaven face that is all angles. His posture towards me is always friendly, though; I make his life easy. He extends a hand as I approach. "Always good to see you, Practitioner." He uses the title because I've never corrected him.

"Good morning, Sergeant. Give me the rundown, please."

"Not much to tell, really," he says as he leads me to the back of the club. "Around closing time, there's a gunshot in the bathroom. The place clears out. No one saw the shooter—probably got away in the stampede."

"Where's the bathroom attendant?" You can't go to a strip club in Miami without a dude in collar and cuffs hawking wares—gum, cologne, single cigarettes. "He's the victim." Richards pushes open the bathroom door. Face-down in a pool of blood is a rather skinny black man. He wears good dress pants and shoes, a well-starched white shirt, and a horseshoe of gray hair. "At least he's already dressed for the funeral. Just need to get him a jacket."

The blood makes my knees buckle. I lean against the door frame and take a few deep breaths until the nausea goes away.

"Pussy," Richards says and laughs.

"Listen, I deal with them when they're cleaned up."

"Well, you know how these things are. The faster we get a name, the more likely we are to get a conviction."

"Is forensics done?"

"Yeah."

I know how messy this is going to get. "I'll need someone to turn the body over. And a chair."

"Sandobal! I need a hand!" A female officer comes in, well-tanned and blonde; she's also in a suit. "Detective Sandobal, this is Practitioner Pablo Diaz." We shake hands. She and Richards don latex gloves from a box on the sink and flip the body. Blood plops and squelches as they do so. Dark gore has congealed and caked this poor man's face.

I put on latex gloves and use a few napkins from the sink to wipe as much off his forehead as I can. "A chair, please, detective." Sandobal runs out and comes back quickly with a black metal folding chair. I set it up at the edge of the pool and try to lean down, but the position is supremely awkward. I sigh. "You're paying for my dry cleaning," I say to Richards. I sit at the edge of the pool of blood.

"Just turn in your receipts with a req form."

"No, you know that takes forever. You're paying, and *you* turn in the requisition."

He bunches up his lips. "Fine, fine."

"My bag, please," I say. He passes my bag over the body. "Hit the lights." He does so. "What was this man's name?" I take out the candle and jar of salt. The pall isn't necessary, just a courtesy for the bereaved.

"Emmanuel Philippe-Auguste," he says as he tries to back away from the door frame.

"Not staying?"

"Hell, no. You know I hate this shit."

"Pussy," I say and light the candle.

Detective Sandobal moves into the light of the doorway vacated by Richards. She holds up her phone.

"What's that for?" I say. "Evidence gathered by magic isn't admissible in court."

"Not every perp knows that," she says.

"Have you seen this before?" I ask.

"No."

"Are you sure you want to?"

"I have to." She swallows. "Say when."

I smirk. Maybe Detective Sandobal would like to get a drink. I light the candle, and I know it will be easier to work the spell, because Sandobal is curious and I want to show off. I throw the salt into the air and speak the syllables. They land in the pattern of veins, glowing blue. I place my hand on Mr. Philippe-Auguste's forehead. "I need you to put some of the salt in my mouth."

"What?"

"From this jar." I motion with my head. She skirts the body, goes around me, and takes a handful from the jar. "Just a pinch," I say, open my mouth, and stick out my tongue. She sprinkles it onto my tongue, lightly at first. I have to mumble the word "more," until she gets the idea.

We have such a unique relationship to fat. Chewy, savory, sickening in excess. Similarly, salt can season as well as slay. I don't need the candle or salt to work my magic. But my mental associations with the items—the rendering of fat into useful tallow, salt crystallizing as seawater evaporates—focus my mind and my will, until I am able to do the impossible.

"Did you see who shot you?" I say. I've done this enough times that I know the usual questions Richards would want answered.

"No," the corpse says.

"Who would want to shoot you?"

"Kayleb."

"Who is Kayleb?"

"My brother."

"Why would he shoot you?"

"Money. And I tried to sleep with his wife."

Sandobal jumps to life before I can end the ritual. "Is there anyone else who would want to shoot you?"

"Yuri Orlov," he says.

"Why?" There is excitement in her voice.

"I was a bagman for him."

"When?" she says.

Emmanuel Philippe-Auguste gives three dates and exact times. In life, he may not have remembered, but in death, his hard drive of a brain spits out details with perfect recall.

"Detective. More salt," I say and open my mouth.

Sandobal pockets her phone before squatting down, grabbing my chin, and throwing more than a pinch of salt in my mouth. She steps in Mr. Philippe-Auguste's blood, but doesn't notice. Her eager eyes and beaming smile look evil by candlelight. She takes out her phone again and resumes recording. "Have you ever met Tamora Orlov or Abram Orlov?" she says.

"No," says the dead man.

Sandobal sneers. "How did you meet Yuri Orlov?"

"Here at the club."

"Who introduced you?"

"Jason."

Sandobal purses her lips. Her voice drops. "Jason Carnero? When?"

"Yes." And he gives a date, almost eighteen months ago.

"Were you also Carnero's bagman?"

"Yes."

Sandobal stops recording. She stands up and yells. "Sergeant!"

I tug at the body's muscles with my mind, and the body rearranges itself: the eyes close, and the arms move to Mr. Philippe-Auguste's sides. I blow out the candle. The glowing blue veins of salt mist away. I exhale the same mist out of my mouth.

Richards runs in and turns on the lights. "What the hell happened?" Richards says.

"Detective Sandobal can tell you." I smile at her, get up, pull off the gloves, and move to the sink to wash my hands.

Sandobal composes herself quickly. "Sir, according to the victim, the perpetrator was either his brother, Kayleb, or—get this—Yuri. *Orlov*."

"Are you joking?" Richards says.

Sandobal backhands his chest. "No! He's the bagman! This—"

"What about the brother?" Richards says.

"The victim slept with his brother's wife," Sandobal says. "But I don't think that has anything to do with any of this."

"I'll radio this in, see if we can't have Kayleb picked up," Richards says. He tries to leave.

"Sergeant," I say, drying my hands.

Richards is pacing. "What?"

"Don't forget about my dry cleaning." There is a line of blood running down the right leg of my pants.

He walks away. I am left with Sandobal. I turn to her. "Would you do me a favor?"

She is staring right into my eyes. "Anything. You just made my case."

I take my keys out of my pocket and hold them out to her. "There is a duffle bag in my trunk. A silver Honda Civic, parked right outside. Would you get it for me? Also, you stepped in Mr. Philippe-Auguste," I say and point at her shoes.

Sandobal purses her lips but takes my keys. She cleans her shoe off with a paper towel before exiting. I pack up the candle and jar, making sure all my things are free of blood. Sandobal comes back and hands me the duffle. I open it and find a pair of jeans.

"I have a question for you," she says.

"I need to change."

"That's fine." She crosses her arms and leans against the bathroom wall, staring at the body.

I go into the largest of the three stalls to change.

Sandobal struggles. "How long have you been a—"

"Practitioner?" I undo my pants.

"Necromancer."

"Since my mother died." I put on the jeans and rummage through the duffle for a black plastic garbage bag. "I've been working with the police for the last couple of years. Ever seen anything like this?"

"Not exactly."

I drop the bloodied pants in the trash bag, along with my shoes. "But you've seen *things*, huh?" I pull a pair of sneakers from the duffle and slip them on. There is a water bottle in the duffle; I chug it.

"Yes. When I was a kid. And recently."

I zip up the duffle and sling it over my shoulder. I grab a card case from my doctor's bag and take out one of my official cards, the ones with the FIU logo that have my title on them. I exit the stall. "Well, if you ever want to talk about it, here's my card." I hold it out to her.

She takes it without hesitation. "Doctor Pablo Diaz?" she says.

"That's me. I didn't get your first name, though."

"Elisa."

I grab my bags, sidle around the body of Mr. Philippe-Auguste, and intentionally brush past her. "A pleasure working for you, Elisa," I say.

I kick myself all the way to the car. *A pleasure working for you, Elisa?* Lame as shit. I throw everything into my trunk and my confidence wanes. Who talks to women like that? As I get in my car, a nickelodeon of all the women I have embarrassed myself in front of plays across my mind. I crank the AC, then kick myself for not getting Sandobal's number.

Elisa knocks on my window.

I scream like a little girl.

I roll down the window. "Holy shit. You startled me."

"Everything okay?" She's giving me a weak smile with a furrowed brow.

"Yeah,"—I sigh—"yeah. Listen, you want to get something to eat?"

She laughs. "Right now?"

"Yes. There's a nice cafe around the corner. Incredible breakfast."

She checks her watch. "It's got to be quick."

"Perfect." I get out and lock up my car.

Sunset Tavern and Deli Lane share the same building, and the two establishments hide Smoke and Lace from the view of pedestrians. The sidewalk is brick instead of concrete, and the facade of the building is covered in sheets of white limestone to contrast with the black wooden trim. Black iron tables and chairs sit under large green umbrellas. There's enough of a breeze to sit outside; otherwise, the humidity would make it impossible.

We don't let the waitress walk away when she brings us menus. We order food and drinks right away.

"Now that I'm officially consulting and drawing a paycheck from this case, can I ask you to clue me in as to what is going on?"

Sandobal cocks an eyebrow at me. "Did you see the newspaper this morning?"

"Sort of. Let's just say I didn't."

"Well, we pulled two bodies out of Biscayne Bay."

"Mutilated."

"Right. One of them was Jason Carnero, a fixer for the Latin Kings."

"I thought the bodies were cut up?"

"Not his tattoos," she says. "I'm pretty sure both men were part of a drug deal gone wrong."

"For them, maybe. But it went right for someone." Sandobal narrows her eyes at me. "How long have you been *consulting*?"

"About two years."

"What made you want to work with us?"

"Bills need to get paid," I say. "You said you saw something when you were a child. What was it?"

"It's silly."

"I promise you it's not."

She sighs. "My boyfriend, when I was sixteen, cheated on me. I broke up with him, but I went into a funk. I started seeing something. Something dark. It felt like it was watching me when I was sleeping, or when I was sad."

"Hmm. Negative emotions can draw all sorts of spirits."

"What?"

"Oh, yeah. There's a line in *Hamlet*. 'When sorrows come, they come not single spies, but in battalions.' That's because there are all sorts of creatures that feed on grief and sadness and hate and they perpetuate the same emotions."

"Are you telling me it was real?"

"Could have been."

She thinks it over, and then purses her lips. "My grandmother did a cleansing when I told her. The house smelled like sage for weeks, but things got better."

"Is she a *santera*?" Santeria is a syncretic religion. African slaves would worship Christian saints in front of their masters, but each saint was used to symbolize a different god of the Yoruba religion. Miami and the Caribbean are full of its practitioners.

"No, but my mother likes to say she was 'sympathetic.'" She gives me the air quotes, then runs a hand through her hair.

"Was?"

"She died last year." She doesn't look at me when she says this. Did someone perform a post-mortem interview for her?

"I'm sorry."

"It's okay. It's funny, actually. I still feel her all the time. And odd things keep happening in the house."

"Like what?"

"The clothes she didn't like me wearing disappear. I always find them under the bed. The same thing happens with the makeup, but only the lipstick that's too red. She always said that shade was for whores."

"Jesus." This woman may actually be haunted.

"Yeah. Abuela did *not* mince words." She smiles to herself.

The waitress brings us our food. Elisa ordered an Elena Ruth, which is a turkey sandwich with jelly and cream cheese—diabetes in sandwich form. I guess she has a sweet tooth. "What about you? What made you want to be a..."

"Practitioner." I smile. "A wizard."

"It feels weird to say it," she says through a mouthful.

"I know." I take a bite of my reuben.

"When I was twelve, my mother died, right out of the blue. Brain aneurysm. My father thought it would help us cope if we did a post-mortem interview. It didn't. But I watched the practitioner who conducted the interview. I remembered everything he did. And then I did the same thing at home, only without a body. I thought I could summon my mother. Something else showed up instead."

"What?"

"Wights. Ghosts looking for a way back into the world of the living. They are usually malevolent, and powerful."

"Holy shit."

"Yeah."

"So what happened?"

"Emérico showed up."

"The Chancellor of the College?"

"Yes. It was after Dead Sunday, only five or six years, and he was still very hands-on. He liked to take care of problems himself, and very publicly. He sensed that something had crossed over and flew to my house and saved me from the wights. He told me to come see him when I was ready. So I did."

"What's he like?"

"Well, when I first met him, he was terrifying and amazing, but he was saving my life. And when I learned magic, he was my teacher, and always very excited about it—full of life, really. He mentored me, and passed me the reins of the Necromancy Department so he could get out of the classroom and concentrate on expanding the College. Lately, though, he's been weird."

"Really? A talking skeleton is weird?" She is smiling.

"*Anyway*, I think the job is getting to the Chancellor, is all." I wipe my mouth with my napkin. "What about you? What made you want to be a cop?"

"Detective."

I admire her for correcting me. "Right. A detective."

"I don't know, really. Seemed right. I'm the eldest of six, and I was always the one in charge. It just felt right."

"Why homicide?"

"That's a story for another day. And don't worry, we'll be getting to know each other a lot better."

I swallow. "What?"

"Richards is moving up in the world; he made lieutenant. I'm your new contact."

"No shit?" For a moment I was very excited but the reality of the situation is a kick to the libido.

She nods. "Advancement is the name of the game."

"For you, too?"

"Of course. I am getting my Masters in Executive Management. 'Time's wingèd chariot,' and all that."

"I don't know that one."

She winks at me, and then her phone rings. "Look it up." She answers. "Detective Sandobal." She listens and frets at her lip. "Okay. I'm on my way."

"Duty calls?" I ask when she hangs up.

"Yes. They're bringing Kayleb into the station." She pulls a leather money clip from her breast pocket.

"No, no. I got this one."

"You sure?"

"Yeah. You have to go. But you get the next one."

Elisa stands and takes a business card from her money clip. "Here. Just in case." She holds out her card to me. "But don't call me if you're summoning demons."

"I would never summon demons. That's bad juju right there."

She shakes her head. "Of course you wouldn't. You're one of the good guys." She smiles, gives my shoulder a squeeze, and walks away.

2
Matters of Honor

I ORDER A CAPPUCCINO and run to fetch my laptop from my car. The waitress is waiting at the table when I get back.

"Oh, thank God. I thought you left," she says.

"No, no. There's no honor in the dine-and-dash. Can I have the check, please? And two to-go boxes?"

The waitress is dutiful so I tip her well.

I take the rest of this afternoon for myself. Well, not really for me; I answer e-mails for hours. But at least I get to sit outside.

I also make the cemetery rotation schedule for September. There are 26 major cemeteries in Miami-Dade County, and a handful of minor ones, and each one needs to have a necromancer on-call for post-mortem interviews and regular warding. Wards are the enchantments that reassure the public there won't be another Dead Sunday; they bar ghosts from entering cemeteries. The College refuses to relinquish their maintenance to the city. It falls to me to make sure that everyone is in place.

I also have to arrange the transportation of cadavers with the Morgue Bureau for the Necromancy Lab. At some point, apprentice necromancers need a safe environment where they can screw up a post-mortem interview; that's lab.

My father calls me at 5:30 p.m. "Hello, Dad."

"Hello, *m'ijo* (my son). The cantina never arrived."

"What? What have you eaten?"

"Nothing."

"Dad! There's food in the house."

"Nothing I want."

"What *do* you want?"

"It's Monday."

"Okay," I say and hang up.

❂

Every Cuban restaurant worth going to has a take-out window. Every take-out window has its appropriate accompaniments: the smell of coffee, a crowd of old men cursing communism, and a plastic tankard filled with ice-cold water.

La Carreta is *the* Cuban food chain in Miami. This is a family place—a sit-down place—and they're not used to anything but sandwiches for take-out orders, but they will accommodate any order. They know me by now because of my father, and no longer look at me like an oddity. Well, the new hires always do, but not the lifers.

At the window this evening is my favorite lifer, Conchita. "*Pablito*!" She waves as soon as I walk up. She's pushing sixty and flirts with me unabashedly. "Come here, handsome." She gives me a kiss on the cheek through the take out window. "How is Tristan?" She regularly waited on my father, when he used to go out.

"Good. He sends his regards."

"Give him a big kiss for me. What do you need?"

"Two Monday specials: meatballs." Each plate comes with four meatballs the size of an orange, cooked in a heavenly tomato and garlic sauce, served over a bed of the fluffiest rice. Every day there are four different entrees, all of them heart-stoppingly good, with two sides. Fried plantains are ready-made.

"Something while you wait?"

"No, thank you."

"You're too skinny," she says, and gives me a croquette in a red plastic tray before moving onto the next customer.

A voice yells from the crowd of old men. "*Coño*, Pablo Diaz! How are you, my son?" The man approaches me. His name is Rogelio. He's tall, balding, and sports a thick gray moustache. He knows me because he knows my father.

"Good, good." I offer my hand.

He takes it without hesitation, even though he knows what I do. To him, I am Tristan's son, and that comes first. "How is your father?"

"Watching television all day. Bored. You should call him. See if you can get him out of the house."

"I am going to do it, but you know how he is." He waits for me to nod. "Take care of yourself, my son."

"I will."

"Grab this, Pablo," Conchita says. She hands me a plastic bag, stacked with styrofoam containers.

"Thank you."

"Take care of yourself. And take care of your father."

"You know I do." I hold up the bag to her and walk away.

When I start my car, a trio of men—one of them much older—begin milling about behind me. When I put the car in reverse, the two younger men move away, but the older of the bunch just stands there, smiling at the other two. He is dressed in a windbreaker, even though it is warm.

I give my horn the absolute softest tap possible.

He doesn't move.

I lower my window and lean out the door. "*Con tu permiso, señor*," (With your permission, sir) I say.

He turns, never losing his smile, and walks up to my window. He puts a liver-spotted hand on my forearm, and I can see that his bottom row of teeth are brown along the edges. Downy wisps of hair float about his head. "*Cuando llega a los noventa años, cual quiera se pone a comer mierda como yo*," (When reaching 90 years old, anyone would eat shit, like me) he says.

The Cuban idiom *comer mierda* literally translates to "to eat shit," but the connotation is loafing about without purpose. This is a light-hearted saying, unlike the much more literal American saying "eat shit." The noun *come mierda* is an insult akin to "layabout" or "good-for-nothing."

All four of us are laughing. The old timer squeezes my arm once more, then lets me leave.

I pull into my driveway and feel a pang. I know where it comes from: the fact that there are two front doors. We may own the whole house, but my father and I only live in half of it. After his stroke, when the medical bills started rolling in, he called in a lifetime of favors from plumbers, electricians, and his former apprentices to convert the place into a duplex. It was the only way we could survive.

At least the lawn is well-maintained and the place looks clean. This comes courtesy of our tenant, Armando; he is a handyman and one of my father's friends from childhood. They grew up in the same village in Cuba. When Armando divorced, my father offered to rent him the other half of the house.

The sounds of the television waft over the driveway. The stroke left my father partially deaf, as well as nosy.

The cramped living room abuts the door and only has space for a television, a loveseat, and my father's recliner. He mutes the television as soon as I enter. He is dressed in pajama pants and a robe. He wears 65 like it is 90. "My son." He speaks to me only in Spanish and expects me to respond in kind.

"Dad." I walk over and give him a kiss on his mottled cheek.

He grabs the back of my head with his good hand—the right—and returns the kiss. "Help me," he says. He grabs his metal cane with his left hand and my shoulder with the right and lifts himself off the recliner. "You have mail."

"Every day." I guide him the few steps to the kitchen table and seat him. He constructed the table, once upon a time, and we had to dredge it out of storage when our old kitchen table no longer fit in the room. This table only seats four comfortably. But it is sturdy, square, and bears no frills, much like I remember my father. I imagine the table being passed down for generations; such is the workmanship. "What do you want to drink?"

"*Presidente*."

Beer raises his blood pressure. So does Cuban food. But what else does this man live for? *The Price is Right*? *Sábado Gigante*? I transfer all the food to plates, set the table, and pour my old man a mug.

"Thank you, my son."

"You're welcome." When I place the food and drink before him, the plate and mug barely make a sound, because the wood is so thick. "Conchita and Rogelio both say hello. They want to know when you're going to leave the house."

He only grunts in response to this. Under the kitchen light, the vitiligo on his neck and hands looks like it is consuming the once-healthy brown. He slowly brings a forkful of rice to his mouth. We have had the fight before so I don't try to feed him. "How was work?" he asks.

"Busy. Two post-mortems. And scheduling."

He nods. "So today you worked and made a lot of money." This has always been my father's primary concern. A lifelong carpenter, he made me his apprentice starting at the age of 10. After school, or when everyone else was on vacation, I was instead helping my father clean job sites.

I poke at the meatballs. "Not enough."

His fork clatters onto the plate. "Why?"

"I owed the College some of my time."

"You owe a lot, it looks like." He points with his lips at the silver tray in the middle of the table, where he stacks the mail, then goes back to his food.

I grab the envelopes and separate them into second notices and final notices. I tear up and throw away the first notices, except for the utilities. "I'll take care of it."

"Your mother and I always paid the bills on time. Whenever the bills came, she always paid them right away."

"I know. I miss her, too."

He nods. "I was watching the television. There was a man, Nick Russo. You work with him, it is true?" I always hear something from *El Nuevo Herald* or Channel 23 when we eat. My father is better than Reuters.

"I've met him a few times." There is no person on this Earth whom I hate as abstractly as Nick Russo.

"The man is rich. And he does the same thing—"

"No, he doesn't."

"He is very rich."

"I know, dad."

"And he does the same thing as you."

"Dad, you know I lost a lot of money in that investment. I need to recoup my losses and try again." I can't really tell my father that I'm drowning in debt because of his medical expenses. He might have another stroke. There's no honor in killing your father.

"When will that be?"

"Day by day, Dad. I'll tell you when we get there."

"Why don't you ask this Nick Russo for a job?"

"I have a job, Dad."

"*Sí. Brujo.*" He uses 'witch' like a curse word.

"I'm a *teacher*."

"You can have more than one job."

"You know I already do. I work at the University, at the cemeteries, and whenever the police call me. When am I supposed to eat?"

"I don't know. But if you can't pay the bills, how do you afford food?" He's talking about the cantina that delivers his lunch. Its cost is reasonable and it gives me the peace of mind that he has eaten. I usually don't even eat lunch. He finishes his beer. "Another, please."

"Dad, you know you shouldn't."

"If the next stroke finishes me off, maybe you'll be able to pay the bills on time," he says, and holds his mug up so I will refill it. He stares at me, bug-eyed, until we both start laughing. I get him another beer and finish my food. I hold his off-hand until he finishes his meal. There's a tremble in it that chokes me.

"Can I help you?" I say.

"For what?" He struggles to stand, shuffles back to his recliner, and before long, he is snoring over the blaring television.

3
Sorrows, Drowned

IT IS 12:20 a.m. I am idling in my driveway.

He's in there, asleep.

I should go in; I know I should. I am drained from visiting every cemetery and morgue in the city, in preparation for the new semester. I have a class to teach in the morning.

But the inexorable sadness of Monday meatballs and *El Nuevo Herald* and *The Price is Right* and Telemundo and bills and oxygen tanks and warfarin and the bedpan force my hand back onto the gear shift, and I creep away from my convalescent duplex.

This late at night on a Monday, the highways are almost empty. I know where I am going but I try not to think. Before long, the orange street lamps give way to neon.

Every broadcast of a Miami sports team and every movie set in Miami needs to include a pan of Ocean Drive. This is what everyone believes Miami to be. The art deco hotels that face the water are an iconic façade, fodder for the naive. The heart of the city beats to the west while its public face looks out onto a hungry ocean that is ready to drown it. But when you need to find the vice in Vice City, there's no better place to look than here.

My escapist watering hole is in a building close to Lummus Park, blocks away from the ocean. The club on the first floor is called Xanadu, and the stately pleasure domes inside are made of silicone. During the day, the place is packed with beachgoers swilling frozen drinks and the dance floor is never free of sand. I don't go in there; I don't fit in there. I wish I did. Instead, I valet my car in the alley and climb a metal staircase up to a fire door that is always unlocked.

The Eight Ball takes up most of the second floor. To the left, eight red-felt pool tables are evenly spaced across the room. Half of them are occupied, and half of the occupants are barely dressed. To the right are booths with red leather seats packed with the debauched, as well as a few tables for two. The floor is glossy sandstone tile in a checkerboard pattern and is unforgiving to dropped glasses. A cloud of smoke—cigarette and other—sticks to the ceiling. The lighting lends itself to chance encounters and loneliness. By some miracle of engineering, the music from the first floor doesn't mingle with the subdued chillwave up here. A wooden bar stretches across two walls; the glass shelves are lit with white track lighting.

The place could have been classy, but the combined lurch of humanity and march of the seasons has taken its toll. No amount of sanding will restore the scratched bar. Cigarette burns and liquor stains scar the felt of every pool table. Warped cues stand in their battered racks. If whatever you're touching isn't sticky with booze or *other*, then it is slick with humidity. The bathrooms are a gamble; some nights, they are clean and free of detritus; on others, you might be walking into a swamp.

I pull out a barstool and take a seat. When I look up, Milka is there. She is a little thing, platinum blonde, with the face of an angel. She swears they make her wear the leather bustier, but I doubt it. She leans over the bar. "Well, hello, professor. Can I interest you in a cocktail, or will you be throwing all your money away on expensive scotch?"

I presided over Milka's father's post-mortem last year. It's how we met. "Good evening. No scotch tonight. Just a *Presidente*."

Milka sneers at me. My part-time bartender, part-time psychologist loves to show off her skills, but I have to drive home eventually. "I am sorry. We ran out this weekend."

My heart sinks. "What else do you have in a bottle?"

She rattles off a bunch of artisanal beers and ends with some domestic swill.

I order one of the higher-end pilsners; crisper, cleaner, but a poor substitute for my father's favorite.

Milka holds out her hand and slaps her fingers against her palm.

I reach for my wallet and produce a debit card. "Leave it open. And I need balls."

She snatches the card from my fingers and runs it. "Isn't it a new semester? And a school night?" she says to me and lays a black plastic tray of pool balls before me.

"Class isn't until 10:50," I say.

She retrieves her phone from inside her bra. The screen lights her face momentarily, and she purses her lips. "You're pushing it. Table seven."

"I know. Thank you. I won't be long." I take the tray to my assigned table and rack. As I break, I drink to my father, who taught me to play pool.

Before and after my mother's death, my father worked full-time and overtime as a carpenter. He regularly took on and fired apprentices. The ones who could swallow his perfectionism and doggedness would go on to find good, stable work at construction companies. My father refused to follow them. Capable as he was, he was also his own man, and he never lacked employment as a subcontractor; there wasn't a foreman in the city who didn't know him.

Clients ogled the tool chest he built: a marvel of organization and a testament to his foresight and ingenuity. Four boxes that nested seamlessly on top of each other, the top one hiding a built-in rack to hold all the drills and hammers and screwdrivers he would need for the job, the bottom one equipped with wheels. Time and again, he would be asked to build one for clients, for construction foremen, for fellow carpenters. They promised exorbitant amounts, but he always refused. He was selfish about his chest. Instead, he would agree to build furniture, but those who hired him would rarely do so again; he created works of art, beautiful, built to last, and often late on delivery—the price of perfection.

Usually he was without help, so he would pick me up after school. I would sit on a milk crate in the back of his powder blue panel van, scribbling into a binder on my lap, the sliding side-door open to expel the demons of heat and welcome in the occasional breeze. At quitting time, I would help him clean up the site: sweeping, vacuuming, packing away tools, carrying out the chest. "*El trabajo campartido es más llevadero*," (Shared work is more bearable) he would always tell me.

If it was a Friday or Saturday, he would take me to shoot pool at a smoky dive hidden in Little Havana called El Güajiro. The spirit of industry had captured the homeowner, inspiring them to convert their garage into a bar. All it took was a fridge full of beer, some stools, a second-hand pool table, and a karaoke machine. My father always ordered two *Presidentes*. When my father would hand me one of them, the bartender said nothing, perhaps because I was covered in sawdust, more likely because there was no beer and wine license to jeopardize.

I scratch on the eight. For the second time.

"You're playing terribly," Milka says when I return with the tray. "And it is getting late."

"Have you been watching me?"

"I always do. You're one of the best when you're steady. But awful when something is on your mind. Tell me what is wrong."

"My drink is empty. Johnny Black on the rocks, please," I say.

"Bad pool and blended whisky. *Tell me*," she says, but pours the drink I ordered.

I down half of it. "Same old shit. It's my father."

"I thought you had it under control."

"Kind of," I say. Before his stroke, my father refused to let me obtain insurance coverage for him. He was his own man, after all. His stubbornness saddled us with close to three hundred thousand dollars in medical bills.

"Money. Always money," Milka says as she wipes down the bar in front of me.

"Those Montessoris aren't cheap, huh?"

"That is nothing! Uniforms, food, computers, toys"—she ticks off the list on her fingers—"my girls will eat me out of house and home!"

"Be happy you have children," I say.

"I am. You know I am. But I would only having one job if it weren't for them."

"Try having three," I say and drink.

"How about having one job that actually pays well?" She stops cleaning the bar top and stares at me.

"If I were normal"—if I weren't saddled with debt—"I'd be fine."

"You work for hire, right? We could help each other."

"I'll listen to any solution."

"Work for my employer. If I bring him someone capable, he may give me a better job than serving drunks."

"Milka, I'm drowning right now. I can't take on something else."

"What you did for me—for my mother—is only a fraction of what you can do. You helped us, Pablo. Trust me and help yourself."

The razzle-dazzle of a post-mortem worked on Milka a year ago. And when I came back here on her invitation, she smiled when she saw me.

Wasn't nervous. Wasn't shy. Was thankful. It's rare for anyone but my father's friends to look out for me.

I rub my forehead. "Fine. When can I meet him?"

Milka cups her hands around her mouth and yells, "Boss!"

I turn around. A large man in a charcoal-gray suit surfaces from a booth full of people. Even across the room, the blue of his eyes reminds me of glaciers. He sports a military haircut and an ordered hedge of red beard. He strides to the bar, not sparing me a glance. He growls something to Milka in what I can only assume is Russian.

Milka turns her hand up, pushes it toward me, and responds in her throaty singsong. She uses a word that he used—*koldun*—but I have no idea what it means.

The man lowers his brow and looks me up and down. His nostrils flare. "Hello. I am Abram Orlov. Milka tells me you're looking for work."

The back of my neck goes cold and my knees tremble: *Orlov*. This man may be the one responsible for the body bags on the front page of the newspaper this morning.

"Would you excuse me for one second?" I glance at Milka, run to the bathroom, and lock myself in. I take out a lead nail and a packet of salt from my pocket. I pour the salt over the nail, speak a few syllables, and rub the nail down both sleeves of my shirt. To make sure the ward works, I try stabbing my shirt with the nail. There is a slight metallic clink. Satisfied that my shirt is bullet proof, I exit the bath-room.

I run face-first into an olive-skinned man with a Caesar haircut in a cream colored suit.

"Sorry," I say.

"No problem," he says and smiles. He has a silver grille over his teeth, etched with a crown. Tattoos cover his neck and disappear beneath his white button-down. He doesn't blink until I reach the bar. Only then does he go into the bathroom.

My drink has been topped off.

Abram Orlov awaits me. He holds a tumbler of brown liquid and has laid his jacket on the bar top. He's wearing sleeve garters, and his blue shirt bunches up under his shoulders. Somehow, he seems even larger.

"Everything okay?" he says.

"Yes. So let's talk about work." I resume my seat.

"How about you tell me your name first."

"What? Oh, of course. I'm sorry. Dr. Pablo Diaz." I extend my hand.

His stone hands do not crush my fingers. "Doctor? Of what?"

"The Practical Arts." Do I always sound so prideful?

Orlov sips his drink. "A wizard, then."

"Correct."

"And you work at the College?"

"I do."

"Anywhere else?"

"I am contracted by Dade South Memorial Park to serve the cemeteries there."

"You talk to the dead."

"I conduct post-mortem interviews, yes."

"Anywhere else?" He cocks an eye at me.

"Is there something specific you want to know?"

Orlov purses his lips. "You work for the police."

"Yes. I am a part-time consultant for the sheriff's office."

Orlov looks over his shoulder. The table he emerged from overflows with people, including the guy who I bumped into when I exited the bathroom. That man and three others stare back at Orlov.

"You are not a police officer, though," Orlov says.

"No." I swirl my drink, unwilling to sip it.

"I need to find someone. I think he may have left the city."

"My consulting fee is five thousand dollars." It isn't, but Orlov doesn't know that.

"Not a problem. In fact, I am willing to double your rate if it will buy your discretion."

My throat tightens. I sip the drink, despite needing my wits about me. That much money would ward off the creditors, keep my father's oxygen flowing. But at what cost? "Mr. Orlov, your offer is very generous. And I would be willing to keep our business confidential, so long as there's nothing illicit behind my working for you. But, it would probably be best if I just finish my drink and we part ways."

"I agree. But those men will follow you."

"What?" I know better than to turn again, but I glance anyway.

"We have a working relationship that has hit a rough patch. Their grievance against me is legitimate. Now they have seen me talking to you. They will follow you."

I could just disappear. A little salt, a few words, a snap of my finger: presto change-o, no more Pablo. Would I be looking over my shoulder forever?

Abram Orlov is offering me enough money to ease my burdens.

And there is Milka, who feeds her girls on Orlov's dime.

I take down half of the scotch. "When would you care to discuss the details?"

Orlov finishes his drink and runs his tongue over his teeth. "Now. We can use the offices upstairs."

"Then let's go. I have work in the morning."

"Wait here." Orlov sweeps up his jacket and returns to his associates in the booth. He places both fists down on the table and looms over them like a gorilla.

Milka runs over. "You need a fresh one?" she says.

I watch the people at the table disperse, leaving only Orlov and the man with the silver grille. "Yeah, might as well," I say. With the more thuggish elements gone, I start to relax. "I'd like a Lagavulin, please. Put it on your boss's tab. And close me out."

Milka beams. "So it's going well?"

"Well enough, I guess. I doubt this will be a long-term arrangement."

"You never know. Abram has a way with people." She pours me my drink as Orlov and the other man walk up.

"Good choice," Orlov says.

"Thank you. You bought it for me," I say. I sip smoke in a glass, with a nice honey finish and barely any bite.

Orlov raises an eyebrow at Milka, who returns with the tab. "Dr. Diaz, I'd like you to meet an associate of mine. This is Augusto Desiderio."

"It's an honor to meet you, doctor." Silver grille thrusts his hand into mine, jingling the gold chains inside of his open button-down. The tattoo inked into the cup of his right hand is of a five pointed crown, each spoke capped with a circle. *Latin Kings.* My heart thumps an extra time.

"Thank you," I say, but my knees and throat are tight. I had suspicions about Orlov, but there is no mistaking that Desiderio is a criminal. How did I get here?

"Let's head upstairs," Orlov says.

"One second," I say. I sign the receipt for Milka and leave her a nice tip, since this might be the last time I ever see her.

Orlov and Desiderio make their way through the pool tables, toward a door with an "Employees Only" sign. Orlov holds the door open for Desiderio and waits for me.

I am expecting seedy underbellies and trap doors. Instead, I get a kitchen, a padlocked stock room full of liquor bottles, and a unisex employee bathroom. At the end of the hallway stands a door with no name on the frosted glass. The lights are on inside. Abram pushes past me and opens the door. All the walls—save for the one whose windows look out on the beach—are tastefully appointed with leather couches. Painted wood carvings of fairy tales hang from the walls. A massive desk squats near the beach-side wall, and there are two leather armchairs in front of it. Desiderio moves to the rolling bar-cart and fills three tumblers from a crystal decanter.

"I like those wood carvings," I say.

"My grandfather made them," Orlov says.

"He was a carpenter?"

"No, a cobbler. I worked in his shop."

I nod. "I know that life."

"Do you?" Orlov chugs half of his glass. "My father went into business for himself when the Iron Curtain fell, but business was not good enough to feed everyone, so he took work on the side. And when I returned from the army, I took the same work, but for different people. And this left me at odds with him."

"What happened?"

"He shot me," Abram says and unbuttons his shirt, revealing the whorl of skin above his navel.

"Holy shit." My father's austere and lonely office never pitted him against me. All he ever did was sacrifice for me—and here I am, drinking with a mobster, while he's at home, probably foregoing sleep waiting for me.

The carving behind Orlov's desk depicts a knight being eaten by a giant frog. The figure carries his helmet under his arm, and has flaming red hair, like Orlov's beard. Someone either cleaned or restored the paint on all the others, but the colors of this one are muted, like it has spent too much time in the sun, or was forgotten in some attic corner. "What is that one about?"

Orlov snips the end of a cigar. "He's going to Hell." He blackens the end of the cigar with a torch lighter.

"What did he do?"

"Nothing. He wants to make a deal with the devil," Orlov says, puffing away until the wisps become cloudy. "This is how a wizard is made in Russia."

"Did you have to get swallowed by anything, Doc?" Desiderio says and grins.

I purse my lips and pretend to check my phone, but I know it is already too late for a full night's sleep. "I have to teach a class in the morning," I say.

Abram rubs his chin. "Business, then?"

I nod. I fiddle with the rim of the glass, then decide to have a sip. Oban. I'm certain of it. I haven't been able to afford a bottle in years.

"I need you to find my cousin," Abram says.

"That should be simple enough," I say. "Do you have anything that belongs to him? The more time he spends with it, the better."

"Wait here. I will get what you need." He strides out of the room.

Desiderio stares at me, unblinking.

I sip the whiskey and give him a tight smile.

His smile is wide. Genuine. "You don't belong here," he says.

I let out a breath I didn't know I was holding. "Jesus Christ, I know!"

"What the fuck you even doing here, then?"

"Man, I don't know. I came to get a drink, then Milka tells me Abram needs work, and now I'm in a room full of gangsters. No offense."

"What offense? You're goddamn right," he says. He leans back and props his elbow behind him on the top of the leather sofa. "So what's keeping you here?"

"Abram is paying me."

"How much?"

"Ten thousand dollars."

Augusto whistles. "Shit. I'd stay, too. But be smart. Abram is a monster. All of these Russians are."

"I saw the papers this morning."

"That is nothing. Stories used go around, you know? He doesn't mind the dirty work." Augusto sips his whiskey and smacks his lips. "Yeah, man. I'm a businessman. I've never had to cut up a body. Miami's my town, and your town, too, am I right?"

I nod.

"Well, think about him. Immigrant. Came over with nothing. He scraped and clawed for every dollar. Now Yuri's fucked him."

"What the Hell did he do?"

He closes his eyes and shakes his head. "You just do what you got to do here, and don't worry about that." Augusto gets up, freshens his drink, and returns. "Could you imagine, being betrayed by your own family? That shit will drive you crazy. It's for sure why Abram hired you. Most of the time, Russians don't like this spooky shit. Magic and whatever. They got some real boogeymen out there."

"So do we," I say and point at his wrist. He wears a woven bracelet, made from three strings: black, red, and white. Followers of Santería wear them, and if they fall off, the belief is that your God prevented something bad from happening to you. "You practice?"

He laughs, puts his drink down, and slaps his hands together. "*Perdónale*," (Forgive him) he says, looks up at the ceiling, and shakes his clasped hands in the same direction. "You better hope no one heard you call them boogeyman. This is real shit."

"I know it is," I say.

Augusto leans in. "Finish this job. Then don't ever come back here. No phone calls, no more side jobs, nothing."

I can hear Abram stomping down the hall. He bursts in. "Look what I found," Abram says. He resumes his seat to my left, drops a duffle bag on the table, and picks up his drink. "Sorry it took so long."

"What is this?" I say.

"Yuri's gym bag. There wasn't a day he didn't paw through it. Also, I can write you a check instead of giving you cash, if you prefer. All nice and legal. You could even report it on your taxes."

I lower my brow at him. "What?"

"Of course! You're my independent consultant, after all."

I tighten my lips and open the duffle. The odor coming from it is the stench of exertion. I try to shift around the contents without touching anything in there. I hear a jingling. "Grab that weight belt," I say to Abram.

He does so, and lays it on the table in front of me.

I drop the bag and kick it under the table. I look around the room. I go to the bar cart and grab an empty champagne bucket and several bottles of water from the bottom shelf. I place the items on the desk, roll up the weight belt, and ease it inside the bucket so it doesn't unroll. I fill up the bucket with water.

"Why do you need something of his?" Abram asks.

"It creates a sympathetic bond. The more he uses the object the better. Do you have a picture of him, as well?"

Abram scowls.

"It will help," I say.

Abram takes his phone out of his pocket and starts tapping away. He shoves the phone across the table. "There." The picture is a selfie of Abram and another man, surrounded by topless women, on a boat, with the downtown skyline in the background. I recognize Milka. I stare at the photo and down the rest of my drink. It is her life. She can do what she wants. But I'd still like to choke Abram with his own phone.

"You don't have another picture?"

"I just thought you would like that one." Abram smiles.

I hand the phone back, but he returns it almost immediately, with a different picture. There is a large man with dark hair, sweaty and disheveled after a night of galivanting, posing with a cigarette in his mouth and a Magnum bottle of Grey Goose gripped in one meaty fist.

"Turn off the lights, please," I say and stand.

Abram hits the lights. Desiderio stands on my right and Abram returns to my left.

"I need a lighter," I say.

"Here," Desiderio says and passes me a bright orange Bic.

I flick the lighter to life and hold it over the bucket, angling it until the meager flame reflects off of the metal innards. I hold the picture of Yuri in my mind and spit into the bucket. I let the flame die, but the reflection of the light remains and spreads through the water. The little lambent pool shimmers and ripples until it coalesces into an image: Yuri, looming over a cheap motel bed, a minxy woman with bright blue hair fellating him.

Abram inhales sharply through his nose.

I pinch the image like I would a smartphone and it zooms out to the room number. I pinch it again, and I find the motel sign. Pinch: closest street. Pinch. West Coast of Florida. "You can turn the lights on."

Abram leaves the table and restores the lights.

A quick search on my phone gives me the answer Abram is looking for. "He's in Naples. The Bonita Inn. Room 14," I say. Desiderio gives a low whistle.

"Excuse me for a moment," Abram says and hurries out of the room, mashing his fingers against his cell phone.

I go to the bar cart and almost pour myself another scotch, but I grab a bottle of water instead. I feel like vomiting but I drink it anyway. I run my hand over the bar cart. Someone spent a lot of time on its wooden top; the bevel could slice my finger if it weren't varnished.

"Everything okay?" Abram asks. I didn't hear him come back in.

"Yes. I need to get going, so if you could write that check."

"Already done," he says. He reaches into his pocket and produces a check.

"How did you know?" I trip but recover as I cross the room.

"I had a feeling." He grabs my hand, shakes it, and steadies me at the shoulder. He slips the check in my shirt pocket. "You've been very helpful, Doctor Diaz. Let me have a business card of yours."

I reach for my wallet without thinking. I look through the pocket where bills should be and rifle through the cards there. Some have the FIU logo and all of my contact information on them. The one I hand Abram is white with just my phone number—no other embellishments.

"You got one of those for me?" Desiderio says.

"I do." I give him one.

"I may have some work for you, too," he says, "since you seem to be in the business of making friends. Abram and I need to talk right quick, though."

Abram pockets the card I gave him. "I will be in touch."

"Have a good night," I say.

I steal one last glance at the two of them as they go to the bar cart. I walk down the empty hall, their mumbling fading.

The metal fire door clangs shut behind me. I trudge down the fire escape and my heart sinks when I reach the clean, humid air.

Milka is out at the valet stand. "Hey! How'd it go?" she says when she sees me.

"What are you still doing here?"

"I just got out. You look beat," she says.

"Yeah. And it's a long drive before bed, and not enough time there before work."

She scoffs. "I have to be up in four hours to get the girls ready."

"Why do we do this?" I say to her.

The valet pulls up in a silver Mazda, maybe a decade old. There are two baby seats belted in the back. He hands her the keys.

"We work to eat. And feed others. And maybe have the occasional drink." She smiles, kisses me on both cheeks, and gets in her car. She lowers the window. "Drive safe!" she says and speeds away.

When the valet brings me my Civic, I get in and draw out the check from my shirt. Caribbean Asset Group, LLC. $10,000. I reach into the backseat and rummage through my jacket until I find the check from Jimenez Peña Dade South. I stare at both of them—side by side—until the valet taps on my window. I wave at him and stow the checks back in my breast pocket. As I put the car in gear, I wonder what possessed me to have a beer in the first place.

4
PRC 1101

"I CAN SMELL YOU from here, *sinvergüenza*," (Shameless) my father says. He is sitting in his chair, right where I left him; he must have dozed off. He looks even more fragile than usual.

I come in and give him a kiss on the forehead. How must I look to him?

"Don't you have work today?" he says.

I sigh. "Yes, dad." I pour myself a glass of water, to ease the scratch of secondhand smoke still clinging to the roof of my mouth.

"Is this how you want to live your life? Drinking and smoking?"

"No, dad. Go to bed." I escape to the bathroom, the one place that has always been sacred in our household. The mirror unapologetically shows me the abuse I've put myself through: sallow skin, shadow of beard, bruised eyes.

I get in the shower, then turn the nozzle as hot as I dare. Rivulets of water wash away the evening. Freezing water blasts my reverie; my father has turned on the washing machine. I do not give him the satisfaction of yelping.

I shave and brush my teeth, but I don't do my hair just yet. It is only a bit past five; I might be able to squeeze in a nap. I emerge from the still-steamy bathroom carrying my clothes, their smell of stale tobacco stifling me.

My father is still in his chair. He is reading the day's newspaper, which must have just arrived.

"I need to get a little sleep, so I can go to work. Will you wake me up at 9:30, in case I don't hear the alarm?"

He throws up a hand in dismissal and turns the page. "*Dios te libre*" (God forbid).

My converted room can only accommodate a twin-size bed, but that let me spring for a pillow-top mattress. I set an alarm on my phone and fall onto my cramped cloud and thence into black sleep before my father shakes me roughly. "It's 9:30," he says, and the strident blaring from my phone agrees with him before he's out the door.

Sleep was a mistake. I grab my keys and stumble out to the converted tool shed. I undo the padlock and open the door.

It should be sweltering, but a slow breeze drifts around the room, an enchantment I set in place when I took over the shed. Bundles of herbs hang from the ceiling. A stool is shoved under the converted workbench—my uncomfortable desk—against the left wall. Spice racks hold vials of ingredients and reagents. There is a small cauldron on a brass tripod. Two squat beige filing cabinets against the right-hand wall cramp the room.

Opposite the door, beneath the shed's sole window, I open a steamer trunk and start examining the eight-ounce mason jars within: invisibility, protection, sleep, but no potion of refresh. I don't even remember using the last one. I curse my irresponsibility, grab a jar of ectoplasm I have saved, and lock up.

I run inside, splash through five minutes of cold water, and style my hair. I almost slip in the hallway. When I open the closet, I panic for a moment, until I remember that my good suit is still in a trash bag in my trunk. First day of class and no suit. I throw on what I can to look respectable: jeans, a white shirt, a sport coat. I sacrifice time to get a tie on right. I look at my phone. 10:11.

"Will you be returning home, or do you have some other way to disgrace yourself in mind?" my father says when I kiss him goodbye.

"We'll see," I say, and lock the door behind me.

I screech to a halt in front of a beefy woman in neon pink tights pushing a shopping cart. She throws up a hand and starts beating the hood of my car. All I can do is cringe and let her have her rage out before she stomps away, leaving me with an echoing "¡*Come mierda*!"

I inch into a parking space in front of The Obedient Apothecary. You can't go a mile in suburban Miami without finding a strip mall, and in half of those you will find an Obedient Apothecary next to a vape store or a cafeteria or a clothing consignment. I hate going into them. The staff are condescending, they represent everything that is reprehensible about how the world treats magic, and every purchase lines Nick God-Damned Russo's pockets.

But I have to go in.

The place smells like Nag Champa incense. Something akin to music leaks from tinny speakers in the ceiling: flutes and wind chimes and a log drum. The floors and walls are stark white and the countertops sport glass display cases, hawking single-use magical wares against blue velvet. To add to the seediness, one of the displays contains blown glass pipes and bongs in psychedelic colors.

"Practitioner Diaz! What. An. Honor." The male clerk knows me by name because he is a former student, but at some point became an acolyte of Russo. This explains his slicked-back hair and beard: he must emulate Nick's looks. His sky blue polo shirt has TOA stitched in gold over his heart.

"I need a refresh." I tap on one of the wall cases.

"Of course! I'm just surprised you didn't make it yourself."

"Please? I'm in a hurry."

"Of course, of course." He checks the wooden clock on the wall. "Your class must be starting soon?"

Everyone takes PRC 1101, Introduction to the Practical Arts. I've been teaching it at the same time for a decade. "Yes, it does."

He takes his time walking over to the shelves. He opens the case using keys attached to a belt loop by a carabiner. "Just a refresh? I can't interest you in anything else? We have some fresh lusts and—"

"No, just that."

"Of course." He locks up the case, takes the stocky, stoppered bottle to the register, and scans the barcode on the bottom. "Your total is $17.11. How will you be paying?"

"Jesus, did the prices go up?" I say, but I reach for my wallet anyway.

"There is a two dollar deposit on the bottles. If you bring them back. But you wouldn't need to, would you? This is just a one-time thing?"

I lower my brow. "Swipe or chip?" I say to him, tapping my card on the credit card reader.

"Chip, of course." He smiles and nods.

I key in my pin and hold out my hand for the bottle once the transaction goes through, taking a little piece of my soul with it.

"Do you need a bag or a receipt?"

"No, thank you."

"Of course you don't. Have a magical day," he says, and waves at me as I leave.

The card attached to the refresh bottle by a thin white ribbon is made of recycled paper. I read the ingredients, to make sure they are up to standard, as it should be with all potions. Whereas spells are variable and enforced by the user, potions are rote, and the slightest change in reagent could spell a different effect. At least Russo hasn't started trying to cut corners.

The verse warning—written in red ink—looks like handwritten calligraphy, but it came out of a machine, of that I am certain: "To stay the effects of a long night, / Imbibe this bottle and feel bright! / A warning for those with this plight: / Straight to bed after or feel the bite!" Shitty corporate poetry.

I unstopper the weighty glass bottle and chug the glowing, orange juice. The stuff takes effect immediately; it feels like I got a full night's rest. "God damn you, Nick Russo," I say. This would make anyone rich. I toss the empty bottle into my backseat and drive to campus.

Home is only a five-minute drive from the University, and the Obedient Apothecary is right across the street from FIU, but even so, I am furious, because it is bumper-to-bumper as soon as I get on campus. The absolute worst thing about FIU is the parking. No one carpools, everyone is late to class, and 99% of the drivers are under 25. It's a wonder that the streets don't turn into scenes from *Mad Max.*

My position affords me a parking spot next to Santa Inés Hall, the official name given to the building housing the College of Practical Arts. Without this parking spot, I would certainly go postal.

I love Santa Inés Hall. From the side, the second and third floors—round like the first—give the impression of a ziggurat, or a tiered wedding cake. Each level is embellished with a terrace and balconies. The exterior of the building is white marble, while all of the accents—the gargoyles, the window frames, the massive double doors—are bronze. Above the massive double doors leading inside, the intact prow of the *Santa Inés* juts out of the building, facing east. The figurehead from the ship has been restored: Santa Inés herself, robed, carrying a lamb under her left arm, her right arm extended and grasping for the sun.

The doors beneath Santa Inés shine like a polished trombone, their surface divided into eighteen panels. For the start of the school year, Archmagus Hellas has sculpted the panels into 18 of the major arcana from the Rider-Waite Tarot. I don't know whether to take it as a compliment or an insult that the Hanged Man in the left central panel bears my face. The Doors open of their own accord when I approach, and the eyes of the flanking gargoyles and Santa Inés follow me as I enter.

The foyer has a semi-circle desk manned by three receptionists. I call them the Moirae, for the fate of your call is in their hands.

Dolores looks at her watch as I enter. She wears a pantsuit, horn-rimmed glasses, and has her hair done up in a bun. I can't remember a day of work that didn't begin with her. The Grand Dame of our institution, she rules with a grandmotherly smile and an iron fist. "Doctor Diaz. The Chancellor insisted that I remind you about this afternoon's faculty meeting. Five o'clock, his office."

"Good morning, Dolores. Thank you. I will be there."

The interior of the base rotunda could not be more different from the exterior. Whereas the outside resembles a mausoleum, the interior is all warm wood. Skylights bathe the room in yellow light. The original keel of the *Santa Inés* bisects the ceiling, and the rafters are the ship's ribs. Beneath them, I feel like I'm standing in the ribcage of a wooden giant.

The central tower that vaults through the building houses a medieval spiral staircase and an elevator leading to Emérico's office. It serves as his living quarters and personal conference room. All of the walls of his floor are made of one-way glass, so that the tower blazes like a torch, a beacon to the magically inclined.

Odd bits of magic float about the hall helter-skelter, some as mundane as levitating paper airplanes, others as ornate as illusory Chinese dragons. As I walk through this area, I am greeted from all angles with good mornings and hellos. I recognize most of the faces, but I would be hard-pressed to name all but a few.

Seven bronze double doors lead into lecture halls devoted to a different discipline within the college. From South to North, the doors belong to Illusion, Conjuration, Abjuration, Necromancy (perfect west), Evocation, Divination, and Transmutation. There's no mistaking my lecture hall. Whereas all the other doors are embellished with scenes of mages performing the most dramatic effects their respective practices can produce, the door to the Necromancy lecture hall just has a giant skull on it.

I open the doors. The hall slopes downward into a tiered amphitheater. Students occupy all of the three hundred seats. The walls and floors and ceiling are made of a light-colored wood, save for the back wall, which is all whiteboard. The central whiteboard is raised, revealing a projector screen. "Good morning, everyone," I say as I descend the central aisle. I still get a bit giddy when my voice bounces off the walls.

A chorus of "good morning" roars back.

I drop my doctor's bag on the desk. "Welcome to Introduction to the Practical Arts. I am Doctor Pablo Diaz. I will be your first guide along the pathways of the Arcane. Everyone raise your hands, please." They all do.

"Put down your hand if you are already part of the College of Practical Arts and know that this class is the prerequisite for all other classes in the College." Most of them do. I remove my jar of salt from my bag. "Okay, wow, good. And put your hand down if you are taking this as a general elective." That's most of the rest. I uncap the jar of salt. "Auditors and refreshers, down." A few more. I grab a handful of salt. "Anthropology or Classics students?" Down to three; two sitting together, and one alone in the front row, right next to the aisle. "Would the two of you stand?" The pair obliges me.

I can see from seventy feet away that their eyes are bloodshot. "Why are you here?" I say.

One of them laughs and takes his seat. The other says, "Yo, for real, though, this class sounds live. And some YouTube chick said it was dope."

"Gotcha. Well, you're both welcome to stay. What about you, sir?"

The man is in his mid-forties, wearing a windbreaker and khakis. He's clutching a Bible like it's a life preserver. "You, sir, are the Devil's right hand! You're corrupting these children into your Satanic ways—" yada, yada, yada.

I pour a circle of salt on my desk, mutter a few syllables, and draw a horizontal line in the air with my thumb and forefinger pinched. The man's face is turning red as he yells, and he is slapping his Bible against his hand, but no sounds emanate.

"Our friend here is a fanatic and will be removed shortly," I say to the auditorium over his silent cursing and stomping, "and you have just witnessed an act of magic. Please, don't be alarmed. I haven't hurt him, and I can dispel the effect at any time. He can still hear himself, and he thinks you all can, as well. I just created a bubble around the man that doesn't allow sound to escape."

Whooping and applause.

"This class, however, is not going to teach you how to perform magic. Instead, I will give you the foundational principles of the Practical Arts. If you want to learn actual magic, you must understand the theory behind magic, demonstrated by passing good old PRC 1101. One moment, please."

I go to the emergency exit, where two uniformed police officers are waiting. "He's the dude standing," I say to them. I snap, and all the sound returns to the man in the front row.

"Saint Agnes is a martyr for the Catholic Church! You have defiled her image, and *yourself*, and you're *defiling* these *innocents*!" He is going hoarse with how loud he is yelling. The police escort him up the aisle and out of my domain.

"Saint Agnes of Rome *is* a Catholic Saint, said to have performed miracles," I say, "and what are miracles if not magic? A little backstory." I sit on my desk. "Agnes was a devout Christian, which meant no premarital relations. One of her suitors didn't take her refusal well, so he reported her to the local magistrate, a prefect named Sempronius. Sempronius ordered her—a *thirteen*-year-old girl—to be marched through the streets, naked, to a brothel. The townsfolk were allowed to 'test her chastity' when she arrived. When the soldiers came for her, her family was nowhere to be found.

"As they marched her through the streets, her hair grew long enough to preserve her modesty. The soldiers tried cutting away her hair, only to find clean robes beneath. When they reached the brothel and tried to open the door, it disappeared. The Romans, undeterred, tried to mete out their punishment in the streets. Every man who touched Agnes of Rome with ill-intent went blind.

"Agnes was led to prison. Sempronius refused to attend the subsequent trial, where she was sentenced to death by immolation.

"Tied to a stake, Agnes continued to stymie the efforts of the Roman soldiers. They tried to set her on fire, but the wood would not catch. When they tried to behead her, their swords bounced off her neck. They had to starve and expose her for *three days* until she passed out, tied to the same stake. Only then was a soldier able to stab her in the throat.

"Keep this story in mind as we move on." I walk to the computer and pull up my introductory presentation. I turn on the projector. There is shuffling, but no one speaks.

The first slide is just a title card: class, instructor, section number.

The second slide is a picture of a balding white man in a Hawaiian shirt, who—in spite of his hair loss—is able to pull off a ponytail. He wears large glasses with thin frames and sports a thick gray goatee. "This is a math nerd." I pause. "What's his name?"

Only a few hands go up. I point to a girl in a pink cardigan in the third row, the person I would least expect to know.

"Doctor Diaz," she says with mock outrage, "you speak ill of none other than the Great Gary Gygax."

"Three points for Gryffindor?" I say.

"Hufflepuff, sir!"

"Oh, excuse me, madam. My sincerest apologies." I struggle not to smile. "In all seriousness, this guy"—I point at Gygax—"was a visionary. In 1974, he and his buddy Dave Arneson produced a series of rulebooks based on a miniatures wargame—army men with rules, basically. This rulebook contained all the math a group of friends would need to create magical characters in a fantastical setting for the purpose of 'playing the role' of the hero. The game they created is called *Dungeons & Dragons*, the first *roleplaying* game ever.

"The creatures Gary populated his game with were taken from mythology, folklore, and popular fiction: dragons, fairies, orcs, you know the like. Problems arose because he also included demons, witches, wizards, and sorcerers in his game. Conservative parents found their children talking about Beelzebub and demogorgons and succubi and thought their precious little snowflakes were going to start worshipping Satan. *D&D* got lumped in with the Satanic Panic of the 1980s, similar to what video games faced in the nineties and at the turn of the century. All the kids really wanted to do was play a personalized game while gorging on pizza and soda.

"But here's the rub: I'm pretty sure Gygax was actually a wizard."

I bring up the next slide. It is a picture of an eight-pointed star, with the names of the schools of magic at each point. "This is magic, according to *D&D*. Does it remind you of anything?"

Mumbling throughout the room. Someone calls out, "Those are the schools here at the College."

"Correct. Now repeat after me." I retake the podium. "The practitioner acted in a powerful manner." Most repeat. "The practitioner *acted in* a powerful manner." Basically everyone. "The practitioner ACTED IN a powerful manner." Same emphasis.

"'Acted in' is your new and most important mnemonic." Next slide: the words ACTED IN vertically. I click once on my remote, and the word 'ABJURATION' fills in the void next to the 'A.' "A, abjuration, the defensive practice of magic. This includes shields and wards."

A cacophony of unzipping and shuffling and furious scribbling.

Click. "C, conjuration, the practice of making something appear from nothing. If I pull a quarter out of thin air, it is conjuration."

Click. "T, Transmutation, the practice of changing things that are already there. If I turn someone into a frog, I have transmuted them."

Click. "E, Evocation, the practice of controlling forces and energy. The ever-popular fireball is an evocative act."

Click. "D, Divination, the practice of seeing the unseen, and knowing the unknown. If I read your future, or the stars, I am divining."

Click. "I, Illusion, the practice of making things appear as they aren't. If I were to disappear right now, I would be casting an illusion."

Click. "N, Necromancy, the practice of manipulating entropy. If I cast a curse or animate a dead body, I am a necromancer."

"What about the other E?" This from a young man in the fourth row whom I didn't select when I asked about Gary Gygax.

"Ah, yes. E for Enchantment. Here, reality and the game differ. When we talk about paradigms and beliefs—the true sources of magic, by the way—you will understand why enchantment is impossible. Magical practices are expressions of an individual's will. You can't force your will on another using magic because you would be manipulating the core fabric of existence. Not to mention, it would topple society as we know it."

Emérico floats in through the back door. His Chancellor's robes drift about him, mist cascading off his bare skull. He gives me a skeletal thumbs up. I barely nod. None of the students notice him, either because I am that good of a teacher, or more likely because he has cast some effect so that only I can see him.

"The only way to control people's minds is through mundane psychology, and while that isn't my department, I would recommend Psych 1101 to everyone."

I click over to the next slide: a classical painting of a woman in an orange tunic down to her ankles, wearing a black robe and a red mantelet, being crowned by a cherub; another cherub is at her feet, hugging a lamb. Her eyes are cast upward, and her hands are steepled in prayer. "*Saint Agnes* by Domenichino," I say.

Emérico taps his left wrist and holds up his hand, fingers splayed. He means to remind me that the faculty meeting is at five o'clock, even though he's giving me the signal for five minutes. At least he is trying. I give him another nod and he leaves.

"Think about the story I told you about Agnes of Rome. What kind of magic did she use against the Romans?"

The stoner who sat down immediately when I drew attention to him raises his hand. I nod to him. "Abjuration," he says. "When?" I say.

"When the swords couldn't cut off her head."

"You can *definitely* stay," I say. "What else? You, all the way in the back."

The guy stands up. I can't make out his face, but he looks large. "Conjuration, with the clothing under the hair."

"Good." I get most of the answers I want: transmutation of the hair, necromancy of the men's eyes, illusion with the door. "What about evocation and divination? Nobody?" I wait. "Evocation: controlling the fire. Divination: where was her family when the soldiers came for her? We know for a fact that her sister was a Christian, as well. Saint Agnes—Santa Inés—was protecting her family.

"A little more from RPGs before we leave." I click over to another slide. "This is a spell descriptor for the spell 'Color Spray' taken from the *Advanced D&D Player's Handbook.* Gygax no longer appears in the credits for these books by this point, but the wisdom has already been passed down. Take a look here," I say and use the remote's laser pointer to circle a section of text that reads 'Components: V, S, M.' "What the hell does V-S-M mean?"

Ms. Hufflepuff answers without being called on. "Verbal, somatic, and material."

"Verbal. Somatic. Material. V-S-M. Very Strong Magic; another mnemonic for you all." I move over to my desk, pass my hands over the ring of salt, and say, "Abracadabra." I look around, confused. A few faces look worried. "Let's try that again." I wring my hands at the salt and say, "Abracadabra!"

Nothing. "Why the Hell isn't it working, class? I have the verbal: 'Abracadabra.' I have the somatic: waving my hands. And I have the material: salt. Shouldn't this do something?"

I let them murmur it out for a bit.

"Nothing is going to happen if I don't *want* it to happen. Or rather, if I don't *will* it to happen. And verbal, somatic, and material components are just helpers, ways to focus the will into producing the desired effects. There are two ways to think about these magical ingredients: training wheels and skis. Training wheels make sure you get your balance until you don't need them; skis help you get to the bottom of the mountain faster, even though you could always hike down.

"Earlier, when *our friend* was condemning my life's work, I used the salt, a few magic words, and a motion"—I pinch my thumb and forefinger and again draw a horizontal line through the air—"to make the effect instant. Casting a spell without foci such as these could take hours to enact. Hence, skis."

"Why salt?" a voice calls out from the center of the room.

"Excellent question." I peer around to find the voice, but no one stands out. "Magic is personal. Your personal beliefs will empower your magic and the reagents you use will reflect that. I use sea salt specifically. Think about the ocean. All that movement, the waves, the storms, the pressure of the deep. Salt must collect that power—at least I think so—so it works for me.

"What's this stuff?" The next slide is a picture of grains of rice.

A somber chorus of "rice" peppered with a few "*arroz*."

"Life-giving rice: the staple of Cuban cuisine and your last mnemonic for the day. Handy for remembering the types of spells."

RICE appears vertically on the screen.

"Rituals are powerful effects that take time to prepare and cast. Once active, they can be maintained with concentration. Post-mortem interviews, summoning extraplanar creatures, and scrying are just some of the many rituals available.

"Incantations are what most people would call spells. They're the quick, single expressions of a person's will. They take little to no preparation and you will usually enact an incantation without reagents. But remember: skis. If you use reagents, you can activate the incantation faster.

"Channeled spells are like incantations that you attempt to maintain over time. Whereas an incantation is instant, channeling allows you to maintain the effect. It's turning the fireball into a persistent flamethrower.

"And finally, enchantments." A flurry of hands go up. "I know, I know. Relax. In our jargon, enchantment does not mean mind control like *D&D*, but rather permanently imbuing an object with magic. Making a magical object like a wand, staff, or charm, permanently transmuting an object, or laying a ward are all enchantments.

"Think of these terms you learned today as guides, but remember there are gray areas. Potions are a perfect example. You use a ritual to brew potions, but they behave like incantations in that they are instant, and can last over time like enchantments."

I check my watch. "Remember, ACTED IN, RICE, and V-S-M, Very Strong Magic. Next class, we'll go over the principles of Abjuration. You should all have bought the course packet from the bookstore already. Inside, you'll find the syllabus, as well as copies of the scheduled readings. Expect a test every four weeks, with a cumulative midterm and final. See you all Thursday."

Students stay for about a half-hour trying to have conversations with me. I entertain all of them. The last one is Ms. Hufflepuff. She introduces herself as Lola de Cardenas and says,

"Do you give private lessons?" "No, sorry. But should you have any questions, my office hours are Tuesdays and Thursdays, right after class, for three hours. Starting next week."

"Why did you choose to focus on Necromancy?"

"I wanted to help people. I was helped by a Necromancer when I was young."

"I'm trying to decide on my focus."

"That's what this class is for. Hopefully by the end of the semester, you have a focus or two in mind. Take the 2000-level survey courses to be sure it's the right path for you, and then you can start on your major coursework. Nothing has to be set in stone, either. If you start down one track and don't like what you find, you can always speak to an advisor and pivot. We're mutable here like that."

"Great, thank you," she says. "It was an amazing lecture."

I take the emergency exit at the back of the hall, where the cops were waiting. Because the lecture halls are actually a full story deeper than the first floor, the exit corridor leads to the basement laboratories, colloquially referred to as the dungeon. The dungeon bears a lurid name but is the most mundane part of the College. The walls are white drywall, the floor is linoleum, the lights are long fluorescent tubes embedded in the ceilings, and the labs themselves are clean and sterile. Along with the labs, there are numerous storage rooms for furniture and non-magical material.

It is slightly disenchanting to think that the College would need such a place and decorate it in this manner, especially when considering all the care that went into constructing Santa Inés Hall. But the plumbing has to go somewhere.

By next week, every lab will be packed with students. There is, however, one room that only staff and alumni can access. Beneath the twin stairwells of the Eastern face of the building there is an empty landing, barely illuminated. Speaking the right magical syllables when no one is around and knocking in a specific pattern causes a portion of the wall to slide down, revealing the best-kept secret in the College: the Well.

The Well is part storage room, part extra-dimensional prison. It serves as job number two for most graduates of the College, and job number four for me. The College purchases magical resources and reagents needed to conduct the labs in exchange for cash, and stores them in the Well.

Most magical reagents are harmless in the hands of the uninitiated, but some are lethal. Others still may be intelligent beings with ambitions all their own; catching them is one thing, storing them another.

I reach for my cell phone with the intent to turn it off, when my vision blurs and all the sleep I didn't get last night starts beating my eyelids. My knees buckle, and I fall. The longer you haven't slept, the less efficacious the refresh. I should have planned for this. No. I shouldn't have gone out last night. I'm a college professor, not some twenty-something working part-time. I force myself to my feet and enter the Well.

The room is so white that it is impossible to see the contours of the walls. Nothing indicates the height of the ceiling. About twenty feet from the entrance, a wooden sign hangs in midair. It reads, in bronze letters, BURSAR.

The Bursar is a demon. He stores the magical goods on Emérico's behalf. He wears a white, pin-striped shirt, a tweed vest, and a green accountant's visor. His skin is red, his hands are clawed, and his teeth are so large and sharp that he must make an effort to close his lips around them, giving him a puckered look when he's not speaking. His overlarge yellow eyes have the thin diamond irises of a cat.

"Welcome, Archmagus Diaz. So good to see you. You just missed Archmagus Coghlan. She told me you might have had a little trouble this morning."

"Yes. The Chancellor allowed a religious fanatic into the building again, and I won the lunatic's lottery."

"From what Archmagus Coghlan was saying, you handled yourself with aplomb."

"Glad to hear news travels so quickly."

He smiles. He could probably decapitate me with one bite. "You don't look well, Archmagus. Is something wrong?"

I swallow hard. I can feel the grease forming on my forehead, the cold sweat invading my pits and crotch. Even the air feels heavy. "It's nothing."

"Hmm. Well, what do you have for me today?"

I lower my doctor's bag in the space between us. I know there is a counter there, but because the room is so white, I never know if it is *actually* there. I open the bag and pull out a mason jar filled with a pale liquid. I situate it on the counter.

The Bursar grabs it once my hands are behind my back. "Ectoplasm, one pint. Impressive."

"I've been saving up."

The Bursar's hands disappear beneath the counter and bring up an inkwell and quill, as well as a large black leather ledger. He opens instantly to my page, and notes my deposit with the most beautiful script I have ever laid eyes on.

My phone rings.

"You brought a cellular device in here, you hydrocephalic primate?!" The Bursar slams his fists down on the counter.

I don't have time to look at who is calling; I am desperate to shut off my phone.

"You are an Archmagus of this institution! You know the rules!"

"I'm turning it off! I'm turning it off!" I power down the phone.

"It is too late for that, simpleton!"

"Relax, will you? What's the worst that could happen? Some imp gets out with me?"

But I know the worst that can happen. I studied it. For my master's thesis, I looked into using modern technology the same way the classically trained might use a wand or staff: to store spells and incantations. The problem I kept coming across was that most cell phones do not function like foci.

Luddites may carry a phone purely for functionality and in theory could store spells in such a device. But the grand majority of people spend so much time worrying about their phones, caressing them, fondling them, cleaning them, that the devices pick up part of our patterns and become spiritual receptacles. This is not dissimilar to how a witch will imbue an animal with a part of their essence to create a familiar; the most skilled practitioners can ride their familiars the same way a ghost might possess a human or a god might use one of his followers as a cheval.

In other words, cell phones are conduits. And everyone is just wandering around, ignorant of the fact that they've imbued something with a part of themselves. Worst of all, because 99.9% of people have no idea how cell phones work, the unfettered belief in their functionality makes them inherently magical.

And I let mine ring in the Well, a clarion call.

"Leave your phone with me," the Bursar says. He holds out his hand and unfurls his fingers one-by-one.

"Absolutely not." There is no way I am leaving what could be a piece of my soul with a demon. If something does sneak out, I will handle it.

The Bursar glares at me and returns his attention to the ledger, recording the rest of my deposit with his meticulous calligraphy. "The Chancellor will hear about this."

"Oh, I hope he does. Now cut me my check." I pick up my bag.

The Bursar slides the ledger under his counter and produces a matching checkbook. He writes a check out quickly, but his handwriting remains a work of art. "Whatever happens to have escaped with you, make sure you bring it back," he says.

"You and I both know nothing is getting out of here," I say.

The Bursar flashes an unctuous smile. "I will see you later."

5
Folktales

THE BURSAR'S TIGER-SMILE stays with me as I climb the East Tower stairs. I was flippant with him, but I start imagining the horrors that could have climbed in my cell phone: ravenous ghosts, a gremlin, maybe even a demon. I try to shake the thought away, but I keep seeing my pocket exploding in the middle of traffic and a pixie flitter away from the wreckage of my car.

It would have taken seconds to turn off my cell phone. God damn me. Last night's trip to the beach keeps paying dividends. My father would say I deserve it.

I exit through the front of the building. When I reach the parking lot, I get in my car, turn it on, and crank the AC to full blast. The car was already hot; the rushing air suffocates me. I lower the windows and turn my phone back on.

Before I can even pull up my recent calls, a different number is calling me.

"Hello?" I say.

"Pablo!" Orlov says.

"Abram?"

He barks in triumph. "I am glad to finally have reached you. I am in need of your services. Immediately."

The clock on my dash reads 2:24. I could be back in time for the meeting. But I am so tired that if I take this job right now, I am likely to kill someone else and myself on the way. "Can this wait until later?"

"I will double your rate again. This is very important."

My father would never turn down work. "I'm on my way," I say and hang up.

I immediately regret that decision. I rub my eyes. Another refresh isn't going to save me. I need a solution. I take out a vial of witch hazel from my doctor's bag and breathe in deeply. I chant a few syllables and allow my vision to drift, so I can perceive the magic in the air. What I see is a swirling, technicolor nightmare, like doppler radar over the College. Each passing car and pedestrian disturbs the liquid rainbow, pulling strings of magic along with it.

This is not abnormal for the College. Performing magic leaves a signature, magical residue. The first day of class can have this effect on new students, eager to learn and perform. I bet my lecture had something to do with it… although the entire campus is awash. Emérico wouldn't have needed this much magic to raise all the dead in the city. Maybe I can use it.

I find a silver needle in my bag and pierce my forefinger. I begin chanting and supercharge the drop of blood. I draw a small diagram on the inside of my wrist.

As I channel the ambient magic into me, a kaleidoscope of color rushes at me, into me, through me. The diagram acts as a valve. The effect is heady. I rub my face and arms, my skin tingles, and with each breath I absorb more raw magic. I sit in ecstasy and use the magic to block the adenosine receptors in my brain and break down the cortisol running through me, feeling awake, alive, so alive, and the flavor is ambition.

Alert. Sensible. There shouldn't be this much magic in the air, even on the first day of class. Day one or not, something is wrong.

I call Emérico.

He picks up on the third ring. "How do you use this damnable thing?"

"Hello?" I say.

"Hello? Pablo?"

"Sir, good afternoon. I am sorry to bother you, but the University is surrounded with residual magic."

"Yes, yes. It is the first day of classes, Pablo. It is to be expected."

"No, sir, not just the College. The whole campus is—"

"I will look into it. Just make sure to be here at five o'clock."

If the Chancellor is on it, I have nothing to worry about. "Yes, sir."

"See you then." His voice gets farther. "Now how do you stop this—" he says and the line clicks.

I turn on my car, dismiss the magical awareness, and drive away.

Almost no time has passed when I'm halfway to the beach. No accidents, mystically light traffic; *something* is going on. I am still floating, full, saturated with chaos, but I know my city. I pull over to the side of the highway and huff witch hazel again, expecting my vision to turn to the monochromatic wavelengths of banality.

My arms break out in goosebumps. The same liquid rainbow is spread over the airport.

The drive starts to make sense. Miami is an aggressive driving city. But we're all so obsessed with getting where we need to go, and the city is so flush with magic, that even the untrained and uninitiated are tapping into that primal mojo and causing everything to work smoothly.

I get back on the highway and call Emérico. He doesn't pick up. I keep calling, all the way to Miami Beach. He never answers. He can work the very essence of creation but he still hasn't figured out his cell phone. I am reminded of my father.

I park in the alley behind the Eight Ball and give my keys to a valet. He refuses to look me in the eyes. I am again associating with these less-than-savory Russians. If I'm late to the faculty meeting, Emérico might scry me. A ward will make me impossible to find. I take out a piece of chalk from my doctor's bag and draw a circle on the inside of my jacket, then a triangle inside the circle, and three symbols at the points: Mars (the circle with the arrow pointing out at 45 degrees) for me, an eye for vision, and Ø to negate. I charge the ward with a whisper and a snap of my fingers.

The back door of the Eight Ball opens. A man in his early twenties says, "*Koldun*?" The sides of his head are shaved, but he's kept it long up top and slicked back. He wears a gray suit and several gold chains. "Come. Abram is waiting upstairs." His English has the meanest aftertaste of Russian.

He takes me to the third floor. All the offices stand empty in the dim hallway. "Abram is in the back," he says and retreats down the stairs.

The frosted glass door shines at the end of the hall. A shadow paces to-and-fro in the yellow light. I tap the glass.

"Bogdan?" Orlov says.

"No. Pablo."

Abram slips out of the door and closes it gently behind him. His knuckles are bruised and bloodied. He reeks of booze. He extends a hand to me and I take it. "Thank you for coming on such short notice."

"Is everything okay?" There are bags under his eyes. Has he slept since last night?

"I could ask you the same."

"What do you mean?"

"You're bleeding," he says, and looks at my left wrist.

"So are you," I say, and point at his knuckles.

"Before I open this door, I have to explain to you what it could mean." His glazed and bloodshot eyes lock onto mine. I'm not sure if he's blinked since he emerged from the room. "Being here, right now, you could already be in trouble. But if you go through that door, it is without a doubt."

He's giving me an out. I should have called Sandobal as soon as I had this man's phone number. I'm not thinking straight, all because I went out for a beer last night.

Could whatever is on the other side of that door be that bad?

"Listen," Orlov says, "I know I'm asking a lot. I will triple your fee. You're the only one I trust to solve this problem for me."

This, plus last night's check, plus the ectoplasm, plus Jimenez's check; this isn't selling my soul, it's winning the lottery. "Open the door."

Orlov raises his chin, almost smiling, and gives me one more handshake. He leads me into the same office where I scried on his behalf. There is a figure slumped on the couch. Yuri, roughed-up. A letter opener sticks out of his chest.

"Of course," I say. The corpse causes me to sigh.

Orlov runs a hand over his head and rubs his chin. "This is why I called you."

I shake my head. How much trouble am I really in, just by being in this room? "I can't bring the dead back to life, Abram."

"I just need to talk to him."

"And I found him for you." This man is dead because of me.

"For that, I have already paid you," Orlov says.

Forget about my career being on the line. I am an accessory to murder. This is fifteen years in a prison cell. This is my father's death before my release. I drop my bag and sit on the arm of the nearest couch.

Orlov walks to the bar cart in the corner of the room. He pours two drinks from a decanter, brings one to me, and goes to sit at his desk chair. "Drink," he says.

There is nothing I can do here. Nothing. If I subdue Abram somehow, I couldn't go to the police. All the magic in Miami isn't making this disappear.

Orlov stares at Yuri and gulps half of his whiskey. "This idiot cousin of mine. You know what he loved? Fairy tales. He knew all of the stories from our grandmother. He loved 'The Tsar and the Thief.' And yet he did this to me." He sniffs and downs the rest of his drink. "You know the story?"

"No." I take a pull off the whiskey and run a hand through my hair. The magic in me crackles like static.

"It is a good one. About loyalty. You should look it up."

"I will." I look at my watch. "What are you going to do about the body?"

"I will take care of it," he says.

"Like you did on Sunday night? You know they pulled those bodies out of Biscayne Bay. It was all over the paper."

"That was Yuri's doing. I know how to handle these situations. I just need to talk to him," he says and rubs his knuckles, those manhandlers. What side of the law am I even on? If I don't help him now, he might kill me. Even if I do help him, he might kill me.

If I can get out ahead of this, I might be able to recover some semblance of plausibility with Sandobal: I was only here last night for a beer and some pool until I was coerced into finding Yuri. I only took the second job because I feared for my life. "Get me a towel, please."

Abram searches the bar cart and finds unused hand towels still in a plastic zip-tie. He tosses them to me.

"Help me. Let's stretch him out." I motion with my head to Yuri's legs. Orlov grabs them while I use the towels to keep my hands free of blood. Yuri's a big boy. It takes the two of us to fix the corpse so that it lies in repose. "Give me a minute."

I stare at Orlov until he goes back to the bar cart.

I kneel next to the couch and open my doctor's bag. I rummage through it and find my jar of salt and the candle; so little salt left. I have to wait for pots full of sea water to evaporate to collect this.

"Explain to me what it is you are doing," Orlov says, squatting down next to me. He snuck up behind me; he's close enough to break my neck.

I swallow and clench my jaw. Here is the first client who actually cares about the process—a potential student. The widow, the cops, they couldn't care less. They want the results. But this man, this murderer, cares. It says a lot about what I do.

"This candle"—I hold it up—"is made from the fat of a yearling calf. To me, it symbolizes life cut short. This sea salt"—I touch the lid of the jar—"is one of the oldest things I can think of, so it works for me. I see my work as old."

He nods, stands up, and crosses his arms. I light the candle and pour the dried sea onto the corpse. The salt on Yuri's body glows blue and shifts to mimic the pattern of arteries running through his body. I hold a pinch of salt on my tongue. I nod to Orlov.

He says something in Russian to the corpse.

"You can't ask in English?"

"No. His English is terrible."

If I can't speak the language, I can't activate the brain properly. This is why being a Cuban-American Necromancer is useful; my parents' tongue allows me to activate more brains than monolinguals.

"Just give me a second," I say. Normally, it is impossible to cast two spells at once; reality will only allow so much tampering. But there's a lot of magic coursing through me. I activate an enchantment with a few flicks of my right hand and a whisper. I sigh when I am not torn apart. The corpse is under my control. "Try again," I say.

"Where is the merchandise, Yuri?" Orlov says.

And now I can understand Russian.

Something is definitely wrong.

Perhaps being supercharged with magic is allowing me to work multiple spells. But I remember the highway. Could the magical essence extend this far, fifteen miles from campus? I have to get back to the College.

"Why isn't he answering?" Orlov says.

"Sorry. Ask again."

"Where is the damn merchandise?" Orlov says.Yuri's brain and body respond, now that I'm paying attention. "Underneath the dashboard of Faina's car," Yuri's corpse says.

"And the money?"

"Inside of the spare tire."

Orlov throws up his hands and slaps his thighs. He paces before falling into his chair. He places his hand on his face and rubs his temple with two fingers. "Did Faina put you up to this?"

"No."

Orlov closes his eyes. "You did this to me? This was your plan?"

And there it is. The same question everyone asks. It's not a widow's 'Did you love me?' but it is close enough.

"Yes," Yuri's brain responds.

"Where is Faina?"

"At the grocery store, buying cigarettes."

"Can he know that, Pablo?" Orlov says.

"No. It is the last thing the brain knew about her," I say.

"Did you involve anyone else in this?" Orlov says.

"No," Yuri's corpse says.

"You are selfish and ungrateful, Yuri. You can stop now, Pablo."

I spit out the vaporous salt, ending the ritual. Yuri goes slack-jawed.

Orlov stands up and pours himself another drink. He downs it in a single gulp, stares at Yuri, and serves himself again. He snorts. His breathing is labored. He drops into his chair and rubs his forehead. "Can you make him talk again?"

If there's enough magic floating about, I could keep him talking for hours. "Almost certainly," I say.

"Do it."

I check my watch. I am running out of time. The thought of driving and the memory of colors gives me an idea. I point at the body and tug. It works: his hand twitches. "This is insane!"

"What?" Orlov says.

"There is so much ambient magic that I don't have to conduct a ritual!"

"Is that dangerous?" Orlov says.

"I don't know." I honestly don't. I feel like I am on drugs. I like it.

"Shouldn't you?"

My heart pounds in my chest. There's only one place to find out what's happening; maybe the Chancellor will explain all this ambient magic at the faculty meeting.

Orlov swills whiskey and falls back into his chair. He says to the corpse, "Tell me 'The Tsar and the Thief.'"

I don't have time for fairy tales. I *have* to be back at the College. I have to tell them about the potential arcane apocalypse.

But I am conducting a post-mortem interview *without a ritual.* It shouldn't be possible.

I pump the corpse full of life; it stands up and starts walking around, speaking with the emphasis and gesticulation of a living, breathing Yuri, the letter opener flashing in the lamplight every time he turns. "One evening, Tsar Ivan, as was his custom, disguised himself and went amongst the people, who he knew suffered. He wanted to lessen their plight, but he knew not how. When he entered an alley, he discovered a young man breaking into a bakery. 'Boy, what is it you do?'

"The young man looked to his elder and said, 'I know this baker. He overcharges for day-old loaves, so I break in and steal them, to keep him from cheating the people.'

"'This is good. Let me help you,' said Ivan Vasilyevich. The boy agreed. The two ransacked the bakery. 'Where shall we go next?' Ivan asked.

"'There is a cobbler down the street who charges by the nail, rather than by the sole. We must steal all the finished shoes and return them to their owners.'

"'This, also, is good. I will help you.' The two entered the cobbler's storefront, ransacked his wares, and delivered them to the just peasantry of Moscow. "'We have done a lot of good,' Ivan told the young thief. He wanted to test the boy's loyalty to the people. 'Why don't we raid the royal treasury?' Ivan asked.

"The boy slapped his elder, not yet recognizing the Tsar. 'I would never steal from the Tsar. He uses those coffers to help his people!'

"'This is best. Come, I know some boyars we can rob.' And so the two went about the town, taking from the greedy princes, who knew not how to rule.

"In the morning, Tsar Ivan summoned the thief to the palace and made him his advisor, since his heart was pure."

Yuri takes a seat and remains still. I let go of his brain.

Orlov is hiding his face.

An old woman's cackle rends the silence. She speaks in Russian. "Abram Volkovich Orlov, your tears are a poor sauce for the stink coming off you."

Orlov jumps up and wipes his face. "Are you doing this?"

"No, I—" Something small and square rips its way out of my pants pocket, the same place where I keep my phone. A tiny wooden hut with a thatched roof lands on the floor, balanced atop two chicken legs. The hut sports a small deck in front of the door, its railing decorated with what looks like human skulls, and braids of garlic hang from the eaves. A woman no larger than a fingernail stands in the doorway.

The crone's voice is louder now. "You have traded your honor for a pittance, Abram Volkovich. Your traitorous blood will make sinful pudding!"

As Orlov reaches into his desk and retrieves a massive handgun, the hut sprints for the door.

I kick at the hut, but it dodges deftly and plows into my other leg, throwing me into the air. I land flat on my back, driving the breath out of me, and slam my head on the floor.

The chicken hut hops onto my chest. I am face to face with the miniscule witch.

She wags a gnarled finger at me. "And you, Pablo, son of Tristan, should know *better* than to bring a cell phone into the Well!" She cackles again, and the hut leaps off my chest and through the frosted glass behind me.

I scramble to get up. Glass breaks twice somewhere down the hall. The crash and tinkle of glass are the symphony of my life falling apart.

"What was that, *sorcerer*?"

Koldun: sorcerer. He thinks I'm a sorcerer. Not a wizard, studied and learned, but a sorcerer, an undisciplined monster that twists magic to their own ends. An evil bought and paid for.

"Why didn't you shoot her!"

"I did not want to hit you."

I try ripping out my hair. "Do you know who that was?"

"Of course," Orlov says. "That was Baba Yaga."

6
Boogeyman

BABA YAGA, the Devil's Chambermaid, Witch of Witches, Devourer of Children. Emérico told me she was born human, a Russian peasant. She was raised on the macabre fairy tales shared with the young to scare them onto the moral path. Those stories of witches and fairies and magic fed her beliefs. At first she was benevolent, ensuring successful harvests, delivering babies, curing the ill. But someone asked her to cast a curse, changing her forever. The villagers' respect turned to fear, and so she became fearsome, until only the darkest paths remained open to her. She became the unrivaled hellion of the Urals.

She is tiny because Emérico hunted her down and stripped her of her magic centuries ago, terror in legend her remaining issue. Faced with those teeth, and that hunger, and a world fat with tourists and children, I start to crumble. I ransack my bag until I locate the witch hazel. I snort too much and almost cause myself to vomit, but I am once again aware of the thaumaturgical hellscape. Not that it is any help. The room is so full of swirling magical interference that I can't locate the trail belonging to the cannibal stalking the streets. I release the effect.

"We need to find her," I say. "Tell your men to start looking in—"

"None of my men will help you," Orlov says. He is staring at Yuri's corpse.

"They have to!"

"None of them would dare cross her."

"If we find her, I can put her away forever!"

"She has escaped once and will escape again."

"She *escaped* because *you* called me!"

Orlov turns to me. "Me? I know nothing of magic. Only one of your kind could have unleashed this horror, Pablo."

"Help me! Please! Innocent people are going to die!"

Orlov opens a drawer and stores his handgun. "No one is truly innocent."

I cram everything back in my doctor's bag and slam the door on the way out.

I whip through the narrow back alleys of South Beach, desperate for any clue as to Baba Yaga's whereabouts, wondering what Emérico is going to do to me, terrified I might not be able to capture the Russian Boogeyman. In each empty corner, in every desolate carport, I find only Emérico's disapproval. I have broken trust with my mentor, the man who gave me power. I deserve to be flayed.

Flayed like this poor rat! I find the pelt about five blocks away from the Eight Ball. Bloody bird tracks retreat from the mangled vermin, due North. She's gotten at least one kill already. It won't be long before she gluts herself on blood and ambient magic. The only one who will be able to capture her then is Emérico.

I run. My doctor's bag hampers me, but I am unwilling to part with it. Two blocks away, I find the head of a cat. I palm the head and charge it, viewing its last memory: the chicken-legged hut—large as a rottweiler—bearing down, Baba Yaga swinging a meat-cleaver from the porch.

A block away, a woman screams, followed by a car crash. Breathless, I arrive to bedlam. Two lifeless bodies on the street, a car inside of a roadside cafe, people running in every direction.

The police will arrive soon. Sandobal will be with them. If I survive, there will be questions. Maybe I should just let Baba Yaga kill me. I scan the area until I find a kid on his phone filming the scene. I run up to him.

"Did you see what happened?" I say.

"Man, I don't know what the—"

"I will believe you. Just tell me."

"There was, like, a *doghouse* on legs, and a midget woman was in it, and she—"

"Where did it go?"

"Bro, that thing hit that fucking car, and like, *pushed* it right into the building, then jumped over—" He points over a nearby building.

"Thank you!" I say as I run away. That kid has this week's viral video on his phone, assuming he has a steady hand.

People are watching her. Human eyes—as hungry for spectacle as she is for flesh, aghast and fascinated by her power—are only making her stronger. Their shock will fuel their belief in her. Belief breeds power.

Behind the cafe, I find a chunk missing from the asphalt. It takes me a moment to realize it is an impact crater. More screaming and tires screeching, this time from the beach. I hit Lummus Park and find a police SUV flipped over. I have to fight against the fleeing crowd, but when I break through the sane, self-preserving mob, a new horror awaits: spectators following the hut. They live-stream and face-time and Tweet and record the bedlam, feeding Baba Yaga, giving her their eyes and their will. The hut tears a path through the seagrape-covered dunes, heading for the ocean.

"Face me, witch!" I say. My legs twitch and my chest is tight, so the challenge comes out a little too high-pitched.

Baba Yaga cackles. The hut, now larger than the lifeguard towers that line the water's edge, disappears over the green hills. She's probably flying around out there right now, capturing children to make her grisly borscht. I can't fight her alone. There is only one person who can help me.

I call Emérico directly. I pace and chew my nails and wring my hands and pull on my hair, waiting for him to answer. He doesn't. I try three more times. Nothing. People are going to die. Have they already died? I call the College. *All circuits are busy now*. I scream. I call Melody Coghlan and Nick Russo, the only archmages who trust me enough to give me their phone numbers. Neither of them answer.

Because they're all in the godforsaken faculty meeting!

I spot a puddle next to a water fountain. I run to it and kneel in the mud. I throw one of my business cards into the water, spit in it, and focus on the reflection of the sun. The puddle explodes into light as I turn it into a makeshift scrying pool. "Oh, God, please let this work," I say. The pool reflects my face; the edges shimmer. I pinch my thumb and pointer together, then slowly draw them apart, causing my image to zoom out, showing me the carnage on the other side of the dunes briefly. I zoom out further, until I have a bird's-eye view of Miami. I draw my fingers across the pool, panning to where I know FIU campus to be located, and start zooming in. I can see Santa Inés Hall for a moment, and then a ray of light blasts me from the mirrored windows of Emérico's sanctum, knocking me onto my back.

Emérico wards faculty meetings. Of course he fucking does.

I could just run. Maintain illusions and wards for the rest of my days. My life insurance will keep my father alive for years. If Emérico isn't aware of this catastrophe, then he may not be aware of my involvement. The Bursar will tell him, but when Emérico catches Baba Yaga, he'll assume she finished me. And I can hide myself.

More screams. I dig frantically through my doctor's bag until I find my boxing wraps. They're white elastic cloth covered in purple runes, drawn in ink made from black tulip extract and my own blood. Evocation is battle magic and doesn't come to me naturally, so I made these wraps for self-defense. Through them, I can control kinetic energy. It isn't as impressive as hurling fireballs or lightning bolts, but it can be just as deadly.

I have to wrap every knuckle multiple times, then my wrists. The time. It ticks by. Screams punctuate each second. Fat drops of sweat roll from my forehead into my eyes or down my nose. Finally, I seal the second wrap, punch my fists together, and the runes burst to light, charging my fists. I take off my jacket, effectively breaking my own ward, and toss it and my doctor's bag into the waxy, broad-leafed sea grapes that hold the dunes in place. I sprint towards the water.

As I crest the sandy hills, my stomach turns. The chicken hut stalks the cream-colored sands between two massive white lifeguard towers that stand blocks apart. The cerulean Atlantic and powder-blue sky serve as a backdrop. Beachgoers closest to the hut attempt to flee, but I can see others hiding in the man-high thickets at the foot of the dunes, pointing their cell phones in Baba Yaga's direction.

The Queen of Conjurers hangs over the balcony, laughing and chucking harpoons attached to ropes at anyone that comes in range. She spears a rather large man through his calf and starts reeling him in like the great, flopping catch of the day.

So far as I know, I am second only to Emérico when it comes to necromancy. But that isn't going to help me battle this monster; she'll deflect any curse I throw at her. "Witch!" I say and pantomime the action of breaking a stick over my knee. The shaft snaps, freeing the man.

With the rope suddenly free of tension, Baba Yaga falls flat on her ass. She cries out, but then our eyes meet. She grins, grabs the railing, and hoists herself to her feet. She wags a long, bony finger at me and clucks her tongue. "You're a naughty boy, Pablo, son of Tristan," she says, as if I had stolen pie off her windowsill. She dives into her house.

Every wizard's magic has a unique resonance that other spellcasters can recognize. Sometimes it's sensory, sometimes emotional. Baba Yaga's putrid brand of magic tastes like curdled milk. It creeps out of the hut, surrounds me, until Baba Yaga flies out of the front door in a giant cauldron. Her stringy gray hair streams out behind her. She wields a giant pestle like a cudgel. Her wart-covered, hooked nose dominates her face. She bears down on the same man she speared. His girth and leg wound prevent him from crawling away.

I throw a punch in the air and my magic magnifies its force. The blow knocks the cauldron off course with a deep *bong*.

"Impudence!" Baba Yaga says. "Kill him already!" She brandishes the pestle at me, condemning me to death with a wave.

The hut's door turns toward me. The chicken legs paw the sand before the living domicile charges at me. Every fall of its tent-pole legs shakes the sand and rattles my teeth. It swipes at me with talons the size of scythes.

I punch and the force sends the chicken leg backwards. The hut goes down on one knee. Baba Yaga—free from my meddling—bludgeons the wounded man in the back of the head, raising a mist of blood in the setting sunlight. Her next meal secured, she zips over to engage the police SUVs and dune buggies that appear to the north.

I try to run after her but the hut stands up impossibly fast. It kicks up a cloud as the chicken legs churn up the sand. I throw a meaty right cross and the projected force slams into the side of the hut, shivering one of its walls. But the hut is relentless. It tries to gore me again. I yank on the attacking leg with my magic, causing the hut to fall into a split. Wind and sand assault my face as the appendage passes within a foot of me.

At this rate, I won't even get the chance to fight Baba Yaga.

I push as much force as I can against the sand, launching myself toward the hut. I hit the door full-on with my shoulder and crash into a realm of despair.

The smoke that fills the hut stings my eyes to tears. It emanates from a crude stone firepit in the center of the room. The open door and damaged wall let in enough light to illuminate the horror. A ceiling decorated with bundles of herbs and butchered cuts of human flesh. A gooey ribcage. A table littered with bones and teeth and limbs. Entrails used as sausage casings. A lifeless woman in a one-piece swaying on the meat hook that protrudes from her chest. And two burlap sacks heaped in a corner. I run to the sacks and undo the ropes keeping them shut. The children I find bear a resemblance to the dead woman swinging behind me. They are blindfolded, gagged, and utterly lifeless.

I vomit.

I did this. I caused this. I try to punch the damaged wall with magic, but nothing happens. My spell is broken. My will has left me. This is all my fault.

How soon before I'm skewered and dangle from this roof?

The hut—wounded, infuriated, and clever—takes off at a gallop. I tumble backwards, nearly breaking my neck. The hut's speed is enough to pin me to the wall, like a carnival ride to Hell. Then the hut stops abruptly, throwing me out of its blackened, sickening innards.

I get a moment in mid-air to take in the scene. Up the beach, Baba Yaga uses her cauldron like a wrecking ball, crushing police cars. The hut races up the beach to join its geriatric master.

The ocean rushes up to greet me. I skip on the water like a pebble until the bath-warm sea finds me slow enough to engulf.

Hanging in salt, pushed by a cool current, I begin kicking my way upwards. It takes an eternity to break the surface, to return to the life-giving air. I cough up more of the Atlantic than I was expecting. I tread water while the hut kicks over a beach cruiser and Baba Yaga brains a cop that took a pot shot at her.

Salt. Weightlessness. Gunshots. Smoke. Pandemonium.

If I don't do something, *all* of those men are going to die. Helicopters begin to circle the beach. Three of them rotate around Baba Yaga, sending live pictures of her wickedness all over the city.

But there's one behind me. It turns to get a shot of her. I see the Telemundo logo painted on the side. If I can get their attention, I might have a chance.

I spit a short incantation and a glowing disk of force rises beneath me, lifting me out of the water. I kneel, stretch out my arms, and inhale. No witch hazel, but I remember the kaleidoscope of magic in Orlov's office; it must be out here, as well. I try soaking it up, gently at first, until I feel a crackle of power in my fingertips. I envision it running through my veins until I can feel every nerve excited with power.

I stand and clap my hands together. The helicopters shake midair. As the force rushes out of my hands, it picks up a wall of water that speeds toward the beach and slams into the hut.

The helicopters turn their cameras on me.

I plug in to every newsfeed in Miami, maybe the country. A million eyes watch me as I take up a fighter's stance, standing in the middle of the ocean. They watched and fed Baba Yaga and now they're watching me; I can feel the weight of their gaze, and with it their hope that something will end the death and chaos. I channel the held breath of the viewing public through my fists.

The hut charges toward the water, realizing where the tidal wave came from. If this bipedal outhouse wants to come get me, I will blast it to pulp.

Let the world watch.

I clasp my hands above my head and bash downwards. When the projected blow contacts the roof, the roof caves in and the air above it erupts in an explosion of wood chips and fireworks. The air shimmers red and blue, courtesy of so much loosed magic. I fling my clasped hands upward and the transferred assault shivers the porch, disintegrating the decorative skulls. Pink and blue and yellow after images of a giant fist fade. The hut falls backward.

My blood is up. The old mad joy is in me. I launch a flurry of punches downward. Each smack of my magically-charged fists flares into multicolored fire. Hydrostatic shockwaves carry away curtains of sawdust. The hut tries to stand. I won't let up. I throw a right cross; the force travels through the hut like a cannonball. Boards and splinters fly. I feel like I am winning. A low groan confirms it.

In the thrill of it all, I forget the real threat.

Baba Yaga cauldrons into me. I've never been hit by a car but the feeling must be similar. The impact of the black iron pot against my body causes all my spells to melt. I once again fall beneath the waves.

I drift through the great blue-green and damn myself for not paying attention. Caught up in the ecstasy of destruction, aware that the world was watching me, I tried to put on a show. It was a Hell of a show.

But I let my guard down. Now I am going to drown for want of restraint.

I try to swim upwards but my chest, shoulder, hip all cry a chorus of pain. I claw toward the surface. I am out of breath too soon. My last breath will be salty. I spit a small stream of bubbles. The green water above me turns clear. So close.

Fingers touch my skull, then clamp down on my hair. The hag yanks me up, almost scalping me. Back to oxygen. I gasp for breath, inhale too much of the sea, and start coughing. "Here's a fine prize for an old woman! Pablo, son of Tristan!"

I hold onto her wrist to keep her from tearing open the skin of my forehead. "Let me go!"

She crinkles up her massive nose, revealing her sharpened teeth. "Spritely, by my troth! You need tenderizing." She smashes my face with her pestle.

I feel my nose break. There's a dull pressure behind my eyes that keeps them closed. I try to inhale through my nostrils and my mouth fills with blood. The coppery warmth pours over my lips and chin. I have to gasp to avoid drowning in my own humors.

"No defenses left, boy? *Hmm?*" She giggles and raises the pestle one last time.

Her shark's grin of iron teeth. Her hooked nose. My executioner. How didn't she get out before? And how did she fill that hut so quickly? She burst from my pocket to ruin my life…

No, she didn't.

The hut did. The hut that she protects. The hut that moans. The hut that grew with each life she took. An expression of her power. She may have birthed it, but it is tied to her as she is to it. I'm willing to bet my life it is her familiar.

I gasp, swallow more blood and power, and extend my left arm. I wrap the hut in as much air pressure as I can muster. "I will kill your pet." I squeeze my fist and the moaning echo turns into something high-pitched and desperate. Baba Yaga screams and dunks me beneath the waves. She tries to hold me under, so I squeeze my fist tighter. She pulls me back up.

"Stop it! You horrid animal! You'll kill it!" Her shrill words, the way she gnaws her bottom lip, the wide-eyed glances between the shore and my face.

I show her my teeth, which must be as red as hers are slate. "Take us to it."

She goggles at me. Her arm, clutching her raised bludgeon, trembles.

I squeeze my fist again. Groaning and cracking on the beach. "Do it, you hoary cunt. Or with my last breath, I'll turn that outhouse to tinder." My balls are somewhere in my stomach. I wonder if this is what a heart attack feels like. It is hard to swallow so much blood. Baba Yaga screams in my face. Some spittle lands on my cheeks. I am ready to die but I'll take the only thing this monster loves with me into oblivion.

The cauldron starts floating toward the shore. She dumps me in the swash like so much flotsam and glides to her pride and joy. She leaps out of the cauldron and coos and rubs the hut like it was a prize horse. I crawl out of the surf holding my ribs. "Get inside," I say from one knee.

She sneers with indignation, petting her occult construct. "You are a cruel man, Pablo, son of Tristan. As cruel as that creature you call master!"

"Emérico is not my master. He is trying to help the city."

"Oh, yes! I see what a fine job he is doing! And soon, you shall see just how much he wants to help, I am sure!"

"Shut up and get inside!" It hurts to yell.

The hut bends down and Baba Yaga flings the cauldron before her with a force no centenarian should be able to muster. She climbs over the few boards that remain of the porch into the front door.

"Wait! Bring out the woman and the children."

"You would deny an old woman of her meal, as well?"

"Absolutely."

She stomps and makes a high-pitched growling sound in her throat, but she eventually brings out the bodies. I do not let go of the air pressure. I begin shuffling around the hut, allowing blood to dribble out of my nose onto the sand. The police arrive when I have finished creating the channeling circle. I put one hand up, but keep the other fist pointed at the hut.

"My name is Pablo Diaz. I am from the College of Practical Arts. Please, go get my doctor's bag. It is somewhere over there, on the other side," I say, and point at the dunes. Guns are pointed at me. "If you want me to neutralize this creature, I'm going to need my doctor's bag. My wallet is in my bag, and you can call Sergeant Sean Richards or Detective Elisa Sandobal of Metro Homicide if my driver's license isn't proof enough."

It takes time to get everything sorted out—well past sundown. Eventually, an officer brings me my bag. I pour the salt out of the earthenware jar and set the container just outside the circle. I plunge both of my hands into the sand and concentrate on all the magical energy in the circle. I envision myself as a magical spigot. I start draining all of the power she's absorbed through me, back into the air. As it pours out, it feels like I'm wading through a fetid swamp, like walking through crusted spiderwebs, like chewing cotton. The hut shrinks down to its original size. I get a good magical grip on it again before I walk over to it and physically place it into the jar.

Baba Yaga, now miniaturized, returns to the porch with a wooden bowl in her hand. She slurps bloody slurry from a large spoon. "Before you jail me, perhaps you would care to listen to a tale?"

"No more stories," I say, and move to cap the jar.

"Even if it is about your master?"

I don't say anything but I don't stopper the jar, either.

"Your master wasn't always as he is. He kept his flesh intact for over 100 years. He was unrivaled in his power"—she eats a spoonful—"and woefully mortal. Do you know what he did?" She cocks a tiny eye and wags her spoon at me. "He ensorcelled every ribbon of flesh on his body. He wasn't happy just controlling magic; he wanted to *be* magic! And he *succeeded*.

"Do you know the cost, boy? His soul. And a hundred thousand others. On All Saint's Day, 1755, he sacrificed most of Lisbon to make a devil of himself." She cackles and pours the remnants of her bowl into her mouth. "And yet, you quarrel with me."

I slam the lid on the jar, seal it with wax from a normal candle, and carve some wards into the wax for good measure. I place the jar in my bag. I limp over to a waiting ambulance, wondering what 18th Century Lisbon and my broken face have in common.

7
Shock and Awe

I SIT IN the back of an ambulance. Police strobes and the EMT's flashlight pair up to birth a headache, just one more on a list of ailments: scalp, face, nose, shoulder, ribs, hips, heart.

"Sit up, please." The EMT's hands shake as he administers my concussion test. I have to push the flashlight out of my face before the man gives me a seizure. He can really only check one of my pupils anyway because the left side of my face has swollen as a result of being tenderized.

"Will I live?"

"We won't really know until you get x-rays and see a doctor. Your nose is for sure broken, maybe the orbital socket, too. No skull fracture... probably. No dizziness, but you did vomit—"

"*Before* I got clubbed," I say.

"You probably have a concussion."

"I haven't slept."

"Yeah, that's not helping, either. Your pupils aren't dilated, but you stumbled on the way here. You can hold a conversation, but your eye isn't tracking right. You *need* a doctor," the EMT says.

The crowd around me starts pointing at the sky, squawking into radios, and yelling at each other. A few officers pull their sidearms. I stand and turn to where everyone is gesturing. A blue comet is blazing a trail towards us. The Chancellor is coming.

"Look, you're already pretty nervous, and I'm not going anywhere. Why don't you go have a smoke while I talk to my boss?" I say and point up at the sky. The EMT glances at Emérico, pulls the pack of cigarettes from his shirt pocket, and scuttles away to join his partner at the hood of the ambulance.

My mentor approaches. As if he weren't the most powerful being alive, I've now armed him with the litany of my carelessness: an abomination loosed on the city, murdered children, the eyes of an entire police department, the confirmed sneers of my city, the failure to follow the rules of my institution. It would be more humane if he just ended me on the spot.

Emérico drifts down from the clouds. His robe billows about him as if he is underwater; I know he does this so that his clothing doesn't hang off him like a wet towel on a hook. Cold mist pours off of his bleached bones, out of his sleeves, and trails behind him on the ground. The hollows of his eyes glow with ectoplasmic light. He wears a white mantelet embroidered with gold, and matching leather gloves. Any cop jumpy enough to have drawn steel quickly stows their weapons.

Emérico looks over his shoulder. Behind him, the police are gathering, talking into radios, eyeing us like we're already in cuffs. His eyes flare up and he speaks through a clenched jaw, but he whispers. The grinding of his teeth sounds like rubbing charcoal briquettes together. He's been in the country for over three decades now, but he still has a slight British accent. If you pay close attention, you can occasionally catch Portuguese intonations. "Do you have any idea how much risk you've put us all in?"

"I know. I'm sorry."

"Everything that I have built over the last twenty years, the trust *you* have worked so hard to engender, jettisoned like excrement! Why?"

"Sir, I wasn't thinking. I was exhausted."

"Oh, you *were* thinking, but about *what* I have no idea! You certainly had enough foresight to ward yourself before a faculty meeting. You shirk your responsibilities to the College like a truant child and take measures to hide your actions in the meantime. By God, you're the one who made me aware of the current magical atmosphere, *Archmagus*. Why on earth would you obfuscate yourself in a time of crisis? Because your phone went off in the Well and you did not want to be punished?"

An officer breaks from the pack of cops and calls as he approaches. I don't recognize him, but I have worked with the Miami Beach Police before. "Pablo Diaz?"

"I sent you here because I felt a magical disturbance emanating from wherever the Hell you were. Understand?" Emérico says.

I nod. He isn't covering for me; he is protecting the College. "Yes, officer," I say to the cop when he arrives.

"I'd like to take your statement."

"Is there a problem, officer?" Emérico says and turns to him.

"I need to—"

"Take his statement. I heard you," Emérico says. "Before you do that, would you do me a favor?"

The detective stammers. "It's important that—"

"Could you tell dispatch that Emérico Abílio Ovídio de Menezes is here on scene and would like to speak to the Chief of Police? Could you do that for me? And could you tell him that one of my professors is in need of medical attention, but that you need to take his statement?"

The detective looks him up and down. "You need to wait here," he says and walks away.

"Chancellor, I—"

"Where is the Hag?"

I retrieve my doctor's bag from between my legs and pull out the earthenware jar. I wince when he snatches it from me. Emérico examines the seal. "Hmm. This is good work. Clearly from a hand practiced with *wards*." He shakes the jar violently. "She rebuilt the hut?" he asks.

"Rebuilt? You didn't trap her with it?"

"Of course not. I destroyed the last one."

I only threatened to destroy the hut in desperation. Destroying a familiar is the magical equivalent of dismemberment. Theoretically, the act could sunder a practitioner's mind. Was she always a monster? Or did the death of her first hut drive her insane? Surely Emérico did it to limit her, not to torture her. "She said something to me after I drained her."

"You cannot trust a thing this monster says," he says. His teeth click inside his skull with every "T". He gives the jar another shake.

His skull, with its glowing blue eye sockets, reveals nothing of his emotions. Is he smiling when he rattles her around her makeshift prison? I cannot tell.

The detective trudges back. "The Chief will be here soon, Chancellor."

"Are you done trying to harass my employee?" Emérico says.

"Yes," he says, and walks away.

"Go get yourself checked out at the hospital. And report to me first thing in the morning." He calls the EMTs. "Gentleman, your patient awaits."

"Again, Chancellor, I am—"

He dismisses me with a wave of his hand and floats over to the water's edge, holding the jar in both hands, head down.

The day before I first met Emérico, my father picked me up from school early. I was not told I had a doctor's appointment, nor a dentist appointment, and when my father didn't say anything to me when I entered the school's office, I could not fathom what I had done wrong. I was days away from my eleventh birthday.

"*Hola, papi*," I said.

"*Vamos*," he said. There was something off about his face, but I couldn't understand what it was. I feared his discipline, so I said nothing as he held the door open for me. He would not look at me as I passed in front of him. He overtook me with rapid steps and led the way to the car. I had to half-run to keep up.

He did not start the car when I got in the passenger seat. His heavy breathing could import anything, maybe even *La Cinta*. If I said a word, the punishment might start early, so I kept my mouth shut. He lay his head on the steering wheel and wept. I had never seen such a thing. My fear took on the bilious flavor of panic. "Daddy, what's wrong?"

He beat the steering wheel with his fist. Each thump echoed in my chest. What could I have done to bring my father to such despair? "¡Ay, mi hijo! ¡Mi hijo! ¡Estamos perdidos!" (Oh, my son! My son! We're lost!)

I knew exactly where we were. Had he lost his mind? "Daddy, we're in the parking lot," I said. "The parking lot of my school."

My confusion, my shrillness, snapped him out of his own misery long enough for him to break the news to me. "*Se murió tu mamá, hijo*" (Your mother is dead, son). There was no lie there, nor any catharsis from the threat of undeserved violence.

My tears were instant and hot and we beat the dashboard together.

The following day—a Wednesday—I dressed in my well-starched church clothing, as my father told me I should. I put up no resistance. After last Sunday's sermon, my mother had lovingly worried over the fabric of my shirt until it was stiff as grace. My shoes shone with the luster that my mother felt was God's due.

The salons of the funeral home were raucous, as is customary for Cubans; their volume reminds the bereaved that there's still living to do. But ours was the smallest salon, and the only visitors were a few of my father's friends from childhood, and some of the other orphans my mother had been raised with. The sympathetic did not stay long; they delivered their healthy condolences, prayed over the body, and departed. The widower and his son were just too much to bear, too somber to adequately console.

The funeral director, Osvaldo Jimenez, joined us at midnight to offer something to my father, something only whispered. Apparently, the College of Practical Arts was willing to provide a radical new service—free of charge—to those suddenly bereft of their loved ones: a post-mortem interview. The Latino Lurch explained the process to my father. I watched my father caught between his faith and the only thing he truly loved in the world. Witchcraft belonged in the Devil's wheelhouse. But to speak to his wife one last time—the temptation was too great.

Practitioner Simón Marrero wore his ceremonial garb. The cloak mystified onlookers. Practitioners wore them, at that time, by mandate of the College. Marrero was enormously fat and bald. He gave me the impression of a nefarious Friar Tuck. His Cuban was so thick and fast that I could only discern every third word, but my father understood him. Marrero began the ritual. I sat away from the casket and studied everything he did. The candle he lit, the ashes he spread over my mother, the chalk line he drew on her forehead then his own. I thought I understood.

My father, who obsessed over my mother, who bought her fresh flowers every Friday, who disciplined me so she wouldn't have to, told her corpse he loved her and that he didn't know how to live without her. He asked her if she lived happily and sobbed when she said yes. He asked her if she loved him and fell to his knees at her yes. He told her he would take care of me and was silent.

"¿No tienes preguntas, hijo? You no have question?" Practitioner Marrero said to me.

I nodded and he beckoned me to the casket. My father moved aside on the portable kneeler. "Are you in heaven, mama?" I blubbered it out, shamefully.

"No. I'm in the kitchen," my mother's mouth reported, her brain suspended in her final moments.

Practitioner Marrero stammered. "She no in kitchen!" But he was too late.

At eleven-almost-twelve years of age, faced with such an impossible prospect, I was ready to go home, expectant that some version of my mother would be waiting for me. No matter how many times my father, Marrero, or Jimenez explained it to me, the thought of contact with my mother would not leave me, could not be taken from me, and I vacillated between openly desperate and secretly hopeful.

My father—disgusted with me, with himself, with the ritual—drove us home. I ran to the porch and bounced on the stoop, waiting for him to open the door. I could see his anger, and for the first time in my waking life, he swallowed it. "She is not inside, my son. And if you think she is, you will only be more disappointed when I unlock this door."

"But—"

"She's dead, Pablo. Dead."

It was the moment we'd both been dreading. "If you're so sure, open the door," I said. He should have hit me, would have under normal circumstances. He unlocked the door, put his hand on the knob, and gave me one last look. Finding no trace of what he sought, he pushed it open. I turned on the light.

Nothing.

I walked around the kitchen table, checked every bedroom, the bathrooms, the back porch. No amount of searching would conjure her. I couldn't look at my father. I went straight to my room, hung up my clothing since I would need it in the morning for the interment, and lay in bed. I waited for my father's snores, which were a long time coming. And as I waited, I went over everything Practitioner Marrero had done, step-by-step.

When the details had cemented themselves into a script in my head, I snuck out of bed and went into the kitchen. I took pains not to be heard. I found a knife, a pair of scissors, matches, a votive candle, but I had no chalk, and no ash. The knife made sense even then: blood magic must be a thing. I took the trash can into my room and dug through it until I found what I was looking for: paper towels, stained with my mother's blood. The aneurysm killed my mother instantly, but the collapse cracked her skull. My father had to clean her blood off the floor to spare me his trauma, but his grief had overridden his sense of duty, and he still hadn't taken out the trash.

I peeled the bloodiest napkin apart and cut a silhouette of my mother's head as I best remembered her: backlit by sunlight streaming in through the living room window as she pored over her Bible. I flattened it out on the ground and could feel something happening. The room was charged. But she wasn't there yet. I went out into the kitchen to find the missing ingredient that eluded me.

My mother kept coarse sea salt in an earthenware jar in the spice cabinet. She said it made her cooking magical. I believed her. I spread the salt in a circle around the grisly silhouette. I pierced my own thumb with the knife and dripped what I thought to be enough onto the salt and the cutout. I knelt before the circle. I lit the candle and positioned it opposite me across the circle of salt. I placed my palms on the floor on either side of the circle and began chanting "*Estoy aqui, mamá, ven aqui*" (I'm here, mother, come here) as loudly as I thought I could without waking my father. I chanted for over an hour, and in desperation, I added my own salt to the circle.

The candle burned out.

The space in front of me twisted and folded like a curtain being grabbed. A lambent fingernail the color of flame pierced the fabric of existence. It was as if the whole of reality were a movie screen, and someone was tearing it from behind.

I kept chanting, whispering, fierce, sweating. Another finger poked through. A gnarled knuckle. A thin hand. The veins on the back of the hand were thick, and I knew that whatever those hands were attached to was not my mother. I stopped chanting, choked by the uncanny.

She peeped through the sundered veil, an old woman with a wicked grin. "It's just a boy," she said. She grabbed hold of existence and pushed it apart, and more hands seized the aperture between life and death, expanding it. The figures poured into my bedroom, three translucent fires in the shape of people. The tatters of actuality hung limp before me, and the space beyond was a cold vacuum.

"Who takes him first?" the old woman in the high-necked dress said.

"We can all get in, can't we?" said a teenager in overalls.

"Let's try," said a rail-thin man in a suit.

They rushed me before I could scream.

Ardelia Black, who beat her sister to correct her idiocy, only to be murdered by the great dullard for the abuse; Silas Young, a porter, drowned by his dock gang because he won a few too many hands of poker; Jonas Wentworth, who cuckolded his wife on their honeymoon and received tea laced with arsenic in return; their rage endured death, and they meant to use me like a marionette. They took turns controlling my limbs, getting the feel for their new vehicle. My hands became unfamiliar to my face.

The tear in the membrane between this reality and the next was mending itself.

"We won't be going back now," Ardelia said, and her smile was in her voice.

"What if *he* finds us?" Silas said.

"Poppycock, how could he?" Jonas said.

On the other side of reality, I could see a dot of blue light, and the stowaway phantasms could see it, too. Their panic was immediate, and I knew that if I wanted to save myself, I could not let them take me from this room. I rooted myself to the spot. They pulled at my limbs, pushed my darkest memories and my mother's image behind my eyes, screamed and cursed and cramped all my muscles. But I would not move.

Emérico stepped through the gash, a singularity of power and light, robed, holding a blue-flamed lantern in one hand and a saber with a gold pommel in the other. He cast his skull-face toward me. "How many?"

I barely managed a wheeze. "Three."

He pointed his sword at me. I thought he would run me through. The souls were torn out of me; I felt their screams fly into his blade.

Emérico loomed over me. "Who taught you to do this?" he said.

I shook my head.

"*Did* someone teach you?"

I kept shaking my head and wiped my face. I was relieved that my face and my hands were mine again. He picked up the bloody silhouette and scrutinized it. "Who is this supposed to be?"

"My mother," I said, and the sobs overtook me.

When my crying began to subside, Emérico bent down and placed a hand on my shoulder. He had saved me. He was no threat. I was determined to be courageous. "What is your name?"

"Pablo."

"Come. Sit on the bed, Pablo." He gave me a gentle push until I moved. He crouched down before me, so that we were eye to eye. "What you have done here is very special, but also very dangerous. You must not do it again."

"I just wanted to see her again," I said, stammering.

He pointed at the crucified Christ hanging next to my door. "Was your mother Catholic?" I nodded. "Then it is likely that her faith led her beyond that blasted land. The only ones that inhabit that dark place are the ones with a vendetta against the living. But she is gone, or she would have come." He held up the silhouette. I nodded, my face coursing with tears. "I am sure you loved her, Pablo, and I am sure she loved you, and you have a duty now. You have to honor her memory by living a good life. Be the good boy she would have wanted you to be." He stood up. "Do you know what the College of Practical Arts is?"

"Yeah," I said. The whole world knew about the College.

"When you are ready, I will be waiting to teach you. But until then, no more of this." He tucked the bloody silhouette somewhere in his robes, gestured with his sword at the remaining reagents on the floor, then pointed into the void. The reagents began floating into the tear in space.

"Wait! Please, don't take that," I said, pointing at the jar.

He plucked it out of thin air. "No more magic until you finish school, correct?"

"Yes. Right," I said, and held out my hands.

He handed me the jar, then stepped into the black. The tear in reality gelled back together.

Good sleep found me. Somehow, I awoke before my father. I showered, dressed, and went to him. "Papi," I said, and shook him.

He started from sleep. "*Hijo*."

"You have to get ready," I said. I went back into the kitchen, made a peanut butter and jelly sandwich, threw out the trash, and poured myself a bowl of cereal. When he emerged from his room, I said, "I made you a sandwich," and pointed at it.

He gave me a look that to this day I don't understand. But he did eat, however mechanically. He kissed me on the head afterward and told me, "*Vamos*."

We drove to the funeral parlor in silence and followed the hearse to the cemetery, along with the few friends of my parents who had come to pay their respects last night. All told, there were five cars in the procession. Father Enriquez met us at the burial site; I forgot his platitudes immediately. I took my cues from my father, and made no noise, but both of our faces spent not a second without moisture. We stayed long after the casket was lowered and all our sympathizers had gone. A backhoe tried to drive up to fill the grave, until the groundskeeper Douglas Bennison interceded and waved him off. My father fell at the lip of that ungracious hole and salted my mother's casket. I stood next to him and put my hand on his shoulder.

I wanted to use the same words as Emérico, to give my father the same comfort I had been given, but I could not find them. I stood sentinel to my father's grief until he made up his mind to leave, well past sunset.

8
In the Public Eye

THE RIDE TO the Eight Ball is short, and I just let myself feel the road and each turn and my aching face all the way there. I pay the taxi driver with a damp credit card. I trudge to the valet stand. I imagine I look like a travelling salesman returned from Hell: jacket slung over my arm, doctor's bag at my side, knot of pain on my brow, cuffs torn, the front of my shirt covered in blood.

Bogdan smokes a cigarette and chats with the valet.

"Get me my car," I say.

Bogdan looks me up and down and takes another drag off of his cigarette. "Abram wants to speak to you."

"No. Get me my car."

He says something to the valet that sends him running. "Mikel will get you your car. I will go get Abram," Bogdan says and goes inside.

My face begins to feel tight and the uneven field of vision caused by my pulsing, meaty eye socket nauseates me. Abram refused to help me. Why would I ever speak to him again?

When Abram throws open the fire door ten minutes later, I am still carless. "Pablo! How is it possible that you are alive?"

"Are you drunk?" I want to rail at him. I want to crush him. I could turn all the oxygen around him into mustard gas. I could twist all his muscles until they snap.

"I have been drinking, certainly. And you! You have been slaying monsters!" Dull of wit, he embraces me. The bear hug sets my shoulder on fire. "Are you all right?"

"Give me a second," I say, and squeeze my eyes until the pain passes. It is hard to believe that this great oaf doesn't know his own strength just because he's had a few whiskeys. What's worse is that he is treating me like this, like he is happy to see me. This brute sent me out into the street alone to fight the creature that haunted his childhood nightmares and I have no idea how I am going to distance myself from his menacing embraces and utter sociopathy.

I sigh. "Listen, we have to be very smart about this. The police are scrutinizing me right now. I think it is best if I stay away from here for a while."

Abram raises his chin, cocks an eye, and nods. "This is very wise. You are a learned man. That"—he taps my forehead and I see spots—"is why you beat her."

The valet pulls up next to us. Mikel holds the door open for me, and when I reach for my wallet, he puts up both his hands.

I try to protest.

"Your money is no longer any good here, Pablo," Abram says.

I sigh. I throw everything in the passenger seat, ease into the driver's seat, and find Abram standing in my doorway.

He looms closer. The fumes flowing from his mouth gag me. "I will be in touch. But not soon. Take care of you, Pablo," he says, closes the door, and pounds on the roof of my car.

I drive away, kicking myself for not withering his tongue.

Driving at night in Miami is an orange dream. But I can't enjoy the drive home. My face hurts too much. My phone is destroyed, a victim of the chicken hut's violent ejection and Baba Yaga's attempts to drown me. No amount of rice or sorcery—both processes really the same—will save my waterlogged phone. My father opens the door when I pull into the driveway. "*Carajo*," (Damnation), "Pablo, you look like shit."

"I feel it." I try to cross the threshold.

He stops me with a hand on my chest and looks me over. "*Ay, hijo*." He pulls me into an embrace. I drop my bag, my jacket, and let myself be hugged. For the first time since this insanity began, I let my anxiety out in a flood. "Don't cry, my son."

"It's my fault, Dad."

He holds me at arms length. "What?"

"They're dead because of me. I killed them."

"*Callate, hijo*," (Shut up, son). He hugs me again. "That monster killed those people. Think of all the people you saved. You're a hero. They said it on the news."

I don't know how to tell him how wrong he is. How I let Baba Yaga loose. I wipe my face. "I need a shower. And to sleep."

"*Dale*. I'm going to bed, too." He shuffles in.

I lug my stuff into my room. I hang up my jacket and I give it a once over. A little sand and chalk—nothing the dry cleaner can't fix. The bathroom mirror, on the other hand, puts the full horror of my face on display. My left eye is completely swollen now, to match my cheek. I run a hand through my stiff hair and immediately regret it. My scalp is hot to the touch. My shirt is crusty with sea salt. I doff my clothing and throw it in the hamper. There is a red line around my neck from where the shirt has chafed me. A massive bruise mottles my right shoulder. Another covers the area from my ribs to my hip. I should feel lucky. I could have been hooked through the abdomen, or harpooned in the leg, or had my neck broken.

I turn on the shower and wait for it to warm up. I step in, but am denied the relief of a cleansing the water hurts my face and head. I clench my jaw and turn the water as close to scalding as I can manage. The sand, the grit, the blood, in a quantum of pain gets washed away. I inch out of the shower and grab two Ibuprofen from the medicine cabinet. I cup water in my hands to swallow the pills. I limp to my room and ease into bed. It should be difficult to rest, but the medicine kicks in and merciful, dreamless sleep finds me.

Sunlight licks my eyelids. I forgot to close the blinds. I peek at the alarm clock in disgust and try to turn onto my bad shoulder, only to find that my ribs, too, have joined the cacophony of pain. No 7:50 has ever been so unforgiving.

I wince out of bed and grab my bathrobe from behind the door. I have to creep into it or feel the tenderized parts of me. I open the door to my room and my jaw drops.

Coffee. Cuban coffee. I don't know how the smell didn't get into my room. The holy trinity of *pastelitos*: guava, beef, and guava and cream cheese. *Croquetas*.

But there's more. Pancakes. Scrambled eggs. Bacon. Sausage. American breakfast that I love, but my father never developed a taste for. My stomach gurgles, in desperation and triumph. My father is seated in front of the banquet reading the newspaper, and the television is on, but muted. "Good morning, my son. I thought you might be hungry."

I go to him and kiss him on the cheek.

He rubs my head.

I suck in breath through my teeth.

"What's wrong?"

"She pulled me by my hair."

"Forgive me."

It seems almost sacrilegious with my people's brew filling the air, but I prepare the coffee maker and turn it on. "Where did all of this come from?"

He doesn't look up from his newspaper. "I made the American food. Armando brought the pastries and coffee."

I stare at him.

He looks up. "What? You think I can't cook?"

"You've never done it!"

"Sit down and eat."

I pour myself a mug of American coffee with cream and sugar, fetch a plate, and sit before the feast. My father pours me a tiny espresso cup of Cuban coffee. American coffee is a drink, but Cuban coffee is a drug. I grab a meat pastry and bite in. The buttery layers of delicate filo crunch like sweetened paper, and the meat inside is warm and savory. I wash it down with the sugary caffeine of my people.

"*Tu amiga*?" (Your friend?) my father says and points at the television.

Melody Coghlan steps up to a podium in front of the doors to the College. She is the Head of the Illusion Department, the spokesperson for the College of Practical Arts, and a punk rocker at heart. To the cameras and the people watching, she appears as the consummate professional in her jacket and skirt, a wholesome, freckled redhead. She must have glamoured herself, because I know she usually wears at least twelve pieces of facial jewelry and keeps half of her head shaved and dyed pink.

"Good morning," she mouths. I jump up, grab the remote, and unmute the television. When the Spanish translator starts talking over her, I switch to an English-speaking channel.

There is a delay between channels, and she repeats her good morning. "Yesterday afternoon, our Divination Department identified a magical disturbance on Miami Beach. One of our staff members was in the area, so we sent him to investigate. The selfless actions of Dr. Pablo Diaz prevented the tragic loss of life from reaching catastrophic proportions.

"Chancellor de Menezes has since been in communication with the mayor, the county's police departments, and the governor. Their statements are forthcoming, but I would like to assure you—my fellow citizens—that your College of Practical Arts is working around the clock to safeguard our city.

"The entity that attacked yesterday shares no affiliation with our institution. We are investigating, at the behest of local authorities, whether or not she was operating alone. For the time being, we have suspended all classes so that our faculty and staff can focus on your safety.

"The College of Practical Arts would like to assure our fellow citizens that we are here to help. It should go without saying that any disturbances should be reported to the appropriate authorities, and not the College. Should our assistance be required, the faculty, staff, and volunteer alumni of the College of Practical Arts will be at the ready.

"Chancellor de Menezes founded the College with one aim: to help our nation. We strive to maintain that goal. Our thoughts and prayers are with the victims of yesterday's attack, and their families. God bless Miami, and God bless the United States of America." Melody walks away from the podium amidst a roar of questions and camera flashes. I mute the television and try to dash to my room.

"Where do you think you're going?"

"I have to help," I say, and take another step toward my room.

"You're not going to help anyone if you faint. Eat."

"Dad!"

"Eat. And bring me the remote."

I want to go, but he's right; one pastry and a coffee isn't going to carry me through the day. I give him the remote and scarf down a plateful of food. He goes back to the Spanish station and listens to the Chief of Metro Police announce increased patrols and a curfew. I don't stay at the table to hear the mayor.

I shower, dare not shave, and opt for jeans and a button down. I emerge from my room carrying my doctor's bag. The voice on the television speaks over cellphone and police dashcam footage of me from yesterday. "—and while we still don't know enough about the College's involvement, one thing should be clear from this clip: this man risked his life to save those officers."

My father, now in his recliner, mutes the television. "Ready?" he says.

"I think so."

He waves me over and gives me a hug. "I'm proud of you, my son. Be careful. Take the pastries."

9
The Reckoning

EVEN THOUGH I HAVE the car's A.C. on full blast, I start sweating under my collar as I approach the College. The consolation I took from my father sublimes under the pressure of the meeting I am about to have with Emérico. What's worse, the doors to my building may not open. If my guilt overwhelms me, if the building smells fear, the doors will sense it and bar my entry. That psychopathic Bible-thumper only got into my classroom yesterday because Emérico let him.

I flash my FIU ID to the cops barricading the parking lot and they wave me through. I take a few deep breaths once I find my parking space but my heart doesn't slow. My arms prickle as I exit my car. The walkway leading to the doors is mobbed by television crews and police officers. I keep my head down and mumble apologies as I push through the mass, ignoring their questions. All of these people are going to watch my will falter—and so will my father, watching at home. The doors will remain closed to my lack of conviction.

When I touch the brass, the doors don't budge. I raise an eyebrow at the gargoyles. Their grins do not change. I clear my throat and the doors ease open. Slightly. I narrow my eyes and squeeze ignominiously through the gap.

Inside the foyer, the Moirae are answering two phones at a time. The buttons on their panels are all blinking. They scratch notes and hand them to interns and push a button to take more notes. Dolores glances at me, points at the ceiling, and goes back to putting out fires. I march past them into a deserted rotunda. Each step I take echoes back from the ribs of the *Santa Inés*. The place should be bustling, but because of me, it is empty. I've killed the magic.

I hit the 'up' button on the elevator panel. The heart of this building is upstairs, and I must seem like dental plaque to him. The front and back doors of the elevator open simultaneously. When I step in the car, the giant skull that guards my lecture hall stares back at me.

Each floor upward brings me closer to something I don't want to think about: reprimand, shame, disappointment, termination. Three more floors, and the doors will open onto my mentor, who entrusted me with power I do not deserve. The fire in his bony sockets will dim, and with it, any hope I might have had for redemption. On the seventh floor, my pulse is so high that my closed eye begins to throb.

Ding.

The dim lift floods with bars of golden light as both sets of doors slide open, revealing Death's Aerie, Emérico's office. The rear doors open on a western panorama: suburban sprawl for a few miles and the green of the Everglades beyond; in the afternoons, the sun reflects off the River of Grass, turning the sawgrass into fire. The door in front of me faces east toward Greater Miami, downtown, and the beaches.

Between the vistas, twisting stone columns support the pointed arches that frame the ribbed vaulting of the gothic office. If the exterior walls weren't glass, the room would look like a tomb; at night, it does. Odd pieces of functionality have found their way up to the Aerie. A large wooden conference table and leather rolling chairs decorate the western exposure. There is a comfortable sitting area furnished with square black couches to the north. Rows of shelves are mounted between the columns to the south, laden with scrolls, grimoires, textbooks, and three-ring binders.

The broad-and-burning sun rises in the east, peering between the columns as if through a dungeon grate. That brilliant orb is obscured by a monolith, and from it emerges Emérico's voice. "Come," he says.

My footsteps bounce off the ceiling and dull on their return, providing the bass drum to the high-hat of my heart. Emérico sits on a throne of marble with his back to the east. In front of him is his desk, a salvaged panel of timber from the *Santa Inés* laid on top of his sarcophagus. The accoutrements are spartan: a leather desk mat, a ream of parchment stamped with the FIU letterhead, and a small stone well filled with pens. There are no chairs opposite him; if you seek an audience with the master in his chamber, you must stand.

I place my doctor's bag on the floor and fold my hands in front of me. I clear my throat. "Good morning, sir."

Emérico turns over a piece of parchment on which he was writing and twists his pen closed. He lifts his head, takes off his gloves, steeples his fingers in front of him, and rests the bony digits where his lips would be. "Walk me through your thought process yesterday, so I can try to understand your contempt for the rules I set in place. Start with your class."

"I gave my introductory lecture to PRC 1101. When class was over, I decided to visit the Well and make a deposit. I had brought ectoplasm with me, and some other things. Before I opened the portal, the refresh I drank—"

"From the Obedient Apothecary," Emérico interrupts, "or one of your own?"

"Russo's. I did not sleep well the night before. I had a private consultation that ran much later than I expected."

"With whom?"

"A new client." Just some mobsters, nothing to worry about, I swear.

"Go on," Emérico says. "Before you opened the portal…"

"The refresh dissipated, and I forgot to turn off my cell phone. I went into the Well, and my phone rang while completing the transaction."

"You *forgot* to turn off your cell phone?" He leans in, splaying his fingers on the table.

"Yes, sir."

"The Bursar claims you were quite flippant. That you refused to leave your phone with him."

Cat-eyes and a too-wide smile, an accountant's visor and a wagging finger. *The Chancellor will hear about this.* "I was exhausted."

"And then, despite your exhaustion and your responsibilities here, you drove to the beach."

I can't tell him about Orlov. But he already knows I warded myself. "I was visiting with another client."

"You thought you had time to drive to Miami Beach, 'visit with a client,' and return to campus in the two and a half hours before the faculty meeting?"

"Sir, I thought it would be a quick consultation."

Emérico rubs his brow. What comfort he receives from the gesture is beyond me. Perhaps he does it to feel human, or to make me think he is human. But the sound is horrendous, like rubbing a dry pestle in a stone mortar. "You know that driving when you are tired is as lethal as driving drunk."

"Sir, I called you about the magical disturbance I perceived outside of the College when I left the Well. I used some of that magic to invigorate myself."

Emérico still has not looked up at me. "Then what?"

"I had to valet because I couldn't find parking on the street. That was when she hopped out of my phone and tore free of my pocket. I tried to give chase, but she got away. I hunted her. The rest you know."

"Where is that phone now?"

"Destroyed. Salt water."

Emérico drums his fingers on his skull, a grisly bamboo chime. I swallow and realize I am wringing my hands. I fold them behind my back. The hollow tapping stops. "Is there anything else, Archmagus Diaz?"

"No, sir," I say.

"Do you still want to be a teacher at this institution?"

I can't keep the shock off my face. I knew it was coming, but you never really *know*, do you? "Of course, sir. This is my home."

"Are you sure? Because you seem to find the rules of this institution too confining. Perhaps you would prefer the private sector."

"Sir, I can assure you, it will not happen again."

"I wish that were enough." Emérico sighs. "Pablo, your behavior displays an alarming dichotomy. You allow Baba Yaga to find her way back into this world, then you risk your life to dispatch her. You draw students to us with unforgettable lectures, and then trample the foundations of our institution. And you are not telling me the whole story of your misdeeds yesterday. I think you would be better off in another line of work."

"Sir, I… teaching is my life. Teaching *here* is my life."

Emérico shakes his head. "My instinct, if I keep you at all, is to cancel your classes for the semester and get you some counseling."

"Chancellor, that is not an option. I have an obligation to my students. The College has an obligation to them."

"Yes. You do. But you were not thinking about your obligations two nights ago."

"I fulfilled my obligations the night before last, reinforcing the wards on the city's morgues and cemeteries. But then I had to take that other job."

"*This* is your career! You missed *our* faculty meeting!" Rasping sounds from Emérico's mouth: he's grinding his teeth. "You have always been one of my brightest pupils, Pablo; your potential has only ever been bound by your insistence on mediocrity." Emérico slams his fist down on the desk, rattling the pens. I can hear his feet clack against the floor. He stands. He never stands. "You really think you can live your life this way? Galivanting about town at all hours of the night for a few extra dollars, like a common drab? If this institution meant a damn to you, you would not take side work. And you say that you consider this place your home!"

He subsides. "You will never know how exciting it was for me when you chose to pursue your Masters in Necromancy. I thought I had finally found my proxy, someone to carry on my instruction so I could instead focus on growing this College. Do you not understand, Pablo? You represent me! And you have brought suspicion upon everything that I do.

"The world wears a caul of banality, Pablo. I chose this moment in time to try and return magic to the world because the masses are hungry. I can feel it. They want something to change, but they have no idea *what* needs to change. I want to help these simpletons see that they can reshape reality in their image. Instead, they let others do the work for them, swilling refresh after refresh and stuffing their pockets with charms. They treat magic like a diversion, a viral video, instead of something to be respected, understood, and wielded. Good, decent, honest *work* will get them everything they desire. Magic is work!

"I made you department head because I thought you understood that. I thought you shared my passion, my vision. I thought you could set an example for these plebeians. But you are no better than any of them. You are just trying to meet your immediate needs, to satisfy your own greed for money and attention. And in doing so, you have put the College at risk. I thought I had made the right choice promoting you. Now I am not so sure." He settles back onto his throne.

"I am sorry that I let you down, Chancellor. Just… please, how do I make this right?"

"What I am about to offer you is not leniency. As I see it, your infraction is tripartite, and you must repair those three parties: the Bursar, the College, and myself. Right now, we are inundated in magical chaos. In order to avert another disaster, the other department heads are overseeing the installation of conduits around the city. Once they are in place, I will be able to cast a net over the city that will pinpoint magical disturbances, as well as allow us to siphon off some of the latent energy. "You"—he points at me—"will be at all of those installations"—he turns the finger upward—"assisting the archmagi of the College. You will continue in your duties as department head for the time being, and that entails organizing the teachers beneath you to maintain our protection of the cemeteries."

He raises a second finger. "The Bursar will have a list of goods that he wishes you to collect. I am sure he will be as creative as he is sadistic."

He lifts a third finger. "I have yet to decide how you will repay me. But you will. When I am ready."

"Yes, Chancellor. Thank you."

"Do not thank me yet. The Bursar will only be a preview. And if I cannot come up with anything, I am just going to fire you."

"Understood, sir." I pick up my bag.

"Visit the Bursar immediately and then go buy a new cellular phone. You are on call with us. Tell your personal clients that you are henceforth unavailable. Now go. You have to be downtown before two o'clock."

"For what?"

"Nick Russo was gracious enough to allow the College to install one of the conduits on some land he has been developing. He will need a capable servant. Treat him with the same deference you would afford me. Show us that you understand humility, even in the face of your undeserved fame." He turns over the parchment on which he was writing when I entered. He shoos me with his fingers. "That will be all, Archmagus Diaz." He doesn't wait for my response, just starts writing.

I try to glimpse him when I get in the elevator car, but he is once again hidden in the shadow of his throne.

The ride down to the dungeon affords me a moment of reflection. I contemplate the other department heads. Melody and Giorgio might be sympathetic to me. But Nick and Rhea are going to abuse me. They're going to make sure I know I am no longer seated at the right hand of the father. And so will the Bursar.

The elevator doors open in the center of the dungeon. When I step out, the motion sensors detect me and the lights come to life. I head to the Well. "Oh, my! Practitioner Diaz, that hematoma looks positively ripe!" The Bursar shows me all his teeth as soon as I enter.

"Good morning, Bursar."

He quickly raises his brow and widens his eyes—a micro-gesture, less than a fraction of a second—but I notice. I have never treated this creature with anything but scorn. "You know, I could take care of some of the swelling," he says and produces his fountain pen. "Just a little incision right at the corner of your eye. People will mistake the scar for crow's feet."

"Bursar, I—"

"Oh, be a sport, Practitioner. The cut alone might be satisfying enough, but if you let me drain it, I might be inclined to put a good word in with the Chancellor. What do you say?" He waggles the pen between his fingers and the nib flashes.

"Your offer is generous, Bursar, but I will have to decline."

"I understand," he says. He nods with his eyes closed and forces his lips over his teeth. "You could let your old friend the Bursar have at those succulent clots and relieve your pain. Instead, you're going to go looking for monster parts, and then some unfamiliar monster will consume not just the clots, but your whole being. And where will the Bursar be? Here, lamenting your unredeemed spirit and wastefulness." He sighs. "Damn humans; always so *selfish*."

"Are you done? I have to go buy a new—"

"Cell phone, yes!" He smiles and folds his hands in front of him. "What ever happened to your last one? Did you just drop it and crack the screen? You humans are known for such carelessness. Or did it perhaps become an interdimensional portal for a disgruntled lunatic?" He sucks his teeth and taps his thumb-tips together, keeping his hands folded. "You can't imagine how delicious your pain smells. Sauced with shame."

"May I have the list, please?"

"Are you in such a hurry? Isn't there something else you want?"

"From you? Nothing."

"Oh, really?" The Bursar reaches under the desk and pulls out my mother's earthenware jar. "Because the Chancellor transferred the former inhabitant of this vessel to another container, but he made it quite clear that I should save this for you—that it was important to you. He is getting on in years, though. Perhaps he was mistaken." He takes a deep breath, flaring his nostrils. "Oh, practitioner. You make it too easy. Would you dare to go against the Chancellor twice? Pray tell, how would you do it? Stab me? Blast me?"

I hold out my hand. "The jar, Bursar. Please."

"Perhaps you'd set me on fire? Oh, oh! I know! You could press me like a witch on trial! I'd make a marvelous Giles Corey! Yes!"

I bounce my hand. The Bursar licks his lips, tosses the jar back and forth a few times, and then lowers it onto my waiting palm. "There, now you have it."

I store the jar in my doctor's bag. "Tell me, Bursar, when was the last time Emérico let you out of this prison?"

The Bursar smiles his shark smile, but I can see him trying to dig his nails into his countertop. "You impudent—"

"Perhaps I will let you drain my eye after all."

The Bursar raises an eyebrow. "You cannot mean that."

"Show me the list."

"Oh, you are a card," he says, but he dives beneath his desk, disappearing completely from view. I am alone in a white void. For the first time ever, I hear a shuffle; somehow, the Bursar has misplaced an item. He emerges and slams a scroll sealed with wax onto the counter. I unfurl the parchment. The Bursar's calligraphy numbers out the grocery list of doom: unicorn blood, dragon scale, orc tusk, troll scalp, kraken beak.

I look up at the Bursar. "I am going to die."

"Of course. You're talking meat."

I sneer at him. "How about a deal?" The Bursar props his elbows on the counter and holds his chin up in his hands. "I'm listening."

"I will allow you to take that pen to my face and squeeze out as much gore as you can, *if* you take care of all of these items for me."

The Bursar stands up straight. "I think all those blows to the brain have softened your skull. Do you know what the Chancellor would do to me if I let you off the hook?"

"How long has it been since you've seen daylight, Bursar? Over two decades, I'd wager. No innocents to corrupt. No misery to feed on. But here I am, at your mercy. All you have to do is take care of this list for me."

The Bursar drums his claws on the countertop. "While my considerable prowess is significantly reduced by my office, I do happen to have some spare items that made their way into my possession, but not onto the ledger."

"What do you have?"

"Blood and tusks."

"Give me both and I'll let you fix my eye."

"Done." The Bursar smiles and conjures a doctor's bed, complete with straps.

"I'm not your victim. You're my cut man. Bring me a stool."

He starts to babble and protest, so I turn heel and make for the door.

"Wait! Fine!" he says.

When I turn back to him, there is a wooden stool in place of the previous contraption. "No funny business," I say. "And when you're done, you're going to patch me up."

"That's not part of the deal!" he says, but he already has the pen in hand, and is on the other side of the counter. I've never seen his legs before. Always standing on the other side of the counter, it was fanciful to think he didn't have any. Now, I am glad he feels the need to wear pants.

"Get an end-swell, too. I need to see out of both eyes."

The Bursar grins and flourishes his hand, producing the little eye iron.

"Coat rack, please." I sit down on the stool. I take off my jacket and hand it to the Bursar, who hangs it up on an antique, freestanding hat stand that pops into existence. I put my bag between my feet and pull out a small hand towel and begin twisting it. I clamp it between my teeth and nod to the Bursar.

The Bursar cleans the pen tip on his shirt sleeve then drives it into the swollen matter where the corner of my eye should be. I am biting so hard on the towel that I feel my molars move in their sockets. He digs around in the wound; it feels like he scrapes bone. I smack his hand away and let the towel fall onto my lap.

I brace my hands on my knees and take measured breaths until the white fades from my vision. "I still can't see."

"Give me the towel," he says and holds out his hand.

"No, use your own." I twist mine up. "Use the end-swell." I bite again.

The Bursar places a towel on my face with no care and then presses the cold metal against my forehead. I nod and he presses harder. There is warmth beneath his hand. My blood. After too long, he draws both items away.

"I don't think it is working," he says and grins.

"Mirror," I say. He hands me one. I hold up the mirror to my face. "I need you to make a cut right here," I say and draw a line right under my eyebrow. I hold the mirror between my knees.

"Thank you so much," he says, shaking his clasped hands in front of him.

"Get to it." Towel in teeth.

The Bursar carves a perfect line and I almost fall forward. He steadies me with a hand on my chest and presses the end-swell again. Blood drips into my eyes, but he catches it before it can get any further.

"I think that did it," he says.

I hold up the mirror to my face. The entire area fluctuates between angry red and sullen purple, but the swelling is almost gone. "Butterfly bandages?" I ask.

"I could cauterize the wound," he says, and holds up a white hot claw.

I grunt. "Quickly this time. Both incisions."

I scream. I have never smelled my flesh burn. I scream again.

"That was magnificent." He is panting and there are tears in his eyes.

I hand him the rolled up parchment.

The Bursar crosses off the unicorn blood and orc tusk and hands the list back to me. "Perhaps now you have a chance of surviving," he says.

"Doubtful," I say.

"You know, I prepared that list myself. Emérico told me I could exact retribution on you, but I thought those things might help you."

I scrutinize him for a moment. "Help me to what?"

"To see a little more clearly." He leaps over his counter and takes his place behind his teller window. "These are dangerous times, Archmagus Diaz. A magical fog over the city. Villains hunting the masses. Should the opportunity present itself, you might find use for some of those reagents."

I scoff and brandish the scroll at him. "It'll take me a decade to collect these."

"Surely, surely. Just keep your *eyes* open." He smiles and retrieves his ledger. "Just going to note these first two deposits." He waggles his fingers at me. "Remember how I've helped you, Pablo Diaz. Remember the Bursar."

10
Logistical Nightmares

THE PRIMARY CIVIC duty of all necromancers is to ward hallowed grounds. This arrangement was established after Dead Sunday, when Emérico emerged. The city fathers weren't keen on having corpses marching about the streets, so the Chancellor mandated that any necromancer working for the College must also work to maintain cemetery wards. It was the first step toward building public trust.

These wards, in particular, are simultaneously powerful and delicate. Their potency allows them to keep the dead from entering the areas they protect. Otherwise, a vengeful spirit could just jump into a corpse to exact their revenge, or float around as a poltergeist wreaking their basest desires on the nearest living soul. Their sensitivity lies in the fact that they require sigils to operate, and those sigils are subject to the elements on the material plane and on the plane of the dead. If a pigeon takes a shit on a ward, the magic might be ruined. If a ghost figures out a way to scratch a symbol, the magic might be ruined. We seem to always be steps away from ruin.

With the swirling magical apocalypse looming over the city, those wards are especially vulnerable. As head of the necromancy department, it is my job to make sure those wards are receiving the attention they deserve. I also have to attend to the conduit installations or else Emérico will fire me. If I can find the time, I have to research the remaining items on the Bursar's list. My chest is tight: the familiar breathlessness of panic.

Dolores stops me as soon as I exit the stairwell. She holds the phone receiver against her chest. "Come here. Your eye looks much better," she says. "You're in charge of organizing *your* people." She hands me a printout of phone numbers. "Yellow for graduates, pink for students. Don't call the students unless you have to."

"Thank you," I say.

"Buy a phone, Archmagus Diaz. Then you call me. *Then* you call them. Clear?"

I nod.

"You call me!" she says, and raises the receiver to her ear.

One need only dream up their desires, envision their fantasies, picture their destinations, and with a few short commands and almost no concentration, a person can teleport, conjure goods, pluck people from their past, and access the majority of the world's knowledge. All this, not from years of eldritch study or a concentration of will, but from a few taps and swipes on a piece of glass. More baffling, however, is the time it takes to retrieve most of the data from my now-salty, former cellular device.

The saleswoman at the nearest electronics store resurrects my contacts and stored photos onto a new phone in less than an hour, and asks me if I want to download all my old apps. Everything saved and returned to me from the mystical "cloud." Humanity treats these devices the same way they treat magic: infinitely disposable. We're happy to upgrade in a series of endless binding contracts.

The cost of my new phone is simple and expected. Monthly payments for two years, which will total close to a thousand dollars. I don't leave the store without dropping an extra sixty dollars on a case that doubles the phone's overall thickness by wrapping it in a tire's worth of rubber. The saleswoman informs me that it is waterproof, as well. That would have been infinitely more useful yesterday.

My first call is to Dolores. "Madame," I say.

"Archmagus Diaz," she says.

"We are up and running."

"Call me once you've mustered the necromancers."

"I'll do you one better. I will send a checklist of everyone's responsibilities through e-mail," I say.

"How bold of you."

"I know. Isn't it amazing?"

"We live amazing. Go do your job," she says and hangs up.

I haven't even crossed the threshold of the store when a slew of text messages assaults my phone. The first, a security alert from FIU proper saying the College is closed. Another message, this one from the College, explaining whom to call if you wish to help. Finally: "Who is checking our wards?" It is from Jimenez, the Latino Lurch.

My response: "Your wards were checked two evenings ago."

Jimenez: "But not TODAY." Caps notwithstanding, he is correct. Two days ago, this mayhem was unthinkable.

I retrieve Dolores's print-out and pull up a running list of the city's cemeteries. I start adding names next to each cemetery. The phone calls are short: *What are you doing? The College needs you. Please go check the wards at ____ and send me a text when you are done. Then, call the College and tell them you're on standby*. All except two calls I make are to former students, and not a one questions me or turns me down. I send the updated list to Dolores. Hopefully this is the hardest part of my day.

Dolores calls me immediately. "What is going on with the necromancers? And why aren't you downtown yet?"

"I just sent you the list I promised. What is happening downtown?"

"The Chancellor told you! The first conduit is being installed. I will send you an address now." The phone chimes as the call ends. An address and a curt message: "Hurry. 2PM start. Go!"

Nick Russo's Plaza of the Tropics, brought to you by Russo Construction Limited, has all the polish and flavor of a doorknob. A massive asphalt traffic circle around a dry fountain serves as the entryway for the open-air slab of coral-colored concrete. Palm trees stick out of the ground in geometric symmetry, majestic derelicts mired in the holes mathematically diagramed for them by an uncaring architect. Micromanaged areas of grass defiantly remain green next to the sweltering stone. Flags of every Caribbean and South American nation hang limp in a line at the elevated seawall. The place screams architectural and bureaucratic precision. Something massive, maybe twenty feet tall, is under a tarp in the fountain.

A stage has been erected in front of the flags. An aluminum scaffold runs the length of the stage. Banners cover the legs of the scaffold. They bear Nick Russo's smiling face, like a douchey Big Brother, above a list of corporate sponsors. A sea of chairs, filled to capacity with men and women in suits, spreads out in front of the stage. Television cameras on platforms await their charge at the back corners of the crowd.

For all his pompousness and self-promotion and slime, I envy Nick Russo's ability to make something like this happen. Years before he broke ground here, he set up two multi-level garages on the other side of Biscayne Boulevard. With the revenue they generated, he established a free trolley that transported people to the up-and-coming Wynwood Art District. He saw Miami's infrastructural ineptitude and filled the municipal gap to further fund his self-aggrandizement and ambition.

The result: revitalization of a dilapidated landscape, nascent projects for his company, and a spot in the public eye. When he's done building the walls of his fortress of riches, and finds all that paper to be green and dry and unloving, he will go into politics and preach his rags-to-riches parable to the lowest common denominator, hoping their love raises him even higher.

I pay his exploitative $20 parking fee, don the robes in my trunk, and sling my sword's baldric over my shoulder. Emérico never considered that black robes might be an impediment in a tropical climate. I barely survived my first time wearing them, and I bound a wind spirit into the lining afterwards. It does a decent job of keeping me cool. Nevertheless, the 90% humidity and 80-something degree weather have me flushed by the time I cross the street.

The man himself breaks away from a pack of suits. I have to force myself not to sneer every time I see him. He's a full head taller than me, and his beard is as manicured and full as the lawn; I have to stay clean shaven out of shame at my sparse whiskers. His green eyes pop against his auburn hair. The gray at his temples gives him a dignified and learned air. He was an all-star tight end in his college days, but turned down the draft to be a wizard. It wasn't enough for him to win the genetic lottery; he wanted to be everyone's prize.

Russo grabs my hand as I approach. His grip is stony. "Heard you might have had some trouble at the College," he says with a smile. His stupid teeth are pearly white, and his canines remain sharp. Mine dulled long ago.

"Archmagus Russo," I say.

"Take off the robe. You have a suit under that thing, right?"

"I wasn't told—"

"You were told, by me, to disrobe. Bet you've been waiting for this day," he says, winks, and slaps my shoulder. "You should keep the sword though. It'll be good for the cameras. Mayra!" He waves at a woman passing a few yards away.

Mayra is in her early twenties. She wears an earpiece with a microphone and is carrying a tablet and walkie-talkie. Her pinstripe skirt suit accentuates her wide hips. Chopsticks hold up her hair in a bun. Her officiousness does nothing to obscure her model-good looks.

"Give Archmagus Diaz the rundown, please," Russo says before he walks away, granting me the dignity of my formal title. It makes me wonder if he actually respects me. In private he tries to break me down with his macho-bullshit jabs. But he's never done it in front of others.

"We're going to have the mayor speak after Mr. Russo's opening comments," Mayra says. "We want you seated on Mr. Russo's right. The mayor will be on his left, so you don't have to say anything to him. The other dignitaries already know their places. We want you on camera as much as possible."

"Why?"

She raises an eyebrow. "Your presence should have a calming effect on the viewers. You're very much in the limelight. 72% of the people we polled said they would trust you with their lives. Do not speak to the mayor or any other dignitaries while you are on stage. Remember that you're on camera, so be the first to clap when appropriate, and don't do anything crude. Nod when you hear something you like. You may give a standing ovation to Mr. Russo, but under no circumstances should you do so for the mayor."

"This is a joke, right?"

"Everyone saw your heroics yesterday. You're the Savior of the Sands. We called all the major news outlets and gave them that nickname. Mr. Russo, myself, and our team need you to look the part. Do you have any prepared remarks?" "No one told me I—"

"Good. Because I don't want to have to look over something that you just threw together." She twitches her lips and flashes her eyebrows at me.

"What is your problem?"

"I've been rearranging all of my hard work because you decided to be a hero on television. So sit on the stage, don't look directly into the cameras, and try to look like an adult who matters. Got it?"

I must seem like an extension of Russo to this poor woman. "You've been juggling so much. I'm sorry if I ruined it."

Mayra's eyes widen for a moment but return to their cold grace almost instantly. "It's not your fault. It's his. Let's get you out of that robe. Did you bring a jacket?"

"No."

She sighs. "Come with me."

Mayra leads me away from the edge of the crowd to a trailer parked behind the stage. The interior is better furnished than my home and the AC is a mercy. "We need the room," Mayra says to the make-up artist sitting in a chair in front of a lighted mirror, who scurries out. "What are you, a forty-four regular?" she says to me.

"*Jesus*. Yes. How did you know?"

She flattens her mouth and looks me up and down. She goes to a rack of clothing at the back of the trailer and brings me back a jacket. "Try this on."

I remove my sword, undo the inner buttons of my robe, and put on the finest piece of clothing that I have ever worn, a blue jacket in a Glen check pattern.

"That's a wool and silk blend." She hands me a red tie and pocket square. "This should go well with it."

I would never think to wear something so ostentatious. I don't recognize myself with the tie on.

"Looks good on you," Mayra says. "Get to the stage. We're starting in ten minutes." She holds the door open for me.

"Nick told me to wear the sword."

"*Mr. Russo* sometimes has unrealistic expectations of control."

"I won't leave it here," I say. In the wrong hands, just unsheathing the sword could be disastrous; in the right ones, apocalyptic. "I'm taking it on stage with me."

Mayra stomps her foot. "No you're not! This whole thing is about Nick. And if he's not wearing a sword, you're not wearing a sword. Plus, you would look like a clown trying to wear a sword with that jacket. I will get an intern to hold it next to me if that's what you want, but there is no way you're taking that thing onto *my* stage."

I narrow my eyes at her. "Fine. Call your intern."

She scoffs and clicks the walkie-talkie. "Ubaldo, come to the dressing room." A young Hispanic man, barely out of his teens but well-dressed, comes running. "Ubaldo, from now on, you don't leave my side, and you carry Archmagus Diaz's sword for me."

"Yes, ma'am," he says and holds out a hand to me.

"Do not draw this weapon." I don't blink or break eye contact until he looks away. I put the sword in his hand, but don't let go. "You understand?"

"Yes, sir."

"Archmagus," Mayra says, still waiting at the door for me. I release my sword and head to the stage, watching that Ubaldo stays by Mayra's side. The jacket breathes like I'm naked, and I hate Nick Russo all the more for it. He just has this kind of luxury on hand, just in case.

"Damn, son," Russo says to me as I mount the steps to the stage. "That's the sharpest you've ever looked. All thanks to me."

"Are we ready?"

"We've been waiting on you, buddy." He motions me to a chair.

Nick walks up to a clear plastic podium, probably selected because it doesn't hide any part of him. He adjusts the thin microphone. "Please stand for the Pledge of Allegiance," he says. A high school color guard materializes behind the crowd and marches the flag down the aisle. When they arrive at the stage, Nick leads the crowd in a recitation of the pledge. "Singing the national anthem today is Zoraida Gomez, from Law Enforcement Officers' Memorial High School."

The girl, dressed simply in an overlarge black skirt and a white blouse, has an afro of blonde curls so big that it shades her eyes from the sun. But the most impressive thing about her is the siren song rendition of the "Star Spangled Banner" that she belts out to violin accompaniment. I get a little teary-eyed. The audience's cheering can barely match her vocals.

"Amazing, Zoraida," Nick says and finishes his applause. "Simply amazing. Zoraida received straight superiors at the state competition last year, and hopes to do so again this year. She's already secured a full scholarship to attend FIU's Werthner School of Music. Let's give her one more round of applause," Nick says. The girl waves sheepishly at the adoration and then takes a seat at the front of the crowd. The color guard brings the flag onto the stage, deposits it into a flag stand, and marches away.

"Good afternoon, everyone," Nick says. "It's going to be a hard act to follow, but I'll do my best. Eighteen months ago, we broke ground here. This space was rundown warehouses cluttering our shores. In the intervening time, Russo Construction Limited and our corporate partners have transformed the blight into the beautiful plaza you see here today."

He waits for the applause to die down. "Our great city deserves to grow up. The congestion, the decay, the corruption that plagues us needs to be eliminated, and with your help, we can and *will* do that. This plaza and the buildings around it will serve as the new hub for our maturation, a place where commerce thrives, where ideas find new ground, and where Miami leads this nation in culture *and* business."

More applause. I realize I am chewing my lip and stop.

"But most importantly, people can come here and feel *safe.* Yesterday, our city was tragically attacked by a malevolent entity, and if not for the heroic actions of my colleague, Archmagus Pablo Diaz, countless more lives might have been lost. It is our shared honor to have the Savior of the Sands here with us today." Nick turns and gestures toward me. I nod and wave at the cheering crowd.

"Pablo was there on the beach to protect our citizens, and the College of Practical Arts is no less committed to the safety of our citizenry, which is part of the reason we're here today. Behind you is the symbol of the College's commitment." Nick gestures at the rotunda. The crowd turns. The tarp falls from the twenty-foot pillar in the center of the fountain.

Massive metal bars form a column supporting a gigantic sphere of blue-tinted glass. An undulating orb of suspended liquid shifts and swirls inside the sphere. It is impossible to see the edges of the bars, since the metal seemingly vibrates in place: cold iron, capped with a wraithglass globe filled with ectoplasm.

I want to run screaming from the stage. I wipe my forehead. There are six of these things in the city?

Cold iron can't be forged in this world, only shaped. The ore has to be mined and smelted by the dead, in Nox. The same goes for the wraithglass. It would take me a lifetime to collect the amount of ectoplasm necessary to fire the forges of the dead.

"This ward, fashioned by Chancellor de Menezes, will ensure that every magical entity and occurrence in a two mile radius is not only recognized, but identified and catalogued, in order to give our first responders the time and information they need to deal with any threat."

The fury of the applause matches my heartbeat.

"Let's take a look, shall we?" Nick says and grabs the microphone. Another tarp is wheeled out from behind the stage. Russo descends the stairs and uncovers the object with a flourish. It is a display the size of a large flat screen television, made of wraithglass and housed in a cold iron frame. I hear him mumble some magical syllables through the speakers and the monitor comes to life, showing a map of Miami-Dade County in ethereal blue lines. He waves his hand over it and red dots begin popping up in the four-mile circle around downtown, Biscayne Bay, and South Beach.

"Here is every magical entity for two miles in every direction," he says. "Oh, look at that!" He works the display like a smartphone, zooming into the map by touching the wraithglass with two fingers and then dragging them apart. "That's me and Pablo," he says, pointing to two dots very close to each other. "Right here, Pablo," he says, and taps my dot.

The crowd laughs, but I saw something else before he zoomed in. I jump to my feet. "Zoom out!" I run to Nick and push him aside. I pan the display east. In the middle of the water, darting toward our location, is a cluster of red dots. "We have to get these people out of here!"

"What? Why?" Nick says.

"Look!" I am pointing out at the bay. A cloud of spray is moving across the otherwise glassy water. People start crowding the shoreline.

"Give me the microphone!" I say.

Nick clutches the microphone against his chest as if it were some bauble, ignorant that it is the only thing that can save the dumb masses rushing to glimpse what's coming for them. The mist grows larger.

I try to wrestle the microphone away from him. He pushes me to the floor, and I sit agog at his strength. "Asshole! Tell them to run!"

A man on the seawall falls onto his back. A driftwood spear is sticking out of his chest. The spearhead is a conch. The miraculously unharmed stand in awe long enough to make themselves targets.

They start to run, but it is too late. The waterline bursts with tentacles. Columns of purple, suckered flesh pluck people from the seawall.

Mermen leap from the sea like dolphins and land on webbed feet as large as scuba flippers. They are surprisingly dexterous on land, bouncing on their clawed toes. I watch one of them dive at a woman and draw back its puffed, angler-fish maw, sinking teeth the size of darning needles into her neck. There is a gout of blood when he rips her carotid open.

Their scales shimmer in the sunlight. One merman impales a middle-aged man through his stomach. The piscine monster turns to toss his catch into the water and I glimpse its back, much darker than its belly. Another merman, its silver eyes the size of teacup saucers, tackles a teenaged boy. The monster's face narrows into a ridge in the middle like a sunfish. It hoists the unfortunate soul onto its shoulder and jumps back into the bay, taking its prize to the salty depths.

I grab Nick. "Desmond's Oubliette!"

Nick nods and pulls his wand from his jacket. I've read the wand's description in his autobiography. The wood comes from a royal palm planted by his father, a tree that survived being struck by lightning. The tail of a salamander (the fire breathing variety) and a thread from his varsity letterman's jacket serve as the core. He transmuted the handle himself to have a football's textured grip.

I draw a circle on the ground with chalk. I place my hand in it and Nick does the same. The rite, designed by Georgina Desmond, the head of Abjuration, requires precision, but Nick's pronunciation is flawed. In spite of this, a bell jar of lustrous white cascades around the stage and the audience.

The few left outside the protective dome are impaled, netted, or carried into the sea. The army of mermen continues to swarm the shore. The kraken hunches at the water's edge, living artillery, watching with unfeeling yellow eyes on the sides of its pulsating mantle. The mermen, an abyssal infantry, surround the dome, trying it for weaknesses. Their spears penetrate the glowing film, but only with colossal effort.

Nick rewards their success with a bolt of lightning from the tip of his wand. Thunder shreds the air, causing the crowd to fall to its knees. All that remains of one intruder is a pile of smoldering meat. It is what I expect of the College's Head of Evocation.

"Your abjuration is terrible," I say to Nick.

"The dome is up, isn't it?"

"Yeah, but for how long? Some are coming through. Your work is shoddy."

"You try and concentrate when months of work goes up in smoke!"

"I fought Baba Yaga *alone*." Saying her name stabs at the darkest corners of my mind. The human cost of her attack makes me want to vomit again, like I did in her hellish hut. "Don't talk to me about concentration."

"That's real good. They can put that on your tombstone. 'Beat Baba Yaga, Murdered by the Catch of the Day.'"

I look around. No one approaches us as we argue. They are cowed by the sight of predators so near. "What the hell do we do?"

"They're fish! Drop the shield and let's fry them!"

"More people will die." I rub my chin. "I could take the crowd into Nox, but if they get lost or possessed, we're going to have even more problems."

"No, you creepy fuck. Where would you even lead them?"

"Anywhere away from the water. Across Biscayne Boulevard."

"They'll suffocate before they get there." Nick scans the area and the crowd. "Can we extend the oubliette into the street?"

"With your abjuration?"

Nick turns and vaporizes a pair of mermen that push through the barrier. "We don't have time for this."

I scan the crowd until I find Ubaldo. He's watching Nick and me, huddled close to Mayra. I point at him, then beckon him with one finger. He scurries up, white-knuckling the sheath of my sword. I snatch it back from him and cinch it to my chest and waist. Mayra was right; it looks ridiculous.

"Give me the microphone," I say to Nick. He cocks his eyes at me, but hands it over. "Ladies and gentlemen," I say over the loudspeakers, "if you would like to go home tonight, please grab the hand of the person nearest you. Make sure you're not making circles. One long chain, please. I will be at the front, and Mr. Russo will be at the back. If you are currently ill, have high blood pressure, a history of heart disease, have or have ever had cancer, you must stay here until Archmagus Russo and I return." I give Nick the mic and he turns it off. "It's Nox or nothing," I tell him.

The planes simultaneously exist in the same place without interacting. Like multi-colored sheets of cellophane that have been twisted together into a rope, they all form a whole, but each is homogenous. From what we understand, our world is the Prima, the Material Plane, and it gave birth to all the other planes. Nox is the Plane of Death. The realm is death itself. The elderly, the weak, this short march could claim them.

"God damn it," Nick says. "I am not going. I will watch your backs as you leave, and then you come back for me."

I unsheathe my sword, Thanatopsis. Crafting it was part of my doctoral thesis. I styled it after a cavalry saber because I knew it would be light and wieldy. The pommel and sheath are carved from a tree that fed from the dead, the leather grip from a bull that gored a man in Pamplona, and the blade is forged of cold iron. It took me almost a year to collect enough ectoplasm to smelt that damned metal.

With a single downward cut through the air, I slice a gash from our reality into Nox. To anyone looking, reality becomes a matte, a projection onto a screen, and the cut edges flap as air and heat rush into the vacuum. I always think I see the tendrils of my breath.

I grab Ubaldo's hand and tell him to grab the hand of the nearest person. I use Thanatopsis to focus my awareness. A glowing green string snakes around my arms, then around Ubaldo's, and around the arms of the terrified woman he is gripping, until it reaches Mayra, our anchor. We are a string of Christmas lights, and each bulb is a human being.

"If the chain breaks, run to the next person! Deep breaths!" I say and pull Ubaldo into the darkness with me. Nox is pitch dark without a lantern, but I've cut a big enough scar in the membrane between the planes that light and air penetrate for a few feet. I hear a muffled thunderclap—Russo's wand again—as I lead the terrified crowd. They follow me into emptiness.

"Faster," I say, my voice muffled. I pull Ubaldo with me and pick up the pace. Each exhaled breath is thick and gets stuck in my throat. I poke the darkness with Thanatopsis—the smallest nick in reality—and peep through. We haven't even made it to the street yet. I look behind me. The silhouettes of the living blend into the surrounding black.

I march on, counting my steps. The aperture between worlds begins to seal itself when I get to 100. Now is when we will lose people. They'll panic in the dark, become one with it. I squeeze Ubaldo's hand and hope he does the same for the person behind him. Reality heals itself. We are cut off from light and air.

Muffled screaming. They are wasting their breath. The first falls. He didn't know he had cancer. It blooms in Nox. The chain is broken, but the people who were holding him find each other. I keep counting. I hiss out air. There is nothing to breathe in. Something appears in the gloom. A blue orb, suspended in darkness. No choice but to keep going straight. So we approach it. Another person falls. She was hyperventilating before she even stepped onto the plane. The lights on the string are dimming.

A gothic lamp on a metal post. It is cold iron. It shouldn't be here, but I am glad it is. The light is burning ectoplasm, and clouds of oxygen cascade down from it. My lamp, if I had it with me, would work the same way. There is a sign fastened to this one, hand-painted: "Biscayne Blvd."

In the distance, a blue haze: is there another light post there? I take a chance and poke the membrane again. Glimpsing the other side, I tear through death for light and life. Air rushes down the chain of humanity. I inhale greedy lungfuls, but don't cross over to Prima. I push Ubaldo through the new aperture and grab the man behind him and force each desperate soul into Nick Russo's parking garage.

Most collapse onto the asphalt. A few remain on their feet, coughing between gasps. When the last person steps through, I follow her. Mayra, our anchor.

"I have to go back for Nick," I say when I catch my breath.

She's sobbing. "He"—gasp—"held open"—confusion—"and it closed!"

"Were you the last one in?" I know she was, but I ask anyway, hoping to focus her. People like her snap at stupidity.

She nods. "He pushed me in!"

We made it. All but two. I shepherded them through the Valley of Death. Alone.

And I don't want to do it again.

Outside of the parking garage, Biscayne Boulevard is packed with bystanders, but these are smart enough not to approach the chaos in the plaza. I run across the street. I can see the mermen massing at the edge of the oubliette, clamoring to get at the conduit. The kraken tries to tackle the shield, pulling its enormous bulk from the water, and gets a lightning bolt from inside.

Knowing the air is still saturated with residual magic, I supercharge myself again. I cast the same incantation I enchanted into my hand wraps, only this time I focus my will through Thanatopsis instead of my fists. As I run across the plaza, I slice vertically through the air. A dozen mermen are cut in half and land in a heap, sending their friends scurrying away from me. "Nick! Drop the oubliette!"

Nick cackles when he sees me. At some point, he must have tossed his jacket and shirt, because he's wearing a shiny white undershirt. "Pablo! You son of a bitch!"

The mermen try to rush me. I cut down the nearest handful, sending the rest scurrying. "Tell them to run towards me!"

"I can't! We won't all make it!" he says and points. There are a dozen people with him, and the cameramen are still on their platforms.

"Watch my flank then!" I say, pointing to my left. I turn to my right as thunderclap after thunderclap turns the anthropomorphic fish behind me into ash. The mermen mass in front of me, jabbing spears and swinging nets in my face. I slice the air and cleave one from neck to navel. The others back away.

"Pablo!" Nick yells.

The pain in my leg is immediate. I look down. One prong of a trident has pierced my calf. I thrust Thanatopsis at the neck of the wielder. The blade is three feet away from him, but a hole opens in his neck and he drops his weapon to cover the gushing wound with his webbed hands. I pull the trident from my leg, limp toward him, and stab him in the eye.

There's too many of them, and only Nick and me. Nick and his charges are fine inside the oubliette. I'm the one in actual danger. I watch Nick build a ball of fire at his waist and then thrust his hips at the mermen, launching a grotesque line of flaming, dripping death at the harriers. He laughs maniacally. When I fought Baba Yaga, did I look like he does now?

A spear flies past my head. Watching his showboating is going to get me killed. I have to end this. How do I scare these monsters?

What does any living thing fear, no matter how dangerous?

I plunge Thanatopsis into Nox and stalk towards the mermen. The rend in reality follows me, widening as I go. The nearest creatures feel the cold winds of death and back away. The ones behind them panic, hurling spears and guttural barks at me with equal effect. So long as Nick has my back, I can knock aside anything that comes toward me.

Nick yells. "What the hell are you doing?"

"Winning," I say. The mermen's collective resolve breaks against my advance and the open wound in reality. Their ranks retreat back into the sea on this side of the oubliette. "Drop the oubliette."

"Got you!" Nick says. When he breaks our spell, Nick raises a wall of fire, separating us, the cameraman, and those unfit to travel through Nox from the remaining mermen and the kraken.

"Why are the cameramen still here?" I ask him.

"I told them I would give them twenty thousand dollars. And that they'd win a Pulitzer."

I shake my head. "I need that kraken's beak." I point Thanatopsis at the beast, still huddled on the seawall.

Nick looks at the people around him. "Archmagus Diaz will guard you to the street. You guys are done," he says to the cameramen. "Go!"

The remaining people break into a run toward Biscayne Boulevard, except for one cameraman. Nick's wall of fire keeps the mermen at bay, but I follow the survivors until they get to the street. "What are you still doing here?" I say to the suicidal cameraman.

"*Compadre*, I'd rather die than miss any of this," he says.

I turn to Nick. "Any ideas?"

"You're bleeding, man," he says.

I look down at my leg. I raise the pants. The wound is small, but there is a thick line of blood leading to my sock. Now that I see it, I can feel my soaked foot. "Jesus Christ! I already went to the hospital yesterday!"

Nick laughs at me.

"I need that beak! You'll have to drop the wall."

"You heard that, buddy?" Nick says to the cameraman. "You'll be on your own." The cameraman gives Nick a thumbs up. Nick allows the wall of fire to fall. The kraken, sensing danger, tries to retreat.

"It's gonna get away!" I say.

"Nope!" Crackling yellow light courses out of his wand, paralyzing the titanic octopod. The creature bellows. The sound shakes my ribcage. I channel kinetic energy through Thanatopsis and slice away flailing tentacles until the beast's mantle is exposed. Blood and saltwater rain down on us as it thrashes about. I use the saber like a baseball bat. Ribbons of flesh fall from the monster, and with a final downward arc, I cut through the mantle, exposing the creature's brain to the air. It collapses.

Nick crosses his arms and stands, trying to look statuesque.

I am bent over, holding my knees, panting. "Show-off," I say. I approach the creature. I have to carve my way through a building's worth of flesh, searching for the beak. I find it. This thing could chomp a man, knees to nipples. I try to drag it out. "Help me with this!"

Nick follows my path into the belly of the kraken and together we muster enough kinetic force to rip the beak away from the surrounding meat. "You're a savage, you know that?" Nick says.

"How am I going to get this back to the College? It won't fit in my car. It might not fit *on* my car."

"We'll throw it in one of the trucks."

"Nice," I say. "Thank you."

"No problem. You can keep the jacket, too, if you want."

"I think it's ruined."

"You just cut your way through an octopus the size of a house, but you can't get blood out of wool?"

"Shut up," I say. I limp back to a chair, stand it up, and fall on it. I raise my pants leg. The bleeding looks to have stopped. As the adrenaline dissipates, the pain starts creeping in. So much pain. So much blood. So much death.

As the chaos settles and the forces of order amass, I can't help but muse over the Conduit. Somehow, the Chancellor forged enough cold iron overnight to build it, as well as five others spread throughout the city. I swallow my envy. He must have tapped some chthonic font in order to amass that much of the metal. The Chancellor said it would siphon ambient magic, but Nick told the crowd its purpose is to monitor magic. Either way, the unintended consequence is that it lured these mermen.

At least this time it wasn't my fault. This time, I saved people.

11
House of Mirrors

NICK RUSSO DOESN'T allow the cameras to stop rolling. They capture him splinting an old man's leg, barking and pointing at his subordinates, and putting the Plaza of the Tropics back in order. People have died, but that isn't his concern. He must control the narrative. To that end, Mayra, Ubaldo, and a squad of interns take to social media, branding the attack as Nick's moment of glory, sharing choice clips from the cameraman's footage to make sure the image of Nick Russo meets the standard the man has already set: powerful, self-assured, capable, and worthy of adoration.

I wonder from the chair I'm slumped in whether or not Nick will even include my presence at this event. Rather than ask him, I wrap bandages around my pierced calf. My phone chimes. A text: "Could use your expertise. Call me."

Despite the near-death experience, I am sorely tempted to throw a "New phone. Who dis?" in response, but I am a *professional*, damn-it-all, so I call the number. As it rings, I pray to God that it isn't Abram. Was he drunk enough to forget our conversation?

A female answers. "Pablo Diaz! Just the man I need," she says. Wherever she is, there is a lot of echo, men shouting, and interference.

"I'm sorry, I can barely hear you. Who is this?"

"It's Detective Sandobal."

I hold the receiver to my forehead for a second and squeeze my eyes shut. When I first met her, I didn't think getting close to her would be a bad idea. If this call is about anything other than mermen, I don't want to have it. "Detective! Please excuse my rudeness. My phone was destroyed yesterday, and I didn't have your number saved."

"Was that before or after you went toe-to-toe with a lifeguard station?"

"During. How can I help you?"

"I am at the Downtown Precinct. We have an infestation. My bosses and I would really appreciate your help."

I take the phone away from my face so I can sigh. Nothing about the Russians; a small miracle. "I am a little busy right now. Can this wait?"

"There are a lot of these little shits, so not really. They are mean. And fast."

"A lot of what?"

"I'm not sure. Little cloaked men with big ears, claws, and sharp teeth."

My mind runs to fairies, and demons, and the most likely candidate, gremlins. "What are they doing?"

"They're tearing apart our squad cars and computers."

Definitely gremlins. Most people think that gremlins crave destruction, but in reality, they are ravenous learners. The best way for them to understand something is by disassembling it. Unlike fairies and demons, who tend to be loners, gremlins operate in familial clans. "No earthquakes, right?" I say.

"No..."

"That's good." Shifting of the earth means something larger following them through their tunnels. "If they're not hurting anyone then they probably won't. They just want your machines."

"Pablo, HQ is under attack. This is the densest district in the city."

I want to blow her off—need to, in fact. But how many more will die if the police are unable to do their jobs? "Let me make a phone call. Fair?"

"Please hurry."

"I will. If you want to try to get rid of them yourself, you can offer them something new and shiny. They probably speak English. Go buy something electronic. The more complicated, the better. Mint in box, for the best effect."

"Are you joking?" Sandobal says.

"No, ma'am." Offering a gremlin computer parts, carburetors, and sometimes even basic tools like scissors can buy their services. They are the blue-collar tech junkies of the magical world. But sometimes, they get their hands on something they shouldn't, like plutonium triggers or magic wands. They take apart the mundane to understand it, but they consume the extraordinary and can be forever altered. Nothing Sandobal can pick up at Best Buy will have that effect, however. "Call you as soon as I can."

"Good bye." She hangs up.

I try calling the Chancellor. It rings twice and then goes to voicemail. Did he just ignore my call? Does he know how to do that? I call the College's front desk. Dolores answers on my third attempt. "College of Practical Arts. Dolores speaking. Please state the nature of your emergency."

"It's Archmagus Diaz. There is a problem at the downtown police department."

"There are problems all over the city, Archmagus. Care to specify?"

"Gremlin infestation. At a police station."

A pause. "I am transferring you to the Chancellor. Please hold." The line clicks.

Emérico answers. "Pablo, are you all right? Archmagus Russo told me you were wounded."

"I'm fine, sir, but—"

"Then why did you take mortals into Nox?" The shift to reprimand reminds me of this morning.

"Sir, we would have been skewered had we stayed in the plaza. Our options were limited." Dead silence for too long. "I need help. Gremlins have invaded the downtown police department."

"You are expected in North Miami in an hour. Archmagus McIntyre's congregation needs to activate the second conduit."

"Sir—"

"Pablo, this is no longer about punishment. After what happened at the Plaza of the Tropics, we cannot activate another conduit without at least two Archmagi assigned to its protection. The activation seems to create a beacon to magical beings, and you have seen the result. Yet without the conduits, we remain on the defensive, reacting to disasters only after the fact. We must regain the initiative if we are to protect the city—and everything I have worked for."

"I understand, sir. But think about the public perception if we don't come to the aid of the police."

A pause. "Very well. But do not dawdle. I will call Archmagus McIntyre." *Click*.

"Nick!" I flag him down. "I have to go!"

He runs over. "What's the problem?"

"Police Headquarters is under attack."

"No wonder they're not here yet. How can I help?"

"Come with me. There are gremlins and you know what that could mean."

Nick lowers his brow. "I won't leave this conduit alone. But if there's anything I can give you, name it."

I give him a look, to which he only responds with a shrug. I scan the chaos, until my eyes land on the prize; I point at it. "Load that up in my car."

I speed through Wynwood—one of the city's street art districts—but as soon as I hit Downtown Miami, the labyrinth of one-way streets and dead-ends swallows me. These thoroughfares loathe the uninitiated. Only the denizens of the looming buildings know how to navigate the contemptuous streets, and even they can be flummoxed by ever-shifting roadwork.

I try to use my phone's GPS as Ariadne's needle, guiding me through the labyrinth, but the artificial voice squawks nothing but lies for fifteen minutes. While I fail to navigate those hostile corridors, my mind wanders to my new charges.

When a gremlin dismantles a magical object, it glimpses the creator's paradigm—that mage's perception of magic—and one of two changes can occur: enlightenment or cognitive dissonance. The former elevates the gremlin to new heights of understanding and cunning; it becomes a gremagus. The latter plunges the creature into obstinance and rage; it becomes a troll.

Trolls are the antithesis of magic. Their very existence denies magic and each denial feeds their size and strength while warping their minds and bodies. Wizards are wary of facing such creatures because their willful banality causes magic to fizzle. Hopefully, I will find neither gremagus nor troll waiting for me.

The Miami Police Department downtown is housed in an odd building. If only the first level existed, it would just be a squat concrete bunker faced with hideous clay tiles. The architecture is unique in that the floors above ground level get successively larger, giving the edifice the appearance of an inverted ziggurat. This suspension of gravity is made possible by massive pillars of poured concrete meant to withstand a Category 5 hurricane. I see no smoke, no cops running around, and the streets are eerily deserted. Right in front of the station, a blue parking terminal buzzes, the keypad hanging from the body of the machine by its plastic-sheathed, multi-colored guts.

The glass door on the first floor is partially open. When I pull on it, something metal scrapes the concrete. The door falls off its hinges. Nuts and bolts tinkle around my feet as I brace my hands against the tilting glass. The thump against my palms makes it obvious: impact-resistant glass. I position the door against its frame and run inside.

"Freeze! Hands up!" A young Hispanic in Metro PD brown, short but built like a tank, points his sidearm at me. So do his two friends behind him.

Until yesterday, I had never had guns drawn on me. I should not be getting used to it. "Don't shoot! I'm from the College!"

The lead cop squints at me. "Aren't you Pablo Diaz?"

"Yes! Yes! I'm here to get rid of the gremlins."

"Weapons down," the young officer says. "This is the guy from the beach." They holster their semi-autos.

I lower my arms. "Detective Elisa Sandobal called me."

"Good luck finding her." His name bar reads Hernandez.

Maybe I don't need to find Elisa. Maybe I can cat burglar this situation and get to North Miami without a word between the detective and me. The station's phone rings; the tinny and warped chime goes unanswered, courtesy of the busted receiver. The chair behind the foyer desk lies in pieces. "How many of them are there?"

"Dozens? We can't really tell. They jump back into the ceiling or the AC ducts."

"You all want to solve the problem? Come with me." I head to the door and turn around. They are milling about. "Come on!"

The officers follow me to my car. I open the rear doors. "You and I will grab the television," I say to Hernandez. "You two grab the sound board," I say, pointing to the panel of sliders and buttons propped up in my back seat.

"You think this will work?"

"Maybe. I'll bet most of your equipment is old. This is top of the line." I slide the 55-inch television out of the backseat. Hernandez grabs the leading edge and pulls it out until I can lift the opposite corner. We wait on the sidewalk until the other two cops join us with their burden.

"Just set it up at the front desk," I say when we get inside. Hernandez and I wait for the other two cops to lay down their loads, then I stand the flatscreen up behind it. This is probably thousands of dollars of equipment and Nick didn't think twice about relinquishing it. I shake my head, caught between envy and gratitude.

"Is there an intercom or anything?" I say.

"I can try an all-call over a working phone," Hernandez says.

"Say this exactly: 'Archmagus Pablo Diaz wishes to treat with the chief of the clan.' Then tell them where we are."

"Davis, go into that office and tell me if this works," Hernandez says. He picks up a receiver at a desk crammed against a wall and punches in some numbers. He delivers the message. He finishes with, "He is at the East Entrance reception desk," and presses a button. Davis comes out of the adjoining office and gives Hernandez a thumbs up.

"You three should go do whatever it is you have to do. They won't approach if there are too many of us here."

"You guys go," Hernandez says. "I'll keep a lookout." The other cops don't stick around. "I'll be in here," he says and points to a nearby office.

"Leave the blinds open, but you have to close the door," I say.

"Got it." Hernandez seals himself in. The blinds shift slightly.

I pace around the lobby. No one tries to enter the building. Phones warble and sputter in every corner of the building, their broken tones wafting around me. A halogen fixture flickers and then goes off. A roof tile slides back, revealing only darkness. "Archmagus?" The click of the 'ch' and hiss of 's' promise sharp teeth.

"Chieftain?" I say and stand up. Thanatopsis hangs at my waist. I rest my hand on its pommel.

"In a sense," the voice above me says.

Down the hall, a stairwell door creeps open. Elisa pokes her head out. I widen my eyes, raise my hand to her, and shake my head.

"Who are you motioning to?" the mirthful voice above me says.

I address the darkness: "An officer." I turn to Elisa. "I am handling this."

"And we really appreciate it," Elisa says as she emerges from the stairwell. A square, bulky bag hangs at her hip, suspended from her shoulder. She draws her sidearm from its holster, chambers a round, and points it at the ceiling. Brandishing a firearm, dark circles under her eyes, her pinstripe suit turns her into a mass of sharp angles.

A sick susurration above—laughter. "Feisty."

"Detective, please leave. I am trying to get them out of here."

"No, by all means, stay," the voice says. "So long as you put away that Beretta."

"I'd be happy to, so long as *you* get your crew out of the server room. Those servers are where we store digital evidence. That's thousands of active cases."

"I will send someone immediately," the voice says. True to its words, a couple of ceiling tiles dip in succession, moving away from our location.

"Thank you." Elisa engages the safety on her sidearm and jams it into her holster.

"My pleasure, detective." The unmistakable mirth in the voice makes me sneer.

I glance between the detective and the darkness. "I have brought these items to barter," I say.

"That's quite a ransom. Do you mind if I take a closer look?" the voice says.

"Not at all," I say.

A ragged figure crawls out of the roof, clinging to the ceiling tiles like a lizard. It drops onto its feet soundlessly, its blue cloak billowing. Standing, it barely reaches four feet tall. Gremlin skin ranges in color from pink to gray to green; this specimen is pale pink, almost human. Its long fingers come to points. Simian feet. It removes its hood. Foot-long, pointed ears stretch behind its triangular head. Its flat face bears sunken eyes, nose holes on either side of a small ridge, and a wide mouth filled with wolf teeth. It is smiling.

"Good afternoon, humans," it says and bows. "You may call me Tetch."

"Gremagus Tetch," I say, and return the bow as best as my calf will let me. "I am Archmagus Pablo Diaz." Rhea McIntyre's conjuring textbook advises us to treat gremagi with respect; they tend to reciprocate diplomacy. Their elevated understanding raises them to the upper caste of their society. They direct groups of their unenlightened brethren toward areas full of machines and magic.

"And you are?" Tetch says and uncurls a hand solicitously at Elisa. Gremlins use their fingers as every tool, from crowbar to screwdriver, and also to communicate.

"Sick of this shit," she says, but grabs his hand. "Detective Elisa Sandobal."

Tetch smiles and nods. "Understandable," he says. "I do apologize for the intrusion. It is difficult to manage so many of my clansmen, and once they start in on a building, it is even more difficult to call them off."

"What brings you to Prima, Gremagus Tetch?" I say.

"The very air you breathe is a smorgasbord, Archmagus. We smelled it all the way in Spiritus Mundi." He smiles. It reminds me of the Bursar.

"What does that mean?" Elisa says.

I start: "Spiritus Mundi—"

"I want him to tell it," she says. "If you don't mind?"

"Happily," Tetch says. "No one knows for certain, but I have always hypothesized that Spiritus Mundi—the spirit plane where I come from—exists because of the belief systems of human animistic cultures. There, one can find all manner of spiritual representatives, from animal and plant spirits, to the spirits of abstract concepts like war and ancestry. The plane itself is inherently magical; its trees bear charged fruit."

Something isn't adding up. "So couldn't you just collect it in your own realm?" I say.

"But someone's already gone to the trouble of amassing it"—Tetch grunts and hops up on the desk—"and I'm tired, Pablo Diaz."

"Who's doing it?" Elisa says.

"A mystery unto itself," Tetch says. "Surely you've been attempting to track the individual yourself, Pablo Diaz?"

"Just Pablo is fine. And no, we are trying to get the situation under control. You and yours aren't the only ones that have thought to make Miami their feeding grounds."

"Are you sure it is an individual?" Elisa asks.

I nod at the question and look to Tetch.

"Almost certainly. You think magic just starts to pool for no reason? Someone is doing some big work."

Elisa turns to me. "That jive with what you know?"

"To be honest, I don't know much. I thought at first it might be Baba Yaga, since she used it to make herself bigger. But what I drained from her was a drop in comparison to what's floating around."

"But you're trying to stop it, right?" Elisa says.

"Right now, we're stuck reacting, like I did on the beach with Baba Yaga.

But the Chancellor has the department heads setting up conduits across the city that can siphon off ambient magic, the stuff Baba Yaga used to run amok—the same stuff that attracted Gremagus Tetch. The beacons also help us track magical activity, so when they're all activated maybe we'll see who's behind this. The problem is that each time a conduit is turned on, it concentrates the magic in the area, and that draws whatever magical creatures are in the vicinity."

"Why are you drawn to magic?" Elisa says to Tetch.

"Clan Screwcap is large, but when I received enlightenment thirteen years ago, we were only seven members. I've done my duty and grown my unruly brood. I thought to come here and find something that might enlighten another. Maybe you can provide what we need," Tetch says and looks at me.

"Funny. I came here thinking to barter you out of here," I say.

"And you still can," Tetch says. "This is a generous offering," he says and waves at Nick's electronics, "but I need more."

"How much more?" I say.

"Something like that would do it," he says and points at Thanatopsis.

I tighten my grip on the pommel. "Yes, I imagine it would," I say. "But this is very personal to me."

"All the better. The more personal—"

I glare at him. "And powerful."

"—the artifact, the more likely to confer enlightenment."

"I'm not giving this up," I say. "And I'm not asking you to. But something commensurate would be helpful."

"Is there nothing else you can give him?" Elisa asks.

The hungry look Tetch gives Thanatopsis reminds me of myself when I started at the College, back when the only teachers were Emérico, Giorgio Hellas, and Rhea McIntyre. The smallest charm, the weakest potion, the smallest acts of prestidigitation filled me with envy. "Why haven't you just made a magical item?" I say.

"With what time? We're nomadic. Those scoundrels in my charge only care about making it to the next sunrise. We can't stay in one place long enough to construct something of value."

"I'm sorry to tell you, that is your fault. You're their leader. You need to lead. You need to tell them when to settle. And if that means spending a few hungry nights for the good of the clan—"

"What do you know of sacrifice?"

I think of my father. "I know enough. How long will these"—I wave at the electronics—"satiate your people?"

Tetch turns his attention to the soundboard. "They're complicated. Many components." He twists a knob, raises a slider, smirks to himself. "A week at most."

"Take them. Find a Best Buy and raid that."

"Pablo!" Elisa says.

"You want them in here or out there?" I say.

"Preferably neither!" She looks at Tetch. "No offense."

"It's understood," Tetch says and grins.

I check my phone. "There is a store on Miami Beach if you head due west. Or just roam Downtown. But if you remain in this building, you keep the peacekeepers of this society from their duties."

"I am willing to do that," Tetch says, "on one condition: make me something."

"No."

"Why not?" Tetch and Elisa say in unison. The gremagus is on his feet.

I raise an eyebrow at Elisa, then turn to Tetch. "Because you should make it."

"I don't know how!"

"Then I will teach you." I extend my hand to him. "Deal?"

Tetch squints at my fingers. "Can we find a place to house my clan during this tutelage?"

The thought of boarding a clan of gremlins in my duplex makes my eyes itch. "You can't just leave them in Spiritus Mundi?"

"Are you insane?" Tetch throws up his hands. "Without me, they'll fall victim to dragons or the elements or each other."

"Fine. We'll house them during your apprenticeship. Deal?"

"Deal," he says and finally takes my hand. Tetch retrieves a silver dog whistle from inside his cloak and blows into it so hard that even I hear a high-pitched wine. Within a minute, all of the ceiling tiles get pulled up, and Clan Screwcap surrounds us.

"Hail to Archmagus Pablo Diaz, who provides us a bounty!" Tetch says. The mass of gremlins raise various implements—from Leatherman multi-tools to machetes—above their heads in salute. "Tunnelers! Dig us home! Let us hide these wonders, then proceed to the nearest Best Buy!" Tetch's tone does all the work; they might have cheered had he said 'trash compactor.'

Eight of the gremlins begin digging into the floor, or so it seems. Instead of throwing back chunks of linoleum and concrete, they throw piles of translucent matter that dissipate into the air, revealing a swirling, multi-colored tunnel. A handful of gremlins grab the soundboard and hoist it above their heads like the day's kill. A few others suspend the television by way of ropes from their spears. As the clan enters the tunnels, they sing what could be a hunting song, full of spitting and warbling and joy. The tunnel entrance closes behind them as the last clan member enters.

"Why are you smiling?" Elisa says.

"Problem solved," I say.

Elisa gives me a look, measuring me up, and gremlins become a surreal memory. The real, the concrete, the stone-cold stands in front of me. "You and I need to have a talk about the real world."

12
Entanglement

"COME WITH ME. We need to talk." Elisa walks toward the stairwell whence she appeared.

"Detective, I really need to go. There are people waiting for me."

"I get that. I promise this won't take more than ten minutes of your time. Richards and I want you to see all the good you've done for us." She waits at the threshold of the stairwell, the LEDs above her flickering, turning her into a silhouette before throwing her back into sharp relief. "Seriously. Ten minutes. Consider it a professional courtesy."

If Richards is involved, it can't be all that bad; we've worked together for over five years. I inhale deeply and make my way toward her.

Elisa waits for me to pass. "Third floor," she says.

I look up the steep, concrete stairs and my calf throbs. "Isn't there an elevator?"

"Sure. Are you gonna trust it after your little friends have been through here?"

"Point taken," I say. I grip the handrail and pull myself up the first stair. I feel my pulse in my leg wound, but no tearing, so I hazard another, then another.

"Suck it up, champ," Elisa says behind me. "This can't be worse than getting bludgeoned in the face."

I ascend, but her mention of my face causes my brow to throb. Each time I step, it feels like a fiery poker in my calf. By the time I reach the second floor landing, my right shoulder and hip scream. The litany of pain feels deserved, but I ascend once more.

"You all right?" Elisa asks as she opens the door for me.

"No," I say. "This was a bad idea."

"Come on. I'll cheer you up." She leads me across a hazy bullpen of cubicles. Computer screens lay flat on the desks, their protective casings ripped apart. The towers beneath are jumbled piles of plastic, wires, exposed circuitry. Acrid blue smoke drifts beneath the few lights that are working. Detectives push past us without a glance, carrying boxes of files. There are only a few bullet holes in the cubicle walls; the detectives learned quickly about gremlin speed.

Elisa opens a door into the first room in a back hallway. "This is the detectives' annex. I've been holed up in here since Monday morning." Filing cabinets dominate the wall opposite the door. On the right, a desk disappears under mountains of paper; posters cover the wall behind it, with notices of benefits and financial planning. The most garish screams, "OVERDRAWN?! ASK HOW WE CAN HELP" in white letters and shows a uniformed officer gripping his head. The only thing remotely new in the room is the flat screen monitor and keyboard that take up a third of the desk. Even those are a decade old, the panel covered in fingerprints and the keyboard crusty with crumbs.

Elisa navigates through columns of stacked file-boxes until she reaches the desk, where she sits in a wooden antique with puke green leather cushions and undoes the clips on her bag. She pulls open the top and retrieves a digital video camera. She flips out the LCD screen. "Take a seat," she says, and motions to something plastic and flimsy that fits only the loosest definition of a chair.

I have to untie my baldric and hold Thanatopsis in order to do as she asks. "What is all this?"

"It's you, champ," she says, eyes fixed to the LCD. She lays the camera next to the television in the corner and digs through the bag until she finds some cables. "I brought these out of storage. I wanted you to see. You had a hand in every single one of these cases. 93% conviction rate; it's outrageous. Made me wonder why you were a teacher and not a cop. With a clearance rate like yours, you'd be the most commended man on the force." She plugs the wires into the camera, then into the television.

"I'm just trying to do my part," I say.

"I know. It's why Richards believes in you. And when I started to read through them"—she points at the file boxes—"it is why I started believing in you."

"Conducting the post-mortem on the stiff from Smoke & Lace wasn't enough to convince you?"

"That's a parlor trick. Seeing it once, I mean. Could just be smoke and mirrors. A hack that got lucky. But the way you beat that thing on the beach? That's some heroic shit. The stuff of legends. It goes a long way around here when you stick up for the shield."

"Like I said, just doing my part." I try to lean back in the chair, but it creaks a warning that keeps my back stiff.

"The soon-to-be Lieutenant Richards owes his promotion to you."

"He would have gotten it without me."

"A *gringo* in Northern Cuba? In this city it has always been who you know, and he is an import." She folds her hands in front of her. "The brass couldn't ignore his effectiveness any longer, though. I'd say you contributed minimum 20%, maybe as much as 50%, to his shine around here. Reading through all these case files, I've become something of a fan of you, myself." Elisa leans back in her chair and props her feet up on the corner of the desk. "You just have so many tricks. It's hard to argue that you're not the real deal."

I smile, but I can't look her in the eyes. Too much praise. Maybe she only sees the Savior of the Sands; she hasn't found the other guy yet, the idiot who got mixed up with the mob.

"Yeah, you know. You can plumb the depths of a dead man's mind. You can touch an object and can see the last person that held it. Super handy with murder weapons." She laughs. "But you want to know my favorite?"

I look up, but I'm not sure I want to. Something about the question, her tone. "Tell me."

"Scrying. I mean, that is just *incredible*. You get something that belongs to a guy, and you can find him anywhere in the world. Is that right?"

The room, already cramped with boxes, shrinks around me. Sweat from my palms glistens on Thanatopsis's scabbard. "That's right."

Elisa sits up straight and puts both hands on the desk in front of her. "How does that work, exactly?"

"The principal at work is sympathetic magic," I say, my mouth going dry. "Having an object with which the subject has made a personal connection allows me to exploit that connection and find them. It has to do with tracing their resonance."

She cocks an eyebrow at me. "You read sci-fi?"

"No, not really," I say.

"Sounds like quantum entanglement to me."

"Could be. Listen, I really appreciate all of this," I say, and when I pat the file box next to me, all the dust on its lid sticks to my palm, in turn leaving a moist handprint, "but I have to get going."

Elisa finds a packet of wet naps in a desk drawer and hands one to me. "I know, you're in high demand these days. Just let me show you a little something before you go. Richards and I could use your advice." She pulls one remote out of the desk to turn on the television and another from the camera bag to control the recording.

"What is this?"

"An interview Sergeant Richards was conducting before your little friends arrived."

The blue HUD projected on the television becomes an image of a girl in a denim jacket smoking a cigarette at an interrogation table. My heart crashes through my ribs and my ears get hot. Faina. I last glimpsed her through a champagne bucket, blowing Yuri at the edge of a motel bed. Echo from the interrogation room distorts Richard's voice, but not out of comprehension. "State your name and date of birth for the record."

"Faina Tomasovna Lukyanenka. The first of February, 1997." Russian accent when she says her name, almost none when she says the date. Been here a while.

"And why are you here?"

She takes a deep drag off of the cigarette. "I want witness protection in exchange for information on the Orlov crime family."

"Please begin with the events that occurred on Sunday, September 2nd."

"Yuri—"

"State his full name, please."

Faina scoffs on the video. "Yuri Denisovich Orlov picked me up from the Eight Ball at 10:00 p.m. when my shift ended. He took me to our apartment and told me to pack a bag with only what I needed. We were leaving that evening."

"Had Mr. Orlov previously made it known that he was planning on leaving?"

"No."

"Then why the sudden rush?"

"I don't know. I think he wanted to get away from Abram."

"Full name?"

Faina wrings her free hand and glares off-camera. "Abram Volkovich Orlov."

"Do you know why he wanted to get away?"

"Yes. Abram had become obsessed with magic since starting business with Augusto Desiderio."

I shift in my seat. Elisa is watching me.

"Do you know any details of their business dealings?" Richards says.

"Augusto supplied Abram," Faina says.

"With?"

"Everything: cocaine, heroin, oxycontin, molly."

Richards writes something down. "Did you pack a bag?"

"Yes. Yuri told me he was going to go get what we needed and to be ready. Then he left."

"How long was he gone?"

"A few hours. I think he left just before midnight and was back after three."

"Did he tell you where he was going?"

"Yes. He said he was meeting Nikodim and Jason."

"For the record,"—Richards interjects—"Nikodim Kuznetsov is one of Abram Orlov's lieutenants. Jason Carnero is a known Latin King and associate of Augusto Desiderio. Are those the men he was meeting?"

"I believe so."

"You'd met them before?"

"Nikodim worked with Yuri. I served him drinks all the time. Jason only once."

"Did Yuri Orlov tell you what happened to them?"

"No. But he came back covered in blood."

"Did he have the drugs and the money with him when he returned?"

"Yes. He showered and then put the money in my spare tire. Then he took the drugs outside and put them somewhere in my car."

"Why are you showing me this?" I ask.

Elisa shushes me. "We're getting to the good part." She fast forwards the video a few minutes, to when Faina lights a fresh cigarette.

"How is Emmanuel Philippe-Auguste involved in all of this?" Richards says.

The gremlins might have taken apart the AC. Sweat trickles behind my right ear. I can't just sit here. "Ah, yes. Emmanuel Philippe-Auguste: the bathroom attendant at Smoke & Lace," I say.

"Pay attention!" Elisa rewinds. She wants my full attention as she continues to dig out my grave.

Richards again: "—volved in all of this?"

Faina ashes her cigarette. "Emmanuel was a dead-drop. An outsider who took messages for everyone for a small cut."

"And so Yuri Orlov murdered him to protect himself?"

Faina shakes her head. "I don't know. I don't think so."

"Could you tell me what happened in Naples?"

Elisa begins fast-forwarding again, until mascara streaks across Faina's face.

"I walked back to the motel but I couldn't see in the room. Yuri told me he would leave the curtains open. I knew they were in there. I waited in the bushes for hours. I saw the curtains move a couple of times. Then Yuri called me. He sounded strange and he asked me where I was. I told him I was still at the supermarket. He asked for Smirnoff. Yuri and I hate Smirnoff. And I knew. We never drink Smirnoff. He was telling me to run. I told him I would be back soon and he told me he loved me and hung up." Faina bawls.

Elisa pauses the tape. "She waited for hours in those bushes until four men carried out her boyfriend and stuffed him in a trunk and drove off. Then she waited until sun-up, got in her car, and drove straight here."

"Is she safe?"

Elisa raises an eyebrow. "Yes."

"Good. Listen, I have to—"

"One more thing. It'll be quick. I promise." Elisa fast-forwards until she finds some frames where Faina dabs her eyes with tissue.

"If you were paying for everything in cash and using burner cell phones, how do you think Abram Orlov's men found the motel?" Richards says.

"I think he finally hired a *koldun*."

"What is a *koldun*?" Richards says.

A sorcerer. A scapegoat. A scryer. An accessory to murder. A man on the precipice of doom. An idiot.

"A wizard. Abram wanted to hire one for months. It was why Yuri wanted to get out of town. Yuri and Tamora kept telling him not to, but Abram wouldn't listen."

Elisa stops the tape and puts away the camera. "I have three dead men on my plate right now: Emmanuel Philippe-Auguste, Jason Carnero, and Nikodim Kuznetsov." Elisa picks up the box next to her and pulls out a case file brimming with papers. "You've seen these before right? Never seen one get so thick so fast. Normally we separate them by victim, but I thought this was all Yuri Orlov's mess, so I put them together. Big mistake, I know."

She retrieves a manila envelope from inside the file. She says, in response to me looking at the envelope, "Traffic camera photos from Alton Road and 5th Street." She pulls out several photographs, reads the backs, and lays one in front of me. "That's Monday night." Another. "This is Tuesday, early morning." Then two more. "Tuesday afternoon and this morning. We don't have eyes on the Eight Ball, unfortunately, but I'm sure we'll find a couple more shots that are close."

All of the pictures are of my license plate. Elisa can probably hear my heartbeat; it pulses in the back of my eyeballs.

"What were you doing on the beach on Monday night?"

"Having a drink and playing some pool. Are you accusing me of something?"

"Where did you drink and play pool?"

"The Eight Ball." My mouth is completely dry.

"Have you ever met Abram Volkovich Orlov or Augusto Desiderio?"

"No." I say it without hesitation.

"Do you know of any personnel or graduates of the College of Practical Arts that associate with the individuals I just mentioned?"

"No."

"Best news I've heard all day. Because I wouldn't want anyone associated with the College to be involved with the Orlovs when this RICO finally goes down. You look at all these boxes around here"—she waves around the room—"there are five times as many for all the shit the Orlovs are into: drugs, guns, prostitution, murder-for-hire, fraud of every color. You name it, there's a file for it. And everyone named in that RICO gets charged the same, as if they were Abram Volkovich Orlov."

My cell phone chimes a text. From Emérico: WHERE ARE YOU?

"Anything interesting?" she says.

"It's the Chancellor. Am I free to go?"

"You were always free to go." Elisa smiles. "This isn't an interrogation. You're not a suspect." She stretches, runs both hands through her long hair, and tucks the strands behind her ears. "You're the Savior of the Sands, after all. You have a city to protect, just like the rest of us."

"Thank you," I say. I stand and attempt as steady an exit as my heart rate and leg will allow, but her voice stops me at the door.

"Don't have any travel plans, do you?" Elisa asks.

"No, detective. There's far too much to do here. You have my number, if you need anything else."

"I'll be in touch," she says.

"I am at your service," I say. I turn.

"Can you imagine what would happen to Sergeant Richards, and this department, and the College, if all of these case files were somehow compromised. Like if someone brought your magic into question. Any perp convicted would have grounds for appeal. Mistrials would just be the beginning. Every case worked by this department in the last two years would be jeopardized." Elisa stands in front of me and half-smiles. "You don't look so good, Pablo. Kind of green."

I rub my mouth and chin. "Black and blue is more like it."

"Cheer up." She slaps my right shoulder and I see stars. "Get on out there. Do some more good. Thanks to Faina, as soon as this search warrant comes in, I'm gonna toss Yuri Orlov's place, and then you can do a little scrying for me, right?"

I swallow. "It's my pleasure to work for you."

Elisa winces and puckers her lips in a rueful smile. "That line is even worse the second time around."

"Sorry," I say.

"I don't really know if you are," she says.

I march down the stairs and out of the police department, numb. When I get to my car, I look in the rearview. Pale, sweaty, scarred: I look like a criminal, not a hero. I get in, lower the windows, and blast the AC. As soon as the air cools down, I raise the windows and try to think about anything other than the noose around my neck

13
Crisis of Faith

DOWNTOWN IS DEVOID of cars. As I drive up the onramp, I find only a few others on the road, most of them speeding. It's lunch hour on a Wednesday; the streets should be teeming. Emboldened by a twenty-year-old green Jeep that roars by me, I hit the gas and brainstorm a way to save myself.

The only ways out are to find Yuri's body and find Emmanuel Philippe-Auguste's killer. Yuri's easy. I can just wait to scry the body once Elisa has something of his. The letter opener might still be in his chest, and if it is, it'll have Abram's prints all over it. Then Abram goes down.

If Orlov gets arrested, does that get me off the hook? Or does he sell me out to Sandobal? Do I then have to confess to helping him and getting paid for it?

Holy shit. The check. It's worthless. My stomach turns. I take a few deep breaths. I have to burn the check. Nothing for it. I slam my hand on the steering wheel.

What about Emmanuel's killer? There are a lot of pieces and still too many gaps. What do I really know?

I conducted the post-mortem interview with Emmanuel, held his bloody horseshoe of grisly gray hair in the bathroom of Smoke & Lace. He had no clue who his killer was. His corpse told me it was either his brother or Yuri. But it couldn't have been Yuri; he and Faina had skipped town before Smoke & Lace closed.

Who benefits from Emmanuel's death? Not Yuri. He was smart enough to make sure I couldn't talk to Jason and Nikodim. He butchered those two, removing their tongues and hands. Abram or Augusto, then: the whale with the icy blue eyes, or the king with the mouthful of gold? Each lost a lieutenant; either is liable to snap. There was no time to give Emmanuel the anti-Pablo treatment.

A whodunit with my freedom on the line.

As I crest a section of I-95, I get a view of the city that makes me gasp. Beyond the empty highway, plumes of smoke dot the landscape. Helicopters hover everywhere. A pair of fighter jets circle the airport; they disappear south, likely returning to Homestead Air Reserve Base. Ahead, an electronic notice board reads "EMERGENCY. STAY HOME. ALL TOLLS LIFTED."

A text. Emérico: WHERE ARE YOU?

I respond: On my way.

The sooner I get to McIntyre and the other archmagi, the sooner we can put an end to this mayhem. My four-cylinder whines as I step on the gas.

This far north, Biscayne Boulevard still hosts a few night spots and restaurants, but you only have to drive a few blocks west before all the houses bear barred windows, old vehicles in front lawns surrender their utility to rust, and spent sneakers, their laces tied together, hang from the telephone wires. I stop at a familiar corner. Freshly whitewashed, McIntyre Grove AME Church gleams. Its small parking lot is full to capacity. Single-family homes crowd around the church, almost touching each other. The church can afford some strips of green on its sides and a small front lawn.

Rhea McIntyre inherited her congregation when her brother died. Heedless of her sex and the complaints of the parishioners, she took over and reinstated some classical notions of Christianity: she would preach, as her brother had, but she would work, as her father and grandfather and Paul the Tentmaker had done. Donations could go straight into the building or back to the fellowship, as need dictated. Any dissatisfaction with this arrangement evaporated the first time the church covered a hospital bill.

Caddy-corner to the church, what remains of McIntyre Grove stands in all its obstinate greenery. The property takes up an entire block—enough for twenty houses like the ones across the street. A tall hedge surrounds the grounds, abutting a short, limestone wall; what little grass remains between the rock and the asphalt is filled to capacity with cars. I can't see it from the street, but I know a hedge runs the middle of the grounds, dividing the lot.

I find a spot and park. I grab the *pastelitos* next to me and check the box, looking for one of the few things that might make my old teacher more amenable to my presence: a guava pastry. There are three. Thank you, Dad.

The noonday sun assaults me as soon as I get out. I retrieve my doctor's bag from the trunk, throw Thanatopsis's baldric over my shoulder, and slide the sword to my waist. I have to walk half a block to reach one of the four entrances to the property. I pass under a limestone arch and through a break in the hedges, feeling my shirt collar stick to my neck. Massive banyan trees canopy this side of the property, surrounding a pool of water so clear that the fish look like they're swimming through air.

Here, Rhea taught me conjuration. Not the theory of making objects materialize or the philosophy behind summoning extraplanar beings. In those halcyon days, I made a piping hot cup of coffee appear in my hand from thin air, brought a *chupacabra* over from Spiritus Mundi, and reveled in what I thought was power. Rhea chided me for my frivolity but was generous with her smiles.

I never questioned being off campus, even though I should have. Despite the warded clean rooms in the Dungeon designed for summoning, Rhea insisted McIntyre Grove was the place magic would happen—and it did—so I stopped complaining about the drive to North Miami every other day. McIntyre asked me once, in this same spot, what I planned to do with my life.

At twenty-two years old, I was always early for class. I feared missing a word.

"Mr. Diaz," Rhea said and waved me over to the pool. The sun was just beginning to set, painting the cloudy sky orange and pink. She wore jeans and a blouse, and her gray dreadlocks were short. Her feet were in the water.

"I brought you something," I said, holding a box of pastries, a *colada*, and a stack of thimble-sized cups.

"That is very thoughtful, young man."

I placed the pastries between us and sat next to her, crossing my legs.

"What do you have planned for today?" She was referring to my final exam. Each student was required to conjure a pair of items with randomized specific components. I drew two of the most difficult.

"Well, I've been reading up on fireworks, which meet the multiple chemical agents aspects, and a nail gun for the moving parts."

"Do it," she said.

"What, right now?"

"Why not? That way you can get out of here early."

"Can I stay, even if I finish?"

Rhea smiled. "You are always welcome here. Now, go on."

I pulled off the ratty bookbag that I'd been using since high school and retrieved my mother's salt jar. I poured out enough to form a casting circle and visualized each part of a rocket: the stick, the fuse, the motor, the payload, the cap. I thought of my favorite effect, the tourbillion. I closed my eyes and kept the picture of the rocket in my head and felt the object coalesce under my hand.

"Do you believe it will work?" Rhea said, looking at the product of my labors.

"Only one way to find out," I said, grinning.

"You're a rascal, Mr. Diaz," she said. She waved her hand at the canopy and the branches of the banyans pulled back, revealing a clear night sky, orange-gray from the light pollution, a few stars visible. "Set it off over there, if you please."

I ran to the other side of the pool, stuck the firework in the ground, and touched the green fuse. I evoked a spark with a power word, igniting the cord in a familiar sizzle. I took a few steps back and watched my rocket lift off, trailing an orange tail, before exploding into spinning heads of silver light, each one leaving an erratic, spinning spark before petering out.

Rhea clapped. "Well done. Now the nail gun."

It took ten seconds to produce a working facsimile of my father's pneumatic nail gun. I'd been using that nail gun since middle school, breaking it down and cleaning it every month.

"Does it work?" Rhea said.

"You would need an air compressor. But look," I said and showed her the nail pusher, the sliding panel on the magazine, the quick coupler, all of them spring loaded.

"You know, this demonstrates advanced technical proficiency. Most people hear 'moving parts' and just decide on a childhood toy." Rhea swirled her feet in the water. "Easy A."

"You're my last exam, too," I said, beaming. That would have been the more appropriate time for a firework, but I've always gotten ahead of myself.

"Well, then, you are a practitioner," she said and smiled. "What comes next?"

"I don't know yet." I didn't look at her when I said it; I already knew full well what came next.

"You do not have to lie to me, Mr. Diaz. I already saw your name on the registry for our masters program. Do you know what you want to specialize in?"

"I haven't thought about it," I said. I knew I would study necromancy the day the Chancellor saved me.

"You have a knack for conjuration. I could be your advisor."

"Thank you, Archmagus. I'm honored."

"Is that a yes?" she said.

"I need to think about it."

"Then it is a 'No.'"

"Not necessarily," I said.

"I have seen your transcripts. Four 4000-level necromancy courses." Her stare only added to her imperiousness.

I felt like a child who had been caught out of bed after hours. "I took those classes so I could start working right away." She was the best teacher I had ever had. Surely she would understand—with us sitting on her massive property—the need to advance in life. "I don't want to live at home forever," I said, but the words stuck in my throat.

"It is disgusting work you will be doing, Mr. Diaz."

I wanted to tell her that it was the most important work a practitioner could do. Keeping the city safe. Comforting the bereaved. Simple, selfless, noble work. "It is an important civil service, Archmagus," is all I could manage in light of her dominion.

"Ah, but whom will you serve?" Rhea pulled her feet out of the water, made the sign of the cross, and the droplets flew off of her in a little arc back into the pool. She laced up her sandals and rolled the cuffs of her jeans down to her ankles. "The Lord saw fit to provide us with an entire other plane of existence to explore. Another place to spread the Good Word. There are untold mysteries in Spiritus Mundi, and it takes a person with discipline and dedication to plumb their depths. Anyone can play with a dead body."

"There's more to necromancy—"

"No, there is not. It is evil and it is unnatural."

"Archmagus, necromancy helps people. It comforts them." I dared not challenge her further in that moment, in her home, with my grade on the line.

"People should be taking comfort in the Divine Plan. And the only one bringing people back to life should be the Almighty at the Last Judgment. What you seek to do is an abomination. You should be ashamed."

She looked up. Voices were approaching from the street. "Go, and take these," she said, sliding back the box of pastries. "I have other exams to administer."

"But—"

"I do not want your presence unnerving the other students," she said.

"It has been an honor, Archmagus."

Rhea puckered her lips. "I wish I could say the same."

I left her property and did not raise my head as I passed my classmates. It was full dark under the trees.

I pass beneath an arch cut into the hedge that separates the pool and glen from the rest of the grounds. McIntyre House dominates this end of the grounds, stately and imposing behind its lawns and gardens and orchards. The property is part of the National Register of Historic Places. A two-and-a-half story American foursquare, it was built at the turn of the last century to oversee the citrus groves that once spread out for miles. A porch wraps around the back of the house, covered with rocking chairs.

Smooth pebbles create the path leading through the lemon orchard to the manse. I sink a few inches with every crunching step. On the porch, McIntyre studies her grandchildren, watching them copy verses out of the Bible, building both their penmanship and dogma.

Lemons as big as grapefruit hang from the branches around me. Before the Haitian diaspora, Little Haiti was called Lemon City. These trees might be the only remains of that moniker; Rhea must have vanquished the city fathers, horse and foot, when they came during the Citrus Canker Scare of the late 90s. I smile, imagining some orange-shirted Asplundh employee trying to explain to Rhea that he was there to mulch her property.

McIntyre stomps her cane on the porch when she sees me. "All right, children, time to call."

A classroom's worth of Rhea's grandchildren, ranging from kindergarteners to teenagers, begin to put away their things. The youngest shriek with delight. She grabs her cane and pushes herself off her cushioned, wicker throne and walks to the edge of her porch. "Afternoon, Archmagus Diaz," she says, more an accusation than a courtesy. "How was the drive up?"

"Good afternoon, Archmagus McIntyre," I say. "The drive was good."

"God is good, Archmagus Diaz," she says and stares down at me. "Come on up."

The children swarm past me as I climb the steps to the porch. Even when I am on a level with her, she still towers above me. Well over six feet tall, big boned, her steel gray hair, braided into long dreadlocks and tied back, contrasts sharply with her earth-toned skin. She wears a green taftan that billows; the thongs of her leather sandals wrap around her feet and calves before disappearing beneath the fabric. Her high cheekbones and sharp chin give her a fierce, regal look. She remains the most elegant woman I've ever met. "You took far too long. I know you did not forget the way."

"My apologies, Archmagus. I had to take care of a gremlin infestation at Police Headquarters."

"Hmph. Filthy creatures," she says, and I have to hide a flinch hearing Clan Screwcap disparaged so casually. "Did you banish them?"

"No. There were too many." In truth, the thought never occurred to me, but it would have been a massive undertaking for anyone except Rhea; she literally wrote the book on extraplanar beings. "I brokered an agreement with their leader instead."

Rhea places her free hand on her chest. "Why on Earth would you do such a thing?"

"I had no other options."

"Of course you did. You just spend so much time playing with dead things that you've forgotten how to deal with the live ones," she says, and begins a rough descent down the porch stairs. I rush to help her down. Rhea stays me with a hand. "Archmagus, I am not an invalid. I just have a bad hip."

"My apologies." But I don't move from the foot of the stairs until she touches the ground. "How many grandchildren are you up to?" I say, satisfied she won't break another hip.

"Nineteen accounted for," she says.

"That's incredible."

"'Be fruitful, and multiply, and replenish the earth, and subdue it,'" she says as she makes her way down the path.

I shake the box of pastries. "Can I tempt you?"

"Those had better not be the real reason you're late," she says. She looks at the box and her nostrils flare. Maybe today will be the day. "And no, thank you," she says, dashing my hopes.

I trail at her side as we head to the glen. "Your children and I are of an age, and they have clearly had children."

"They knew what advice to listen to," McIntyre says.

Stymied by her curtness, I look up into the glen. Her grandchildren are running around the pool in the green shade, laughing. Children shouldn't be close to the work we're about to do. "Archmagus McIntyre, I know your family and religion are important to you, but we really need to activate the conduit."

Rhea tilts her head. "That is exactly what we're going to do."

"But where is it?"

"Same place you came in."

"Unguarded?!"

"Do you take me for a fool, Pablo Diaz?"

"Never, Archmagus. I am just confused."

Rhea shuffles down the path. "'There is nothing covered, that shall not be revealed; neither hid, that shall not be known.'"

The sweat pooling in my pits has nothing to do with the heat. I have hidden my actions, but they shall be known. Sandobal knows too much. Maybe everything. The Chancellor will figure it out, as soon as he is not preoccupied with the conduits. If Rhea were curious, she could just squeeze the Bursar and my life would be in her hands. I don't know how to fix any of this.

"You look sick, Archmagus," Rhea says to me as I pass under the arch and re-enter the glen.

"I haven't eaten since breakfast," I say, and I realize it's true. I could just have a *pastelito*, but it feels wrong eating in front of Rhea.

"Well, this'll be over soon. Give me your shoulder." Rhea lets her cane fall to the floor and grabs my good shoulder. She uses her free hand to undo her sandals. She places them next to each other, along with the cane, and wiggles her toes in the grass. She claps. "All right, children. Gather round."

"What are we doing?" I say. I stow the box of pastries in my doctor's bag.

"Praising the Lord, and taking His lesson from what happened to you and Archmagus Russo this morning. Crosses children," Rhea says. "We need some divine intervention today."

The children all produce small wooden crosses from inside their shirts. Rhea does the same. "Lord, recognize our need, and in Your mercy, send us servants fit to face Your enemies. And so we pray the words You gave us. 'Our Father, who art in Heaven, hallowed be thy name.'" As they move through the verses of the Lord's Prayer, halos appear over their heads. The light, golden and warm, washes over me, and I know my misery and my failings and my faithlessness. "'Thy kingdom come. Thy will be done on Earth, as it is in Heaven.'"

Heads emerge from above the halos, some with four faces, others small and curly haired, one with a blazing head and eyes. I can taste Rhea's magic, hers and her family's. It is ordered and dry, like a communion wafer. "'Give us this day our daily bread; and forgive us our trespasses, as we forgive those who trespass against us; and lead us not into temptation, but deliver us from evil.'" A lambent figure floats above each member of Rhea's family. A person of faith would call them angels.

I know better. These are extraplanar beings, avatars of goodness, and the auras radiating from the figures feel that way. A little Gospel from Rhea, along with some favors done, sets these outsiders preaching the same way she does. Her belief in the Good Book fuels her magic, but it also makes her shortsighted and haughty, single-minded in her belief that any magic that doesn't come from God comes from the Devil.

Looking at the children running around and playing with their personal spirits, I can't help myself; the irresponsibility chokes me. "Rhea, what have you done?"

McIntyre raises an eyebrow at me, smiling. "I haven't done anything. The Lord saw fit to send us protectors in our hour of need." She sighs and relishes her smile, watching the children try to catch each other's angels.

"You taught the children to summon spirits!"

"Of course. 'Train up a child in the way he should go: and when he is old, he will not depart from it.'"

Normally, I would keep my mouth shut: her family, her choice. But a memory yells in some recessed corner of my brain, a memory of being at the mercy of three wights. Rhea stands beside her grandchildren now, but what might a child—alone, wrathful, or sullen—summon? "This is the most reckless thing I have ever seen! Do you know the danger you've put these children in? I would never—"

Rhea wheels on me like a falcon and jabs a finger in my face. "How dare you question me in my home?"

I turn my palms up and shake them. "Because you're out of control!" The children's heads swivel between their grandmother and me, and I am conscious of the fact that I have yelled. I clasp my hands behind my back and clear my throat. "Can we, perhaps, discuss this alone?"

Rhea takes a moment to scan the faces of her grandchildren. "Everyone, back inside, but tell your servitors that they are now in my charge." Only a few of the children complain and they are quickly silenced by the teenagers. One boy mean-mugs me on the way out of the glen. It feels like a tiny, male Rhea cursing me. The angels congregate around Rhea. "You may speak freely now," she says.

"How gracious of you."

"Grace comes from God."

I have to think about keeping my face level. "What do you think the Chancellor would say about all of this?"

"I do not care what he thinks, Archmagus. I was practicing well before he showed up. And you do not know him at all if you think he would somehow disapprove of me instructing my family." I had no idea that she was practicing magic before Dead Sunday. That's probably where she gets that chip on her shoulder.

"Rhea, can't you see that you're endangering their lives?"

"I see plenty! Like a grown man entering someone else's domicile and having the audacity to second-guess their host."

I have always imagined her rage as white hot and shaking. Instead, her steady voice and stare bore into me. "As always, Archmagus, you are correct. I apologize for my impertinence. Perhaps you would allow me to explain myself?"

"Apology accepted. And there is no need for an explanation. I know who you are, Pablo Diaz."

"The second most powerful necromancer in the city? Maybe in existence?" I say, instantly realizing I've taken the bait.

"A prideful fool who needs saving. But instead of giving your allegiance where it is really due, you ally yourself with the Chancellor. You made him your idol. And once he had trained you up, you made yourself your own monument."

"Archmagus, this—"

"Lord have mercy. Pablo Diaz, open your eyes!" She smacks the back of her hand into her cupped palm. "He trucks with demons!"

"He imprisons demons to serve the College!"

"You only defend it because you take shekels from that wolf-toothed toad. You are no better than that huckster Nick Russo, but at least he has the honesty to sell himself heart-and-soul, instead of sniffing around for crumbs."

I clench my jaw and take a few deep breaths. The tune is updated, but the beat is the same. "Archmagus, I came here to do a job. The path I chose was the one that most interested me, provided the most stable work, and—I felt—was the most noble."

Rhea throws her head back in laughter, a clucking chuckle that might have been infectious under different circumstances. "Is that how you see yourself? Russo could take a lesson from you." She wipes a tear from her eye. "Repent your vanity, Diaz. Tell me, what have you reaped from your good work?"

"I don't owe you an explanation."

"No, but you owe yourself one." She raises her eyebrows and tilts her head down at me. "Let me tell you what you have garnered. A position at an institution that treats the miraculous like cold science. A friendless existence, where even your closest colleagues are strangers to you. And an inability to take care of you and yours.

"And why? Because you, just like Russo and Coghlan and Hellas, think that magic is control. Magic is not bending the world to your whims, Pablo; it is letting God do His work through you. Had you stayed with me, you could have had all of this," she says, and throws up her hands.

I try to think of a way to tell her how wrong she is, but I can't say anything to her. Her legacy is secured; even the youngest can conjure angels on faith alone. Scary as that might be, she has taught babes to do what most adults fail to do: summon.

"You only sought money. 'What shall it profit a man, if he shall gain the whole world, and lose his own soul?'"

"I could ask you the same thing, bringing your grandchildren into this. Please, don't interrupt me," I say, seeing her inhale and move her foot toward me. "I tried my hand at magic as a child and it almost killed me. What happens when you're not around and those children decide to summon something other than an angel? What happens when one of those teenagers gets heartbroken or bullied or shown up and they start hurling curses?"

"Those children are better trained than you ever were." She sneers at me and turns to the banyans. The angel hovering over her, the one made of fire, looks at me without pity or love. An afro of flames, copper skin, spear in hand, armored cap-à-pie. Merciless.

"It's time," she says to it. Her servitor dives into the pool. An I-beam of cold iron begins to rise from the water. As it reaches the height of a man, a crossbeam appears. Where the two beams meet, the bubble of ectoplasm encased in the orb of wraithglass undulates. She shaped her conduit into a cross, naturally. Its tip reaches the canopy. Her angel returns.

"That object has necromancy written all over it," I say to her.

"The Lord works in mysterious ways, Pablo. Who are you to question Him?"

The conundrum of Rhea McIntyre laid bare. Her faith gives her power; that much is undeniable. She reckons the faithless having power as part of God's mystery or the Devil's handiwork. Yet, she's willing to hold up her faith while working with the conduit, an item made of cold iron, which can only be produced by the dead. That knowledge came from Emérico.

What probably keeps her up at night is Emérico's power. Why would God allow such a creature to wield His might? Unravelling that knot is probably why she teaches at the College: to observe him, study him, and counter him when necessary. She brings the uninitiated out here to lure them away from the Chancellor. She treats me this way because I denied her. I am the wrench in her holy rolling.

I set my jaw. After beating Baba Yaga, after getting my face pressed and seared by the Bursar, after fighting a battalion of mermen, after dealing with Tetch and Elisa Sandobal, I won't bend to this woman's hypocrisy. When I started teaching, she made me think I was a fraud, but if the last two days have taught me anything, it is that I am a force to be reckoned with. An idiot. But a force.

Determined to teach her a lesson, I retrieve my mother's jar of salt from my bag and open the top. There isn't enough left for a casting circle. "May I have some salt?" I say.

Rhea's allows herself a single, seething breath. "Still leaning on that old crutch?" She passes her hand over the jar of salt and says, "'With all thine offerings thou shalt offer salt.'" The jar replenishes itself. "You think you're going to prove something to me?"

"Yes. You're not my better, Rhea McIntyre."

"Nor did I ever claim to be," she says, but the set of her mouth, the raising of her chin, say otherwise.

"I am just serving the College."

"No. You serve yourself. And you serve the Chancellor." Rhea picks up her cane.

"I needed the Chancellor to learn magic. I owed him." He saved me that night as a child. He asked me to take over as department head. Those who deny their benefactors end up in the deepest circle of Hell.

"Had you had faith in the Lord, you would never have needed Emérico. I didn't. I was God's instrument well before Dead Sunday. When I saw Emérico erect that tower, I knew I was witnessing an even more profane Babel. The very next day, I marched down to that abode of the damned and those doors flew open for me. They flew! And when I came face to face with that demon, he had no choice but to give me my due. I haven't been able to save everybody but I've saved a few, and that was God's will and my own.

"That's faith, Pablo Diaz. Putting your trust in the Lord. Haven't you wondered yet where all this came from?" she says and waves an arm over her head. "My family has always believed in two things: the Gospel and hard work. Everything that we have, we prayed and worked for, and God saw fit to grant it, because we work in His name.

"I can't even imagine what you work for"—she points at me—"if not yourself. And don't you dare blaspheme these grounds by calling upon some abomination."

I won't dishonor Rhea in her own home by summoning something dark. I will call out to something—anything—good, and hope for a response. I take a handful of salt and weigh it in my hand. I severed my ties to religion long ago. My mother's death sundered my faith. What remnants lingered were banished into Nox by Emérico the following night. I've tried to hold onto my morals, however.

My services are needed, by the bereaved, by the city. And yes, I get paid, but a man is worthy of his hire. Involving myself with Orlov was a mistake, and the price was Baba Yaga. I was willing to lay down my life to fix that. Where does that come from? Vanity, as Rhea says? I can feel the grains of salt crack as I clench my fist.

No. I fought the witch because it was right. I marched mortals through Nox because it was right. I bartered with Clan Screwcap because it was right. My parents would think it was right. I look down at my mother's jar. Baked clay. Thick. Weighty. I fall to my knees and let the grains of salt pour out of my fist, drawing a small conjuring circle with connecting cursive letters. It takes several handfuls to finish, and I dare not look up at Rhea as I do it. Rose is a rose is a rose? No. I connect the two names who bestowed goodness on me: "Elena" and "Tristan."

I place my hand in the circle. I chant their names. I think of their lessons. My mother starching my shirts. My father always cleaning up a job site. Fresh eggs. Charity when we had nothing, to beggar and church alike. Duty above all. The portal to Spiritus Mundi appears, massive, a beating oval taller than a man. A golden, spiraled horn emerges first, attached to a bearded, horse-like head. The fur is so white it hurts to look at.

A thick mane covers the creature's neck and shoulders. Its meaty legs resemble those of a rhinoceros and end in golden hooves.

"You wretch," Rhea says. "Are you mocking me with that creature?"

There is no voice in my head, no words, but I understand its question. I look at Rhea. "It wants to know why it has been summoned," I say.

Rhea rubs her tongue against the roof of her mouth and then over her teeth. "Tell it to wait," she says, and snatches up a handful of salt.

I stow the jar, grab my bag, stand up, and brush the dirt and grass off of my knees. I reach my hand out slowly to the unicorn, my fingers trembling. It moves its shoulder beneath my hand. It wants me to know it is real.

Rhea stomps to the edge of the pool, jabbing her cane into the ground with each step, and tosses in the salt. She raises her hands. "'And I saw another angel fly in the midst of Heaven, having the Everlasting Gospel to preach unto them that dwell on the earth, and to every nation, and kindred, and tongue, and people, saying with a loud voice, fear God, and give glory to Him; for the hour of His judgment is come: and worship Him that made Heaven, and earth, and the sea, and the fountains of waters.'"

The pool's glowing shifts from blue to white. I glimpse my old teacher, matter-of-fact, regal, unconcerned, as clawed, crystalline, scaled legs—each the size of a cow—grip the edges of the pool on either side of her. The purple talons dig into the soil for purchase, attached to blue legs. The head emerges, reptilian, red, jagged, with human eyes. The orange neck and frills follow, until the rainbow dragon towers as high as the conduit, but only half of its body has emerged. It shakes out its wings, buffeting we mere mortals.

"Sister McIntyre," the dragon says, "why have you summoned me?" Its voice makes my chest quiver. The unicorn sidles against me.

"The forces of evil will be upon us. Defend us, that we may continue to serve. Allow nothing to approach these grounds or the church."

"They shall tremble before the strength the Almighty has bestowed upon me," the dragon says. It pushes the rest of its body out of the portal, its tail equipped with a vicious thagomizer bristling with green, glass spikes. It tries to find purchase to stretch out between the pool and the trees, but some of the trunks groan and snap.

Rhea studies the dragon for longer than I would expect, then turns to me and raises an eyebrow. "Shall we get this over with?"

What did Tetch say? Spiritus Mundi only exists because humans believe in it. I walk over to her and whisper. "I thought dragons were supposed to be evil?"

"I called for protection. Moral and lawful. What else do you want?"

"Not a thing." As Gygax and his cohort taught us, dragons come in every flavor. The children's summons come from purity of heart; this *thing* only serves dogma. Her face reflects back from every scale and I realize she got exactly what she wanted: unquestioning obedience.

"How do we activate it?" I say. "Nick had a panel."

"The panel is for the police," she says. "Stay on guard and don't move."

Rhea grips her cross and says, "*Fiat mandātō meō*." Is she quoting the Bible in Latin? Her forebears would call that papist arrogance. The heart of the conduit flashes, and I have to shield my eyes, just like this morning. *Fiat mandātō meō*: *that* is what I heard Nick speak this morning. Aside from their egos and self-aggrandizing and magical potency, there couldn't be two human beings more different than Rhea McIntyre and Nick Russo. Why, then, are they working in the same paradigm? They might have made the conduits together, but even so, if they personalized the objects' appearances, they could have done the same for the activation.

Beyond the tranquility of the grove, a horn blows. Roaring echoes in the distance, followed by screaming and the crunch of metal. "We must defend this house," Rhea says.

The dragon leans its head down to Rhea. "I shall wait in the skies until you signal me," it says. It leaps into the canopy, leaving deep prints at the pool's edge. Once above the trees, it flaps upward, sending a hail of leaves down on us.

"Come along," Rhea says and waves an arm at the angels. Her host gathers. She leads them out to the street. I follow and the unicorn keeps pace. Beyond the overgrowth of the glen, the roaring a few blocks away rises in pitch.

"What is that, Rhea?" I say.

"Hmph. Nothing good." Rhea holds her palm out to the hedges and the entrance to the glen closes behind us.

An orcish warband turns the corner onto Rhea's block. They range in height from five to seven feet, wearing rusted armor and carrying tarnished swords, axes, and spears. Two yellow tusks jut upward from their lower jaws, and their mottled, green skin reminds me of turned meat. They just keep coming, massing in the street. There are easily a hundred of them.

"Rhea?" I ask.

She points her cane at the oncoming enemies. "No quarter," she says, and the angels charge to meet their opponents. She lifts her cane into the sky and a firework shoots from the tip into the air, exploding in a red peony—an old standard and exactly what I would expect from her.

The unicorn nudges me. It intends to engage, and I only have to nod. It takes off, sparks flying every time a hoof strikes pavement. It gores the first orc it meets through a bloodshot eye. It jerks back, ripping the head from the body and tossing it into the air.

"Lord, guide us and keep us," Rhea says. "You ready?"

"No," I say. I run to drop my doctor's bag behind the limestone wall and unsheathe Thanatopsis as I return.

"What are you going to do with that?"

"Turn them against each other," I say.

"There's no need for that," she says and points at the sky.

The dragon drops from the clouds, wings folded against its body. It hurtles toward the orcs like an intercontinental ballistic missile. Before it hits the street, it unfurls its wings and somersaults. As it flips in the air, its tail rakes the ground. Whatever fighters aren't impaled on the spikes get launched a block away. It flaps twice, then breathes heavenly fire on the war band, leaving burnt flesh and slag.

When the dragon lands, the orcs rush it. It bats a few aside and unleashes another flaming torrent on the bloodthirsty, relentless mob. They cling to its claws and knees and wings, but their rusted blades break against its scales.

Emboldened by the dragon, McIntyre's summoned chorus does its best to beat back the orcs. But where each berserking menace falls, two take its place, and they just keep swarming the streets. The cars on the strip of grass have corralled the orcs thus far, but a few are starting to climb the cars for vantage.

"Rhea, they're going to get in!"

McIntyre points her cane at the hedges and a wall of spears shoots forth from the leaves, impaling the nearest orcs, driving the rest back onto the asphalt.

Rhea smiles next to me. "The day is ours," she says and waves her fingers at the hedges, opening an archway.

"What? No! Just because their line is broken, doesn't mean they're retreating!"

"Look," she says and points with her cane.

The army of orcs stalls half a block away from the dragon. Between the horde and the winged battalion, a no-man's-land of charred bodies smolders. Faced with the enormous and incomprehensible reality of being consumed by flames, the orcs turn to the nearby houses, leaping fences, pushing aside cars, battering at barred doors that bend all too quickly.

"We have to save those people!"

"Don't be a fool, Pablo. You have a job to do. Get to the next conduit and all of this stops."

"Rhea, people are going to die! That's your congregation!"

She laughs and my skin crawls. "The ones that matter are in the church, and the Lord's house is impenetrable."

"Help me save them!"

"You can't save everyone, Pablo," she says. "Lord knows I've tried." She enters the archway and the hedges close behind her, leaving me and the rest of the faithless to face a green-skinned apocalypse.

14
Street Smarts

DOWN ON HIS luck, the crackhead goes to his corner to beg change for his next hit. With rock-bottom in sight, the gambler relies on scratch-offs to scratch his itch. When addiction meets opposition, the debased rely on rote.

Drooling, tusked, green-skinned, clad in hide armor, the orcs teem the streets surrounding Rhea's property, trying her defenses. Conjured spears shoot out from the hedges, impaling any who approach the grounds. A dozen fiends stand skewered.

A horn spits three quick blasts and the orcs retreat across the street. They flex and roar and tremble, seeking deliverance. An orc in mustard yellow robes aims to give it to them. He drops a horn suspended on leather thongs to his waist. He pounds his staff on the sidewalk three times; small skulls—goblin or gnome—top the staff, their jaws clattering like castanets. "Brothers and sisters!" he says and waves a rolled-up parchment in his hand to silence the mob's murmur. "Gormar Thrill-Gore"—he pounds his chest once, crumpling the scroll—"brought you here to feast! But a witch ensorcells this land to starve us!"

The warband gnashes teeth, stamps, spits.

"She cowers in her thorny brush. She refuses to face us. She knows the Thrill-Gores will eat her heart!" Gormar shakes his staff to silence them. "Bring me fresh blood from these homes"—he waves behind his head—"and I will give you the rites my father, Helbar Thrill-Gore, gave me. We will tear down this witch's walls and take what she tries to keep from us!"

I take it that Gormar must be a member of the Hallow Order. These are orcs who shun industry and big game hunting in favor of nomadism. They pursue magic and all its related ecstasies. Whereas magic exalted Tetch, it has warped Gormar's tribe into junkies. Jonesing for a hit, faced with insurmountable odds, the horde rushes the tightly-packed homes across from Rhea's property.

Instant panic. I drop to the asphalt and ransack my bag until I find a fat stick of chalk. I draw an octagon in the street—a stop sign to stop them—connecting the corners with lines that meet at the center. I draw the eyes of eight deadly creatures in the triangles, lay my hand on the intersection, stare at the houses, and begin chanting.

The facades of the houses warp and distort into faces: a kraken's beak, a merman's maw, Baba Yaga. The illusions snap, lunge, and cackle at the oncoming orcs. The horde falls back. "They can't eat us all!" Gormar says.

An orc armed with a crude sword tries to slice the tiger's head. She whiffs through it. "They're not real!"

Gormar bellows in triumph: "It's the witch!"

As quickly as my ruse is exposed, they are pounding at the walls. I curse myself. I love chalk as a tool; it will draw sigils on most substances. But I learned to use it for Abjuration, not Illusion. The rote has failed me. I could ward the houses if these villains weren't already knocking at the gates. If I make myself a target, they will dogpile me before I have a chance.

In my inert moment of consideration, the unthinkable inevitable happens. They drag a wizened black man in flannel pajamas out onto his front porch. Gormar pulls the oxygen tubes from the man's face and slices his throat. The man doesn't have time to scream, but I do. A purple fountain pours from the gash.

Gormar presses the scroll against the old man's chest until it soaks up enough blood to turn brown. He calls up one of his subordinates and rips a tab off of the scroll. "Pray the words my father gave us," Gormar says.

"I hunger, but my flesh is weak." The orc cracks his knuckles; he shivers and rubs his upper arms. "Grant me your strength." He opens his mouth and extends his tongue. Gormar presses the gory piece of parchment onto his tribesman's tongue. He pantomimes, pushing air at his fellow, and every vein in the follower's exposed flesh pulses. The subject grows taller, more muscular.

"Show her our power, brother!" Gormar says and points at Rhea's property. Someone brings the imbued orc a crude, flat sword; I would have trouble gripping it in two hands, but he handles it in one. He takes three running steps toward McIntyre House and bounds into the air; he will clear the hedge with room to spare.

A shadow passes over me. A blur of shimmering iridescence bats the orc to the street. The marked one bounces once on the asphalt. The dragon crushes him into a gooey pulp, bellows at the orcs watching the display, and takes flight.

"More!" the yellow-robed orc yells. "More blood for the sacrament!"

I watch the grisly rites from the crossroads. Ahead of me and on the left, McIntyre Grove, where Rhea has bunkered down and abandoned her neighbors. To the right, the houses under assault and Gormar surrounded by his kin. They clamor for the disgraceful paper. Those without patience make for the houses again.

Rhea's dragon lands behind me in the grass of McIntyre Grove AME. It stretches its wings and neck, scales rising and glinting in all its multi-colored glory. I run to the church. When the creature sees me, it lowers its head and drops into a prowl. "Not another step, *practitioner*."

I swallow the insult and stop short of the curb. I try to gauge how long those houses will stand, then turn back to the creature. "Please! Strafe the street! You have the power to thin their numbers," I say.

The dragon curls back its lips from its fangs. "My orders were to keep anything from approaching the grounds or the church."

Was that disgust or glee? "There are innocent people in those homes! You could save hundreds!" It could clear the street in a single sweep.

"That is not my concern. I have been given a task, and I will finish it. If you step any closer, I will roast you where you stand."

I turn to the screech of metal. A seven-foot-tall berserker rips a guard door made of iron bars off of its hinges. It kicks open the wooden door into the house and roars into the darkness. Bullets roar back. The home invader crumples before what remains of the door slams shut. Orcs of every size rush the home, but none proves brave enough to try the front door again.

Whoever lives in that home—armed as they may be—won't last long. I glare at the dragon and run toward the house. The setting sun leaves floaters in my vision. My head starts to throb, then my calf, then the rest of me. Had I eaten something, now would be the time to throw up.

I need to end this, but I can't face an army of addicts. I hear them bashing doors and breaking windows and choking their victims' screams. Because death is kinder than withdrawal, the only pity they have is for themselves. Another summons won't be enough. Rhea can summon dragons; one would never respond to my call.

I have to meet these animals with my own soldiers. I can think of one way to do so. McIntyre warned me against it, then left me with no recourse. If she didn't want this, she should have stayed and fought with me.

Reanimation requires a ritual similar to that of a post-mortem interview. A few reagents, such as my blood or ectoplasm, can supplement a corpse with life. I crafted Thanatopsis, however, with three inherent abilities: cutting a path into Nox, exorcism, and the reinvigoration of corpses. I run up to the smoldering orc bodies the dragon dispatched. Most are charred to a crisp. The least damaged specimen has half of its face and the left side of its torso blackened Cajun-style. I take one last look at the hedges; she'll judge me afterward.

I hold my breath. I turn to the corpse and plunge Thanatopsis into its abdomen. I channel my desperation from my stomach, down my arm, and into the blade. The orc uses its undamaged arm and leg to push up from the ground, its remaining eye glowing ectoplasmic blue. The zombie is incapable of thought, but it reacts to my intent. It takes up a boxer's stance.

My heart beats a little faster as the dead servant snaps to defense. Some of the reanimated fighter's skin is on the verge of sloughing off but the muscles beneath are intact, ready to rip a man in half. If Rhea were to emerge now, she would be livid. I stab another corpse. A rictus grin freezes its scorched face; boils cover the taut skin on its arms. It tries to get to its feet, but both wrists snap. Its head hits the pavement with a wet thud.

I gnash my teeth. By the time I raise enough of these creatures, the neighborhood will be rubble. I limp amongst the corpses, slashing bodies with abandon, trying to build an offensive line of green and black flesh. As soon as I have created five servitors on steady feet, I send them to rush the orcs trying to get into the houses, and continue my ghoulish search for the least damaged candidates.

A battle cry from across the street. I've been out in the open too long; I should have kept one zombie with me. An orc leaps into the air, blocking the sun. "Sorcerer!" it says, hurtling toward me with an iron pipe. I feel the sweat in my pits, on my chest; my knees are jelly. I scream and raise Thanatopsis above my head. Maybe I can cut him down before he impales me.

Metal clangs rapidly to my right. The unicorn barrels into my would-be murderer. The two of them go down in a thrashing ball. The unicorn brays—a high-pitched scream that raises the hair on my neck—as the orc drives the pipe into its shoulder. I dash after them and drive Thanatopsis through the orc's temple. Its jaw goes slack. I channel my pounding heart through the blade. Its face goes from lifeless to stoic; blue, forced life lights its eyes. I send it running into the fray with a thought.

The unicorn finds its footing. It whinnies; I duck. It turns around, plants its front legs, and kicks over me. When its hoof meets the chest of an armored orc, the sound is like the crumpling of a fender. I push Thanatopsis through the felled orc's back. My posse swells in number.

The unicorn sidles next to me and whickers. When it brushes me, I feel its pain in my shoulder and my gorge rises. It pushes the pipe under my hand. I recoil, but the creature paws the ground and pushes against me again. I sheath my sword, grab the iron with both hands, and yank. The unicorn stamps its hoof down in bonging protest then shakes out its mane before galloping to the house.

The nausea didn't come from the pipe in the creature's back; the unicorn disapproves of my reanimation. But I can't avoid it; force must meet force.

Unable to find any more able-bodied candidates, I give hobbled chase. Orcs swarm the fourth house on the block, ripping off every piece of siding, iron bar, and gutter they can grab onto. The unicorn rears up and pummels a raider with its front legs. Each kill gives me a new, mostly undamaged servitor. They prove much more effective than their dragon-fried brethren. Orc by orc, stab by slash, we clear the perimeter of the house.

I mount the porch using Thanatopsis as a cane, stand to the side of the front door, and pound on the wood with the side of my fist; the door rattles in the frame. "If you're still alive, please don't shoot!" I say.

"Get the fuck off my porch!" a man says.

"I can get you out of here!"

"You think we're stupid? You got these things crawling all over my damn house!"

"Sir, please, you don't understand—"

A crash of glass and a child's scream.

I run to the edge of the porch. A green gang jumps over the chain link fence from the neighboring house and then into a window.

The booming report of a shotgun. Three quick shots from something smaller.

I summon my zombie to the porch and they charge in, knocking the door off its hinges. The dark room—tight because of a sectional couch, lit only by a television—fills with chaos. Three of my servitors tackle the first orc they see and rip off her jaw. A living raider tries stabbing one of my reanimated orcs, only to have his victim headbutt him until his skull fractures.

An orc bellows in the other room; the sound is cut off by a meaty crack. My heart thumps double-time in the silence of the house. The dead man in the hallway is missing an arm. An orc lies crumpled in the bedroom doorway. Inside the pink room, a woman has had her intestines ripped out. A shotgun lies next to her. The little girl and orc in there have been peppered with pellets and lie in gore.

I run to the bathroom and vomit bile onto the floor; the force of it raises blinding tears. I wipe my face and find the man's arm—still gripping a shiny semi-auto—in the shower. Hands on my knees, I dry heave until I fall onto my ass.

I don't know how long I sit there.

Something bubbles to my right. The pool of blood next to the man's arm undulates and its center rises, heedless of gravity. As the blood levitates upward, red threads coagulate and knit together, coalescing into the form of Gormar Thrill-Gore. I scramble to shaky feet and brandish Thanatopsis at the orc made of blood.

"Leave this place to us, necromancer," Gormar says. His voice reverberates, as if in a cave: the echoes of scrying.

"You're getting your tribe killed for no reason. You'll never reach the conduit."

"We have as much a right to this 'conduit' as you."

I scoff. "What claim could you possibly stake? You didn't make the conduit. This isn't even your realm. Practice your profane magic elsewhere."

"Profane? Look what you've done to my people!" He motions to the zombie standing around like terracotta soldiers.

"What about *these* people?" I say and point at the man whose blood serves as Gormar's body.

"What greater honor could they find?" He toes the dead man. "Weak sacks of meat. At least they found a purpose. What are they to you, sorcerer?"

"Everything," I say.

"Then you will lose 'everything,'" Gormar says. "When you stand alone among the smoking ruins, I will make your blood our strength, and we will take what you deny." Gormar's sanguine projection explodes, splashing the walls, the ceiling, my face. I wipe the gore from my eyes and mouth.

Just because he's scrying me doesn't necessarily indicate he knows my exact whereabouts. I command the zombie to move against the walls, into the doorways, and to the windows; if Gormar sends more into this house, they will be met. I dash through the rooms, revivifying any dead orcs with a wound from Thanatopsis.

Weak sacks of meat. That's how Gormar sees the living. Just another reagent. I walk around, studying the three human bodies. I want to blame Rhea; she destroyed this family by doing nothing. But Gormar exemplifies the worst kind of villainy. Violence for self-empowerment, selfish self-aggrandizement.

I don't want to look at the little girl. I try to focus on the mother but she's still holding the shotgun. The room is a misery. That dragon could have prevented all of this. Rhea chose her servitor well: obstinate, prideful, an obedient soldier.

Can I turn that to my advantage?

I know what I want to do. I know what would work. I also know I shouldn't do it. If the news reports it, I could be dragged by the mob, or cause another mass panic. They'll see me like I see Gormar, another debased spellcaster. But the city has its eyes elsewhere. Who in Miami would turn their attention to the ghetto in the midst of a catastrophe? They'll ignore it like they do every other day.

I pity these dead. I do. I really do. But their souls have crossed over to Nox, and hopefully gone toward the great unknown. I can do no further harm here; these decaying vessels only resemble something that mattered. I can make them matter once more, if only to punish Gormar, who stripped this meat of its true essence. I start digging through the drawers and cabinets in the kitchen until I find what I need: a barbeque lighter, a ceramic bowl, and a pair of scissors. I pluck a hair from my head and drop it into the bowl. I go to the man's corpse. His hair is too close-cropped, but his goatee is long enough for some snips. From the woman, I take a short, crinkled lock. I can't bring myself to take anything from the child. I dig around her bed instead, until I find a long, suitable strand.

I don't leave the zombie that much dignity, just yank coarse hairs from their arms. I put all the hair in a bowl and cover the tuft completely in salt. I chant and hold the flame to the grains until a puff of magic snuffs the fire. The enchantment is in place. I poke Thanatopsis into the tip of the man's finger until the skin surrenders to the point. His eyes glow blue. I do the same to the woman.

I stand over the child. I close my eyes, exhale, and scratch her calf.

I creep out the front door, crouched against the doorframe and walls, eyes darting at every movement and grunt. The church is close, but there could be orcs around every corner. I stay low. Take slow, deliberate steps. Bite my lips. Try not to breathe. I can see the church once I reach the sidewalk. The dragon sits on the lawn, preening itself, looking as pristine and opulent as Murano glass.

It's only four houses away. I break into a run. My doctor's bag jingles and clanks with reagents; I hold it to my chest. I keep my hand on Thanatopsis's hilt to point the scabbard behind me, afraid to fall. My lungs burn. My calf feels like it might just split.

They're going to see me.

The dragon lifts its head from beneath its wing as I cross the intersection. "Why are *you* still here? I doubt there's anything left alive in those houses."

It takes me a moment to slow my breathing. "I wanted to give you one more chance to help." I am on the church lawn, caddy-corner to Rhea's property.

"How magnanimous," it says, "but I must decline."

"You'll regret this," I say.

It laughs, a staccato hiss.

All that power, and no sense of duty; I can feel my blood pressure behind my eyes. I gave this recalcitrant a chance and he laughed at me. I grip Thanatopsis's hilt and shuffle in place. My malice moves my feet, and I shuffle a two-step, charging kinetic energy, which I channel out to the zombies.

When I was a child, my mother made me take dancing lessons. She said no Cuban girl would ever fall for a man who couldn't dance. When they teach you Salsa, they start with *Rueda de Casino*. I didn't know the names of the other children around me, but in those moments, watching us all struggle with—and eventually understand and share—the rhythm, I felt a connection.

With each step, I can feel the location of the bodies under my control. Once I am aware of all of them, I stamp my feet and clap the beat I know best: *la conga*. The family comes screaming out of the house. I send them down the block, away from myself and the church. My servitors run after them.

Confusing them for potential victims, the living orcs pour out of the houses to give chase. Somewhere, Gormar says, "No! Do not follow!" but it is too late. His tribesman cannot hear him; they only see fresh blood to abate their weakness.

The dragon lifts its head again, snorts, and turns to me. "Did you reanimate a dead family?"

I purse my lips and nod.

"You're a disgusting person," it says.

I close my eyes, pray he's wrong, and keep shuffling. The little girl's shrieks carry far, and each second-long wail of terror is answered by orcs, either mine or those that emerge from the houses. They turn a far corner.

"I hope you're ready," I say to the dragon.

"For what?"

"Your just desserts."

Something clenches my heart; they're in trouble. I clap harder to the 4/4. I bob my head and spin in place. The feeling passes. But the tightness is still there. I jump in place and shimmy. Whatever was holding the family loses its grip.

The little girl cries out. They're close now, on the opposite side of the block. A rumble and murmur approach with her. "You look like an idiot," the dragon says.

I turn up my lips and shake my head. "This is your last chance. Say you'll help me do the right thing. You can save yourself."

It snorts. "You don't scare me."

I clap and slide backwards. "I should."

The screaming family appears around the corner, a short block away from the church. The one-armed father carries the little girl with his remaining limb. Her arms are wrapped around his neck; she is missing one of her pigtails. The mother's robe flaps in the wind, tatters flailing. Her hands hold in her entrails.

Behind them, an army appears. The orcs closest to the family have glowing blue eyes, but the eyes of the mob behind them are bloodshot yellow. The dragon whips its head toward them. "Are you doing this?"

I throw my arms at my side, palms up, and stamp my feet. *Tada*.

"You are truly useless," it says. It raises its head. The scales on its neck glow. Like a cobra striking, it spits a torrent of flame at the oncoming bodies. The orcs giving chase fall into piles of roast meat and ash.

But the already dead, enchanted against fire, barely smolder. My plan worked. So why is my heart still in my throat?

"Very clever," the dragon says. "Why didn't you just summon one of my brethren? Archmagus McIntyre could have."

Every muscle in my body tightens. My army charges. The dragon's eyes go wild. It spits fire at them. Mother and father and child and close to twenty orcs leap at the creature's mouth. Spurts of flame explode from its throat, useless against my warded undead. Orcs latch onto the dragon's feet and shove their arms under its cuticles, trying to pull out claws. Those that have weapons ram them beneath its scales to pry them up, tearing at the soft, hidden flesh with fist or tusk.

The dragon jumps and thrashes, trying to throw them off. Gouts of flame jet into the sky and disperse into black smoke. It flaps its wings once in an attempt to buffet the assault, but bodies weigh down its wings. In its desperation, it smacks orcs off its back with its tail, looking momentarily like a scorpion; it impales two, but stabs itself.

The dragon's knees buckle under dozens of bodies. It collapses onto the lawn. I feel the vibrations in my feet. The zombies tear strips of magenta and cerulean scales from its legs and neck and rend the exposed flesh. They attack anything they can latch onto—except for those brilliant wings. It takes three orcs on each side of its head to force open its jaws, but when the passage is clear, they ram themselves down its neck. They rip its tongue apart, clawing their way toward the inside of the jugular.

There are simply too many dead for the dragon to swallow.

One-by-one, the zombies tumble out of its mouth. The family emerges last, followed by a rattling gust of foul air. The dragon is still. I pose the corpses on the steps of the church, the parents holding the child. Let Rhea see what she destroyed.

I unsheathe Thanatopsis and cut the dragon's lolling tongue. Its scales become muted. Its eyes turn lambent blue. I walk down the block, beyond the second patch of scorched bodies. There are more orcs in the neighborhood, concerned only with violence and pillage. I point Thanatopsis at them.

The dragon rushes them like an alligator. With one giant bite, it chomps an orc in the abdomen; it swings its head from side to side, sending its legs and head flying in different directions. With one swing of its claws, it cuts another orc into gory ribbons. Swipe after giant swipe, it begins to clear the street.

Gormar appears from the dead family's home; he must have been looking for me. He blows a long note on his horn. "Thrill-Gores! To me!" His tribe begins to emerge from the houses and mass around him.

A band of orcs steel themselves to attack. The dragon burns them where they stand. It slinks toward the orc in yellow and lowers its head. "Leave," I say through its mouth.

"Sorcerer?" Gormar says. "So you've made the most notorious hoarder your mouthpiece. Fitting." He spits on the ground.

The dragon bites down. It raises its head, chewing, bones cracking and crunching. It swallows Gormar Thrill-Gore with a gulp.

The rest of his tribe scatters. I raise Thanatopsis. The dragon takes ungainly flaps of its wings until it wobbles in the air. Sword to the sky, I fly the deadliest kite in creation on an invisible tether, raining down chaos. My newest servant deals death and destruction with its remaining talons, flambéing those who run away. I scour the neighborhood, chasing down every orc I see until I can't find another.

I return to my car—the dragon circling above me—to find the insult heaped upon my injury. The passenger-side mirror is on the asphalt, and the window must have broken when something crushed the door. There are dents in the hood and the roof.

I look at the hedges and glimpse flecks of yellow. With a thought, the dragon flies over the lemon trees. I release it from my control, and the corpse drops onto Rhea's grove. I pick up the mirror and throw it in my passenger seat, along with my doctor's bag and Thanatopsis. I have to brush glass off of my seat before I can get in.

As I pull into the street, the sun in my rearview makes me squint. My car lurches over orc bodies as I stop opposite the church. I briefly wonder what happened to my unicorn but the answer seems obvious as I look at the dead family: it knows what I've done.

15
Craftsmen

I PULL UP to a red light, utterly alone. No people. No cops. No birds. The city has gone to ground. Only hurricanes empty the streets like this. My phone starts ringing; it's the College. Before I answer, I glimpse a notification on the screen: four missed calls. Am I in trouble? I could refuse to answer… but that got me on gopher duty in the first place. "Hello?"

"Hold for the Chancellor, please," Dolores says.

The line clicks. "Ah, Archmagus Diaz," Emérico says, "I suppose now that you've finished your rampage through Little Haiti, you can get to the Bird Road Art District where Archmagus Hellas is waiting for you?"

Either Rhea tattled or he's been scrying me. I turn toward the highway. "I needed to deal with those orcs."

He sucks his teeth. How, I don't know; he has no lips. "You could have left that to the police, Pablo."

"They never came," I say. They would have just been torn apart.

"Pity, after all that time you wasted in the middle of the day," Emérico says. "That was petty, by the way: dropping a dragon on Rhea's trees. She'll just banish the corpse, mend the trees, and hate you for making her expend the effort. How about a little post-mortem, you and I?"

My breath catches in my throat. He *was* watching. "Is there a corpse?"

"What? No. You don't play chess?"

Why would he compare our most solemn ritual to a game? "I'm not following, sir."

Emérico sighs. "After a chess match, players who have annotated their game will go back and examine the board, looking for moves they may have missed, moves their opponents didn't make, and most importantly, blunders: the catastrophic failures that lead to their or their opponent's defeat. You may feel you've won some victory, but in actuality you have committed an egregious offense."

"To shift the metaphor, sir, I had to play the hand I was dealt."

"Ugh," Emérico says. "Cards are for peasants, Pablo. And do not lose sight of my point. You have taken an aggressive posture toward one of your esteemed colleagues. How do you plan on rectifying that situation?"

He's taking her side. I grind my teeth. "I don't."

"Foolish and narrow-minded. I will not have your impulsivity and obstinance driving a wedge through my faculty."

I knead the steering wheel. "Sir, with all due respect, Rhea had her entire property enchanted to repel the orcs. Moreover, being so close to the enemy and not acting is only going to draw scrutiny when this is all over. She retreated and left those people to die."

"Rhea McIntyre saved her parishioners, Pablo."

"And left the rest of the neighborhood to be ransacked!"

"You know, PRC 1101 aside, your department's enrollment numbers have always been low. This semester in particular is abysmal; only six students with the qualifications to take the senior-level necromancy laboratory. I may have to look at revising the course catalog for Spring. Liquidating a department for lack of demand is shameful, but sometimes necessary. Especially if the department head cannot find some manner of making amends with their peers."

I raise my fist to my mouth and bite my knuckle, keeping the wheel steady with my elbow. When I withdraw my hand, the teeth marks are purple grooves. I take slow breaths, careful not to make a sound. "How would you propose I go about doing that, Chancellor?"

"Publicly, in front of your peers, at the next faculty meeting."

It wasn't enough to treat me like a whipping-boy all day. Now I must prostrate myself before the other archmagi. I thought this wasn't about punishment anymore. "Very well, sir."

"Glad that's settled. See that you do not upset Archmagus Hellas."

I could rail. I really could. "I will not."

Click.

Showing my belly to my boss when I am so clearly in the right. My father would be ashamed of me.

Magic hasn't always lived at the Bird Road Art District. Once upon a time, the only things tucked away in that forgotten corner of the city were a concrete producer, a towing yard, a few mechanics, and small workshops. What do these things have in common? Noise. From dawn to dusk, the cacophony endures: trucks reversing and chewing up gravel, impact wrenches whirring, saws buzzing through wood or iron. The sounds of creation play harshly.

That's when rents fall.

The artists move in, bringing their own noise, piped in through headphones, happy to lose themselves in personal melodies, adding a personal touch to the fruit borne around them. In studios as in machine shops, the spirit of creation thrives. The brewers arrive last, plying their art and cementing the place in hip.

I arrive at sundown. I have been running through every scenario for fifteen minutes, and in no way do I make it out of the next faculty meeting with a shred of dignity intact. That smug bitch will have justice for her lemons.

I pass a low concrete wall that's been turned into mural space. The works are as varied as the artists: sharp, neon, blue and pink lettering in an 80's subway splash spelling "BRAD;" a bearded fisherman done in black-and-white staring me down, confounding the very idea of spray paint; and a mermaid rendered in the new-school tattoo style, cartoonish and cute, like a giant sticker.

As I turn into BRAD, I almost crash into a gas station. A floating pyramid made of glass cubes hovers over the streets. It's the size of a courthouse, and at its heart, there is a globe of wraithglass, hovering between two concentric rings of cold iron; the inner ring has two orbs attached at diameter points, while the outer ring sports four orbs, one at every ninety degrees.

The parking lot of Giorgio Hellas's shop is narrow and surrounded on three sides by subdivided workshops. His place is sandwiched between an automotive paint shop and an ironworks. The man himself waits outside for me. He wears a black leather apron over a thick, blue jumpsuit. He holds a Churchill cigar in one hand and an old-fashioned glass in the other. Somewhere between butcher and blacksmith, his bushy gray beard would identify him as a wizard to anyone. He shakes his head as soon as he sees me.

"Something wrong, Giorgio?" I say as I exit my car. He was the first archmagus to insist I use his name instead of his title after I earned my doctorate.

"The city is going to Hell, Pablo," he says to me. He serves as the College's Head of Transmutation. He was also the first Archmagus to graduate from the College. He calls his discipline the Protean Arts, but there's no steadier individual; punctual, level, and grounded, he teaches people to change the molecular properties of creation. He hasn't changed a bit in the decade and a half that I've known him.

"Makes you think it's our fault, doesn't it?" I say. I cinch my baldric and grab my bag before slamming the door shut.

He works his lips a moment and puffs his cigar. "The worst of the media pundits have been speculating such, but we know better," he says and sips whatever brown liquor he's made his poison for the day. "Now that I've seen you, you can go. I'll tell Emérico we activated the conduit together."

I smile at him, shake my head, and try to walk into his shop.

Giorgio puts the hand holding his cup against my chest. "I'm serious."

I glance down at his hand, then stare at him until he blinks. "I'm here to help you stop anything that attacks."

"I understand your intentions. But as I told Emérico, you aren't needed. I can handle this on my own. In fact, if you get back in your car, you can go find a corner of the city that actually needs your help."

I turn my face to the sky, and take several deep breaths. "Giorgio, respectfully, you are not equipped to handle this situation. I've almost died twice today. Nick and I almost died together. Rhea wasn't even willing to fight."

"I know all of this. I've watched the news. That won't happen here."

Old men and their obstinance. I wonder if I'll be as intractable when I'm his age. "You're going to get yourself killed."

"I've been doing this much longer than you have, Pablo," he says.

"I am on orders from Emérico, Giorgio, so please just let me in."

"If I don't, are you going to drop a dragon on my shop?" he says.

My heart jackhammers. He must have spoken to Rhea… or the Chancellor. "I needed her to see her mistake."

He puffs his cigar. "You're in the business of correcting people's mistakes now?"

I look down at my shoes. The leather is shredded beyond repair. Blood stains my shirt cuffs. What must my face look like? "I just want to do my job, Giorgio. I'm begging you, as my former teacher, to let me help you."

Giorgio sucks his bottom lip into his mouth and chews on his beard. "One condition," he says. "No magic from you whatsoever."

"Your house. Your rules," I say.

"Did you say that to Rhea, too?" He turns on his heel and heads into his workshop.

The blood rises to my brow but I follow him in. The scents of sawdust, varnish, and oil mix. Before his stroke, my father would have loved a space like this; such a workshop would have filled him with more wonder than my classroom ever could. Now he only loves his recliner.

Every machine stands clean and ready for creation. A lathe, drill press, belt sander, and acetylene torch kit line the left wall. Nearby, a table saw bears several pieces of half-cut lumber that provoke the imagination; what is Giorgio building that he couldn't just conjure? Overhead, all of the piping and air conditioning ducts remain exposed, and run alongside a large, bulbous sack that leads to a vacuum hose. Against the back wall, a giant pegboard holds every hand tool imaginable. Beneath it, one of the red tool chests my father envied before he built his own. The concrete floor grabs my feet with every step, and this too is by design, to prevent any slipping. "This shop is amazing, Giorgio."

Hellas grunts but I can see him puff his chest. He leads me to a brick staircase built against the right wall, pallets of raw materials stacked beneath it. The loft at the top could be an office or an apartment. He takes a seat in a black leather chair behind a large desk and motions to the cushioned rocking chairs in front of him. Across from the door, diagrams, architectural plans, and drawings cover every inch of the wall, including charcoal sketches of each archmagus's face: studies for this year's College doors. His drafting table is placed beneath the sole window in the room. A television hangs on a wall opposite his desk. Arranged before it are a coffee table and a couch. There is a wet bar and a coffee station, complete with an espresso machine and a minifridge, to my left as I enter.

"Sit," he says.

I almost drop into the rocking chair but I have to take off the baldric. I reach into my doctor's bag and pull out the box of pastries I crammed in there before I began reanimating everything dead in Little Haiti. "I have to eat. Do you want one?"

"No, thank you," he says and knocks a head of ash from his cigar into a massive, glass ashtray.

I scarf down a whole *pastelito* and look around. "May I have some water?"

Giorgio lowers his brow. "There are bottles in the fridge."

I chug half of one before returning to my seat. Semi-satiated, sitting, I realize how tired I am. My body has been a tight, aching nerve all day. If it weren't for Giorgio's hostility, I could melt into the chair. "Why do you think you can handle this alone?"

"I've weaponized the conduit."

"Did the Chancellor okay that?"

"It was his idea." Giorgio goes to his drafting table and picks up a cube of glass. "This is nothing as serious as Emérico suggested. Each container can capture, shrink, and store any creature that wanders into the area. Self-contained, self-replicating atmosphere, and they'll light up if they've caught something. Like I said, nothing fancy. Practical." He hands me the cube and returns to his chair.

I examine all the sides of the cube. Aside from the fact that it is seamless, there doesn't seem to be anything magical about it: a box made of glass. Giorgio's style has never been ostentatious, but this is downright Spartan. "I would love to know your definition of complicated."

"You saw it already. I made all of those machines downstairs by hand."

"Giorgio, that is impressive, but you don't think that monstrosity you have floating outside is more complicated?" I say and place the cube on his desk.

"Absolutely not. That thing is magic, so it took vision, but there are no moving parts, no real soul to it. A desk like this"—he pets the desktop—"will last for centuries under the right conditions. A hurricane will take out that structure."

"You could make it permanent."

"That would take time. And I imagine we won't have any need of it once we take care of the ambient magic in the air."

I stop rocking. "I was curious about that," I say. "How do the conduits function?"

Hellas drums his fingers on his desk. "The cold iron is actually insulation for the transfer of energy. The wraithglass and ectoplasmic orbs are the transistors. They aren't sucking up the ambient magic. They are siphoning it."

The residual magic has to be going somewhere. "You didn't call them capacitors," I say.

"No, I didn't." He relights his cigar, getting an even burn all around.

I start rocking faster. "You're just going to leave me in suspense, then?"

"A teacher is always teaching," he says. "Tell me, when was the last time you surveyed an area to actually see the ambient magic? Certainly not since you've activated a conduit, or else you would know exactly how they work. When I turn this one on, see if you can't figure it out."

Hellas reaches into his desk and pulls out a block of cherry wood. He draws his finger over the top, turning sharp angles, chanting, and seams appear. He slides the lid off. Inside, resting in velvet slots fit to each, are a dozen wands. The carvings could indicate what each is for: one is two-pronged and oddly asymmetrical, another covered in scrolled vines, a third is shaped like a candle with a long flame.

I try to keep a poker face. That many wands in one place is dangerous, even if the man wielding them is the person who taught me to craft such artifacts. "Why do you keep so many?"

"Don't worry. You would need to know basic transmutation just to open the box, and even then I have keyed each one to my fingerprints and a few power words," he says. "Each of these stores the most common spells I need so I can focus on what I love: working with my hands." He selects a thin stick made of colored cubes. He flicks it at the ceiling and speaks a long string of syllables I don't recognize.

The roof above us becomes transparent, but it somehow continues to hold up the AC handler and motor for the giant vacuum downstairs.

"What language is that?"

"The greatest language of creation. Homeric Greek."

"I never took you for a classicist."

"I studied organic chemistry, engineering, and the language of my forebears well before Chancellor de Menezes came along."

Organic chemistry? The conduit had the two concentric rings with the orbs at the cardinal points. I thought it was a compass of some sort. "You shaped it to look like a carbon molecule," I say.

Giorgio nods. "Clever, yes?" He swirls the wand in the air, pointing it at the heart of his pyramid. "*Fiat mandātō meō*," he says. Spears of light shoot from the wraithglass heart of Giorgio's conduit, connecting to each cube of the pyramid, until the entire structure glows blue.

There it is again: *fiat mandātō meō*. Nick and Rhea and now Giorgio. "You speak Latin, as well?"

There is a glint in his eye, something mischievous. "Do your homework, and it'll explain everything," he says.

I purse my lips and find the witch hazel in my bag. I exhale until my lungs are empty, but before I inhale, a beam shoots out of the cube on the desk, lighting up my entire chest. The room around me expands, Hellas becomes a giant, and a force sucks me into the cube. The glass turns red.

The son of a bitch shrank me.

"God damn it, Giorgio!" I say and pound on the glass.

Giorgio stands. Every step he takes rattles my surroundings. He retrieves Thanatopsis and resumes his seat. We are eye-to-giant-eye when he sits back down. He lets out a long sigh.

"Let me out of here!"

"What do you think of my work?"

He warned me not to use magic, then tempted me to do it. I study the now-visible carved inlays of the Greek alphabet. "This is... pretty incredible," I say through gritted teeth, and the glass remains red.

"I know!" he says and clenches his fist in front of his face.

His excited yelling makes my ears ring. I touch them, but there is no blood. "And you're an asshole."

He smirks. "My apologies."

It takes a minute for the ringing to stop. "What do the colors mean?"

"Hostility and power level. Red for hostile *and* powerful. Yellow, just power. And green for benign."

"You can let me out now," I say.

"No, I don't think I will. Red isn't filling me with confidence at the moment. And you still think I am incapable of handling this situation."

I scowl at him. "More capable, certainly."

"The walls are warded against force *and* magic. See if you can get out," he says and begins to stand.

"This is kidnapping!"

Giorgio puffs his cigar, looks up at the ceiling, and rubs his chin. "I suppose you're right. What do you call killing a sentient being and then using it to cause destruction of private property?"

"If you mean the dragon, then the answer is simple," I say. "Justice."

He scrunches up his face and closes one eye. "Some might call it murder. In which case, I've caught the rogue necromancer Pablo Diaz and can turn him in."

"I'd love to hear you explain that to the police."

Giorgio scoffs. "We're of a mind there. The police wouldn't know what to do with you. But the Bursar might."

The Bursar, commissar of reagents, turnkey to Baba Yaga. "Emérico would never allow that."

"Are you sure? I get the okay from him, turn you over to the Bursar, and you spend the rest of existence in a pocket dimension where time and space mean nothing. Meanwhile, we tell a little story to the press. Pablo Diaz, beloved necromancer, rushes around the city saving lives. His exploits abound to the point that people wonder if there aren't two of him. Sadly, the College of Practical Arts loses contact with him. Presto, change-o, no more Pablo. Lost like so many others.

"The result? Disaster is averted, we forge a link to the common man, the College claims glory, and we gain a martyr to boot. Our enrollment numbers will skyrocket. We could put your face on t-shirts. Like Che."

Genetic habit causes me to scrunch up my face. "Che Guevara was a murderer."

"You're one to judge." He leans back in his chair.

I pace around my prison, following the lines of the Greek letters under my feet. If I were out of this box, I would flay this man. The thought causes me to clench my fists. My breathing is short and choppy. I glare up at him. "I just don't understand why you're throwing in with Rhea."

"We have worked side-by-side for the better part of two decades without incident. Coincidentally, we are the people who ensured your own success."

I stretch my jaw when I realize I am grinding my teeth. "When the chips were down, she left me in the street."

"She's over sixty years old, Pablo. Those were *orcs*."

"She could have summoned an army!"

Giorgio lowers his face to mine. The wrinkles on his forehead stand out like valleys. "That's not her job, my boy."

"Yes! Yes, it fucking is!" I pound the glass and he recoils. "These people cannot handle what we handle! It is her job and she isn't doing it."

"If that were true, it is not your responsibility to correct her. Nor is it your responsibility to tell me what I can and cannot handle. That falls to Emérico."

I stare him down, but he doesn't blink this time. I close my eyes and press my forehead against the glass. "Is it so wrong to do the right thing?"

"No. Of course not. But it is wrong to think your way is the only way. And it is deluded to punish others for not following your logic."

"She let those people die, Giorgio."

"Not everyone is ready to be a martyr, Pablo."

I look up at him.

He raises his eyebrows.

"Point taken. Is my timeout done yet?"

He purses his lips and shakes his head. "Still red."

I push myself off of the cube's wall. I pace. When I hear the shlink of metal on wood, I spin around. "What are you doing?!"

Giorgio holds my blade at eye level. "You seemed very concerned about my wands. One would need the ability to make a wand to find my stash. But you just walk around with this," he says and turns the blade. "Each of my wands serves a single purpose. Enlarging or shrinking objects for logistical purposes, changing the properties of materials"—he waves at the transparent ceiling above him—"and sure, a fireball wand, but only for defense.

"But *this*"—he flourishes the blade—"has got to be the most reckless artifact any of us has ever created. There is a reason exorcism and reanimation and crossing into Nox require rituals: to give us time to think. You are so sure of yourself that you believe your decisions don't merit consideration. Overconfidence is a slow and insidious killer, or so I have heard."

"Before today, I had only ever unsheathed that blade to go into Nox."

"Then why not limit its abilities to just that?"

"Originally, that was the plan. But if I was going to walk around Nox,

I would need to defend myself, so exorcism became a necessity. And when I told Emérico, he insisted that I add the ability to raise the dead."

Giorgio sucks his teeth. "The Swiss Army Knife of necromancy. Reckless."

"In the hands of the ignorant, perhaps. I trained to be worthy of that blade. You hold nothing less than the manifestation of my craft."

Hellas leans in. "What is our craft, eh? To you?"

"I don't know, Giorgio. It isn't something I think about."

"Liar. You're constantly thinking about it. I know this, because you're a craftsman and the son of a craftsman. I have seen you work. I have watched you pace the corridors, or brood in your office, or—most astounding—when you get in front of a crowd. You are always finding new ways to explain your craft to others. But how do you explain it to yourself?"

"It's just what I do."

"Ah, art for art's sake," he says and flashes his eyebrows.

"No, no. Fine." I look up at the ceiling of my prison and crack my knuckles against the base of my skull. "My craft is my obsession. I will always find new ways to learn about and better my craft. At first it was from the gut. Sloppy mimicry. I could create, but nothing good.

"I knew I had to learn more. My craft is my own, but it is also yours and Rhea's and Emérico's. I took the best parts of you all, the things I admired the most, and tried to make them my own. Problem was, nothing functioned as it should. It didn't fit together. Bad puzzle pieces. My imagination and your technique. I took everything you all gave me, an unrefined mass of knowledge, and had to poke and prod and whittle and carve, until I honed my craft down to what worked for me. The work could then be refined. Smoothed out. Until it was perfect. Until it was mine."

I hold a finger up as Hellas inhales. "I realize there is no perfect. One work gets judged by the quality of another. Artists, athletes, archmagi, each compared to the other. The next best thing is always waiting in the wings. I want greatness in my own right, but I also want to live up to the example you all set for me. I am nowhere without you."

"Killing the dragon and trying to barge in here uninvited aren't exactly getting that message across," Giorgio says.

"Rhea rebuked me long ago. That slap is fresh every time she turns her nose up at me. I try to come in here and help you, and you do the same thing. I find the entire situation wanting. The disappointment of a lifetime, in fact."

"You should not be surprised. Arrogant. Workaholic. Quick tempered. Too private. Lean and hungry. Willing to challenge your colleagues on a whim. Your goal should not be to live in competition with your fellows. You should enjoy their work, take what you can from it, and continue to create, until you breathe life into something that you believe is worthy of living." He nods and raises his chin. "That may be the only point to all of this. It is why I teach, and why I believe you teach: to feed posterity. Nourish what comes next."

"You and Rhea have that belief in common," I say.

"We are right to think so. *You* think so. Instead of antagonizing your peers, you could, I don't know, write a textbook! Like Rhea's. With all of your knowledge of necromancy, it could be another *Poetics* or *Origin of Species*."

"Those are foundational texts."

"You think Aristotle and Darwin knew that when they created them? Those men had arguments to make, and they prayed people would listen."

"They are also two of the most divisive works ever written. Very *antagonistic*."

Giorgio smirks. "Of course, you can't create something like that if you're already dead. I'm sure when Rhea saw those creatures outside her home, staying alive became her priority. Weren't her grandchildren there?"

"The house is warded."

"Family first. You know that."

When was the last time I spoke to my father? He's been nowhere near a conduit. He should be safe. But he must be worried about me, even though he pretends not to. The nights that I stay out, he's up until he can't keep his eyes open. Has he eaten? My heart begins to thump in my chest.

I look up and the walls turn yellow.

Giorgio smiles, drags his finger over my new roof, speaks his lilting Greek, and snaps his finger. I am ejected from my prison, right back into my seat. My face must register my surprise, because Hellas is laughing. I smooth down my shirt and pick up the bottle of witch hazel from the floor. I take the measure of the man for the first time since I was his student. I want to call him a shit. But there's no point to it now. The fight's out of me. I just want to see my dad. "Nice design," I say and point at the cube. "May I have my sword back?"

"Of course." Giorgio sheaths Thanatopsis and passes it to me, handle first.

I drape the sword across my lap. "You have things well in hand."

"Thank you, Archmagus, for being such a willing test subject."

I shake the bottle of witch hazel. "May I?"

He holds up a finger, whispers a few words, and draws an image in the air with his wand. The glyph glows like a floater in my vision; he's warding me against his defenses. "Now you can, yes," he says.

I inhale the fumes until my eyes water. The air outside explodes in color. I see the cubes shoot beams of blue light, only to have each beam return to its respective cube, which in turn causes the cube to turn green or yellow or red. A lot of red cubes. But even through the haze of ambient magic, a solid, rainbow chord shoots toward the southwest from the wraithglass orb.

I turn to Hellas. His wand shimmers, and some residual magic drifts around him, but the orb pulls it from the room, slowly at first. Once it passes the roof, the mist beelines for the molecule of carbon with the ectoplasmic nucleus.

I lean forward; the chair creaks. "The pyramid, the scanner, they're just tapping into the magic that the conduits channel—to where? The College?"

"Very good, Archmagus," Hellas says.

"What's at the College?"

"The Chancellor."

"What is he doing with it?"

"He has a capacitor." Hellas crushes his cigar in the ashtray.

"What is it?" That much magic in one place could warp the fabric of existence. I have no idea what could hold that much.

"The Chancellor did not tell me."

I scowl. Emérico could use all that magic for a grand work, like making another lich, or causing an earthquake. Baba Yaga's words echo: *On All Saint's Day, 1755, he sacrificed most of Lisbon to make a devil of himself.*

Emérico would never. Why save me—a worthless child—when you've killed tens of thousands? "So the Latin, then," I say, trying to ignore the witch's manipulations, "it's his command word. What does it mean?"

"Just that. *Fiat mandātō meō* means 'this I command.'"

They're all working in Emérico's paradigm. That makes no sense. A practitioner's paradigm is unique. Maybe the Chancellor made all the conduits himself. Except, each has been shaped by the individuals turning them on. "Why wasn't I included in this process?"

"I believe it has something to do with you warding yourself from scrying and fighting a Russian boogeyman." He flashes his eyebrows over a cavalier grin. "An impressive piece of work, I might add."

"You were planning the conduits during the faculty meeting?"

"That's correct."

I rub my mouth and chin. The Chancellor knew, the afternoon I fought Baba Yaga, that he would have need of the conduits. When I called him at—what, 2:30?—he waved away my concerns like so much prattle. Can so much change in less than three hours? From dusk 'til dawn, he managed to procure enough cold iron for all the conduits. How?

"Are you all right?" Hellas says.

"What? Sorry. Lost in thought," I say. Every department head has been responsible for a conduit except me. I missed the faculty meeting, so the Chancellor gave me no details about how he created the conduits, only orders to protect the people when they were activated.

Giorgio sips his whiskey. "It must be frustrating, being the only person who tries to go about their job honestly. Rhea has her family and church, Nick his businesses, I have my shop, Melody has the news, Carmen is *the* prognosticator to the stars, and Georgina trains mercenaries for—"

"Private—"

"Yes, yes, 'private military contractors,'" he says and waves a hand in my face. "Call them what you will, she still does it."

"She only teaches them protective spells, though," I say, defending Georgina Desmond, Head of Abjuration.

Hellas stares at me, cockeyed. "You're not so naïve."

I grimace. "Once they know how to cast protection spells, all they need is a textbook or a little imagination, and they can cast any spell."

Hellas taps his nose. He gets up and makes for the wet bar, having finished his drink. He returns with two glasses and hands me one. I take it and sip it without looking. I almost do a spit take, but then I sip some more. I needed a drink, and this one is smokey.

"You're not all bad, Pablo," he says. "Capable, occasionally respectful, but I feel even now I may be indulging your narcissism."

I nod. I find the box of pastries and take another out. I bite in. It is so stale that the guava sticks to my teeth; I didn't notice when I wolfed down the one prior. I offer the last one up to Hellas again. This time he takes it.

I dust the crumbs off my fingers into the empty pastry box and down the whiskey in one go. I don't want to piss this man off anymore, and if he has things in order, then I can get home to my father. "Giorgio, it has been a pleasure, as always," I say, trying not to sound strained, "but the situation seems under control here and I have other responsibilities to tend to."

"Yes, you're a very busy man. Although I don't think you'll be taking too many odd jobs tonight. Melody, Carmen, and Georgina have taken similar precautions to my own."

"One can hope," I say. I get up, toss the box into the wet bar's garbage, and gather my things.

"You should come by more often," Giorgio says. He opens the door to his office for me and motions down the stairs. "You are not so disagreeable as your job may imply," he says, smiling.

On the way out of his office, I catch a glimpse of my profile drawn in charcoal, hanging upside-down. I snap. "I meant to compliment you on your work on the doors, and ask you why you thought I deserved to be the Hanged Man." We descend the stairs together.

"You see things differently than the rest of us. It is what makes you so fine a teacher. For us, magic is a means to an end. For you, magic is the end."

"Thank you, Archmagus. I really appreciate that."

"It's also why we all think you're a fool," he says and slaps me on the back.

"Real nice," I say. "Why didn't you make *that* my card?"

"The Fool is a man beginning a journey, beholding a life full of options. It is a man to envy. That's not you," he says. He pushes past me and opens the door to his shop. "Go. Work your craft everyday. Greatness is reserved for those with the will to claim it."

I extend a hand to him. He shakes it and slams the door shut, leaving me in the shifting shadow of his pyramid.

16
Expectations Tempered

AS I TURN onto Bird Road, steel-gray clouds gather on the horizon. Afternoon thunderstorms roll over the city from June until November: hurricane season. I might be able to make it home before the deluge. Even a tumultuous sky can't dampen the fact that the conduits are in place. Whatever magical creatures remain will find the pickings slim and slink back across the veil into Spiritus Mundi. Any debris left in the streets will be cleansed. A fitting end to a sordid nightmare.

As I call the College, the first sortie of raindrops arrive: fat, tropical splashes that leave half-dollar sized dollops on my windshield. I put the call on speakerphone so I can concentrate on the road. "College of Practical Arts. Dolores speaking."

"Good evening, Dolores. No more emergencies?"

"We're still getting a few calls, but nothing major. Shall I direct you?"

"Yes, please."

"Good night, Archmagus. Hold, please."

A click, a few seconds of silence, and another click. "Archmagus Diaz," the Chancellor says. Is that a smile I hear? I mean, he has no flesh, but could he actually be merry?

"Good evening, sir."

"We are in receipt of a beak capable of biting a man in half," he says.

True to his word, that beautiful bastard Nick delivered my goods. "A memento from this morning."

"Your callous frippery on Tuesday and your myopic regard for the public remain troublesome, but I don't want to wear you too thin. We have the situation well in hand, and the Bursar reports you are making progress on your obligations. Get some rest."

"Thank you, sir. I plan on it."

"Dolores will call should the need arise," he says. "Good night." *Click*.

He's not done with me yet. But at least I can get some sleep. As I pass

La Carreta, I see a few people standing outside. *La ventanita* (The little window) is always the first place to open after a disaster, natural or otherwise. I turn on the radio. A few notes play from "Bad Moon Rising" by Creedence Clearwater Revival; I don't want that juju on me, so I start hitting buttons until I find Celia Cruz, Queen of the Cuban Diaspora, belting out "*Ríe y Llora*." A few trumpet blares, a little cowbell, some uncharacteristic electric guitar, and I am dancing in my seat. I can be happy, if only for a moment, lost in the simple distraction of song: *Ríe. Llora. A cada cual le llega su hora.* (Laugh. Cry. To each one, their time will come).

That's when my phone rings.

I tap the screen without looking at it and turn down the volume. "Hello?"

Abram Orlov's voice creeps out of the speaker. "Pablo."

Ahead of me, a curtain of water that obscures all vision. "Abram! Are you insane? The police are watching me, man!" I pass into a monsoon. My wipers and headlights on max give me five feet of visibility, tops.

"I would not call unless it was an emergency."

I turn onto my block, white-knuckled. "Listen, I have had an incredibly long day trying to avert apocalypse. Are you sure this isn't something you can handle yourself?"

"Yes. Fine. Just a question, then?"

"What is it?"

"When you bring someone back from the dead, are they normally hostile?"

The hair on my arms and scalp and legs all stand at once. "Explain," is the only word I can manage through my tightened throat.

"I did what I saw you do. I brought Yuri back."

He's talking about the impossible. He must be delusional. You can't bring the dead back to life. "No, Abram, no. Fucking no! That is not how it works."

"I am telling you I did it. And he is out of control."

I flinch. A bolt of lightning crashes a block away with a booming crack of thunder.

Out of control. This coming from a Russian gangster, a tried-and-tested killer. "Where are you?"

"The Course. My restaurant on the Miami River."

I park on the street, just across from my house. I look at the screen and realize the number he's calling from is blocked. I pull up a notepad app. "Give me the address."

He does so and I record it.

"I will be there shortly." I throw my phone into my passenger seat and massage my forehead and cheeks. I find a pen in my glove compartment and draw a ward on my shirt sleeve, the same sigil I drew inside my jacket before reanimating Yuri's corpse. I refuse to give my boss any more ammunition against me.

The lights are on in my living room. He's in there, watching T.V., worried sick, sneaking beers to calm his nerves. I'm less than a hundred feet from a warm meal, a hot shower, and my bed.

Instead, I keep driving through the storm.

In Miami, if the traffic doesn't murder you, then the weather might. I feel my tires try to abandon themselves to the rain. The overly-spaced lights on the 836 (The Dolphin Expressway to the locals) create pockets of darkness that hide pools of water. I have to drive under 40 to avoid hydroplaning. When I exit onto 17th Avenue, I'm manhandling the wheel like it's a life preserver.

Would it be wrong to blame Creedence for this harrowing?

The streets are as slick as the highway. I park at a small funeral home and crematorium a few blocks from the address Orlov sent me. If Sandobal tries to link me to any illicit activity in the vicinity, I will have the alibi that I was checking the wards here. The stoplight cameras might even be blinded by runoff.

I can't take any chances. I refuse to give Elisa any more ammunition. I pull up the NOAA doppler radar for the area on my phone, then sniff some witch hazel. The ambient magic has diminished, but there is still enough to give me a good charge. I siphon off as much as I can and begin chanting.

Because of the personal connection, reagents tend to be more effective when you make them yourself. Chaos magicians prefer sigils derived from letters but I have always been partial to pictographs. They better convey intent. I take out a sheet of homemade paper, a quill, and a vial of

DIY blue ink. I draw the tip of the quill over the fibrous sheet, watching it soak up the pigment, until I finish drawing a raindrop. Then I draw three identical wavy lines over the drop. I chant as I burn the paper using a lighter, literally putting my intent in the air.

The rain abates. The blacktop steams. The air goes from water to vapor. A thick fog surrounds my car. If the doppler is right, it should extend for miles. I get out of my car with my doctor's bag, ease the door closed, and creep to my trunk. I turn the key slowly and wince at the heavy release. I put on Thanatopsis's baldric, grab my cold iron lantern, and lower the trunk back into its lock. I pray the *chunk* wasn't heard.

There is no way to get to Orlov's restaurant except by crossing a bridge, so I whisper-chant the entire way, condensing a cloud around me. Muted dog barks reach me, the moving water beneath my feet barely a murmur. The orange lights of the warehouses on the south side of the river stand like will-o-wisps in the fog; they belong to shipwrights, dry docks, and yacht salesmen. I keep to the darkness and double-time it under the street lamps. A few homes and condominiums appear ghostly in the obscuring air.

Beyond the marinas, closer to downtown, the buildings on the river become clubs, bars, and restaurants. The day's events and torrential rain have rendered the night inhospitable; no music plays, no headlights fall on me.

Abram's restaurant, The Course, sits right on the water. Long and low and square, it has the shape of a warehouse, now repurposed and stuccoed. Modern accents like large barn doors and wooden shutters have been placed all over the building, giving it a rustic feel, poorly disguising its original purpose. The floodlights on the corners of the building only deepen the shadows beyond them. When I am almost at the door, the shape of a man coalesces on the steps. He takes quick, biting puffs from a cigarette. I recognize him.

"Bogdan," I say as I enter a pool of light, but have to keep chanting, or else the mist around me will thin.

He jumps to his feet and squints in my direction.

"Relax, Bogdan." More chanting. "It's Pablo Diaz. Open the door."

Bogdan flicks away his cigarette. "*Koldun*," he says, holds the door open for me, and nods as I pass him.

Inside, the place has the feel of a dining hall after a tornado rips through it. Chairs and tables are overturned and smashed. A table cloth hangs bloody from an iron chandelier. A third of the bottles behind the bar are broken. A barn door leading out to a veranda has a man-sized portion missing, while the other dangles from one hinge.

Cigarette smoke clings to the ceiling. A dozen of Orlov's men sit in silence, nursing black eyes, gouged arms, and several bite marks. One of them is missing an ear. Only a few tables weathered whatever disaster tore through them. As I navigate through the rubble, I can feel their eyes on me.

I turn to the footsteps behind me. "What happened here, Bogdan?"

He swallows and lights another cigarette. His hands shake. "Yuri."

Biology limits the human body. Strenuous activity causes the buildup of lactic acid in the muscles, which in turn causes soreness and fatigue. A corpse under the control of a necromancer suffers from no such impediments. The cessation of biological function means the muscles work more like ropes and pulleys than meat and bone. This efficiency made my reanimated servitors in North Miami dangerous.

"Where is Abram?"

"I can take you to him." Bogdan says something in Russian to the men. They won't look at me as we pass, but a few acknowledge me with a single word: "*Koldun.*" It smacks of salute. Bogdan takes me to the far end of the restaurant, into a narrow hall; my shoes squeak on the wooden floor. Water drips in the darkened kitchen. Bogdan fumbles with a key to open a heavy door marked "Employees Only."

Another small hallway. In a room on the right, one of the four can-lights flickers and sizzles. A chunk of hair and flesh sticks to the ceiling; parts of the drywall crumble. A couch remains intact, but something splintered the chairs and table. Cards and poker chips lie on the floor, spattered with globs of gore.

Light seeps out from beneath the door on the left. My footsteps drowned out the murmur of voices, but as I stand in front of the door, the syllables rise. Abram and someone else speak. A thick, gurgling chuckle raises gooseflesh on my arm.

I turn back to Bogdan and point at the door. He nods and exits the way we entered. The lock slides into place as soon as the door shuts. Iron teeth and fish scales and orc flesh. What new horror awaits me?

I knock.

"Come in," Abram says.

I take one measured breath and turn the knob.

In the darkness, a computer monitor paints Abram's face in shades of orange and blue. He has toilet paper stuffed in both nostrils, bloody splits glisten at the corner of his mouth and on his fattened lip, his nose sits at a crooked angle, and he holds an icepack to his jaw.

I get a dim layout of the room. All function, no style, the opposite of his office at the Eight Ball. To Abram's left, filing cabinets. Behind him, weekly time charts, OSHA posters, and framed newspaper clippings. To his right, two chairs, one occupied.

"Hello, Pablo," he says. He points at the door frame.

I flip the switch next to me. The lights in the ceiling click to life.

As soon as it sees me, Yuri Orlov's corpse starts yelling at me in Russian. The body struggles against the chains binding it to the chair. The steel rubs the gray arms down to purple meat. Chalky skin, limp hair, mottled face, letter opener still glinting in the chest at every movement. The wraith tries to make the body stand, but the feet are tied behind the legs of the chair. The cloying sweetness of death stifles me. A fly buzzes past my ear.

I flick my right hand and whisper. The Russian doesn't become English, but I understand it now.

"—this American mongrel so I can gut him! He's responsible! He's the one—"

"Tell it to be quiet, Abram," I say, not taking my eyes off of the corpse.

"—that told you how to find me! You would never have killed me, cousin!"

"Yuri, please, he is our guest," Abram says. Dry gore cakes his chin and shirt.

The chords in Yuri's neck creak as the head turns to look at Abram. It snaps back to me and tries to spit on me, but the moisture in that mouth dried up yesterday.

"This cur came between us! I would have come back! I just needed time to think! You know me, cousin. You know I would not have been gone for long! Release me and we can make amends to each other over this bitch's corpse!" A crust of something brown falls from the corner of Yuri's mouth.

"He sounds like himself," Abram says.

"The wight inside him has access to his brain," I say. "The same way that I did when you asked him for information."

"He's lying!"

"You know I'm right," I say.

"Remember Rada Semyonavich? He tried to come between us," it says. "He thought to win you to his side! You let him play you, and I lost a tooth!" Yuri's head nods as Abram smiles. "Remember what we did to him when you found out the truth? Do not let this foreigner divide us. We are family, Abram Volkovich."

"You're being manipulated," I say.

"Not another word, sorcerer," Abram says. He lowers his head and shifts the ice pack from his eye to his lips.

The wraith flashes me Yuri's mossy teeth.

I take a deep breath. "Abram—"

"No!" Abram slams his hand on the desk and recoils with a hiss. The bandages wrapped around his palm bleed through.

"Kill him!" the wraith screams, rattling the chains.

I know Abram has no idea what he has done, no idea that he made his cousin's corpse a door to Nox. Worse, I have no idea how I can convince him short of driving the wight out. Worse still, if I do it, he's liable to kill me. I cannot blame him; as a child, I was convinced I could have my mother back. Who could act differently, hearing a voice thought lost?

In front of Yuri's feet, there is a puddle of wax inside of a circle of bloody Cyrillic letters. It takes me a second to spot the candle under the corner of the desk. "Casting circle and blood—yours, I assume?"

"And his power!" the imposter says. "He could strike you down where you stand!"

I cock an eye at the body and tap Thanatopsis's pommel. Yuri's eyes go wide, then they squint. This one knows of me and my sword. "Is that all you used?" I say to Abram.

"No. There was one other thing."

"Show me," I say.

"Don't do it, cousin! It could kill me!" the wraith makes the body say.

"That is not how this works, cousin." He's already so comfortable. It took me years to build that level of confidence. "I have already brought you back." Abram stands and goes to Yuri. "Behave," he says and reaches for the chair.

Yuri's kicks so hard that the chair leg beneath him cracks.

Abram dodges backwards and brings his hands up reflexively.

"I can immobilize him," I say.

Abram points at me. His finger definitely trembles. "Don't. Do. A fucking. *Thing*," he says, hunched over and wide-eyed.

I exhale through my nose and try not to blink. "Your show," I say.

He turns to the corpse. "If you do that again, I am going to let him work on you."

"You wouldn't!" the wraith says. He even makes the voice crack.

"Do it again, if you don't believe me." Abram stares Yuri down and inches closer to him. He reaches his good hand toward the corpse. He grabs something beneath Yuri's seat and tries to pull. "Lift your ass," he says.

The wraith works Yuri's lips. "Please, cousin, don't—"

"Lift your fucking ass!" Abram says.

I grip Thanatopsis.

Yuri stares at Abram, then shifts his weight forward.

Abram produces a panel of wood smeared with blood from beneath his cousin's body. It is the wood carving depicting a knight entering the mouth of a giant frog. I've seen it before—in Abram's office, before I fought Baba Yaga. It was the only one of the panels that had not been restored.

"Your grandfather's," I say.

"*Our* grandfather's," Abram says and glances at Yuri.

"Strong work," I say. "Good practice. What else did you do?"

"What do you mean?" Abram says.

"Well, I get the connection to the family: the blood and the carving. What do the letters say?"

"It's his name," Abram says.

"And the candle?"

"Just something I found in the kitchen."

"Interesting. Why did you choose it?"

"I thought…"

"Yes?"

"I thought it would guide his soul back."

I lift my eyebrows and purse my lips. "It didn't."

Abram's face goes slack. "How can you say that?"

I hang my head. "I'm sorry, Abram, but that is not Yuri Orlov."

"Fuck you, you cunt!" The arm of the chair breaks, but the chains are so tight that the wraith can only manage a foot of reach.

If I don't do something, this will just continue. The longer the ghost has to plumb Yuri's mind, the higher the likelihood of it finding something to turn Abram against me. "Give me a pen and those sticky notes," I say. I put down my bag and lamp and hold out my hand. "You've asked it all the things that Yuri would know, right?"

"Yes," Abram says.

"Do not trust him, Abram Volkovich! He treats with the devil!"

Abram hands me the items without taking his eyes off Yuri.

I write down: *Tell him something he doesn't know and watch.* I pass Abram the note. It's a gambit, but the play's the thing.

Abram looks at the paper as if it were Sanskrit. "I don't understand."

"Do it and you'll see." I lean against the wall.

"Don't do anything that sorcerer tells you, cousin!"

Abram sighs. "I slept with Faina."

Yuri's eyebrows raise. "What?"

"Faina. I slept with her." Abram looks down at the table.

"Watch him, damn it!" I say.

The pair lock eyes.

"I will rip out your throat, you dog!" Yuri's body starts rattling the chains, but the chair doesn't budge.

Abram blanches. He turns slowly to me. "It isn't him."

I purse my lips. "I told you."

"How can you say that?" Yuri's stunned face darts between Abram and me.

Orlov moves the ice pack to his forehead. "Yuri Orlov loved three women in his life: his mother, my sister, and Lada Lukyanenka. Faina meant nothing to him."

"Cousin, please," it says. "Don't talk about me like I'm not here."

I lift my cold iron lantern off the ground and open one panel. I shine the light into my own eyes. "Normal. See?" I say to Abram.

He folds his hands and brings them to his lips. "Yes," he says.

I turn the light on Yuri. The whites of his eyes turn flaming blue. "Your cousin's body is currently possessed. You would need training to exorcise it yourself. Allow me to do it, so you can lay this body to rest."

Yuri's corpse bleats dry, high-pitched laughter. "What a bloody, frightful thought, teaching this Cossack your arts," Yuri's corpse says with a British accent. "Have you no dignity left, man? I suppose years of fucking corpses will steal that from you. But it won't bring back mummy, will it?"

I swallow. "What did you say?"

"Mummy. *Mamá*. Elena de la Caridad Díaz. You know, the seamstress, the baker, the orphan, the one who you made cry when you got lost at the International Mall. The one who couldn't look at you after you stole that candy bar. The one who allowed your father to belt you when you got detention for cursing."

Those memories. He's used them to try and break me before. But he couldn't then and I can only imagine punishing him for it now. "Jonas Wentworth," I say.

"In the flesh, as it were," he says and smiles through Yuri's mouth.

I turn to Abram. "Are you satisfied this isn't your cousin?"

He covers his face. "Yes."

"Good," I say. "I won't damage him any further."

"Do your worst, blackguard," Wentworth says and bares Yuri's teeth.

I draw Thanatopsis and lunge for Yuri's letter opener. There is a tink when metal meets metal. An unearthly scream echoes through the corners of the room and shakes the walls. A dim halo of blue surrounds Yuri's body and gets sucked into Thanatopsis. The blade glows momentarily. The body slumps.

Thanatopsis glows. A disembodied laugh rises from it. "*My word*, Pablo. Is he actually crying?" the voice says.

I look at Thanatopsis, turning the blade over twice. The voice is a part of me. I've been hearing it in nightmares since my mother died. "You miserable shit," I say, barely a whisper. I run to my doctor's bag and pull out an empty mason jar.

"What is happening?" Abram says.

"Is this any way to treat an old friend?" the wight trapped inside Thanatopsis says. "Do try and remember the good times, Pablo. Like mummy making flan? You love that, don't you? Or how about when she watched with approval every time your father spanked you?"

"I'm going to stuff you in this jar"—I hold it up as if he could see—"and I'm going to collect all but the tiniest bits of you. Then, I'm going to leave the jar in Nox until you reform. And I'm going to play 'God Save the Queen' every time I come back. Your entire existence will be darkness, broken up only by the moments I come to take your essence." Wentworth should grovel. He should beg. He should plead and sob and throw himself at my mercy.

Instead, he laughs. "Do your worst, Pablo Diaz. Make *mamá* proud."

I twist the lid off of the mason jar, place it on Orlov's desk, and hold the sword vertically over its lip. I pinch the blade at the guard and it begins glowing. I push my fingers down the blade, and otherworldly goop condenses below my fingers, pouring into the jar. I cap it and scratch a lock into the lid. I seal the ward by spitting.

The jar glows the same blue-white as a ghost. I seethe.

"What is in there, Pablo?" Abram asks.

"The thing that was pretending to be your cousin." I grab the chair next to Yuri's corpse and drag it in front of Orlov's desk. I fall into it.

"How did it know your name?"

"He knows my name because he once possessed me." I close my eyes and hold my head. "As a child, I made the same mistake that you did. I tried to resurrect my mother. Only, I didn't have a corpse. So when the wraiths arrived, they possessed me instead. Jonas Wentworth made me watch every time I made my mother cry, every time she scolded me, every time..." I sit there, blank.

"I'm sorry I didn't listen," Abram says.

I wave my hand.

Abram sits there for a moment. He leans forward slowly and grabs the jar. He rolls it around in his hands. "There's no going back now," he says.

I smirk. "You could just forget the whole thing. Go back to your gambling and racketeering and whatever else you do."

"I have made magic," he says.

"Undeniable."

"It's better than drugs."

I nod.

"I need more. You have to teach me."

I run my hands through my hair. It's never a question with this guy—always a command. Since the moment he surfaced from that booth, he's been trouble. I should just wash my hands of the whole affair. What exactly went through Emérico's mind when he found me? He was kind enough to comfort me and proffer a road. Is this like that? "I *could* teach you," I say.

"When?"

"Monday, Wednesday, Friday, ten a.m. to eleven fifteen."

Abram raises an eyebrow. "That is very specific."

"That's when I give my lecture."

Abram laughs. "You want me to enroll?"

"I don't give private lessons." Georgina Desmond has no compunctions about teaching magic to soldiers. There isn't a gray area here, though. This is the black that falls in an open grave on a moonless night.

"But you're such a good teacher," he says and smiles.

"You're not wrong," I say. "But I can't knowingly arm a criminal."

"My record is clean."

"But there is a record." Two days ago, I reanimated that corpse in Smoke and Lace who couldn't tell me who murdered him. This morning, Elisa Sandobal decided to bring me to task for it. If this is going any further, I'm going to have some answers. "Who killed Emmanuel Phillipe-Auguste?"

Abram stares at me. "Are you sure that is a conversation you want to have?

"It's the conversation we're going to have if you want this to continue."

"Yuri killed him."

I stand up and grab my lamp and doctor's bag.

Abram pushes himself up from his chair. "Where are you going?"

"If you're just going to lie to me, I have better places to be."

Abram extends a hand, like a spent swimmer. "Stop. Fine."

I don't move.

"Bogdan killed him."

"Why?"

"Because Sergeant Sean Richards told him to."

I make to grab the door knob.

"It's true!" He glances at the computer screen and his eyes go wide. "Shit. The police are here."

I dash to his side. Eight camera feeds are paneled across the screen. The ones showing the street feature armored trucks, fully-geared cops pouring out of them. A fly buzzes past my face. I look at Yuri. "Your men won't fight the police, will they?"

Abram scoffs. "They know better." "Good." I drop my bag and lamp on the desk and draw Thanatopsis. I cut Yuri. The body strains against the chains. "Where's the key for these locks?"

"What are you doing?"

"The key, damn it!"

"Here!" Abram reaches into his desk and tosses me a key.

I let it hit my chest. "Don't be stupid. I can't touch anything in here!"

Abram scoops up the key and undoes Yuri's restraints. He watches as his cousin's body stands up.

"You need to trust me. I can get us out of this. Tell them that Yuri is the mastermind. He murdered Emmanuel Phillipe-Auguste, he killed the men on the docks, he is the one who shot you, and *he* is the sorcerer they have been looking for. But you don't know where he learned it." I point at the magical accoutrements on the floor. "Say he was going to sacrifice you and that's the first time you ever saw him do magic. You understand me?"

"Yes. Except I haven't been shot."

"Do you have a gun?"

Abram's face tightens.

"We don't have time for this!" I say.

Abram returns to his desk and produces a nickel-plated .45 semi-auto. He holds it by the barrel and offers it to me, grip first. I control Yuri's body and it goes over to Abram. Abram's eyes soften as he hands the gun to Yuri's body. "Where do you want it?" I ask.

Abram sits, closes his eyes, and inhales. "The leg." He grips the arms of his chair.

I stick my fingers in my ears and nod. Yuri shoots Abram on the flank of his right leg; Abram screams. All the cops in the security cameras duck in unison. Abram takes in sucking breaths. "You okay?"

Abram nods. He breathes heavily through his nose.

I pull the letter opener out of Yuri's chest and wrap it in some newspaper before dropping it in my bag. I point at the door. Yuri goes charging out of it. I point at the monitor. Yuri runs down the hallway and kicks the fire door off of its hinges. In another panel, he runs past Abram's men, who look up from their prone positions on the floor. Yuri runs out of the restaurant and starts firing into the tactical vests of the police officers.

Two dozen semi-automatic rifles flare to life. From inside, it sounds like the finale to a fireworks show. I keep Yuri standing until they have to reload. I keep glancing at the monitor, looking for Elisa. She has to be out there.

"How will you get out?" Abram says, surprisingly calm.

I use Thanatopsis to cut a long, vertical sliver into Nox. I sheath the sword and take the watch off of Abram's wrist. I hold it up. "So I can find you later. We're not done talking," I say and pocket the watch. I tuck the jar of Jonas Wentworth under my arm, grab my bag, and open one panel on my lamp. "And don't forget this, Abram Orlov: I just saved your life. Temper your expectations about magic and me before you try to use either again." I step into Nox and thick smoke pours from my lantern down my arm. "Start yelling once this rift is closed. They'll call you an ambulance."

Abram slumps over and watches the gash in the fabric of existence seal itself.

17
The Heart of the Matter

I AM THE only interruption in the sea of darkness. Without my lamp, the night would choke me. The lantern is beautifully wrought, with four filigreed panels and claws at its bottom corners; if it were not made of cold iron—difficult to look at, fuzzy at the edges—it could have been stolen from the streets of Victorian London. Three of its flat panels are covered. The fourth is partly open, and its slits cast bars of light on the spongy floor and allow a steady flow of smoky oxygen to pour out, giving me a means to survive Nox's unforgiving expanse.

To stow the jar of Jonas in my bag, I have to put down my lamp. I hold my breath against the greedy press of the realm. I loop the baldric strap through the handles of my doctor's bag so that when I fasten the baldric again, the bag hangs on my hip. I take my lamp and Thanatopsis in hand. I need to see what is going on out there, but my pulse races. I gulp down clouds until I stop wheezing.

Despite the press and the dark and the isolation, the fact that I have a man on the outside who can clear my name with a few choice phrases keeps me calm. But I only need to think about that man, and what he said about Sergeant Richards, for my blood to go cold.

If what Abram says is true, Sergeant Richards wanted the bathroom attendant eliminated. Richards was the first detective on the scene at Smoke & Lace. That would give him the opportunity to tamper with evidence. But why kill Emmanuel? What end could that possibly serve? Richards will be the most vulnerable if Abram is exposed. What connects these two men?

I cut the tiniest of slits into Prima, just enough for a few seconds' peek. In the thinning fog of the material plane, all the cops keep ten feet away from the corpse of Yuri Orlov, all but one: the most tenacious and determined and scowling of detectives. Elisa wears blue latex gloves. She hunches over the body, studying every bullet hole, bruise, and missing fingernail. Trained to aim for center mass, Elisa's brothers-in-blue pulped Yuri's chest, including his stab wound.

I wheeze and bring my lantern closer to my face. Elisa turns toward the slice between the planes just as the gash closes.

Too close. She could have seen me. I need to walk away. But that glimpse didn't satisfy me. I have to know if I've cast her off. I hazard only a few paces backward and wait a short eternity before I cut a horizontal slice for a better view. Elisa removes her bloodied gloves and presses the heel of one hand into her forehead. She hunches back down and stops herself short of prodding the body. She ignores the parade exiting The Course. Handcuffed mobsters are loaded into the paddy wagons. She's beaten. She has to know it.

Abram Orlov, wheeled out on, and cuffed to, a gurney, draws her attention. "Isn't this your cousin?" Elisa asks.

"I never thought he was capable of such treachery. We are lucky you came along." Abram snorts and spits on the floor. He winces. "That sorcerer is dead to me."

Soon all of this can finally be over. He listened to me and dead men only tell *me* tales. I draw no small satisfaction from someone else being called a sorcerer, though. Elisa should frown or grimace or curse. But she does the worst thing I could expect. She smiles. A wolf baring teeth.

"I thought it was pronounced *koldun*?"

Abram roars at her. "He shot me! He was ready to kill me!"

"We can talk all about it at the hospital. Seen your friend Pablo Diaz around?"

Abram lifts his eyebrows and tilts his head. "Who?"

Elisa smirks. "Get him the fuck out of here."

Unflappable, insightful, determined, dangerous. Whatever entity conspired to pit me against this relentless creature clearly had no soul or mercy. She steals all my joy in an instant, replacing it with bitter uncertainty. She'll find nothing.

I hope.

I march toward my car, occasionally peering into Prima to get my bearings. Geographically, Nox's features match those of Prima, but the ground doesn't feel like ground, so much as a force that resists your feet. There's a little give with each step, almost like walking on skin. It takes some getting used to and newcomers tend to lose their footing. If this realm was designed, the architect never expected the living to walk its inky, umbral hellscape. Each step only raises a whisper. Beyond my lantern, I can't see anything, so my eyes fill the void with sinister wisps.

As the last gash I made to reckon my path closes, I see a faint glow ahead. I try to blink it away. I take a big gulp from my lantern and hold it behind me, but the image doesn't dissipate. A blue halo floating above me in the black.

Few venture into Nox, even fewer come here to study it. Potential necromancers learn to traverse the Realm of the Dead, but the planar disposition to kill you means that trips don't last very long. Sadly, taxonomy has suffered. We know there are ghosts—all of them hostile—and there are mimetic personifications of death called reapers that look exactly like you would expect them to (cowl and sickle in the West, white robes and black hair in the East, the list goes on). Beyond that, we're no better off than other people.

Whatever glows blue in the distance, it could be benign, or have designs on me. I inch towards it. I knead Thanatopsis's grip, my slick palm slipping. The halo solidifies. I bring the lantern closer to my face to breathe.

A pole of cold iron blurs at the edges. Suspended from a visually-buzzing arm, a wraithglass globe hangs in sharp relief. The post points toward Biscayne Boulevard, where I saw the last one. Two in one day. Where did it come from? After the day I've had, curiosity takes a backseat to weariness. I shake my head and peek into Prima.

A squad car has its strobes on next to my car. Why does the universe conspire against me? The question's futility is immediately apparent. This has nothing to do with the universe and everything to do with Sandobal. Of course she was going to find the car. She's found everything else so far. Either I'm really bad at this, or she's really good at this. Probably both.

A uniformed officer circles my vehicle, and I drop to my knees before realizing I don't have to. The rift in Nox seals itself above my head. The floaters from his roof lights fade, leaving me with my lantern and this streetlamp. How long will he be out there? Will they tow my car? I can't go out there right now. It will only confirm Elisa's suspicions. She'll accuse me of working with Orlov, suspect I had something to do with Yuri, and mount her case on mere (awfully incriminating) circumstance.

Two pictures of my license plate taken from traffic cameras on the beach the night after Yuri Orlov skips town. Two pictures of my license plate the next day, when I conducted the post-mortem on Yuri's body and fought Baba Yaga. Now, the car, less than a mile from his restaurant on the same night Yuri Orlov magically reappears.

Coincidence nothing. There's no smoke screen here, just a bonfire that I set. I can't go home right now. Knowing this city, I might be able to get an Uber. Some intrepid, naïve soul is out there trying to cash in on the panic. But that leaves my car at this funeral parlor. I look around but there's only me and the ghostly lamppost in this place. If I can't save myself, maybe I can get some answers.

I sigh, sit, and lay the lantern next to me. I unbuckle my baldric and retrieve the jar of Jonas from my doctor's bag. Using a red artist's crayon, I draw lips on the glass. I breathe onto the jar until my breath condenses, then watch the moisture get absorbed into the drawing.

"Hello, Wentworth," I say.

"Hello, twat," he says. The lips move on the jar as he speaks.

"Can you see?"

"Well enough."

"What is this? Who made it?"

"I can't say for certain, but I hypothesize that it may be the lost stick someone buggered you with long ago. As to its creator, I haven't a clue."

Hostile, as expected. I don't have time to exchange snipes with some impertinent philanderer. "Do you remember pain, Jonas? The physical sensation of it?"

"You don't scare me," he says.

"I don't think I should. But *you* should scare you. You died in 1932. It has been over ninety years since your wife poisoned you. You probably haven't felt anything in that time. I remember your pain, though. Felt it, when you took over my mind. I could recreate that pain. I know that doesn't scare you. But sensation, any sensation, what if you enjoyed it? Came to beg me to hurt you, just so you could feel?"

A long silence before he finally answers. "It was made at the Necropolis Tropico."

"How?"

"The path is set before you, Pablo Diaz. Enlightenment awaits. Just follow."

I set out in the direction the streetlamp pointed. My lantern keeps me from suffocating, but the pains in my head, shoulder, hip, calf, muted in the real world, have flared to life. Each step prods a different wound or bruise. I should have called my father before I came to see Orlov. He must be worried sick. That consternation could raise his blood pressure. There's no honor in worrying him into a stroke.

My calf itches. I raise my pants leg and see the puncture starting to stretch and ooze. Nox wants me dead. The only remedy is to leave the realm. Or maybe I just want to assuage my guilt.

I peek. An empty alley. I tear a rent and step across. The stink of brackish water and garbage assaults me. I dig in my bag for my cell phone. No texts. No voicemails—only my father leaves voicemail anymore. I pace as I call him.

"*Mi hijo*," he says.

"¿Papi, estas bien?" I grimace. I don't wear desperate well.

"Yes, my son. Why wouldn't I be okay?"

I sigh. "Nothing, dad. I just wanted to know. Did you eat?"

"I'm confused. Are you my son or my mother?" he says, the mirth obvious.

"Stop, dad. What did you have?"

"A sandwich," he says, causing my stomach to gurgle. The swish of liquid in a bottle. He exhales.

"Are you drinking beer?"

"I am allowed a beer with dinner."

"Check your blood pressure."

"Enough. When will you be home?"

"I still have to work."

"Remember," he says, "*el obrero es digno de su salario. Pues gana*" (The laborer is worthy of his hire. Therefore, earn). "Don't stay out too late."

"I won't. I love you."

"And I you," he says and hangs up. *Gana*: earn your keep. That, I'm doing. *Gana*: to win. If this is a game, who am I playing against? *Ganas*: desires. Like bed. A shower. And maybe an *empanizado a la milanesa* (breaded steak Milanese).

I brush the thoughts away and go to work on my calf. I roll up the pant leg. The blood crusted over as soon as I entered Prima. I can't have it open up again, though, so I tighten the bandages around the wound. Tied off, the pain hums more than screams, but that's not going to heal without stitches at this point.

Red and blue lights splash the walls around me. I freeze. A grotesque thought crosses my mind: *finally*. The lights fade. I never even see a police car.

Did I leave Nox for my father, or did I leave Nox to give up? The cloying garbage and fetid water nauseate me. I cut my way back into Nox and try to hurry, but I am limping when I arrive at the second street lamp. The strange luminescence casts no shadow behind me, doesn't illume the ground, adds no definition to what's ahead. A reprieve, nothing more.

I stand under it and roll my shoulders. The tightness returns to my upper back and hips: Baba Yaga's club. My eyebrow throbs anew: the Bursar's sick joy. The creak in my knees: mermen or gremlins or orcs? It's unclear. Two days of abuse have led me here, battered. I can hear my breath.

The clink of metal.

I have my sword drawn. It could not have touched my belt. Maybe my doctor's bag? But the handles are strapped to me. A mumble. I dash from the glow of the lamppost and crouch, my lantern by my face.

In the distance, ghastly eye sockets and lambent grins appear inside darkened helmets. The ghosts glow the same color as my lantern's flame. The outlines of their armor buzz: cold iron. The largest of the group, almost seven feet tall, carries a warhammer in both hands. A girl—too small to call her a teenager—brandishes a thin, serrated rapier. The last of the trio is a woman holding a shield and a machete. Like their armor, I have difficulty discerning the edges of their weapons.

Their words don't carry far enough to distinguish. They keep looking down at the floor. They move across my field of vision then recede into the darkness. I suck in a few breaths and creep forward. After what feels like half a mile of darkness, the ground ahead of me begins to glow.

An immense pit spreads out before me, dotted with ectoplasmic lanterns. It is divided into descending terraces, each level being slowly excavated. The glowing dead in the quarry work by lamplight with shovels and picks. Ten feet below me, what was once a man picks up something blurry and tosses it into a wheelbarrow next to him. Ramps have been carved between each level, and ghosts from every generation ascend from the depths, pushing carts and wheelbarrows brimming with chunks of ore.

I walk away until only the sounds of pickaxes and shovels reach me. I pull out the jar from my bag and hold it up like Yorick's skull. "What is going on here?"

"Well, judging from your uneven gait, it would seem that Nox has decided to attack your living tissue from the leg up," Jonas says.

"Not that. There were ghosts working in a quarry," I say.

"Ah. Under new leadership, our community has found industry."

"Which psychopathic shade was able to unite you monsters?"

"If you don't take care of that wound, you'll never find out. I can taste the rot. And I'm afraid if I let you die that I'll be trapped in this jar for the rest of my days—a prospect unbecoming of a gentleman. You have one option remaining to you, much to my delight."

I sigh. "I have to use your ectoplasm to block the effect."

"Quite right."

I look at the glass, the same way Emérico looked at my mother's earthenware. What is my mentor doing to Baba Yaga? What could I do to Jonas? I have hated this entity my entire life, but it's either his imprisonment or my survival. The lack of justice here galls me. I sigh. "I thought to make you my well, but it turns out you're just a sponge."

"Don't dismay, Pablo Diaz. We'll meet again."

"That's... likely." I wipe the wax mouth off of the jar.

Wentworth remains trapped because the jar contains his ectoplasm. With no planar matter tying him to it, Jonas will escape his *ad hoc* prison.

There's nothing for it. I poke holes in the lid. I raise my pant leg and pepper my bandages with the goo until I get an even coating. I then spread what's left across every inch of my exposed flesh. Unlike on Prima, the ectoplasm doesn't evaporate.

The disguise won't hold up to any amount of close scrutiny, but if I come across any more shades, I will look the part from a distance. I hold my lantern up and march on, into the gloom.

I follow the train of ghostly miners, passing under three other streetlamps before I reach Biscayne Boulevard. The lamps stand on every corner and bear cold iron signs. The lamp-arm here sends me south. That's when the shacks start appearing: squat, free-standing lean-tos with lamps lighting their hazy innards. Industry has bred suburbia. Ghosts chat or lounge or stare out into the darkness from their ramshackle homes.

I turn my face away and gulp clouds of oxygen whenever I'm out of sight of them or when my lungs burn. Close to Bayfront, I find a park and an arena, right where any Miamian would expect them. The park swarms with ghosts, like a bloom of jellyfish, all of them crowded around small tables. I stand agape at the cold iron gates. I turn to the sound of laughter: a man wearing boots and a suit out of the Wild West slams a domino down in front of three young men in long-sleeved guayaberas. At another table, a woman in a Miccosukee dress calls "Gin!" to a Bahamian in a straw hat and a man in a yarmulke.

I know these people are evil to a man—or woman. The only dead that remain in Nox are the ones with an agenda. The rest make their way to the Aperture, a pinprick in the night sky that is invisible to the living and sings to the dead. These shades are hostile, and they deserve an eternity devoid of light or happiness. And yet, looking at them, knowing the reason they don't move on is fear of what awaits them, knowing that some of them might have been here for centuries, seeing them find joy in what should be damnation, I smile.

The arena next door buzzes with excitement. I make my way inside, and whatever sympathy the park elicited in me evaporates. Scaffolding made of cold iron upholds rows of benches tiered like a stadium without walls. On the makeshift fields lit by dozens of glowing orbs, the ghosts spar, using every weapon imaginable to dismember each other. They need only pick up their severed limbs and move them to the right spot to reattach them, but each victory sends the crowd to its feet. It could just be blood sport, but the number of combatants waiting on the sidelines, and the racks of different weaponry, make me think this spectacle is more training than entertainment.

What else is violating the emptiness of Nox? I slip out of the arena and move on. A block south, the tower appears. It deposits into existence from the darkness as I approach, glimmering blue because of the wraithglass exterior, a crude replica of Santa Inés Hall. The park, the arena, those things were palatable, if inexplicable. But this mockery insults everything I believe in. I cannot wait to tell the Chancellor about it. Hopefully, I can be there when he brings it crashing down on their disrespectful heads.

I make my way toward the travesty, which is when I start hearing my heart beat. Am I having an infarction? Nox *can* kill me, as my leg attests.

The irregularity of the pounding belies anything living, and I realize the thumping isn't coming from me, but from inside the grim parody of what I hold dearest. The unadorned doors of the College of the Dead stand closed but unguarded. A crowd of ghosts has amassed in the square in front of the building. They carry shovels and pickaxes and maneuver wheelbarrows made of cold iron. The doors part and open faster than I could have imagined; the ones at the college creep, but these fly.

The miners shuffle into the building and I follow, stopping just beyond the door, flabbergasted. No foyer of greeting or Moirae. Just a large, open rotunda, its center decorated with a lattice-work of beams holding up a double-helix spiral staircase where I would expect to see a tower. The room is lit in blue from the seven massive smelters lining the walls. Ectoplasmic flames burn within each. The ghosts push their wheelbarrows beside the smelters and begin shoveling the base minerals that can be converted into cold iron. Black liquid oozes from each smelter, down into a mold where the molten goo hardens into billets. Ghostly smiths in aprons grab the ingots with tongs and take them to freestanding, blue-flamed forges, where they reheat them and pound the metal into shape on anvils.

A ghost in a jumpsuit walks around to each forge and anvil, taking notes with a pencil onto a clipboard. "*¡Vamos, vamos, vamos!*" The complaints from the smiths range from cockeyed stares to outright curses. "*¡Oye! ¿Que haces?* What you doing here?" he says and points the pencil at me. His Cuban accent garbles up the last consonant of each word. He stomps up to me and pokes me in the chest. "You need something?" Ju. Somesing. I would smile.

He looks me over and his eyes go wide. "Listen, we no want trouble. You go, and I no say nothing."

"How long has this factory been open?"

"*¿De vera?*" (Really?) he says and taps his clipboard. "Two days."

"You made all of this in two days?"

"Is no so crazy." Cray-see. "The dead no sleep, no eat, no rest. We work for what we need, *porque no hay de otro* (Because there is no other way). *Me llamo Legión, porque somos muchos*" (My name is Legion, for we are many).

"Why the weapons? *¿Las armas?*"

"*Protección*. From you." The foreman whistles and backs away. Every smith wields a hammer, every smelter a shovel, and guards appear from behind the smelters and pour in through the doors. "Drop your weapon, *mi hijo*," the foreman says. "You no win here."

I raise my sword for a final stand in the realm of the dead.

"That's enough," a voice calls from the top of the tower.

Every inch of me starts sweating. Why is he here? Did he come to find me? I lift my lantern because I'm hyperventilating.

A lambent figure descends the staircase, heedless of gravity. Smoke pours off of him, cascading downwards until it spreads across the floor. Two orbs of blue fire nestle in the eye sockets of his skull. "Pablo," the Chancellor says as he alights, "I think it's time we had a talk."

18
To Make Matters Worse

EMÉRICO HOVERS ABOVE me, his robes shifting as if suspended in water. Cold mist pours from his neckline and sleeves and down his skeletal feet. "You should be at home, Pablo, taking care of your father," he says. He raises a hand.

The ghosts surrounding me halt their advance, all of them brandishing pikes or shovels. They do not lower their weapons. They snarl at me in silence. "I found lampposts when I traversed Nox this morning. I had to know where they came from." The words are out of my mouth before I realize I'm making excuses.

"The lampposts have been there for months. You would know that, except that you allow yourself to become distracted by other matters." He points to the cold iron double helix. "Take the stairs." The Chancellor floats upward and through a circular opening in the ceiling. His glowing eyes illuminate the walls above him as he ascends.

The room defiles every memory I have of Santa Inés Hall. Gone are the skylights that honey-glaze the wooden walls. Cold iron rafters buzz where the salvaged ribs of the *Santa Inés* should be. A forge roils in place of each door that is supposed to lead into a lecture hall. When I grab onto the railing of the intertwined spiral staircases, I long for the tower that ascends to my office, the libraries, and Emérico's quarters. If not for the chaos engulfing the city, I would have class in the morning.

The ghosts below me grin and break up into small, gossiping patches. Some with shovels return to their piles of raw ore and forges. Others stow their pikes on wall racks. The backs of my eyes itch. My shoulder clicks and pops as I raise my lantern to my face.

The raw materials for the conduits had to be sourced from Nox, that much had occurred to me. But who else besides me could light the forges of the damned? I can't find my breath.

I make the landing. Stealing up from the furnaces below through the lattice-work flooring, blue light speckles the stone walls. The entire platform is suspended from the ceiling by chains. It shifts ever-so-slightly with each step I take, never meant to hold something with mass. A circular opening in the middle of the lattice makes me feel like I'm suspended above a blue grotto.

Emérico casts a bright blue ripple wherever he looks. He sits on a cathedra formed from hundreds of bars of crudely-welded cold iron. The back of the throne rises ten-feet into a pointed arch, but the inherent static of the metal makes it look pixelated. Seven other chairs surround the opening in the floor, but none as forbidding as the Chancellor's seat. They look more like garden furniture formed of flattened strips of metal and prove the other chairs an afterthought to the throne.

"How can you allow this place to exist?" I ask, wheezing. "This building is a hollow mockery."

Emérico scoffs. "This is how Santa Inés Hall looked the day I completed construction. I taught for those first two years from a platform like this in the main atrium. The Hall as you know it is a garish testament to opulence, made to assuage the university and the city. This was what I envisioned."

I frown. "I thought you and Archmagus Hellas—"

"Hellas was the first meddler," Emérico says, his eyes flaring. "He thought that the building should be grander, more imposing, and more *luxurious*. When I refused him, he went to the dean. I acquiesced to remain politic."

If the first thing I saw when entering Santa Inés Hall was Emérico looking down from the rafters, I might not have entered. Especially after having my senses assaulted by the gargoyles, and the doors opening of their own accord. Point Hellas. "He was right. I don't know how anyone could learn in a place like this."

"And yet they *did*. Giorgio and Rhea and Dolores and all the others would practice in the rotunda while I lectured amongst them. Whenever a newcomer would enter the Hall, I could see them from the second floor, and they could see me. There was no division between teacher and pupil. No isolation. No mistaking our purpose. It was glorious."

Emérico sighs and takes the throne, his robes settling about him. He motions to his right. "Sit. Put your lantern on the chair next to you."

I remove my baldric, unloop the leather straps from the handles of my doctor's bag, and place the bag under the chair. I prop the scabbard up next to the chair, the tip nesting in the spaces of the latticework. Every joint in my body creaks when I sit down. I can still see the ectoplasm covering my skin, but the tightness in my chest makes me wonder how much protection the ghostly matter provides. I set the lantern down next to me, but it is too far. "I'm sorry, sir," I say and raise my lifeline to my face, "but I can't breathe."

Emérico sighs. My need to breathe only annoys him. He doesn't account for the life functions of others. He's forgotten. He points at my chair with two fingers. A tendril of mist streams from his fingertips toward me. The mist wraps around the back of my chair. A strip of metal moans as it twists out of alignment and into a spiral appendage beside my head. "There," he says.

I've always conjectured that the mist that sluices off of the Chancellor is similar to the oxygen that pours out of my lantern. But the clouds my lantern produces are a result of ectoplasm combusting. Perhaps ectoplasm replaced his marrow. I place the lantern in the makeshift sconce and the oxygen pours over me. My breathing approaches normalcy.

His skull turns to me, tinting the vapor around me blue. "Who is Abram Orlov to you?"

I rub my neck. I can feel my pulse under my fingertips, a jumpy hammering in my veins. I take a deep breath. The lantern's vapor chills my lungs. "My client. How do you know his name?"

"What do you think it says about you, that you are willing to associate with a known criminal?"

I try to swallow away the tightness in my neck and end up choking on my own spit. Once again, before my mentor and idol, I have fallen. I wheeze out, "It makes me a criminal," between coughs.

Emérico makes a fist and taps his thumb against his teeth. He then points at me with his whole hand, the leather of his gloves creaking. "Why did you do it?"

My father's medical bills have kept me drowning in debt for six years. I work myself to death, but I can't seem to move forward in life. "I needed the money," I say, with all the gravitas of a mis-flipped pancake.

Emérico scoffs. "You are poor because you do not know your own worth." He takes off his gloves and motions to Thanatopsis. The sword flies into his hand.

I grip the arms of my chair and move my feet to jump.

Emérico's head snaps in my direction. "Is something wrong?"

My hands shake. "N-no. No, of course not." The darkness must be getting to me. This man has been my mentor for years. "Sir, to return to the matter at hand, you must understand, circumstances beyond my control—"

"What circumstances? Your father's stroke? Medical bills? They may have beggared you, Pablo, but the only thing chaining you is your scruples."

"I have been paying off that debt for the better part of a decade."

"Why not charge more for post-mortem interviews? You should have made yourself rich by now."

I purse my lips. The most learned man I know echoes the suggestion of Benito Jimenez, the Latino Lurch, a snake who makes his living off the dead. "It would be criminal to exploit the bereaved."

"Your life seems to be filled with criminals these days," Emérico says. "With little exception, that ritual is a sham. You decide what thoughts get pulled to the fore. As easily as you can make a corpse answer 'I love you,' you could make a corpse say 'I'm hungry.'"

My eyes go wide. I sit up in my chair and stop myself from crossing my arms by gripping the chair. "I provide people with closure. I make the most trying time in a person's life slightly less painful. I give them a chance to say goodbye and reconcile with the dead."

"You provide a fantasy. No matter how you may prompt them, those people believe they are talking with their loved ones. But it is nothing more than a macabre puppet show. Either you are exploiting them, or they are exploiting you," Emérico says. "And nowhere is *that* more obvious than with the police."

"I provide a valuable service to the police!" Sandobal may be dogging my footsteps, but she also has box upon box of cases that were solved with my help. "Do you know the clearance rate in my cases?" I glare but I also have to lean into the smoke pouring from the lantern.

Emérico says nothing. Behind the flames, the dark of his eye sockets could be the expanses of Nox.

I gulp cloudy oxygen from the lantern before saying, "I make a difference."

Emérico's voice betrays his amusement. "How many times have you had to testify in court?"

I stay silent. I know the answer as well as he does.

"Not once," he says. "They do not admit magic as evidence. Instead, they use the threat of you as coercion. At best they use you as a dowsing rod to find admissible evidence. You are the lynchpin of their investigations, but giving you credit would be tantamount to giving you power." Emérico leans forward. "Has it occurred to you that they keep you off the books because revealing your involvement would make them obsolete?"

I won't look him in the face. Clouds of oxygen cascade over me but I still feel light-headed. Emérico unsheathes Thanatopsis. He runs his bony fingers along the blade. He flicks the metal once with his middle finger. "So much talent, so much imagination, yet you live like a pauper. For some reason I cannot fathom, you are content to work yourself to death. All sowing, no reaping.

"I do not imagine you as a constable, but for argument's sake, let us say you were. Your knowledge of necromancy would mean that only the most seasoned criminals would be able to elude you. You could teach other detectives your techniques and effectively neutralize the highest orders of criminality in this city.

"The world should be ours, Pablo. *Ours*. And instead, we are a diversion. Something to fear or trivialize. And now you have turned to a common thug for deliverance when the means have been at your disposal this entire time." He sheathes the sword and props it up against his throne. "It is vulgar."

The praise coupled with the back of his hand makes me shift in my chair. He doesn't care about the crime, and he wants me to take advantage of people. That's not who I am. I never intended to get involved with the Russians. So why did I help Abram? "Orlov is one of us," I say. "He summoned a ghost."

"I know that. How do you think I found you? At first, I thought it was you, actually."

"Why would I do that?"

He nods and turns up his palm. "My exact reaction. I scried the location of the ritual, when lo and behold, my scrying is broken by what could only be a very powerful ward. So I notified the police."

My jaw drops. Elisa showed up because Emérico called her. She will see Abram's little song-and-dance for the farce it is. I stare at him. "You've destroyed me, sir. Detective Sandobal is going to implicate me in a RICO case, and I am going to prison." A sea of troubles has opposed me since dawn and at its heart is Emérico Abílio Ovídio de Menezes. He's sent me all over the city, and now, with a phone call, he's ruined me.

"Nonsense," Emérico says. "In a day, none of this will matter, and any questions concerning your character will be dispelled under your brilliant leadership. The city already trusts you, but by week's end, they will beg you for guidance."

"Forgive me, sir, but you just aren't seeing the way the world works."

Emérico's entire head blazes. He spits gouts of fire with every word. "Had you been at that meeting, you would understand the way I am going to *make* the world work!"

I clench my jaw. I won't have this conversation again. "Sir. I was contrite this morning. I have put my life on the line multiple times to make restitution, to you and the College and the Bursar. I've been stabbed, bludgeoned, and shrunk in your service. I've endured Nick's showboating and Rhea's scorn and Giorgio's experiments. What could have been so important that I couldn't miss that meeting?"

Emérico tilts his skull. "You mean aside from the facts that, one, I am your direct superior, and two, a stipulation of your employment is your attendance at all faculty functions barring documented emergencies?"

Damnable facts. I cover my mouth with a fist. "Yes."

Emérico sighs. "At the beginning of the summer semester, I came to a realization: I was unhappy. The world that I had thought ready for a change was actually more banal than the one I abandoned centuries ago.

"This city, this current humanity, has no idea how to deal with magic, let alone anything else, unless it is to market it and consume it. I brought about the means to change the world, a vehicle by which anyone can shape reality, and all they want to do with it is bottle it or take a selfie. Disciples of Nick Russo, one and all, without having met the man.

"The masses have no concept of sacrifice or ambition. They elevate celebrities—utter non-entities—to positions of leadership, ignorant of the consequences.

"Their entire goal in life is to take anything dynamic and volatile and transform it into something static and consumable and safe." Emérico slumps into his chair and rubs his skull.

My molars itch at the mortar-and-pestle grating. "Sir, I—"

Emérico slices the air with his hand. "I will not be ignored, Pablo. I have come too far, given up too much, to be relegated to the appendix of history."

"Then why open a school? Even the greatest teachers are forgotten within a generation. You really only ever impact your own students." I wince. There is a real pain in knowing that your sacrifice means so little in the grand scheme of things. "It is a life of service."

"You are an amazing teacher, Pablo. Better than I ever was. That idealism and dedication will be incredibly important in the days to come. You have just the right combination of patience, empathy, and imagination to reach any student. People may recognize Nick and Rhea and the others, but I believe you will shepherd our new flock to their true potential. I am almost glad you were not present at that meeting."

I lower my brow and rub my chin. "It's still pandemonium out there and I'm probably going to be arrested."

Emérico laughs. "I have told you already. None of that is going to matter." The way his robes flit about him as he leans in, you would almost think he was excited. "As I have said, I recognized my dissatisfaction, and came up with a tripartite method to dissolve everything stopping our progress.

"First, I would need the means to focus a large amount of magic at the College, which is why I impressed the local haunts into producing cold iron and wraithglass. I promised them Downtown in exchange."

"Sir! You can't—"

He cuts me off with a raised hand. "A promise I do not intend to keep, Pablo. Prima is for the living. But, with the forges in place, they've been producing for me at top speed.

"Second, I would need to enlist you and the other archmagi. I decided to present this plan to you all at the first leadership council of the year.

If any of you balked, I would have no recourse but to change your minds. Not a single one of your peers accepted my plan."

I lower my brow. Nick, Rhea, and Giorgio have been going along with the plan. They are even working in the Chancellor's paradigm. How did he convince them?

"Now, follow my logic and you will understand the final step. The option to learn magic is not the same as actually performing magic, which has been my ignorance all along," he says, placing a hand on his chest. "I thought the option to learn would be enough. But this world is so banal that it believes reading or hearing or streaming is the same as experience. I know if the masses were given one chance,"—he holds up one finger—"given the meanest morsel of power, they would be breaking down our doors.

"The final step, then, must be to channel all of the stored magic into the citizens of Miami, infusing every living soul with enough power to perform a single spell." He sighs and his robes deflate briefly as he sits back.

The room begins to spin. I knead my lips. I balked at Rhea for *teaching* her grandchildren, providing them with guidance, supervision. What the Chancellor is talking about would be nothing short of cataclysmic. There has to be some kind of mistake. I have never known my mentor to be reckless.

I lean toward the lantern. "You're going to *give* everyone magic?"

Emérico nods. "Enough for one spell."

"Without telling them?"

"Correct."

Trying to contact my mother was the most traumatic experience of my life. If Emérico hadn't saved me, I would still be a marionette to those wights.

I am choking. "You're going to destroy everyone's lives!"

"Some may suffer, Pablo, that is true. Some may even die. Whatever children and elderly aren't able to handle the magic, they will find their place here in Nox or beyond the Aperture. But you have to see that we are getting nowhere."

"Sir, please, think about yesterday,"—an eternity ago—"and how packed the Hall was, how many students were in my lecture alone, and multiply that by *seven*. That has to be more than two-thousand students who are willing to follow in our footsteps. By the end of my lecture, the entire building was swimming with magic! There's no need for—"

Emérico holds up a hand. "Only *you* draw crowds that size. Everyone else's intro classes are less than half capacity. Far less." The fire in his eyes dims. His robes cease to undulate. The cloth hangs off his shoulders, empty, save for a centuries-old skeleton. "As for the residual magic, that wasn't your students. That was me preparing an enchantment."

I check to see if there is still ectoplasm on my hands. My heart is pounding in my chest. I scratch at my face. "Sir, I have never heard of an enchantment creating the kind of residual magic that has been tearing through the city."

"Changing someone's mind against their will is no small feat. It is enough to cause an earthquake, in fact. That is why I refuse to teach it to any of you."

The words that just came out of his mouth are nuclear. Since I was eighteen, the one rule of magic that seemed inviolable was this: no amount of magic can affect another person's will. The talking skeleton in front of me was the one who taught me that. The very idea of spells in the School of Enchantment became inconceivable, because Emérico said the idea could not exist. It had become metaphysical law.

He's been lying to us all this time. Has he also been using us? How many small adjustments has he made to our attitudes? How many people are under his influence? Can I trust a single thought I'm having?

I behold the monster for the first time.

"I am trying to build a better world, Pablo. A place where we are all appreciated. Where the philosophy we espouse is accorded the proper respect."

"You're a tyrant. You're not trying to bring anyone up. You're trying to force magic down their throats when they haven't taken it from your proffered hand. The only new world you're going to create is one where people come crawling to you because they literally have nowhere else to turn. I looked up to you. You saved me. But you're no teacher. You're an autocrat dissatisfied with his empire."

Emérico pushes himself to a hover and his eyes blaze. He is so close that the mist pouring off of him allows me to breathe. "This world and its people have been yoked by decades of crises. They are already afraid. Of everything. So much so that they give up their privacy and individuality for the anesthetizing fiction of a connected world. All that does is subject them to even more laws and scrutiny. They make themselves willing slaves to a realm of data and numbers and electrical signals, that could disappear at a whim of man or nature."

If I tried to shake some sense into him, would the bones rattle? "That is their choice! If they want to find comfort in video games or TikTok or the next platform to come along, then so be it. That is where they want to be. The world has always been terrifying. For you, and for me. If that's their choice, then who are we to wrest it from them?"

"My plan will make the world better," Emérico says.

"No. It will destroy it."

"Had you been present on Tuesday, I could have changed your mind, as well. Instead,"—he snaps, and two of the chairs behind me fly apart into strips of cold iron that wrap around my wrists, ankles, waist, and neck—"you'll just have to join us once we've finished."

The metal bends me into a sitting position but I don't fight it or test the restraints. There is no use. He could crush me as easily as he's fettered me. "Baba Yaga was right. You're a devil. Did you cause the Lisbon earthquake?"

Emérico tucks his chin against his chest. "Yes."

"You killed tens of thousands of people to become a lich!"

"You have no idea what you are talking about," he says. "I tried to change the minds of my followers. I wanted them to see the New World we would create. But the residual magic was too much. I absorbed as much as I could and it still devastated the city. *That* is how I became a lich. I tried to save Lisbon."

"You're just making the same mistake! What's going to stop the city from falling into the Atlantic?"

"I learn from my mistakes, Pablo. The conduits have helped control the residual magic of the enchantment I cast, and I will use them to enact the final step of my plan."

He glides around the platform with his head down, avoiding my gaze. At least my lantern is close enough that I'm not asphyxiating on top of being trussed up. I try not to think about what that much magic could do, but I keep seeing babies throwing tantrums and blowing up their mothers, finger-guns firing real bullets, and rapists turning themselves invisible as they stalk the streets.

I am awash in blue light.

"Have you thought about what your father is going to do with his share of the magic?" the floating skeleton says.

"You son of a bitch! You're going to kill him!"

Emérico holds up a palm. "Circumstances *could* lead him to kill himself. Unless you are there for him when it happens. If you remain here until I complete the ritual, I will make sure you get to him in time. Otherwise, you're gambling with his life."

My head begins to swim and I realize I am hyperventilating. I concentrate on slowing down my breathing.

"I know you'll do the right thing, Pablo; it is your nature to sacrifice for your students. The new world we build will need someone as selfless." Emérico grabs Thanatopsis and dons the baldric. He floats over the opening in the latticework floor. "Do not worry, Pablo. I have all of this under control. By tomorrow, you will be living in a world where you will not have to struggle to survive. You will thrive."

He descends into the forge, leaving me to contemplate the anarchy he will unleash, wondering if he's right about the world that will emerge, desperate to know if my father has paid attention to anything I've said about magic in the last two decades.

19
Bargain Your Soul

GHOSTLY WISPS OF vapor rise off my skin as the realm slowly erodes the ectoplasm. When it is gone, my body will have no defense left, the hole in my calf and split eyebrow will necrotize, the infection will spread to my blood, and the sepsis will kill me. I need to get out of Nox immediately.

The problem is, if I struggle, the strips of cold iron around my wrists, ankles, and neck wipe away some of the ectoplasm. Every time I move, I am moving toward death. Giorgio would know how to slip these shackles. He wouldn't need a wand, either. He could probably just command the metal to move.

Trapped by two of my teachers in one day. I grind my teeth at the thought. What did Giorgio say about Emérico? He called him extreme. In light of the current situation, the understatement sickens me. Giorgio only tried to hide that extremism. Emérico was unwilling to adapt to the world, but Giorgio could at least adapt Santa Inés Hall, make it presentable. Maybe that's why he stayed at the College.

Those changes infuriated Emérico. Giorgio had to build his workshop as a refuge. Yet he never tried to steer me away from Emérico, as Rhea did. Was he as naïve as I was, or just too self-absorbed to care?

Rhea retreated from the College to North Miami. Her students had to follow her. She extracted them from Emérico's influence, one lesson at a time. Is that why she was so upset with me the day of my final? She thought I had chosen the monster over her.

I made that choice well before I met her.

The two of them were right to stay away from Emérico. But they couldn't bring the monster to heel. Two mortals could never hope to curb such a lavish spirit.

Yet they could see what I couldn't. I never suspected Emérico because I never had the time. I was too concerned with my own problems, my own business, my own self-interests. The only things separating me from Nick Russo are genetics and circumstance. Completely self-absorbed assholes, one and the same.

How could I have been so stupid?

I try to reckon the tightness in my chest. Shame? Betrayal? Nox? Yes, yes, and yes. My own thoughts are killing me. I need to get out of here. Bound by strips of cold iron, stranded in the dark, my lantern my lifeline. How do I make an escape?

A crash below me. "*¡Inútil!*" (Useless!) the manager of the ghostly crew yells. Through the latticework, I see another shade grab his own crotch, then begin shoveling spilled ore back into a wheelbarrow. The angry dead are my only hope.

"*Oye! Asere!*" I yell. *Asere* translates as "savage." It is the quintessential Cuban word and, colloquially, means "friend." The manager looks up. "Come here," I say in Spanish.

"*Que tu crees?*" (What do you think?) he says, and goes back to checking the forges.

"I am going to die!"

"*Perfecto. Así no te tengo que oír más.*" (Perfect. That way I won't have to listen to you anymore.)

"What do you think Emérico will do when he finds out you let me die?"

"*A mi no me dijo ni un coño.*" (He didn't tell me a damn thing.) *Coño* is as useful in Spanish as "fuck" is in English, and just as vulgar.

"He didn't kill me. He wants me alive."

The foreman frowns. "What do you expect me to do?"

"The forges run on ectoplasm, right? Bring me some."

"*Pa' que?*" (For what?)

"You have to cover me in it."

"*Me cago en su madre!*" (I shit on your mother) he says, but he goes to a nearby forge and picks up a bucket with a latched cap. He makes his way up the spiral staircase, cursing the entire time. When he arrives on the platform, he unlatches the bucket, unceremoniously dumps the ectoplasm over my head, and tries to walk away.

The cold, goopy shock of ectoplasm causes me to gasp. I cough so hard that the manager stops to check on me. "*Compadre,*" (Comrade) I say, "thank you very much, but if you don't spread it all over me, I will still die."

"*Vete para el carajo*," (Go to Hell) he says, but he approaches me and starts slapping the ectoplasm around. When I am completely encased, he says, "*Ya. Jódete*" (There. Fuck yourself).

"*Que Dios te bendiga*," (May God bless you) I say.

He sneers and throws up a hand as he descends the stairs. It may be enough ectoplasm. I'm not really sure. Either way, I'm not going anywhere if I don't get out of this chair. Somehow, I'm going to have to convince the haunts to free me.

Being a necromancer doesn't require a mastery over death. But the ability to manipulate what is dead does demand an acceptance of the state of death and acknowledgement of the immortal soul. Interacting with dead bodies isn't what scares people away from the discipline. Most often, it is coming to terms with the metaphysical reality that confirms the existence of the soul and its complete lack of necessity for a living body. A potential necromancer's capstone project must demonstrate an understanding of this incongruity.

The surest way to demonstrate this comprehension is to exorcise your own soul.

I close my eyes and begin taking deep breaths through my nose for a count of five, holding that breath for seven seconds, then exhaling for ten seconds. Emérico recommended meditation to me as part of my initial practices, but I never found a use for it until I needed a way to divorce my mind from my body. I know I am in a rhythm when I stop counting the seconds.

I have a mantra: "the breath." It helps me silence the most intrusive thoughts and centers my focus back on the breathing process.

The breath. I'm sure my father is fine. I'm sure I'll get to him in time. *The breath.* Here I am, using what Emérico taught me to escape. Would he be proud? *The breath.* I reach out and "check" every part of my body. My heart rate slows. My split eye and punctured calf pulse. My hip and shoulder are tight. Why are my arms so tired? *The breath.* I can feel the ectoplasm on my skin, cool and slick.

The breath. The breath. The breath.

The darkness around me is devoid of feeling. It is loud: a wet chug, a vacuum whoosh. I move up through the dark and find moist meat and enamel. I force the jaw open and stick my disembodied arm out of my own mouth. I wriggle out and brace my hands on my shoulders. I push upwards, freeing my soul from the prison of flesh.

I stand and face my body. It is barely breathing. I used the ectoplasm as a reagent to power the effect, but I may have stolen too much. The thin coating sublimes away. My flesh will die. Would that be so bad? Flabby, beyond its prime, the heir to a thousand natural shocks, prone to a million different pains and desires. Is there a difference between those two? One a feeling that gives pleasure when it's over, the other a feeling that is over once it's pleasured.

I sigh, out of reflex. I had forgotten the nihilism that accompanies shunting your soul out of your body. The exorcism dulls emotion. I fled that sinewy prison with one goal: to be free from the chair. But all I can see is frailty, unfit to continue. I descend the stairs, resigned to at least follow through with the initial impulse. I make a clanking show of it, banging the banisters, kicking the posts, drawing the attention of the ghostly crew.

I've only ever auto-exorcised at the College's labs. When I did so, the appearance of the room didn't change. But the spiral staircase here in Nox surprises me. The cold iron isn't the usual buzzing, distracting metal. Instead, it looks like Damascus steel that breathes; the pattern shifts like wind-blown lake water. Above me, chimes. I look up into the tower's darkness. When I hear them again, I am certain they are coming from outside.

"*Que le pasa*, Kiki?" (What is wrong with him, Kiki?) a ghost says to the foreman.

Every worker in the foundry stares at me, having once again taken up their tools and weapons. I see no malice, however. "*Perdonenme*," (Forgive me) I say. "I've never seen this before," I say and rub the cold iron banister.

"Are you dead?" Kiki the foreman asks.

"Not yet. I just needed to get out of that chair."

"Get back in your body, before we make you," he says, and motions to the ghosts around him.

No heartbeat. No adrenaline. No fear. No pain. No quarter. "Emérico has betrayed you." No filter or tact either, apparently. "He's never going to let you have Downtown. 'Prima is for the living,' he said." The assembled ghosts break into groups of yellers and conspirators. Their sentiments are divided. The foreman looks ready to retch, if such a thing were possible.

I descend to the floor of the false College and they raise their weapons, but back up. To them, I am plagued. I scan each of the forges. "Ah," I say and move toward one of them. The ghosts part in unison. I find a bucket like the one Kiki brought before.

"*Que coño tu crees que haces?*" (What the Hell do you think you're doing) Kiki says.

Before I can grab it, the chimes tinkle again. "What is that noise?"

Kiki looks around at his peers, then back at me. "The Aperture," he says, and his tone is full of regret.

The Aperture. I've never seen it. The mere mention of it tugs at me. "Where is it?"

Kiki's eyes dart around. None of his fellows will look at him. "It is outside." The crowd murmurs.

I rush up to the foreman. The ghosts scatter like sardines before a sailfish. Only a few raise their weapons. To his credit, Kiki doesn't flinch. I laugh, but there is no real joy in it. I miss mirth. Does Emérico? "Open the doors," I say.

He blinks. Surely he doesn't need to. I know I haven't since I left my body. He raises his chin to the guards at the door. He dismisses me with a gesture: palm turned down, a flick of his fingers. The guards push open the doors to the false Santa Inés Hall. I make my way to the entrance, every eye in the room following me.

Outside, the darkness remains. Even to the dead, Nox is a vast nothing. Why stay here? I look up. A single, unblinking star in the black. It sings. The song plucks a string in me that shouldn't exist. If all the ghosts feel this, then they are masochists, denying the most righteous sound in existence.

"Having a gander at the last, great mystery, old boy?" a disembodied voice says.

I don't look away from the Aperture. "How do you get to it?"

"Just give up the will to stay."

I keep staring and something grabs my leg. A hand appears around my ankle, pulling me down. I was floating five feet above the ground, which

I now see is made of hard-packed sand, cracked like desert earth. When I was in my body, I felt it as flesh instead of dust. The hand fades. The ectoplasm it absorbed from me disperses throughout the ghost's form. The brief outline of a face vanishes.

"Jonas," I say. I feel blank. I recognize his predatory nature, but my rage has abandoned me.

"Hello, Archmagus."

"Respect. That's a new flavor for you," I say and return my gaze upward.

"You can hear it, can't you?" he says, and looks up. "You were drawn to it. Like we all are. But you're not dead yet."

I nod.

"Why not just go?" Jonas asks.

I rub my mouth out of habit. Why indeed? Would it truly be so bad to let the world burn? They're all going to die anyway. I sigh. "I can't let the city fall further into ruin. And if I find my mother beyond the Aperture, I don't think she would forgive me for abandoning my father."

"You always were a mama's boy."

"Why are you here, Jonas?"

"You can get me something I need."

I raise an eyebrow.

"Go back inside. Grab a bucket," Jonas says.

He wants the ectoplasm "Hmm. I need it to save my worthless body. What do you need it for? You can just make it yourself." As I understand it, the effort to remain in Nox generates ectoplasm, and the more willful you are, the faster it accrues.

"Don't be daft. It took me weeks to gather the jar's worth you wrung from me. But you could just waltz in and grab some. Save me the effort."

Another person looking for shortcuts. Somewhat ironic, considering that I used it as a reagent. "I will get a bucket. For me. You can have whatever's left, provided you help me get out of here."

"You can't get yourself out?"

"Emérico stole my sword."

Wentworth grins. "What. A. *Pity*."

"And for you all. All this work you've done for him, and he's betrayed you, too."

Wentworth massages his chin. "Can you prove that?"

"No, but you can."

"How?"

"Jump in my body." A twinge only, where there should be disgust. "Find the last conversation I had with Emérico and you can report the truth to the others." I head back into the false hall, unsure if Jonas follows. "Do you feel it when you laugh? Because I feel nothing."

His voice emerges from empty space. "It takes time to get used to it. And it is... muted," he says. "Kiki!"

The foreman approaches. "What you want, *pendejo*?" (Pubic hair.)

"Our guest is going to allow me to enter his thoughts to determine whether or not we've been lied to," Wentworth says.

The foreman nods. "*Bien. Dale.*" (Good. Go ahead.)

"I'm going to need one of those," I say and point at a bucket.

"You waste one already!" Kiki says.

"You'll never know the truth if you don't give it to me."

Kiki lowers his brow and takes a long time to measure me up. He snatches a bucket from the nearest forge and pushes it into my arms. "*No me jodes más*" (Don't fuck with me anymore). We three proceed up the stairs. All industry has stopped in the foundry. Their hope has evaporated.

When I make the landing, a cloaked figure crouches over my body. The tatters of its robe wave like the arms of an anemone. It holds a sickle.

"*Coño!*" Kiki yells and retreats down the stairs.

"I swear I wasn't helping him!" Jonas says as he flees.

I approach my body, unlatch the bucket, and dump the ectoplasm all over the living parts of me. The reaper speaks in a voice like iron gates moaning. I WAS WONDERING WHERE YOU WERE. READY TO GO?

"Not today."

SOON?

"Hopefully not."

SOONER THAN YOU THINK.

"Thank you for the reminder."

JUST MY JOB. The reaper walks through the wall.

Wentworth and Kiki are frozen at the top of the stairs. "Thanks for the assist there," I say to them.

"You handled the situation marvelously, Archmagus," Wentworth says.

"Yes, yes, very good, my friend," Kiki says.

"Climb in there already, and don't go poking where you don't belong," I say.

Wentworth's dim outline moves behind the chair. He plunges his hands into my body's back. I don't know if I'm imagining it, but for a moment, it looks like the skin of my arms rises with the impression of his fingers. My body's hands grip the chair. My body starts screaming.

"For Christ's sake, Wentworth. Get a hold of yourself. You're going to give me a goddamn stroke."

"How are you in so much pain?" he yells through my mouth.

"Just breathe through it," I say. "In through the nose. Good. Hold the next one. Good. Out through the mouth. Slowly. Good. Good. Feel better?"

"No," he wheezes.

"The sooner you find the memory, the sooner you can get out."

My body takes three quick breaths, as if it's about to plunge into cold water, and then my eyes roll into the back of my head. He works my jaw as if speaking, moving through the memory. I see Jonas mouth, "*You're going to kill him.*"

All motion stops. No breathing. My hands go limp. I lean in. "Wentworth?" I look at Kiki. He shrugs.

Ghostly hands dart from my mouth and pull at me. "*Ayúdame, cabron*!" (Help me, you bastard!) I say to Kiki. The foreman runs over. We each take an arm and pull Wentworth out of my body.

Wentworth's panting subsides quickly as he returns to his own sense. "Oh, my word. Never again." He's absorbed some of the ectoplasm that was covering me, so he looks almost as solid as Kiki.

"Finally had your fill?" I ask.

He cocks his eye at me, then looks at the foreman. "The Archmagus is not lying. Emérico betrayed us."

Kiki throws up his hands and lets out a string of rapid-fire curses that I wouldn't be able to follow with subtitles. "*Nos ha traicionado*!" (He's betrayed us!) he says as he descends the stairs.

"They never had his trust," I say. "He only cares about himself."

Wentworth looks down his nose at me. "You're pretty well buggered, I'd wager."

Through the opening in the lattice, I can see Kiki yelling at the other ghosts. They surround him as he slaps the back of one hand into the palm of the other, stomps his feet, gesticulates wildly. "Even in death, Cubans are still animated," I say.

"You have no idea." Wentworth's form has solidified into the same man I had nightmares about for decades. I'm not scared of him now, but I do know what I am going to do to him, once this is all over.

"You ruined my childhood," I say to him. "I had night terrors about you until I was an adult. You're the reason I had to become a necromancer."

"So I gave you a future," he says with a smirk.

"My childhood ended with you. You made it impossible for me to be normal. Do you have any idea how hard it is to not be able to sleep at night, thinking someone might take away your free will? Your personhood? For what? Your pleasure?"

"Listen, old boy. You see what it's like here. There is no feeling. No life. Wouldn't you do the same?"

"If I were dead, truly dead, I would just go into the Aperture." I let him chew on that for a moment. "Death would have been preferable to living with what you did to me. I just wanted to be normal."

"Think about how powerful you are. You would never have achieved this greatness if I hadn't possessed you."

"I need you to understand something. I've been working with you because I needed you. Nothing more. Now, I am going to treat solely with your brethren. We *will* come to an agreement. I am going to give them a semblance of life. It has become painfully clear that *that* is the only thing motivating any of you. But you, and Ardelia Black, and Silas Young, you will have no place in what is built. You're not safe from me. Consider this warning a courtesy for helping me to convince Kiki."

Wentworth sneers. "I suppose this is goodbye, then."

"Don't forget. I'm coming for you."

Jonas Wentworth descends the stairs. "Poor Pablito Diaz. Macabre to the very end."

I am left with my miserable, piece-of-shit body. Dark bags under my eyes. Shadow of patchy stubble. Sitting, the love handles are even more evident. I move around to the back of the chair and realize I've never truly seen myself from this angle. At least I still have a full head of hair.

The Aperture's chimes swell in the silence.

I dig my ghostly hands into my back, then dive in with my head. Instant darkness. Pushing through meat. A constant pressure. I dig farther. I find my thrumming brow, so my head is in the right place. I shift until I find the shoulder that is hanging on by a few tendons. Hip and calf scream as I settle into reality. My sinews bear up my neck.

I open my eyes, panting. Kiki and a horde have completely overrun the platform. No weapons this time. "He no give us Downtown," Kiki says. "What you going to give us?"

"For letting me out? Nothing."

A murmur spreads through the assembly.

Kiki holds up a hand. "Then why we should help you?"

I low-ball them. "Revenge?"

"No is enough."

"I can't allow you to run amok. There's a reason we ward everything. People are afraid of you. They're afraid of possession, and of the dead coming back to life. You are all where you belong."

"Is no life!"

"I'll keep the forges lit. You can build whatever kind of city you want. But it has to be here. And I can bring people here who want to talk to you. Necromancers, historians, anthropologists. Maybe even some that *want* to be possessed."

"What about cable?" a voice calls out.

My eyes widen. "What?"

Kiki nods. "*Sí. Cable*. Premium channel. HBO."

My jaw drops. "You want television?"

"*La muerte es aburrida, consorte*." (Death is boring, friend.)

"Fine. We'll figure it out. But I'm going to need some things from you." I explain what I want from them.

Kiki whistles. "*Estás quemado, asere*" (You're burned out, my friend).

"*No hay de otra*," (There is no other way) I say.

"We be right back. You wait." They all return downstairs.

I can hear them deliberating. What might they be saying? That I'm insane, clearly. That Emérico will kill me, then destroy or imprison all of them. My heart sinks, not for my imminent demise, but for the betrayal of my mentor. To Emérico, we're all recorders, our stops governed all too easily. He saved me when I was child, welcomed me into the College, guided me through the hardships, and elevated me to a position of power. Nothing would have kept me from trusting him.

I should have been wary of a talking skeleton that runs a school of magic. Rhea and Giorgio certainly were. I should have taken him at face value. I could have spared myself this misery. And yet, that level of cynicism would have barred me from any advancement. I would have no life, education, no career. Evil or not, he saved me. He taught me. He made it possible to keep my head above water when fate conspired to drown me.

Fuck his betrayal for ruining that.

After I beat Baba Yaga, he had the audacity to tell me I was putting the College at risk. That I put *his* College at risk. When this plan of his fails and turns the city—Hell, the nation—against us, it's back to Salem 1692 for all of us.

Unless his plan works. But for it to work, I would have to do nothing. Sit here, possibly die, while three million people marvel at the flood of power I've spent close to two decades learning to control. And if I do stay here and wait, I have no guarantee I will make it to my father in time. Jonas found the memory of that conversation. He mouthed the last thing I said to Emérico: "You're going to kill him." I was talking about my father.

What happens when Tristan Díaz comes to terms with magic? What does that look like? Does he turn off the T.V. with a gesture, confusing magic for coincidence? Does he transmute his ratty armchair into a leather La-Z-Boy? I smile at the thought, but then the more likely outcome intrudes upon my reverie: does he blow up his oxygen tank? Or does he just have another stroke before discharging the magic?

Instant, bilious panic. "*Donde coño estan?*" (Where the fuck are you all?) I say.

Someone starts working at one of the forges. After a while, I hear the hammering of an anvil. I wish the sound matched my heartbeat, but it is much slower. Kiki returns, followed by the blacksmiths, all of them armed with hammers and tongs and crowbars. "*No hay de otra,*" (There's no other way) the foreman says, and then they are upon me.

20
Blood from the Stone

KIKI'S STEPS MAKE no noise on the spiral staircase, but he's careless with the hammer he holds, banging it against the banister. With the forges dead, the sound rattles my teeth. As he makes the landing, he furrows his brow and taps the hammer against his leg. He looks like a man unsure about leaping off a bridge.

Three ghosts follow him, a grim crew that continues to work, just like Kiki. A black man in a linen shirt and shorts, a frontiersman in a wool coat and collarless shirt (Florida's humidity probably killed him), and an indigenous man in hide pants, a long-sleeved tunic, a vest, and a turban. A Bahamian, a homesteader, and a Seminole, some of the people who laid the foundations of Miami. They carry various tools—a sledge, massive tongs, a crowbar. They surround me in silence.

It is difficult to swallow. The strip of cold iron around my neck disrupts the ectoplasm there. Nox must be poking at my shield, looking for weaknesses, trying my defenses to get at my too-vulnerable flesh.

No amount of effort draws a sound from the ghosts, and the only indicator of strain is when one of them asks another for help. Free of muscle and sinew and lactic acid, they float around me—moving through me when necessary—to twist the iron wide enough for my hands and feet to slip through. It takes all four of them to budge the metal around my neck, and the cold shocks of their ghostly matter passing through my trachea send me into coughing fits so strong that I am lightheaded afterward. The bar binding my waist moans when they bend it backwards.

"*Levántate*," (Stand up) Kiki says.

My knees crack as I do so. I stretch for so long that white spots invade my vision, forcing me back to my lantern for oxygen. "Thank you all so much," I say as they make for the spiral stairs.

"Remember your promise," the Bahamian says, sparing me one last look.

"*Cómo escaparás?*" (How will you escape?) Kiki says.

"I don't know yet."

"*Suerte*" (Luck). He returns to the forges. I spread the ectoplasm over my exposed flesh. There must be more buckets downstairs. Will any amount check the ravenous realm?

Emérico took Thanatopsis, my key to the doorways of Nox, but he left me my doctor's bag and lamp. He thought the only way I was getting out of here was with the sword. But I standardized the curriculum by which all wizards are trained. If the last two days have taught me anything, it is that I truly live in these moments. Somewhere in this bag, I will improvise my deliverance.

My sword's connections to death allow it to rend the veil between the realms. If I want to get back to Prima, tear through the iron gates of life, then I need to make connections to the living. I start digging through my doctor's bag. I spread the silk pall over the latticework floor so that nothing falls through the gaps. I lay out my boxing wraps, bloodstained by my fight with Baba Yaga. The blood didn't mute the indigo of the runes; they should still work. I pull my leather bag full of reagents, fashioned from the same hide I used to make Thanatopsis's grip. A pencil case full of ash and bone fragments—earthly remains collected from societal derelicts. A candle made from the rendered fat of a yearling calf. Too much death here.

A blood drawing kit and a first aid kit, but the only life here is my own. Can I afford to give up any more of my own essence? Sticks of white chalk, wax crayons, a ball of clay, homemade paper: the materials of an artist. Every creation is an act of life, isn't it? Matches, a tin of earth, orc tusks. In the reagent bag: a golden eagle feather, a bag of diamond powder, some dead spiders in nickel bags, iron nails, cosmetic containers full of different herbs, fish parts (tongues, gills, fins) vacuum sealed in plastic. Provocative and esoteric junk.

I spread it all out before me, looking for a way to put it all together.

"Kiki!" I yell.

"*Que coño quieres?*" (What the hell do you want?) he says from beneath the opening in the floor.

"How was Emérico going to let you onto Prima?"

"*Que se yo?*" (What do I know?)

I curse under my breath. I grab the phlebotomy bag and look at the orc tusks. That orc shaman made his avatar out of blood. The memory of the little girl intrudes, jellies my knees, turns my stomach. The leader of the orcs, Gormar, fed the addictions of his tribe. Could I do something similar on my own? "Do you have any bowls or dishes?"

He squints up through the latticework. "We no eat."

"Can you make me three?"

He throws up his arms and starts tossing raw ore into one of the forges.

I roll up my left sleeve, exposing the veins in the crook of my arm, and then dab the displaced ectoplasm back over my skin. I tie off my upper arm with my boxing wraps. I uncap the needle at the end of the plastic tubing connected to the blood bag. I smack my arm, raising the vein, then push the needle into it.

It takes longer than I expect to fill the bag. The entire time that I am rocking the bag back-and-forth in my free hand, a forge breathes and a hammer pings. I pull the needle from my arm and hold a bandage over the drawsite by bending my elbow.

Kiki arrives with three tea saucers made of cold iron. "*Eres loco?*" (Are you crazy?) he says, looking at the blood bag.

I shrug. "Set them down in front of me."

Kiki does so. "*Vas a perder ese brazo*" (You're going to lose that arm).

"*Espero que no*" (I hope not). I wrap the bandage with gauze from the first aid kit and spread ectoplasm over it.

"*Haya tu*" (Do as you will). Kiki leaves again.

I pick up the bag of diamond powder my father abandoned after his stroke. It always held a special fascination for me. Mixed with mineral oil and applied to a strop, the dust would sharpen knives and polish tools to a mirror finish. But how could my father afford such extravagance? As I learned the truth about industrial diamonds and how cheap they were, a metaphor for my craft slowly formed. When worked, things have value, but when made en masse, even the most costly substances cheapen. It's the difference between Thanatopsis and a Refresh™.

I pick up the ball of clay and roll it in my hands, warming it as I knead it like fresh dough, adding blood as I go. I fold diamond powder into the softened clay, then add an equal amount of salt from my mother's jar. I mix the two granular substances into the unformed loam. My fingers and wrists ache as I pull, roll, and mold the clay into three small figurines. I poke them in the head, drip blood into the impression, then cap the divot. I smooth out the clay with spit until I am sure the little blood bubble is secure. I break a tongue depressor and carve my name into the clay. I begin chanting. I stand each imitation on one of the saucers and pour blood over them.

The clay begins to absorb the final drop of blood, and as it does, the little golems morph from formless figurines into effigies of me. They move, but without purpose, without personality. They need more life; they need more of me. I begin chanting and scour the hodgepodge of reagents for something significant.

The griffin feather. I hold it up in my lamp's light. Even in the blue haze, the gold plumage remains brilliant. During the first year of my doctorate, I was desperate for money. My father was hounding me to go work for him. To avoid starvation and Tristan's knowing glances, I took a job in the Redlands hunting a griffin. I found the eagle-headed lion by illuminating the trail of blood it left after gorging on a cow. It would have eviscerated me, but it pounced on an illusion of me instead and triggered a kinetic cage. I kept a feather as a memento. None of the archmagi congratulated me, but I knew I was their equal.

In feudal Japan, samurai and other warriors would wear a small banner on their backs into battle. The flags were called sashimono, and such is the impression I seek to emulate as I dig the quill into the back of the first effigy.

The matches are homemade, as are at least half of the reagents. There's something about an unstruck match, the possibilities it holds, that seems so like life. Will it warm? Will it destroy? A scratch, a spark, a minor act that could light a path or burn down the countryside. I dig two matches into the arms of the middle figurine, giving him hands with the potential to blaze.

The iron nails were used to shoe horses, that much I know. They were given to me by my father when I started at the College. He thought they would get me to return to carpentry—give up my dream for his reality. I understood his intention because it made me doubt my own. I would hold one in my hand when I studied as an undergrad, drawing the point under the words in my course packets. I push a nail into the core of the third effigy. As I finish chanting, they open their eyes. The clay shifts and takes form, until each figurine becomes a miniature copy of my current, physical state.

"Masterful technique," Griffin says. "We're quite good at this."

"Thank you," I say.

"Do you really believe this is going to work against Emérico?" Nails says. "I doubt you're *that* good."

"Can you see what I see?" I ask. Nails nods, shuffles in place, wrings his tiny hands. Sharing their perceptions is about as distracting as watching four televisions at once. I need only shift my focus to a different "screen."

"This place is fascinating. We have to come back," Matches says.

"We need a way out," I say.

"Don't worry, we'll think of something. We always do," Griffin says.

"Because we keep putting ourselves in these situations," Nails says.

"Don't act like you don't love it," Matches says.

"Focus, please," I say. "Four of us will be more difficult to pinpoint than one."

"True, and some illusory wards might confuse the Chancellor," Griffin says.

"He'll see right through us," Nails says.

"We have to risk it. Otherwise, we might as well stay here," I say.

Matches cackles and scrapes his hands together. "I think I have a plan. Will the wraps still work if we take a few strings from them?"

"Are you insane?" Nails says. "What if you destroy them? All that blood might have already compromised them, and now you want to pull parts from them?"

"Don't be such a pussy," Matches says.

"You're the worst, you know that?" I say to Nails.

Nails scoffs. "You know I'm right."

"We do know," Griffin says. "But we don't have any other recourse."

I rub my chin. "So: a ward, boxing wraps, and…?"

"Celia," Matches says.

We all look at him. "You're goddamn right," I say.

"Fucking A," Griffin says. "She does work."

"Line up," I say and sit crossed-legged. They do so, and I pick each up in turn and draw a ward in chalk on their backs: a circle with a triangle inside the circle, and three symbols at the points—Mars for us, an eye for vision, and a closed eye for the illusion. I draw the same ward on my shirt pocket and charge all three wards with a whisper and a snap. I ease an elastic thread free from the boxing wraps and rip it into three pieces, handing one to each of the golems.

"We should get going," Nails says, ripping his thread in twain and then wrapping his feet with the pieces. "I can feel the blood congealing. We three have an hour, maybe less. If this has any chance of working, we should attempt it at shallow points."

Certain locations on Prima build connections to other planes of existence: frequent wildfires make it easier to reach the elemental plane of fire; study and contemplation weaken the veil between Prima and the Astral Plane; places associated with death draw closer to Nox. I pocket the wraps again. The golems scatter as I bundle up the pall and reagents and throw it all into my bag. "Kiki!" I yell down through the opening in the latticework floor. "I need you to take me back to the crematory next to the river."

"*Dale. Vamos.*" I grab my lantern. When I stand up, my head is swimming.

"Slowly!" Nails says. "Take a breath. You've given up too much blood."

Griffin snaps at him. "We don't have time. He can take it."

"Enough," I say and scoop them up. I lean on the railing as I go down the spiral staircase. Kiki is waiting. The three ghosts who freed me from the chair are back at the forges. The false hall has once again become a hive of industry. I call out to them. They arrive in turn, and I hand each of them one of my golems. "They'll tell you where to go," I say.

"The Miami Circle," Griffin says. He hops into the Seminole's hand, and the man darts away. His trip is the fastest, a short jog. Brickell Point Site, part of the National Register of Historic Places, is home to the Miami Circle, the remains of a Tequesta Indian shrine. The tribe itself was devastated by disease, and what few members escaped small pox, dysentery, and syphilis were rounded up by the Spanish and taken to Cuba as slaves. The Seminole consider the Tequesta their ancestors.

"Jackson Memorial Hospital," Nails says. I watch through his eyes as the frontiersman carries him through the town of the dead that has sprung up around the false Santa Inés Hall. They arrive at the first of many buildings that would eventually become Jackson Memorial Hospital. In 1918,

Miami City Hospital began as one building. It was built to service those affected by the Spanish Flu. 87 people died that first year. Jackson is currently America's largest transplant center, and while a lot of people walk out of that building with a second chance, not everyone does.

"Miami City Cemetery," Matches says, and the Bahamian takes him as his charge. The cemetery is the oldest modern burial ground in Miami, the only municipal cemetery in Miami-Dade County, and serves as the final resting place to many that built the city. The Bahamian drops Matches off at the west end. "The first man buried here was black," Matches says as they arrive.

"I know. The city wouldn't even give me a headstone," the Bahamian says and disappears into the darkness.

I look at Kiki. "I won't make it by foot," I say to him.

"*Cabrón*" (Bastard). He grabs a wheelbarrow. "*Agárrate fuerte*" (Hold on tight).

I get in the wheelbarrow, my lamp and doctor's bag in my lap.

We leave a cloud of oxygen from the false Santa Inés Hall all the way to the other side of the river. Kiki doesn't breathe or need to rest, so he runs the three miles in what feels like minutes. "Thank you, Kiki," I say.

"*Ojalá que la próxima vez que te veo, es con un televisor*" (God willing, the next time I see you, it's with a T.V.).

"I'll do my best."

"*Hasta ahora lo has jodido*" (You've fucked it up until now), he says and leaves.

Without Thanatopsis, I can't peek onto Prima to see if there are any police. But the wards floating in midair translate to the four corners of the building in the real world. Griffin, Matches, and Nails see similar wards at the Circle, cemetery, and hospital, respectively. "Y'all ready?" I ask. Across the distance, I can feel my golems respond in the affirmative.

"He'll know as soon as we cross," Nails says.

"Better have your balls on tight, 'cause he's coming for you," Matches says, meaning me. "He knows you were at Orlov's restaurant."

"True," I say. "But he might go for Griffin. The Miami Circle is the closest spot to the false tower."

"I can take him," Griffin says.

"If we're doing this, then let's do it. Otherwise, you're going to have to find another means of escape," Nails says.

I take off my shoes and wrap my feet in the boxing wraps. I make sure to get as little ectoplasm as possible on the wraps. "Together then," I say, "One-two-three-four five-six-seven-eight," the 4/4 time having been engraved in my memory at an early age, the rhythm possibly a part of my DNA.

"Left two three four right six seven eight," my golems improvise in unison.

"Left two three rest," we shuffle the two-step of the salsa, "right six seven rest. Left two back rest right six front rest."

Celia Cruz was the Queen of Salsa and soul of the Cuban diaspora. Her music has bolstered the exile community since before the Revolution. When she died, her body was held in state in the Freedom Tower—the Ellis Island for Cubans arriving in Miami—before being flown back to the Bronx for her burial. Tens of thousands packed Biscayne Boulevard for their chance to see the legend one last time. Her cover of "I Will Survive" by Gloria Gaynor is cocaine for my soul.

"*Oye mi son*[1]*, mi viejo son, / Tiene la clave de cualquier generación*," (Hear my son, my old son, / It has the *clave* of every generation) I sing.

"*En el alma de tu gente,*" (In the souls of your people) Griffin says.

"*En el cuero del tambor*," (In the leather of the drum) Matches says.

"*En las manos del conguero*," (In the hands of the conga player) Nails says.

"*En los pies del bailador*," (In the feet of the dancer) I say.

The song and dance and rhythm and blood charge the spell, but the force exerted by our feet and my heartbeat pushes at the membrane of Nox. The realm resists. My arches begin to ache.

"*Yo viviré!*" (I will live!) we all chant.

"Stronger, damn it!" Griffin says. We kick up a dusting of death. The runes on my wraps glow an otherworldly red. I can see my veins pulse beneath them.

"*Yo viviré!*"

1 Son cubano: syncretic musical stylings mixing traditional Spanish and African music.

I feel the spongy terra at our feet give way. Beneath it, a sinewy mass. Thanatopsis cuts through it so easily; Nails and I barely budge it. We feel the chords of the realm resist. Griffin and Matches keep pushing, biting into the matter.

"*Yo viviré!*"

Nox vomits Griffin and Matches into Prima simultaneously, as if the realm was purging itself of their liveliness. I feel my connection to them sundered. But Nails and I are still in Nox, and as we struggle, the fibrous membrane of the realm burns away more ectoplasm, seeking my vulnerable flesh. "Come on, man! We're almost there!" I say.

"We knew it! We knew this would happen!" Nails says.

I did know. But I also have hope. "Don't quit now! We're halfway there!"

"We're not strong enough!"

"How many monsters have we beaten?"

"Why even fight it? Whatever we find on the other side is going to kill us."

"We're leaving this place, God damn it. I shouldn't have to point out the obvious to you. You know what I know."

"The reaper isn't here." There should be strength, but I only hear resignation.

"You're goddamn right. We're not staying here while Emérico goes after our father."

"Dad doubts us, too, you know."

"He always has. But do you remember that look he gave us this morning?"

"I never thought he could be so proud of us."

"Shows what you know," I say. "One more push."

"*Yo viviré!*" we chant, stomping the realm until the sudden lack of resistance sends me sprawling.

My hands and knees hit asphalt. "Holy shit," I say, panting.

"Took you long enough," Griffin says. He stands at the Miami Circle site. It was turned into an urban park a decade ago, and the Circle itself remains buried to better preserve it, although limestone walkways were built around it. No paths have been placed above the circle, a headstone-in-absentia to the Tequesta, a culture murdered by rapacious colonization.

"My fault," Nails says. He's staring at the Alamo (named so because of its resemblance to the eponymous Texas structure), an exemplar of the Spanish Colonial Revival style popular in the early twentieth century.

Arched entryways adorn the first-floor facade, the second floor alternates between bay and thermal windows, and the terracotta tiled roof bears a domed cupola along its ridge. Anton Cermak, then-mayor of Chicago, died in this building after being shot by a bullet intended for Franklin Delano Roosevelt.

"That was too close," I say.

"Fucking intense," Matches says, with all the glee of a child dismounting a rollercoaster. Mahoganies and oaks are the primary shade trees in the Miami City Cemetery, but palm trees line the central thoroughfare, and the odd rainbow eucalyptus grows in resplendent defiance of the pervading headstones and occasional mausoleum. A circular memorial built to Julia Tuttle—the Mother of Miami—stands close to the East entrance, obscured from where Matches stands by another circular monument, this one erected by the Daughters of the Confederacy.

"Stay frosty," Griffin says. "You know he felt that."

"Let him come. I'm ready," Matches says.

I stand and walk to my car. It is blessedly free of police. I stow my lamp and doctor's bag in the trunk. When I walk around to the driver's side door, I notice the boot on the front left wheel. "God damn it," I say.

"We've got bigger problems," Griffin says. Through his eyes, I see a shimmer in reality above him. A pinpoint of light appears and spreads into a fiery window, Emérico at its center. I run back to the trunk for salt. My chest tightens as the air above me wavers like heat off of asphalt.

"Pablo?" Emérico says to Griffin.

"Chancellor," Griffin says. He puffs out his chest. With my ward in place, Emérico should be seeing an exact copy of me, instead of a tiny golem. Moreover, if the wards hold, he shouldn't be able to see where we are, either. He'll need to come find us.

"You just could not help yourself, could you?" Emérico says.

The air above Matches, Nails, and myself shimmers like fata morgana at sunset, then solidifies into scrying portals. Flaming holes in reality float above each of us. "Absolutely reckless," Emérico says. "How have you divided yourself?"

"I'd say my recklessness is merited, seeing as you left me to die," Griffin says. While my golem distracts him, I pour a ring of salt around the booted wheel.

"There is nothing you can do to stop me. All you are doing is spreading yourself thin," Emérico says.

"There is nothing I won't try," Matches says. He begins chanting and attacking a ward at the northeast corner of the cemetery, one meant to protect the grounds from rebellious ghosts. Emérico placed it after Dead Sunday as part of his covenant with the city, but I'm the one that has maintained that ward for over a decade.

"You cretin! I thought you cared about the city!" Emérico says. His skull bursts into flames; behind him, I see stars blur into lines, and the occasional cloud zooms by.

"Oh, I care," Matches says, scrubbing the ward. "And so do my new friends."

"I doubt you have any allies left," Emérico says.

"I do, though. You know them. They built you that grotesque monument to your own pride, and for their service, you betrayed them." I visualize the bolts in the boot turning and mimic the action of unscrewing them with my thumb and forefinger. The boot falls off with a resounding clang. I wince, and so does Griffin.

"I will find you, Pablo, and when I do, there will be no escape." Emérico makes a fist. Pain lances through my abdomen. I double over and vomit what little is in my stomach onto my shoes. The others go down as well, mimicking my pain. He's using the same spell I employed against Baba Yaga's hut, only he makes it work through the scrying portal. Emérico's eyes flare. "That should have killed you! How are you still standing?"

The metaphysical interaction between the golems, the scrying portals, and Emérico's incantation must have dispersed the force generated by his spell. "You cannot understand what is at stake," Emérico says.

"I know all too well," Nails says. "Emérico, the great and powerful, can't stand to live behind a curtain anymore. It won't make them fear you any less."

Emérico laughs. "Why would I ever want that?"

Nails scoffs. "All you've ever wanted is to be set upon a pedestal. You burn for it. But you failed in Lisbon, and you'll fail here."

Emérico makes a fist again. It feels like a beartrap shuts around my skull. Nails's head pops in a spurt of blood. "Golems? Brilliant!" Emérico says. "Such a shame to lose such a sharp mind."

"You can kill us all," Matches says. "I've already escaped. You think I would just gamble on this? I know who you are, but you clearly have no idea who I am." As Matches begins to attack the second ward of the cemetery, a comet appears in the air above him.

I do my best to stand, but it still feels like my innards and head are in a garbage compactor. I paw at the door handle. I manage to open it and crawl into the front seat. I toss my doctor's bag from the asphalt into the seat next to me and try to recover my breath. Emérico alights in front of Matches, his robes billowing as if he were held in a current. Smoke cascades from his sleeves, spreading on the grass below him. Two scrying circles float around him, showing Griffin and myself.

Matches laughs. "You've chosen poorly," he says. I fumble the chalk out of my pocket. My hand shakes violently. It is impossible to draw on the dashboard.

Emérico darts through the air and tries to stomp Matches, but the miniature proves too fast for him. "You couldn't play the human game, Emérico, and now you've nothing to resort to but sorcery. You're every bit the monster they say you are," Matches says. His brashness helps me steady my hand. I draw a ward on the dashboard, charge it with a whisper, and wait.

Emérico roars and makes another fist, lifting Matches into the air.

"Do your worst," Matches says, grinning. In my most Cuban-accented English, Matches says, "There's nothing you can do to me that Castro has not already done—" Emérico crushes him. Crushes me. My eyes feel like they might pop out of my head. However weak, my snap discharges the ward.

Emérico flinches as the fresh ward activates. Through Griffin's vision, I see one of the scrying windows around the Chancellor dissipate. "You could have had the city, Emérico," Griffin says. "You could have been the greatest leader Miami has ever seen."

Emérico scoffs. "And now you expect otherwise."

"Should I not? You're afraid of *me*," Griffin says. "If you didn't see me as a threat, you wouldn't have stirred from the Aerie."

"You are a peasant!" Emérico roars.

"Kings have fallen to less," Griffin says.

"This is your last warning. Stand down, or I will take away everything you love," Emérico says.

"Try it. See if I don't end you," Griffin says and reaches for the feather in his back. A tiny effigy of myself remains in Emérico's scrying window, holding a griffin feather above its head in one hand, brandishing a middle finger with the other.

21
Visitations

HE'S COMING FOR me. I have to put as much distance between us as I can. My tires squeal onto the 836. I pass a rainbow-colored toll station and crest a hill of highway—one of the only breaks on the flat plane of the city. As the road dips, Marlins Park baseball stadium dominates the vista on my left. I gun it on the straightaway. The rain has stopped. Sweat dampens my collar. 110 on the speedometer. The steering wheel vibrates.

I crest a low rise. After a weightless moment, my tires chirp and I hit my head on the ceiling. Metal grinds on asphalt and sparks fly around me. On my right, the airport spreads out before me, a vast field of orange against a backdrop of concrete, glass, and jutting terminals. Red and white runway markers waver in the humidity.

In my rearview, a blue candle-flame rises above Downtown, trailing a string. Just above the rooftops, the flicker becomes a comet that turns west, toward me. The blue ball of fire gets larger as it approaches. Do I imagine the skull in the center?

My ward will hide me from his vision but the swash from my car could give me away. With no cars on the road and nothing but wet asphalt ahead of me, I take my foot off the gas and coast, praying. I slow to a stop in the middle of the highway, not daring to leave tracks that point to the shoulder.

Blue light bathes the cabin. Emérico's glow bends bars of shadow onto my face. Does he know I'm here? Can he find me?

Of course he can. All he would need is my blood to form a sympathetic connection, like the blood I used to fashion my golems. I cover my mouth with my fingers. I'm a dead man. Emérico continues to circle my car. He won't be stopped. Why did I defy him?

My doctor's bag sits on the seat next to me. I try to keep my hand in the shadows as I move toward it. My shaking fingers make it impossible to push in the clasp. It sticks. To be undone by a latch. A click. It opens.

What can I grab that will save me? I pull the salt to me and hold it to my chest. I remove the lid and the little whoomp of air rushing into the jar stops my heart. I grab the door handle. I drew the ward on the dashboard. I'll be visible the moment I am out of the car. If I throw the salt around me, I might be able to close a circle of protection.

If I can't? Nothing is going to halt his wrath. He'll blast me, crush me, suffocate me, flip my car onto me, or hurl me onto a tarmac. He will have won, and all my pain—traversing Nox, dealing with the ghosts, the golems, all of it—will have been for nothing.

Ultra white headlights appear in the rearview. I wince away from them. Emérico hovers a few feet above the road in front of me. If I don't exit the car now, I'm a dead man. If I exit the car now, I'm a dead man. I grab the door handle and take in a long breath.

A cell phone begins to ring. The headlights are getting closer. I have ten seconds before it slams into me. Emérico reaches into the sleeve of his billowing robes and retrieves a phone. He passes his hand over it and brings it to the side of his skull.

"Hello?" he says. "Yes, I believe I have found him."

Sweat beads on my brow. I chew my bottom lip into a meaty ruin; I taste blood. The car pulls up right behind me. The driver turns off their car. As my eyes adjust, I can make out the front vanity plate: DR COPA.

Carmen Espinoza, Head of Divination, plants her boots on the pavement before she slithers out of the driver's seat. She tucks her cellphone in her back pocket and Emérico hides his own up his sleeve. She wears tight jeans, a flannel shirt, and a thick belt with a massive oval buckle. The only thing she's missing is the cowboy hat. She dresses like a gaucha to honor her roots, but all her finery—necklace, earrings, rings, bracelets—is made of gold; half of Hollywood has her on speed dial.

"Chancellor, it is almost two in the morning," Carmen says. "The plan was to begin at midnight."

"Do not lecture me about my own plans, Archmagus," Emérico says.

"My apologies, sir. I am merely pointing out that we are two hours behind schedule, and you aren't even at the College."

"I will be satisfied."

"I've told you, sir, there is nothing he can do to stop it," she says. "But if you don't hurry, they will give him the credit."

Emérico's flaming eyes blaze. I am awash in blue. The droplets of water on my windshield scatter as he takes off to the West. Carmen takes a few steps forward, following the Chancellor's progress, until the comet disappears over the horizon of the highway.

She taps on my window. I cap the jar of salt and place it in the passenger seat before I lower the window. "Good evening, Archmagus," she says.

"Hello, Carmen," I say, and I feel myself deflate.

She props her arms on the window frame. The shadows on her face make her sinister and alluring. It is not the first time I've seen her looming in the dark. The memory turns my knees to water. "You look stressed," she says. "Let's go have a beer."

My heart thumps once and drops into the pit of my stomach. She plucks some dusty chord in me. "I need to—"

"I'll meet you at your place," she says and pushes herself off the window frame, rocking my chassis. I find her perfume and can't stop myself from sniffing after it. She still moves to a rhythm, some unheard beat that I nevertheless feel. In the driver's side mirror, she slinks back into her car.

I gave her the idea for the vanity plate. I wanted it for myself. But I suggested it when she asked me, and in truth, the twin meanings—College of Practical Arts and the Spanish word for cup—suited her better. In the tarot, cups are a suit of mindfulness and emotion; in life, vessels can hold the water needed to scry. Her headlights once again sear my retina.

None of this has anything to do with old times. She wants nothing more than to distract me, keep me from stopping Emérico. He made her his thrall days ago. I cannot trust her. But what did she say to him? *There is nothing he can do to stop it.* Could any of her be in there, working? She wouldn't proffer a beer if she knew I wouldn't accept. She tuned me up by leaning into the car.

She taps her horn twice. I put on my seatbelt, and turn on my car. I keep glancing at her, confirming that she is there, but after a mile of tailgating me, her Mercedes blows past me, and I can see her flipping me the bird with a smile.

My much-abused four-cylinder engine cannot keep up with her. Chasing her now, I know too many things at once. She serves as Emérico's overwatch, plotting the immediate trajectory of events all over the city. She has divined far enough into the future to ensure his success, which makes any effort on my part fruitless. She probably came up with the plan to send me all over the city. We aren't driving toward an execution or a memorial; we're heading straight to the retrospective.

The other thoughts are just as frustrating. Decade-old memories of a time when I thought I was on top of the world and thought I could be with a woman who regularly peers into the future. The worst part, of course, was not knowing whether anything I said could sway her, whether the words coming out of her mouth weren't predetermined or rehearsed or lies to spare my feelings.

But she let me get on a plane to Pamplona and knew that, on the night of my greatest triumph, the night I completed Thanatopsis, I would find myself in a bar and get drunk with the first woman I laid eyes on, a woman who found my poor, Cuban Spanish as charming as it was vulgar. Ever after, I approached my lecture hall doors from the south, because the northern-most door was Carmen's.

YELLOW LIGHT POURS out of the windows on our side of the house. Dad must still be watching television, waiting for me. Carmen leans against her car, her hands resting on the grip of an umbrella. I pull myself out of my car, doing a terrible job at hiding my weakness. I go to the passenger side, retrieve my doctor's bag, and grab my lamp from my trunk. I hear her boots on approach. Carmen leans against my back passenger door. "You hear that?" She is smiling.

I was too busy trying not to look at her. I bend my ear toward my house.

"Sounds like someone is having a party," she says. "Are you going to invite me in, or are you going to wait for your father to do it for you?"

"How much have you seen?"

"Enough to keep myself safe."

"Typical."

"You want to know so badly? Look for yourself." You can use divination to scry, understand other languages, and read magical auras, all of which I find incredibly useful. But the reason I hate this particular practical art is because it allows you to see into the future. This is one of the most dangerous things a practitioner can do. From what we understand, the future is immeasurable, its possibilities innumerable—until you start trying to read it. Divining events that are yet to come narrows the possibilities down to what you read. Put another way, your future is unknowable, unless you look at it, at which point it becomes inescapable. The Schrödinger's cat of magic.

"Hurry up," she says. She pushes me with her eyes toward my own front door. The deadbolt slides out of place. "Oh, too late." My father throws open the door; he is fully dressed. Have I gone back in time? He looks ten years younger.

"*M'ijo*!" He embraces me and I know time has not reversed itself; there is strength in his limbs, but the tremble remains.

"Dad? Are you okay?"

"Yes, yes," he says. "Your little friends are here." Dominoes clink in the backyard accompanying the soulful trumpets of the *Buena Vista Social Club* soundtrack, played low enough so as not to disturb the neighbors.

"Who?" I say.

"*Los duendes*" (The elves).

Ceramic smacks onto our glass table. "Domino!" Tetch yells.

I try to push past my father but his fingers bore into my chest. "*Y tu amiga*?" (And your lady friend?)

"Carmen Espinoza, please meet my father, Tristan Diaz," I say.

"*Un placer*" (A pleasure), Carmen says and leans in. They kiss each other on the cheek.

"*Encantado*" (Enchanted), my father says. "*Adelante, por favor*" (Enter, please). He sweeps his arm behind him and Carmen enters. My father grabs my shoulder. "*Estas cojo. Te ves muy jodido*" (You're limping. You look fucked up).

"It's nothing," I say.

He furrows his brow but turns around to his guest. "*Algo para tomar*?" (Something to drink?) he says to Carmen.

"*Una cerveza, por favor*" (A beer, please), Carmen says. Carmen motions to a chair at the kitchen table, smiling. "*Se puede*?" (Can one?)

"*A la orden*" (At your command), he says to her request for a beer. Gesturing to a chair: "*Como no*?" (Of course).

"One minute," I say as my father pulls out a chair for Carmen. My father moves into the kitchen and fills a wooden bowl with plantain chips, setting them before Carmen, then pours a *Presidente* into a mug for her. I drop my lamp and doctor's bag at the foot of my bed and head to the backyard.

Clan Screwcap crowds around the table of the covered patio. Tetch and three other gremlins stand on the seats of the chairs and reach into the pile of dominoes, stirring the bones. The gathered gremlins hold open bottles of beer. One of them takes the lid off our garbage can, tosses in his bottle, and sways back to the crowd. "Archmagus!" Tetch says and throws up his arms. Clan Screwcap echoes him, lifting their beers.

I shush them. "What the Hell are you doing here, Tetch?"

Tetch scowls. "Your father was much more hospitable. The situation is resolved, is it not?"

"In no way!"

"Odd. The city is no longer saturated."

"The Chancellor is siphoning all of the magic. He plans to infuse everyone in the city. He wants everyone in the city to know what magic feels like."

Tetch takes a pull off of his beer and takes up two handfuls of dominoes. He holds them like a cop holds his tac-belt. "Funny how you won't do the same for us."

"Gremagus, it has only been a day!"

"And still we starve," he says, laying down the double-nine. "*La fea*!" (The ugly one). His clan whoops.

My father appears in the doorway behind me. "*Cállanze*!" (Be quiet!) he says, then looks at the dominoes. "*La fea*!"

"*La fea*!" the clan responds.

"*Te espera*" (She is waiting for you), my father says and motions me inside with puckered lips. My father has a beer in his hand as he hovers over Tetch. He watches their game in satisfaction. "*Dos Gardenias*" starts on the portable CD player set up on the planter. It is his favorite song, and he'd sing it to my mother occasionally. A rueful smile plays across his lips.

When was the last time he got dressed? Had company? Listened to music? Had the opportunity to play dominoes? Did anything but feed himself and stare sullen at the television? He looks so happy.

"Your father is quite the host," Carmen says as I enter the kitchen. She sips her drink and plucks a *platanito* from the bowl.

"Didn't know he still had it in him," I say. I crouch down and search under the sink until I find a fingerhole in one of the cabinet panels. The wood moves enough to reveal my father's stash. I grab a contraband bottle of Havana Club and hold the dusty vessel up to the light. It is the dark rum—not my preference—but I will have to make do. I pour myself a *Cuba Libre* and sip it. I look in the fridge and find a lime already cut into wedges. I twist a wedge above the drink, then drop it in.

"Isn't this nice?" Carmen says and leans back in her chair. "Old friends chatting. Dominoes in the backyard. A rejuvenated father."

"Don't act like you planned this."

"Can you be sure I didn't?" Her knowing smile.

I take a sip of my drink. "Have you seen what happens if Emérico wins?"

She licks the salt from her lips. "Then we all win. Even you."

"How much blood does that victory cost?" I see children in a burlap sack and a little girl shredded by her mother's misplaced shot.

"Some of that blood is on your hands," she says and crosses her legs. "I don't remember Emérico loosing a fairy-tale witch."

"Every family in the city will have that level of suffering thrust upon them."

"The price of progress is always the same, Pablo. Grow up."

"You sound like Emérico," I say. A cheer from outside. The back door opens. My father jaunts to the fridge and grabs fistfuls of bottles. "*Oye. Suave, viejo*" (Hey. Easy, old man), I say. He grunts. The door slams.

Carmen leans back in her chair and crosses her arms over her chest. "When was the last time he had guests?"

I tuck my upper lip into my mouth. I can feel the shadow of a mustache. "Not since the stroke."

"He's one man. Imagine the entire city just as happy. You above all people should know how gratifying magic can be."

"He's acting like this because of the elves." I grimace at her laughter. "Gremlins, I mean. The rest of the city is going to panic and burn. It might change some for the better. But for every Tristan Diaz, there is an Abram Orlov out there, who will use it to take advantage of others." I down my drink.

Carmen tucks a strand of hair behind her ear. "Final answer, then?"

"There is no other."

She checks her watch. "Well, all I can say is, you brought this on yourself." She stands up slowly, leans over the table, and turns her head to offer me her cheek. I stretch to kiss it. Carmen opens the front door and speaks over her shoulder. "If you want him to survive, take him to Jackson Memorial Hospital."

"Excuse me?" I say and stand.

As she closes the front door, she opens her umbrella. The back door flies open. I hear the handle bury itself in the drywall. "*M'ijo! Algo esta pasando!*" (My son! Something is happening!) my father says. I run outside. The dominoes have been abandoned. The gremlins have all crowded around my toolshed. Light spills out of the open doorway.

"Who told you you could go in there?" I say, approaching the shed.

The gremlins clear a path. I push through them and throw open the door. On the left, the workbench converted into a desk, covered in papers bearing sigils. Above it, the clear plastic drawers my father once used for screws and nails, now filled with different reagents. One naked bulb hangs from the centerline of the ceiling, its cord dangling like a noose. Tetch stands over one of his clanmates.

The cloak—if you can call those tatters such—hangs limply off of the gremlin's bony body. A steaming ball of ectoplasm hovers above his palm until it dissipates. At his feet, my disassembled lamp—every cold iron panel, screw, wraithglass pane, and filigreed strut are arranged on an old towel. He must have snuck into my bedroom while I was talking to Carmen. "Oh, fuck."

"It is fine, Archmagus. We'll make you a new one," Tetch says.

"I told you that *you* needed to make it! He won't understand!"

"Give him some credit, Pablo. He's my eldest son. He can handle it."

I rummage through the drawers until I find a vial of witch hazel. I snort it until my eyes water and try to focus my vision. The air shimmers into a kaleidoscope of color, and Tetch's son is mesmerized by it, pawing at it. "Tetch, can't you stop it?"

"Why would I?"

"Oh, no," Tetch's son says.

"What is it, Weir?" Tetch says.

"That can't be how it works," Weir says. "That just... doesn't make sense."

"What is he seeing, Pablo?" Tetch says, his hands hovering over his son's back, afraid to touch him.

"He's seeing me. All of me." When a gremlin dismantles a magical object, it glimpses the creator's deeply personal understanding of magic. One of two changes must occur: enlightenment or cognitive dissonance. The former elevates the gremlin to new heights of understanding and cunning; it becomes a gremagus, able to cast spells and make enchantments. The latter plunges the creature into obstinance and rage; it becomes a troll.

"This won't work! There aren't any moving parts!" Weir says and slams his hand on the counter. Bottles and vials tinkle from their shelves, spilling all over my papers.

"Tetch, do something!" I scramble to save my work. "How do you stop the transformation?"

"You can't," Tetch says, his eyes wide. "He has to work through it."

I crouch in front of Weir and tap him on the cheeks. "Weir. Weir! Look at me. Look at me! Stop looking at the magic!"

Weir scrunches his face. "It doesn't make sense. It's impossible."

"It does make sense, son," Tetch says. "You've seen him do magic."

"Not a lot of people can understand it," I say. "But I need you to try."

"It isn't like a machine," Weir says, looking at Tetch.

Tetch looks at me, gnawing his bottom lip. "Explain it to him, Pablo!" he says. His pleading gives me goose flesh.

How can I impart years of understanding to Weir in a sitting? Everything from PRC 1101 to NEC 4001 in... I don't even know how much time I have. Weir mentioned parts and machines. He can't get away from what he already knows. If he had taken apart one of Giorgio's wands, none of this would be happening.

"Listen carefully, and try to understand. Magic takes will, and will comes from belief. The germ of my belief began with my mother's death. I came to believe death was the sole absolute in the universe. Everything living has a one-way ticket back to non-existence. But there was something I couldn't reconcile with that belief: Emérico. How could he defy death, when the rest of humanity marches toward the grave?

"Then I realized the truth: we all defy death, just by existing. That was the key, Weir. Everything *will* die—that remains a fundamental truth. But *will* is strong enough to break that rule. Existence spits in the face of the one absolute of the universe." Tetch and I look at each other. In his eyes, there is fear—fear of what he sees in mine. A stream of magic floats too close to Weir's face. It condenses and crystallizes into a dust that tinkles to the floor.

Trolls are the antithesis of magic. Their very existence denies the possibility of magic and each denial feeds their size and strength while warping their minds and bodies. A troll's simple mind is limited to the comprehension of consumption, sleep, and violence. Their willful banality nullifies magic, converting it into worthless, brittle crystal.

"But what about the parts?" Weir says.

My pulse beats behind my eyeballs. I've done everything I can and he refuses the explanation. "That's tricky. Once you know what you believe, you can exert your will through practice—established systems of work. Like machines. The foci are the parts, and they are interchangeable, just like cogs and springs."

"Machines only work one way!" His face starts to shift, his chin and neck ballooning out.

I told Tetch to wait.

"Magic is different than a machine," Tetch says. "What you're trying to understand is the fuel. Pablo's ideas. His beliefs."

Too many metaphors and similes. He's already broken. I scan the room; the machete leans against the corner behind me.

"Pablo, please," Tetch says.

"You're a miracle, Weir," I say, trying to stand my ground, not understanding why I am failing to convince him. "We all are. We came from nothing. We'll return to nothing. But in the middle, you can do anything! Limit yourself to that one rule, and nothing else can rule you!"

Weir grabs his head and starts stomping around the room. I creep backwards, toward the machete. I could take off his head with one swing. But I'd be left holding a troll head and with his bereft father to console.

I could scalp a troll's head. The last item on my list of things to collect. *Remember the Bursar.* Carmen isn't the only one who has been sifting the seeds of time to see which will bloom.

Weir grabs his father with his ballooning hands. He's a foot taller now. "What lies do you believe, father?"

Tetch won't let his son go. "Weir, you're crushing me," he wheezes.

The blade of the machete clangs against the walls of the shed as I rip it from its peg. I rear back to strike down Weir. The troll roars at me and lets go of his father.

"No!" Tetch yells and jumps at me. He pulls on my arm with such force that I fall flat on my ass. I turn over, trying to scramble to my knees. Pain lances through my back and stomach. I expel rum and Coke out of my mouth and nostrils. I turn onto my side and look up at the troll: five feet tall and growing, fists clenched, arms tight with muscle. He must have stomped me.

And Tetch is gone. He abandoned me to the whims of his cannibal son.

Weir grows half a foot as he raises both arms, ready to crush me. The shed is too small. I won't be able to roll away. Cracks of multicolored light form under Weir's feet. He looks down. The floor gives way beneath him, revealing a swirling, rainbow tunnel. Dozens of tiny hands grab at his legs, trying to pull him back into Spiritus Mundi. Weir roars. He reaches into the tunnel, pulls a gremlin out, and throws him through a wall of the shed. He punches downward and connects with a meaty smack. He is almost large enough to completely plug the hole, so he tears at the floor and the tunnel, fighting for space.

The more he rages, the larger his muscles balloon. Half of him sticks out of the tunnel, but that half is as tall as he was when he stood ready to pound me into a paste.

They won't win. The whole clan couldn't drag him in. And he's distracted. I push myself to my feet and swing at the back of his head. He rears at the blow and bellows, exposing his throat. I drive the machete toward his neck. An arm the size of an I-beam slams into me, sending me flying back.

I hit the door and it crumples around me. I try to suck in air, but only manage a moaning gasp. My shoulder blades are numb. Maybe they broke. White spots form in my vision.

Weir manages to pull two gremlins from the tunnel, crushing one in his fist with a sound like crackling fire. With a grisly chomp, he decapitates the other.

I pull myself from the door. The gremlins below him are able to pull his chest and arms into the tunnel. All I can see are his shoulders and head, but the force of his struggling shakes my entire shed. Glass breaks all around him and muffled gremlin cries rise from the tunnel. I pick up the machete, put all my weight behind it, and lunge at his eye.

Weir stares at me with hatred until his body goes limp. The gremlins below try to pull him into Spiritus Mundi, but the portal closes too quickly, severing his head. I fall to my knees. I stare at the boulder of a head, a machete sticking out of one of its eyes, the skin graying, the purple tongue lolling out like a giant slug, saliva and blood pooling on the floor in front of me.

Remember the Bursar.

Something crackles behind me. I turn. Tetch stands in the doorway. The porchlight behind him renders him a shadow. "You monster," Tetch says. "We had him!"

"He killed three of you in an instant. He would have killed you all."

"That was my son!"

"Not anymore, Tetch. I'm sorry."

"Death is too good for you, Pablo Diaz. I will find ways to make you suffer." He jumps feet-first into a portal that closes before I can blink.

The adrenaline dies, leaving me an inheritance of pain. My shed lies in ruins. Everything, everyone is gone: my lamp, Tetch, Carmen. What do I have left?

"*Hijo?*" He's on the steps leading into the house.

"Help me up," I say. I brace myself between my father and my splintered bench, agonizing to my feet. Every step toward the house is a crucible. The patio is as bad as the shed. I'll never find all the dominoes.

My father tries to lead me into my bedroom. I put my hand on the frame of the door. "No," I say. "I can't."

"What else are you going to do? You can't even walk."

"Just leave me on the sofa."

My father grunts but he walks me over to the couch. He tries to ease me down, but I just let myself fall, almost pulling him down with me. He shuffles over to his recliner and his age returns to him. He turns on the T.V.

I close my eyes and try not to move. There's no part of me that doesn't hurt. But I deserve it. My every action wills this misery into being. I killed Weir. He had to die. But it didn't have to be me. And Carmen. How long will she be under Emérico's enchantment? I should have made her stay, tried to work on her. Then maybe I would have caught Weir. Maybe I could have freed her.

How am I going to fight Emérico if I can't walk? I can't even keep my eyes open.

The television volume rises. I lift my brows before I open my eyes. There's Melody on the television, the words "EN VIVO" in the bottom right-hand corner. She speaks in English, and then the Spanish voice-over begins. She repeats the words that woke me: Pablo Diaz.

"The police have the suspect, Abram Orlov, in custody. Dr. Pablo Diaz is wanted for questioning." Every word she says is going to echo from my father's mouth. "We have not been able to verify for Metro whether or not yesterday's events are directly linked to his involvement with the witch Baba Yaga, or the murder on the docks Sunday evening, but we strongly urge Dr. Diaz to turn himself in to the authorities peacefully and for any citizens with information to call Crime Stoppers."

"*Desgraciado*!" (Wretch!) my father yells.

"Dad, stop. She's working for the College. They are trying to frame me."

"*Que coño has hecho*?" (What the fuck have you done?)

The scrolling banner at the bottom of the newscast reads, "*La policia buscan el salvador de la arena*." (The police seek the Savior of the Sands.)

The College has been aiding the police and is telling them I summoned Baba Yaga on behalf of Abram Orlov. They are pinning every magical misery of the past day on me. So where are the police? Why is Melody making the announcement and not Richards or Sandobal or any other cop?

"Are you consorting with criminals?" he says.

"I took work from him. I had no idea he was a criminal."

He paces around the living room, running his hand through his hair. "The witch"—*la bruja*—"was Russian?"

"Yes, but—"

"Shut up! Shut up!" He grabs the side of his head. "This smacks of every kind of rashness. Stupidity. Laziness."

I seethe through my nose. He would collapse if I told him I took that job to pay his medical bills. "Take it back."

"Your mother and I didn't raise you to associate with criminals. Look at what you've done to your reputation. To the name I gave you!"

"I needed the work—"

"You have a job! To think that I felt proud of you this morning! You arrived, and I thought, 'That is my son. A hero.' You let me believe it!" He sweeps his hand behind him at the television. "This would have killed your mother!"

I don't know what overcomes me. The day. Emérico. Carmen. Rhea. Orcs. Gremlins. Orlov. Sandobal. Weir. "You don't know what it is to work three jobs just to chip away at a mountain of debt." I grimace as I rise to my feet. "You don't know what it's like to face other professionals in threadbare clothing while they make themselves rich." I limp toward him, his face reddening with every impertinent step. "You don't know what it costs to keep you alive!" I poke him in the chest. I have never touched my father without love.

He looks down, where I touched him.

He looks up at me, the skin of his face blood red.

He falls.

With a touch, I have given my father another stroke.

22
The Cost

"911. WHAT IS your emergency?"

"It's my father. He's unconscious."

"Is he breathing?"

"Yes."

"What is your address?"

I give it. I give it again when he asks me to repeat it. Then the cross street. I can hear the hollow sound of my voice. "Are you trained in CPR?"

"Yes. But he's breathing," I say.

"Count out the breaths for me, please. Say 'now' each time he inhales."

"Now. Now." A pause that makes me gulp. "Now."

"You need to turn him over on his side in case he vomits. If he does, you have to scoop out anything in his mouth with your fingers. You have to keep his airway clear."

"Okay."

"The ambulance is on its way, Pablo. You can hang up now. If the situation changes, you can call back."

"Okay. Thank you." I hang the receiver in its cradle on the wall.

My father retches onto the floor in front of him. No heave, just the slosh of a mop bucket spilling onto the floor. I run to roll him over. Bile and beer soak my knees and shins. I open my father's mouth and push his tongue aside, rooting amongst his molars to make sure no offending detritus proves mortal.

I kneel beside him, mute, wondering if my father will die if I go get a towel to clean up the mess. Strobing red lights pull me up from the floor and to the front door. One EMT jumps from the ambulance's passenger seat. She already has gloves on, and she's carrying a blue plastic toolbox. The other two techs unload a gurney from the back of the ambulance. Is that all the equipment they're going to use to save my father?

I rush to open the front door. "In here," I say, and the desperation makes me sick.

The woman kneels at my father's side and scans the room. She checks his breathing, pulse, blood oxygenation. "Tell me what happened."

"We were having an argument and he collapsed."

"Any history of heart disease? Diabetes? Fainting?"

"He had a stroke about a decade ago."

"Do you have a list of his medications?"

I run to the kitchen cabinet, the one where the orange vials stand like toy soldiers, and pull the list of prescriptions taped to the inside. The gurney barely fits through the door. The two techs roll my father onto a yellow plastic stretcher, then lift that onto the gurney. They raise the device with a metallic clack and begin wheeling my father away. "We're taking him to West Kendall Hospital," the woman says to me.

If you want him to live, take him to Jackson Memorial.

"No. Jackson."

"Sir, that is much farther."

"I know." I grab my pocket things—keys, wallet, cellphone—and lock up. The EMTs don't close the back of the ambulance until I get inside. I have to bend over to fit next to my father.

The tech in the back sticks a few sensors onto my father's chest. "L1," he says to the driver after checking a small panel. They gun the engines, but only turn on the sirens when they approach an intersection. Otherwise, we ride in silence. At some point, I slip my hand into my father's. Whatever synaptic maelstrom rages in him, it causes his fist to clamp down on my fingers. I wipe a line of drool from his face with my shirt sleeve.

He's dressed. I haven't seen him in anything but pajamas and slippers and a robe in years. Will he make it back from this one? How much of him will be left this time? But his grip is so strong. If he can pulp my fingers right now, surely he can still walk, talk, hold a hammer. He only gave up on his tools because he was too ashamed to keep going. He'll make it out of this one. The EMTs aren't even working on him.

He's fine.

The paramedics scramble out of the ambulance as soon as we arrive at the receiving bay. They pull me out of the ambulance. I stand by and watch them unload my father. They run the gurney across the concrete, through sliding doors that open automatically. I follow in silence.

My eyes dart to every corner of the emergency room. No one looks at me, or if they do, they avert their eyes before I can catch them. A cop reaches for his radio at the front desk.

"Sir?" This from a twenty-something in a lab coat and scrubs. At my nod, she leads me through the labyrinthine corridors of the hospital and motions to one of the rooms. "You can wait in here."

"Not the waiting room?" I ask.

"You have a lot of paperwork to fill out. Your father will be brought in here." She ushers me inside. The walls are ultra-white, antiseptic. The clipboard she lays on a thin counter strains to hold the stack of documents I have to fill out. Before she leaves, she asks for my father's name and birthdate.

I take a seat on a wooden chair with a green cushion, prop my elbows up on the counter, and hold my head in my hands until my fingers tingle. There's no comfort in the walls, in the chair, in the smell. It is an alien place, where you bring the sick, the maimed, the dying. And there's always paperwork.

I find my father's insurance card in my wallet and write until my hand hurts. I'm only halfway through the documents when two nurses wheel my father and his bed into the room, a doctor trailing them. They align the bed with the outlets on the back wall and situate two standing monitors on his left hand side. "Mr. Diaz? I'm Dr. Camillo," he says. He tries to walk me through what has happened to my father: the heart attack, the stroke, the stents, the vegetative state. "Do you have any questions for me?"

"Is he going to be okay?"

"It's too early to tell."

I don't even know what questions to ask. "How long…?"

"We'll have to wait and see," he says and extends a hand. I take it and he leaves. I sit back in the chair and stare. IV, feeding tube, diode clipped to his finger, oxygen in his nose, the intermittent beeps of the heart monitor.

A nurse appears. "Mr. Diaz?" I nod to her without taking my eyes off of my father. I hear her shuffle behind me. "I need this page right now," she says. She's holding the clipboard. I only glance at it. "His list of medications," she says.

"Right. Sorry." I retrieve the paper from my pocket.

"I'll give you a minute," she says and leaves.

I carefully scribe the medicines onto the page in my neatest script when a drop of water falls onto the pages. I look up at the ceiling. When I touch my face, I realize my own stupidity. The next time the nurse arrives, I give her the finished paperwork without meeting her eyes. I stand at my father's bedside. He grimaces and shifts his legs. There's some life in him yet. Some fight. I bring the chair to his bedside and have to pry his fingers apart to hold his hand.

They are still so strong.

I have never held my father's hand this long. His spotted skin is as thin as a latex glove. Dull, blue veins worm through his metacarpals. When did he get so old? Nurses keep wheeling other patients into the cavernous room. They're too busy to mind me as they enter, but each time they leave, they pause when they catch sight of me. I straighten out my shirt and run a hand through my hair. They're going to ask me if I need medical attention if I don't clean myself up. I push myself to my feet and regret it. My back has become the soprano in a chorus of pain. I limp out of the room, doubled over. The sign on the plastic wall: ICU3.

A massive, circular desk dominates the ICU floor, giving sight lines into every room. Eight people man it, typing away at computers, while two dozen others check-in at the desk briefly before hustling away to their tasks. The halls are filled with gurneys and the sounds of misery. I brace myself on the desk. "Where is the bathroom?"

The nurse's eyes widen when she looks up at me. She checks my wrists for an admittance bracelet before pointing down the hallway. "Thank you," I say and shuffle away.

Before I can reach the bathroom, a maintenance worker bursts through the doors of the ICU. Green flames wreathe his body. "Please, someone help me!" He keeps slapping himself and flailing his arms. Four nurses follow him, yelling at him about oxygen tanks, but keeping their distance. One in the front keeps bobbing on the balls of his feet, holding an aluminum blanket like a matador.

"Stop!" I say. There is a ringing in my ears afterward. I shuffle up to the man and the nurses back away. "You were in the dark, right? And just wanted light?" I say to Burning Man.

"How did you know?" he says.

Every novitiate learns this most common of transmutations. When you don't have an object ready to turn into a source of light, you just make yourself the object. "Save yourself the bills. It's just faerie fire. It'll dissipate in a few hours."

He squints at me. "You're Pablo Diaz."

I pray no one else heard him. "Yes."

Burning Man marvels at his arms a moment, then walks away from the ICU, followed by a single nurse. The three that remain mutter in a group.

Emérico has started. He's flooding the city with magic. The only thing saving people right now is the fact that it is the middle of the night and the city is on curfew. Most will be asleep. By sunrise, though, this hospital won't be able to handle all the new cases. It can't even handle the current ones: nurses and technicians are treating patients in the hallways.

Before I reach the bathroom, I find a blind alley between two of the ICU rooms. An EMT hunches over a body. He has two fingers on the patient's heart and two on his own. His lips move as he stares down at his tattooed arm.

"No!" I say. Hobble towards him but it is too late. The EMT crumples to the floor. A spot on his shirt spreads into a purple mass. I squat down next to him, heedless of the lament of my back and hips. "What happened?"

He looks up at me. "G-S-W," he says through gritted teeth. I survey the body on the gurney. There is an open bottle of rubbing alcohol between the victim's legs, a damp cotton ball beneath the gurney, and a rapidly-evaporating symbol drawn on the wall. I grab the alcohol. It isn't witch hazel, but I can will it to produce the same effect. I inhale the fumes, burning my sinuses, causing my eyes to water.

The ICU swirls with a rainbow mist. The tattoo on the EMT's arm pulses a deep red, and I can see the same symbol drawn on the wall: two snakes twined around a staff. The rod of Asclepius, god of healing and symbol of hospitals everywhere. A red spot floats above the sternums of the patient and the EMT.

When most people think of healing magic, they envision wounds miraculously knitting themselves shut, lifting ill-humors out of the body, and other such nonsense. The last thing they would think of is necromancy, but that is actually the only magic that can repair a body, living or dead. When it comes to the living, however, the only way to fix a wound is to transfer the damage from one body to another. Trauma can't be repaired without sacrifice. "What is this spot?" I say and point at my own sternum.

"Heart chakra. For healing," the EMT says.

I worry my bottom lip until I taste blood. "What do I do? Who do I tell?"

He inhales sharply and grabs the gurney. He takes my proffered hand and we both struggle to get him to his feet. He drapes his arm over me and points down the hallway. "Just leave me at the main desk." We two cripples make our slow way there, only to be swarmed. As they pull him from me, I spot the true horror.

"You can't make this shit up!" a teenager in a baseball cap and skinny jeans says, filming a gurney parked against a hallway wall. On it is a minotaur in a Dolphin's jersey emblazoned with a giant 13. "Dan Marinotaur! Tell them what happened!"

That is how it will spread. How the city will catch fire. How Emérico will win. When the masses wake up and start scrolling, tens of thousands of cameras will be live-streaming the apocalypse, inspiring a million more to try the unimaginable, to will their dreams and my nightmares into existence.

I limp back to ICU3 and lean over my father. So small. Thin. Sunken cheeks. Tubes everywhere. A rank smell makes me wonder if he hasn't shit himself. This is where I belong. I need to be here. I take a deep breath. "*Te quiero. Por favor, no te mueres. Tengo que trabajar*" (I love you. Please, don't die. I have to work).

I may never see him alive again. I walk away, ashamed by my own relief.

❁

Lights stutter to life as I enter the hallway outside of the ICU's double doors. The corridor stretches into darkness to my left and right, automatic lighting adopted as a cost-cutting measure. I try to remember the twists and turns we took to get here. I was too concerned with my father to pay attention.

I take the left-hand path. Along the corridor, lights shudder to life. A sound at the end of the hall: rhythmic clicking and wooden chimes rattling each other in the breeze. Gooseflesh spreads across my arms and scalp. I've heard the sound before, two days ago on Miami Beach.

I stop and wait. The clicks slow down.

I am breathing too loudly. I try to soften it, exhaling through my gaping mouth. The blood pulsing behind my eyes becomes louder, until my ears twitch with each beat of my heart.

One last click.

Baba Yaga's hut leans around the corner, as stealthy and as small as a toddler. Shocked, I cough so hard that my vision blurs. How did Baba Yaga get out? Would Emérico release her just to spite me? With all the magic in the air, all the weak and dying coming in, how long before she makes her first kill? How long before the hut towers over the hospital itself?

The chicken legs bound away under the lights. I throw myself after the hut, trying to give chase, but the best I can manage is a hobble. I suck in ragged breaths as I turn the corner. I hear my wheezing. Bile rises in my throat. The hut is so far away. It banks left and disappears down another hallway. By the time I make the turn, the stitch in my side feels like a spearhead. The hallway is empty. I bend over, bracing my hands on my knees. I can't fight her again. But I can't let the hut get away, either.

Ding.

The elevator doors to my left open. Elisa Sandobal stands inside, hands in the pockets of her windbreaker. She lifts an eyebrow. "That *thing* almost killed you when you were healthy," she says. "Did you actually expect to beat it if you caught up to it?"

I point my right hand down the hallway and try to speak, but the sound that comes out of me is somewhere between a bark and a cry. "Wheh!"

"It's an illusion," Sandobal says.

The antiseptic of the hospital, snuffed deeply through my nostrils, is enough to help me shift my focus. As the world becomes a kaleidoscope,

I see the magic hanging around me. I smell cigar smoke and feel the violence of the magic, like crunching teeth. The clicking sound emerges down the hallway. The hut comes into view, does a couple of Kazotsky Kicks—that mind-bending Ukrainian dance—and fades out of existence.

"Whose?" I say, but I can feel the answer. He knows me too well, knows that I would throw myself back in the path of that monster to save innocent lives.

Sandobal sticks her foot in the path of the elevator doors, halting them from closing. "Abram Orlov's."

I clench my jaw. Of course they brought him here; it is the closest hospital to his restaurant. He's tapping into the ambient magic. Otherwise, there's no way he could cast such a complex illusion and maintain control of it.

Elisa purses her lips and beckons me. "Get in." Lilac whisps curl away from Elisa's fingertips. She's in it now, too. She's gotten a taste. As if she wasn't dangerous enough. What spell did she cast?

I push on my knees to stand straight and hear a few too many pops. "I am in the middle of something, detective. But it was good seeing you." I start walking away.

"I found your car," she says. "At Gustanvil's Mortuary."

Sweat dapples the inside of my collar. "Of course. Yes. Gustanvil's. I was checking the wards." The excuse seemed brilliant a few hours ago. Now I recognize its fecklessness as soon as the words are out of my mouth.

"Sure. When you were done, did you happen to stop by any local restaurants? There's a real good one nearby. The Course."

"What do you want, detective?"

"I want you to get in this elevator."

"I don't think so. I have work to do."

"There's a squad car waiting at your home. More at the College. I'm your only way out of this, Pablo Diaz."

She could call off the manhunt. With her help, I could get to Emérico before dawn. Without it, I have to work against Emérico *and* the cops. But what if she's trying to trap me? I sidle past her into the elevator.

"Thank you," she says, swipes a security card, and hits the "29" button.

The elevator begins to rise. I peer at the button, try to suck down as much oxygen as I can. I smell sweat and cordite and the streets. It was stupid of me to expect perfume. She watches me in the reflection of the elevator doors. "I got to take some potshots at Yuri Orlov earlier. Funny thing is, the coroner tells me he died Tuesday afternoon."

"I don't know who that is."

She taps her lips. "I guess you've never met him. Living, anyway."

Ding. The doors slide open. "Let's go," Elisa says and marches out with all the subtlety of a hangman. She waits for me to exit the car.

I push myself off of the wall and limp forward. "We don't have much time, detective. Emérico is going to destroy the city."

Elisa smiles. "Really? He said the same thing about you." She walks down the hallway and knocks on a wooden door. A uniformed officer opens it and Elisa brushes past, but I recognize him as the cop who helped me yesterday in the Downtown Precinct, when Tetch and his gremlins were stripping the place for parts.

More than a decade of teaching have impressed upon me the importance of remembering names. "Officer Hernandez. Good to see you."

Hernandez smiles and extends a hand. "Archmagus Diaz."

I shake his hand. "This is not the greeting I expected."

He shrugs. "Maybe you can't believe everything the news tells you."

"Guess not." I shuffle through the door. Elisa sits in a massive armchair on the right side of the room. The walls are paneled with wood, a light is on in the *en suite* bathroom, and a writing desk has been positioned under a window. "This is very posh."

"It's for long-term patients. Transplants mostly," Sandobal says. "Close the door behind you."

I do so, and when I turn around, I find Orlov on the left side of the room, handcuffed to the bed, smiling. I try not to move. Should I be moving? I clasp my hands behind my back. I hiss at the pain.

"The floor requires a keycard to access, so there's no chance of this monster's goons getting in here to spring him," Sandobal says.

"How could they?" Orlov says. "You've jailed them all."

I should just escape. But I need Sandobal. Damn her. I grab the chair from the writing desk and plant it next to the door. "Do you remember yesterday's chaos?" I say to Elisa. "All of that was just a preamble to what happens at dawn."

"Then you don't have any time to waste," she says.

I grimace. "This is all your fault," I say to Orlov.

"I have done this for you!" Orlov says.

I run my tongue over my teeth. I flex my hands. Nothing this man has done has netted me a positive. "You've brought me as close to ruin as any monster I've dealt with."

"Shut up," Sandobal says. "His cousin killed two men on the pier Sunday night, booked it to the West Coast using his girlfriend's car, then showed up five hours ago at his restaurant to suicide by cop."

"That has nothing to do with me," I say.

Elisa smiles and reaches under Orlov's bed. She drags out a metal bedpan filled with water. My business card floats inside of it. "Are you sure? Because I think that you scried Yuri Orlov Monday night, just like I scried you tonight."

I look at the card the same way I might examine a final notice. The moment Sandobal needed to find me, there was enough magic in the air to do it, and she had Orlov to instruct her. He must have outlined my method.

Sandobal points at me. "Your scrying allowed him to kidnap his cousin, bring him back to Miami, and murder him. Then, Tuesday afternoon, you performed your puppet act and got Yuri to spill the beans about God-knows-what right before you went ten rounds with Baba Yaga and her bungalow. And five hours ago, you pulled Yuri Orlov's strings *again* and sent him into a SWAT team, trying to cover for *him*," she says and points at Orlov.

I want to respect her. She's dogged my steps and has me dead to rights. Instead, I imagine a gust of wind sucking her out of the nearest window. "What do you want?"

"I want you to stop. Just stop."

"The city is about to consume itself and—"

"The sun will rise, Pablo Diaz, same as it always does," she says. "Orlov and I have been talking, and we've come up with a solution to how I'm going to arrest *him*"—she jabs her finger at Orlov—"without arresting you, too."

"It's all very easy to solve," Orlov says.

I thought Orlov's money would solve all my problems, but it evaporated in the spotlight of Sandobal's investigation. Now here is Orlov again, playing a savior. *Playing*.

"Tell him," Sandobal says.

"This all began when Detective Richards said he could get around your methods. He said I could find out information from my dead enemies without being caught. To prove it, he murdered a bathroom attendant."

"Bullshit," I say. Richards is Elisa's mentor. He was the one to hire me as a consultant in the first place, and he has been promoted for it. He was the sergeant in charge of Elisa's homicide shift until Monday, when he was promoted to lieutenant.

"I thought the same thing," Sandobal says and jams her hands in her pockets. Yesterday, she thought I was a threat to all of Richard's cases; the glamour's off now.

Orlov smiles. "I have receipts. Phone logs. Pictures. When all of Richard's cases go to appeals, Detective Sandobal will still have me."

I thought she'd been hunting me. Turns out I'm just a nuisance keeping her from her real prey. She told me as much, once. I refused to listen. We all sit in silence for too long.

Sandobal crosses her legs. "I have to arrest Richards. And him," she says, pointing at Orlov. "When I do, he's promised to turn state's evidence."

"Da," Orlov says. "And you leave him out of it," he says, pointing at me.

Sandobal rubs her forehead. As if answering my stare, she says, "He'll serve some mandatory minimums, depending on the evidence presented, but the D.A. will probably cut him a deal."

I think about the illusion Orlov made. He knew he was torturing me. He's a predator. Yet here he is, laying down on the sword he's been avoiding his entire life. "What are you getting out of all of this?" I say to him.

"You are still to be my teacher," Orlov says. "And for my men."

"You're going to prison, Abram. You could be in there until you die."

"Ah, but if I live? What then?" There is mania in his eyes. "Something new."

"And that's enough for you?"

Orlov lowers his brow, tilts his head, and smirks. "It is everything."

They are waiting for me. What choice do I have? I nod.

Elisa stands. "Glad all of that is settled. Now, what about this chaos you're expecting?" She says to me. "What do you intend to do about it?"

The weight on my chest remains. To storm the College, I would need an army. Even if I raise the dead, as I did to the orcs outside McIntyre Grove, they would just be fodder. Without protection, the College's defenses will tear them apart. I need wizards. Orlov was so quick to learn, and with all the magic in the air, I might be able to teach a few people how to serve as guardians. "I have to stop the Chancellor," I say.

"Do you have a plan?" Elisa says.

Not so much a plan, exactly, as a series of half-formed, ill-conceived, and self-destructive gambits. The perfect capstone to the last three days. I explain this 'plan' to Detective Elisa Sandobal of Miami-Dade Homicide and Abram Orlov, disgraced head of the Orlov Crime Family, my last two allies in this world. I tell them how Emérico uses the conduits. I outline how I could disrupt one of them, and how that would help me storm the College.

What I don't share is the cost of all this madness: less than a pin's fee, if the Bard is to be trusted.

23
Field School

THE CLOCK ON the wall reads 3:42 a.m. The sun will be up in less than four hours. Emérico's Armageddon won't be heralded by trumpets and the breaking of seals but by tens of thousands of retweets. Any person could throw out an *abracadabra* or snap their fingers or level a finger gun and *poof*, fireworks.

Officer Hernandez appears at the door of Orlov's hospital room, pushing in a wheelchair. He moves to Orlov's bedside. Orlov hisses his way out of the bed and lands in the wheelchair with a loud exhalation. "Thank you, officer. So helpful," says Orlov, grinning.

Hernandez, to his credit, doesn't engage.

"Let us proceed to the police station," Orlov says. Sandobal shakes her head, but motions Hernandez toward the door.

Hernandez has to brace the wheelchair against his thigh to get it moving and out of the suite. Sandobal keeps trying to make calls until her phone signal disappears as we enter the elevator. Sandobal, Hernandez, and I watch the red digital numbers click down from 29 to L. Only Orlov doesn't look up. He hums softly to himself, taps one foot against the footplate, stares at his reflection in the polished brass door. He catches me watching him and gives me a wink. He's actually excited.

When we reach the street, Hernandez shoves Orlov into the backseat of his squad car, behind the driver's seat, and slams the door before tossing the wheelchair in the trunk. He throws himself behind the wheel and squints up in the rearview at Orlov. Elisa climbs into the passenger seat, busy with her phone. I sit behind her.

The journey to the Downtown Police Station takes less than ten minutes. The cruiser's abused suspension sags as we climb the spiral ramp and enter the motorpool. "The news isn't good," Sandobal says to me. "Besides Hernandez, I can only get four officers to come out."

Six cops, myself, and a half-assed plan are all that stand between Emérico and Miami. "They won't be enough."

Orlov leans forward. "Go get Bogdan and the rest. That is twelve more."

Elisa turns around, glares at Orlov for a moment, and then turns on me.

I purse my lips. "We need them."

Elisa kicks open the door as she gets out of the squad car. She manhandles the wheelchair out of the trunk and opens the backdoor for Orlov. "Out."

"You'll have to help me," Orlov says. He shifts his weight, rocking the chassis. He pulls himself out of the backseat with his good arm and Elisa guides him into the chair. He lands, panting, and says to me, "We'll be back shortly."

"Like Hell," Elisa says and slams the back door shut. She and Orlov disappear into a hallway beneath an elevator sign.

I release a breath I didn't know I'd been holding. The extortion, coercion, manipulation—all of it was just wheeled into a police station. The seat of the police car doesn't seem so rigid any more. "How long do you think she'll be?" I say to Hernandez.

"Not long. Orlov's men aren't under arrest, they're just being interviewed." Hernandez doesn't turn around. Instead, he watches me in his rearview. "You think it's a good idea to arm these criminals?"

"No choice. Wake me up when she gets back," I say. "

"How can you sleep?" Hernandez says.

"Field napping," I say, taking the phrase from the U.S. military. I lean my head on the cool glass and close my eyes. I hear Hernandez clicking away on his phone for some time, but each keystroke could be leaping sheep for how long I listen.

Sandobal pounds her fist on my window, jumpstarting my heart. She throws open the door when I sit up and thrusts her hand at me. We clasp hands and she yanks me out of the back seat. My right shoulder and hip are on fire. I try to blink away sleep, taking in my surroundings.

Orlov sits in his wheelchair behind the police car.

An icy fist grips my heart. "I thought you were booking him," I say.

Elisa shoves her fists into her jacket pockets. "His men refused to follow me up here unless he was allowed to be a part of your little magic show."

Orlov's presence is a cancer on this plan. When this all goes to shit, he'll be the one walking away.

Elisa sees my horror. "You were the one who told me how much we needed them." She moves to join Hernandez, who leans against a nearby SUV, and greets the four other police officers who are with him. They wear kevlar vests, fiddle with their firearms, and make a grand show of never looking at the nearby Russians.

Orlov's men huddle in a pack two cars away, smoking cigarettes, mumbling, occasionally laughing, always watching the police.

I limp between the two groups. "When the sun comes up, yesterday is going to feel like a joke. Three million people casting spells will cause absolute mayhem. People will get hurt. We are the only ones in the city who understand the problem enough to stop what is coming." I swivel my head between both groups. I feel the tremble in my knees, so I pace to keep it from showing.

"Right now, you're all juiced up. It won't take much effort for any of you to cast a spell." I rub my chin, finding stubble. "Problem is, you need to practice to achieve the desired effect.

"The goal of today's lesson is simple: create a shield to protect you and those around you. Nothing more, nothing less. Who's the best shooter?" I say, looking at the policemen.

In unison, the men turn to Elisa Sandobal.

"Detective," I say, walking into the middle of the motorpool, "do you have your sidearm?" I wait for her nod. "Please, stand in front of me. The rest of you,"—I sweep my hand at cops and gangsters alike—"back up against the cars."

I raise my hand, brandishing Orlov's phone. "This is not *my* phone, but right now, it is the single most important thing I have on me. This is my lifeline, the only way we're all getting through the next three hours together. If I lose this, I have nothing. I know I have to protect it. Clear?"

I look around, holding eye contact until I have the assurance I'm looking for—a nod, a thumbs-up, a spoken "yes." "Now, detective, I need you to shoot this phone out of my hand." I hold the phone away from my body.

"Absolutely not. Even if I trusted you to stop a bullet, I'd still have to take a drug test and fill out a report explaining why I discharged my firearm."

"You have to do this," I say. "You all need a demonstration, if you're going to learn this tonight." My knees have turned to water. A bead of sweat rolls down the middle of my back. "Clock's ticking, detective."

"Diaz," Hernandez says from my right.

"Yes?" I turn to look at him.

"Catch," he says and hurls a knife at me.

I watch the knife tumble end-over-end as it flies through the air, the blade flashing orange in the motor pool lights. A second of pure panic flutters through my chest, between my legs.

If I die, this city burns, and my father with it.

A bubble of blue light expands around me. The knife sticks in the haze as if it had buried itself in a wooden target. I take a breath, let the fear melt away. "Thank you, officer."

"You're welcome," Hernandez says.

I turn so that everyone can see the knife floating in midair. "Kinetic shield. Basic effect. I need each of you to find something that means something to you, something that makes you think about protection. Show me, and then we'll get to work." I let the shield drop, and the knife clatters to the floor.

Of the Russians, two of them show me crosses, which I expected, but the third has a photo. "What is this?" I say.

"My parents," the Russian says.

"Why will this work?" I say and reach for the photo.

He moves it out of my reach to look at it, through it, beyond it to the realm of memory. "No one took care of me like they did."

"What is your name?"

"Stepan Pavelvich," he says.

"Very good, Stepan."

As I approach the officers, a cop asks me, "Will this work, professor?" He holds up a jagged chunk of material that looks to be composed of several different layers. There's a bullet hole in its face and strings of fiber sticking out from the point of impact.

"This is broken. Why do you think it will work?" I say.

"It saved my life," he says.

"And you kept it?"

"It saved my *life*," he repeats.

I nod to him and read his name tag. "It may happen again, Sergeant Buitrago."

"What about you?" I say to Elisa.

She holds up her badge. "They call it a shield for a reason."

I walk back into the middle of the motorpool. Good talismans all around. "I tell my students on the first day of class that there are two ways to think about reagents: training wheels and skis. Training wheels help you learn to balance; skis help you reach the bottom of the mountain faster.

"What you're holding is even stronger than a reagent, because it isn't just an ingredient. It matters to you. We call these foci because they help you focus your will. You need to visualize the reason you're holding these items, the feeling. Why are they important to you? Did they protect you? Do you need to protect them? Those feelings, your attachments, your belief in their power, will fuel your own magic. As we practice, the foci function as training wheels. When we get to the College, they will be your skis."

I look at myself in the reflection of a car window. I should be tired. But I'm alert. Pedagogy is a hell of a drug. "Spread out. Six feet between each person and stay away from the cars. Everyone needs to give it a try. Once you all get it, we can leave."

The motor pool becomes a laboratory as my newest students fill the lanes between the rows of cars. I limp around, watching them. "With your focus in hand, and in your mind, picture what makes it so important to you. Try to find the feeling you attach to it—security, love, hope, whatever it may be. Then, visualize the shield you wish to create as a barrier *made* of that feeling. *Push* the feeling out into the world. It may help some of you to think about the strongest part of your body as the epicenter of the bubble."

Red light explodes around us. Metal shrieks and tears. The cops and gangsters duck in unison. We all turn to the first shield caster. Abram Orlov sits in the center of a lambent red bubble. The trunk of Hernandez's squad car has been crushed like a soda can.

"I told you to get away from the cars!" I say.

"My apologies," Orlov says.

"God damn it!" Hernandez yells. "That's my ass right there!"

Lights flash again—white and gold. Undeterred by Hernandez's outburst, Stepan and Elisa produce their own shields. "Very good," I say. "The rest of you, don't get discouraged. Find the feeling inside of yourself, then throw it out around you."

Purple, blue: Bogdan and Hernandez. "Yes, yes! Excellent!" I know it is naïve to hope this will work, that Emérico won't just levitate me up to his office and drop me, but each flash feels like a victory. "If you're having trouble, try closing your eyes, counting your breaths, and kneading your focus in your hand." A disco erupts around me. "Hands if you haven't been able to practice yet. Is that everyone?"

They congratulate each other, marvel over their shields, whoop.

"How do you stop it?" Bogdan says in the center of his purple bubble of light.

"You can pull it back into yourself, or just let it go," I say. One by one, the lights go out. I check the cell phone's clock. "We need to get going."

Elisa moves toward Orlov's wheelchair. "Give me your hands," she says.

Orlov doesn't say a word, doesn't smile. He presents her the cuffs.

Sandobal finds the key on her key ring and undoes one cuff, then locks it onto her own wrist. "Time's wasting, teach. What's the plan?"

It takes a while to convince Sandobal to use department vehicles. Eventually she turns over three paddy wagons: two cops and four Russians to each van. Lastly, Hernandez finds me an old Crown Victoria that he says no one will miss.

It is still dark when four vehicles exit the motor pool toward an uncertain destiny, fueled by nothing more than the words of a sleep-starved madman.

24
Grievances Foregone

THE CITY STREETS are hurricane empty.

Untenanted police cruisers stand sentinel on the highway every two miles. Strobe lights fill my cabin as I pass. I turn on the radio. Every station plays the same message: "This is a state of emergency. Curfew is in effect until further notice. Shelter in place." The message then repeats in Spanish and Haitian.

A fine mist dapples my windshield, melting the orange cityscape into an impressionist panorama.

I slap my cheeks hard enough to sting, trying to fight back sleep. Even the blaring tones of the emergency broadcast do little to combat the anesthetic of rolling concrete.

Will he make it to dawn? I could die and never see him again. Worse, I could live and never see him again.

How long have I been running away from his death?

How much farther can I get?

I try to focus on the task at hand. Anything to get my mind off my father.

Six Conduits around the city channel energy to Emérico. He's stored all of the siphoned magic at the College, most likely in the Well, but possibly in the frame of the building, or even his soul cage. Right now, he's reversing the flow, forcing the magic into every person in the city. If I could tap into one Conduit, I could raise an army.

Which Conduit, though? There's the rub.

I have visited three of them already. One of the Conduits sits at the Plaza of the Tropics. Rhea guards one in her backyard in North Miami. Giorgio has floated another hundreds of feet over the Bird Road Art District.

When Nick Russo brought up the map of Miami two days ago—before the mermen attacked—I glimpsed enough to guess at the other locations. Melody would have had hers installed at the Telemundo building in Doral. Carmen likely has her Conduit in Hialeah, which would give her the most coverage over the city's northern and central corridors.

Nick would blast me. Rhea would overwhelm me. Giorgio captured me yesterday. Melody's illusions would take hours to unravel. It won't matter where Carmen's is—she'll always have foreknowledge of my arrival.

That leaves only Georgina Desmond, Head of Abjuration.

If Emérico wants to break me, she's the only archmagi who could do so.

A month into my first semester of college, I was drowning.

My first academic advisor, to whom I was more number than name, had enrolled me in fifteen credits worth of general education courses. I had let her because I didn't know better. It was only five classes, after all. High school had made greater demands of me.

Midway through the semester, a column of C's assaulted me when I opened my grade report. I understood "C," was quite familiar with it. A year ago, it meant I needed to get my act together, pay attention in class, do all my homework, and actually study.

Only, I thought I had my act together. I never missed class. I spent my nights and weekends poring over my notes and rereading all the required materials.

Most damning of all, one of those accursed letters stood next to PRC 1101.

Disturbed, I approached a librarian, clearly another undergrad on work study. He was highlighting every line of a chemistry textbook and did not look up at me until I coughed.

"Can I help you?" he said, pushing up his glasses with his middle finger.

"Yes. I need to find a study group."

"Postings are in the second floor lounge, by the small group rooms."

"Yes, I know. I have been there."

He tapped the line in his tome to which he wanted to return. "Then what is the problem?"

"I can't find a study group for PRC 1101."

His Adam's apple bobbed as I heard him swallow. "You need to go to the library in the tower—Santa Inés Hall. Sorry if I was rude. I was reading," he said, and swept his free hand over his book.

"Yeah, no worries. Thank you." I hitched up my bookbag and made my way across campus. Santa Inés Hall is the southernmost building on campus. By the time I reached it, I could feel sweat pooling in all the undesirable places.

Small groups crowded the walkway leading to the carved doors and leering gargoyles. The huddles stared or mumbled. The most daring would egg on one of their members to try the doors. The wary would approach, only to have their bookbags open of their own volition, spilling their contents, or have their caps blown off their heads.

For students who actually belonged, the doors would fly open and slam shut once they entered.

They had opened for me on the first day of class, but something strange had been happening since. If I was alone, one door would slide forward—just a crack—so that I had to slip my hand in to pull the door open. During this little struggle, I could feel the grain of the wood under the brass panels. I felt more than heard the sigh when I would close the door behind me.

Dolores sat at the front desk, flanked by her two undergrad assistants, officious as a judge.

I loosened the straps on my bookbag and mopped my brow with my hand, wiping the offending sweat on my jeans. "Excuse me, ma'am?"

Dolores glanced up from her computer screen, sizing me up over the rim of her glasses. She typed something into the computer. "How can I help you, Mr. Diaz?"

I pursed my lips. This woman remembered my name after orientation, despite never having had a conversation with me. "Does the library have study groups?"

"For PRC 1101? Yes," she said. "Library starts on the third floor, but tables are up on the fourth. And don't you ever go to those general advisors again. The College has its own." The phone rang. "Is there something else you need?"

I wanted to tell her it was all too much, that I couldn't balance work and study, that my father's demands on my time were ruining me. I only managed a weak, "No. Thank you, ma'am."

"Call me Dolores. You're welcome."

"Dolores." I nodded. "I will remember."

"I know."

Back then, the atrium was more dungeon than cathedral. My footfalls rebounded between the stone floors and rafters, each one an accusation. *Failure. Impostor. Failure. Impostor.* Is this why the doors didn't open fully for me anymore?

Shelves lined the walls of the fourth floor library, with breaks at the four cardinal compass points. Faux-gas lamps decorated the northern and southern alcoves, illuminating the large leather chairs beneath them. The northern shelves held books, while the southern shelves were stacked with scroll tubes—some leather, others wood, and a few metal.

Each table was an island of light in a sea of darkness, illuminated by a hooded, stained glass lamp. There was a folded place-card at each table announcing which class was meeting.

The twelve chairs at the PRC 1101 table were occupied. At least thirty other students were standing and scrawling notes as the seated few spat out tidbits of information helter-skelter. I checked my phone. I only had an hour before I had to meet my father to help him clean up his current job site. I took out a legal pad and began recording any facts that made it out of the hubbub.

"This is for PRC 1101?" a voice whispered behind me. She was my height and beefy. Her hair was tied back in one big afro puff. She wore an FIU singlet under sweatpants, and was carrying a bookbag and a gold-and-blue duffel.

"Yes, but it's chaos," I said to her.

"I'm not standing for an hour. I have practice."

"Wrestling?" I said and pointed to her singlet.

"Excuse me? I am a *lady*," she said. "I toss hammers."

I checked my watch. Fifteen minutes. I was late. "You think they'll be here later?"

"I will be. Is your major practical arts?"

"Yeah," I said. "You?"

"Uh-huh. You've been to every class?"

"Every one."

"Eight o'clock, then. We'll find our own kind," she said and shouldered her bags.

"Pablo, by the way," I said, extending a hand.

Her grip was iron. "Georgina."

My father's van was idling in the driveway. I threw my bike in the house and hopped in the passenger seat. He was white-knuckling the steering wheel.

"*Que te paso?*" (What happened to you?)

"*Nada, papi. Tuve que estudiar*" (Nothing, dad. I had to study).

"*El acuerdo era que llegarías a tiempo*" (The agreement was that you would be on time). He reversed out of the driveway.

"*Perdóname*" (Forgive me).

"*Quieres seguir estudiando?*" (You want to keep studying?) He hit the gas a little too hard, throwing me against the seat.

I put on my seatbelt. "*Claro*."

"*Pues no me eches a mierda*" (Then don't throw me to shit).

I refused to show up at the College with sawdust in my hair and grime under my fingernails, so I was late to our first meeting.

Georgina waved me over when she saw me.

She sat at the head of the table, though there were a few empty seats. "I thought you wanted to be a practitioner."

I took a chair and began unpacking. "Nothing I want more in this world."

Georgina cleared her throat. "Everyone, this is Pablo. He'll be adding his insights to our little cabal." Her island lilt and sing-song prosody crept in as she tried to lead.

"What day are you on?" I said.

"One," someone at the table said.

"Share what you got. We'll fill in the gaps," Georgina said.

"Sure," I said, the word scraping my throat. I flipped my legal pad open and began rattling off everything I could from the first class. I skipped through pages of notes from other classes until I came to the scraps of information I had collected in the afternoon. A few people at the table scribbled the odd note here and there, until I could hear blood pounding in my ears. No one spoke.

"Okay, well," Georgina said, unclicking her pen, "that was a good overview. Who wants to take over?"

The scratchings of graphite cascaded around me as someone took up the call. I tried to keep up, but it was hard to concentrate. What had I said? What had I *not* said? Why are all of their notes better than mine? Were we really taking the same class?

We got through four weeks in a little under four hours. It was close to midnight when the table began its exodus, but Georgina tore a sheet of paper from her notebook and asked for everyone's e-mail addresses, promising a mailing list.

I made a show of packing up my things until we were alone. "I just wanted to say thank you for including me."

"No problem," she said, reading over the list.

"Do you think there will be other meetings? Weekends?"

"I have practice and work outs and studying for more classes than just this one," she said, drumming her fingertips on the tabletop.

"Yeah, of course. Sorry," I said. "It's just... I really want to be good at this."

"Are you always going to be late?" she said.

Making excuses to my father was a pastime, the price I paid for room and board. "I have to work for my father. He's a carpenter. By the time I get home, there's barely enough time to shower." My stomach gurgled, pleading my case.

"If it's worth doing, it's going to take time." She put her notebook into her bag and slid something across the table.

I caught it under my hand: some kind of fruit bar. "Thank you," I said, tearing the wrapping, taking slow, purposeful bites to keep from wolfing it down. "My notes were useless."

"Almost completely." She fetched one of her many notebooks from her pack, turned with precision to a pocketed divider, and plucked a printed flyer from it. "Without discipline, you'll get nowhere." She handed me the piece of paper.

I read it over. An advertisement for *Learning Resources* from the library's *Center for Academic Success*. The kind of bullshit I had been ignoring throughout high school: note taking, study skills, memory, procrastination. "How are you so good at this?"

She scoffed. "I actually read. Start there," she said and pointed to *Reading and Study Strategies*.

"I will."

"See you next week," she said, and stomped off into the darkness.

When I got home, I read through most of the website. I was taking what I thought were notes until I read the *Taking Notes* section, at which point I crumpled up every page I had filled with garbage and tried Cornell Notes. I didn't go to bed until close to three. I changed my alarm, sacrificing thirty minutes of precious sleep to give myself time to make lunch and pick up a *colada*. I still hit the snooze once, which forced me to hustle through the morning, but I was the first one in class.

Two years later, Georgina came within striking distance of making the Olympic team. FIU had been chosen as the site for the state competition.

The day was made for glory. Waves of clouds afforded respite from the sun. By the afternoon, the shadow of Santa Inés Hall was creeping over the lip of the track and field stadium.

Georgina surveyed the stands. She waved at me when she found me and entered the throwing cage. As she padded around the circle, the clouds parted and the sheen on her shoulders glowed.

She took the grip of the throwing hammer in both hands, held it at her waist, and let the head hang at ankle height. She allowed the head to pendulum twice and then twisted her torso in a massive arc, swinging her arms overhead, drawing a full circle with the weight. Twice she twisted, putting the weight in her orbit, and then she began spinning.

Once, twice, and released right into the cage.

Foul.

It was her third throw of five and her first foul of the meet. She came out of the circle watching her feet. Droplets fell from her nose, and I knew they weren't sweat.

I ran down from the stands. "Georgina!"

She snapped her head in my direction. Her face contorted. She ran to me, favoring her right arm, and buried her face in my shoulder. I almost lost my footing beneath her. "I heard it pop," she said.

Between her red eyes and quivering chin resided all the misery life could throw at a person.

I spoke without thought. "If you qualify for nationals, when would you have to throw again?"

She had to choke down sobs to answer. "Middle of July, maybe." That was four months away.

Rhea McIntyre, in Introduction to Conjuration, had dispelled the myth of magical healing. But Intro to Necromancy had revealed a loophole: damage could be transferred from one living body to another. "What if I held onto the tear until the meet is over?"

"You would do that?"

"I mean, you'll take it back, right?"

"Of course!"

"Let's go, then. You're up in nine minutes."

"My necromancy is terrible, Pablo," Georgina said.

"Mine isn't."

We escaped into the tunnels of the stadium and found a family restroom. I used a piece of charcoal to draw a circle of sigils around Georgina's shoulder. I tried to be delicate, but the need for precision forced me to press down more than once. I saw her eyes roll back into her head.

"Almost there," I said. I sprinkled salt from my mother's jar into the drawn circle and onto my own shoulder, then started chanting the old nursery rhyme my mother would employ to heal scraped knees and elbows. "*Sana, sana, culito de rana. Si no sana hoy, sanará mañana*" (Heal, heal, little frog's ass. If it doesn't heal today, it will heal tomorrow).

"Stop," she said and put her hand over my mouth.

I tried slapping it away. "Are you fucking crazy? I'm in the middle of the spell."

"Don't finish it," she said. Tears rolled over her cheeks, met at her chin, and fell to her chest.

"George, this is your last chance," I said. Her classes put her a year ahead of me, about to graduate.

"It doesn't matter. I can keep throwing. But not if I cheat."

"How is it cheating? It's not like I'm making you stronger."

"No one else gets a personal healer, Pablo." She stood up. "No cutting corners."

I followed her out of the tunnel and took my place in the stands. My breathing was shallow. I felt the heat of the stadium as Georgina walked up to the judges' table. Her last two throws were marked as giant X's on the scoreboard.

If it meant so much to Georgina, how could she refuse my offer? If it meant so little, why did she continue to compete? The athletic trainer came up to her and began scrambling for bandages. Her teammates approached her individually, until they swarmed her. They patted her on the back, in time with her heaving.

I couldn't watch. The shadow of Santa Inés Hall had reached the throwing circle.

The Sunday before I graduated, I did everything as Georgina had coached me. I bought my father's favorite from La Carreta, acquired a smuggled bottle of Havana Club from the shadiest liquor store on Eighth Street, and set the table.

"Papá, tenemos que hablar" (Dad, we need to talk). I took my seat and motioned to his chair across from mine.

"*Hoy no es lunes*" (Today isn't Monday). He began forking the meatballs, breaking the monstrosities into massive but edible chunks over their bed of rice.

I poured us rum and Cokes, adding a twist of lime. A drop of juice flew into my eye. "*¿Y esa botella?*" (And that bottle?)

"*Una celebración*" (A celebration).

I watched him chug half of the drink to wash down the meat.

"*Voy a empezar a trabajar*" (I'm going to start working).

He stared at me, chewing methodically, thoughtfully, patiently. "*Ya tienes trabajo*" (You already have a job).

"*Para la universidad*" (For the university).

"*No entiendo. Explícamelo*" (I don't understand. Explain it to me).

I gripped the seat of my chair. I had yet to take a bite of my *pan con bistec,* nor had I taken a sip of my *Cuba Libre*. "*Ya no puedo trabajar para ti*" (I can't work for you any more).

"*¿Por qué?*" (Why?)

"*Porque necesito tiempo para estudiar. Para realizar investigaciones*" (Because I need the time to study. To conduct research).

"¿Y ellos te pagarán por eso?" (They're going to pay you for that?)

"*Es cierto*" (That's right).

"*Entonces puedes empezar a pagarme el alquiler, ya que prefieres las brujas a tu propio padre*" (Then you can start paying me rent, since you prefer witches to your own father).

"*¡No es así!*" (It's not like that!) I searched for something to keep him at the table. "*¿No vas a terminar de comer?*" (Are you not going to finish eating?)

"*Eres bárbaro. No me apetece*" (You're a barbarian. I don't have the stomach). He slammed the door to his room.

As teaching assistants, Georgina and I shared an office on the second floor of the tower. We were both charged with the introductory courses while simultaneously working on our respective doctoral theses. Georgina still threw hammers, but her newfound love for yoga had slimmed her down. She could still toss me across the room if she so desired.

I paced in front of the nascent schematic for Thanatopsis, which I had been applying to a whiteboard all morning.

"Back to work, Emérico, Jr.?"

I had never told anyone how the Chancellor saved me, but whenever I turned my attention to the diagram, Georgina would take shots at me, implying that I wanted to be him. "Why should he be the only one who gets a sword?"

Georgina held up one hand, as if weighing an orange. "Centuries old Lich." She then extended her other palm. "Cuban-American teaching assistant." She bobbled her hands like a juggler. "Something's off."

"We're not all capable of having spells named after us," I said. Georgina's thesis, articulating a channeled and malleable dome of protection, was under consideration as an addition to higher-level abjuration courses. They were calling it *Desmond's Oubliette*.

"No, I suppose not," she said, smirking.

"Well, I do believe I am done here," I said, stepping back from the schema, folding my arms across my chest.

"Oh, really?"

"It's just a plan, of course. But I think I've finally nailed it."

"Let me see," she said and nudged me aside. She pointed to the pommel and the list of ingredients. "Damn, my necromancy is rusty. I get wood from a tree that has fed on the dead, but why would you need the leather of a murderous bull? Are you using this on people?"

"If I'm trying to replace two high rituals, why not go for the hat trick?"

"Come again?"

"Well, if I am replacing the ritual to enter Nox, as well as the exorcism ritual, why not also use the sword to reanimate the dead?"

"Pablo, that is grotesque. What if you lose it?"

"Then I'm shit out of luck."

"You make something like this, you're bound to make some enemies, too." She took her seat and threaded her fingers behind her head. "Just because you make it with your hands doesn't mean Tristan is going to forgive you."

"No, I suppose not." I sat across from her. "But it would be nice."

"We've only been friends for six years. What do I know?"

I phoned my father before my return flight from Madrid. He insisted he could pick me up, but I told him I would take a taxi home. I didn't want him to forego sleep. He told me I was throwing away money. We left it there.

I carried my suitcase over the threshold at one o'clock in the morning. All the lights were off. I crept to my room, weighing every step, lay my suitcase on my bed, and shut the door before turning on a light.

I opened my suitcase. Thanatopsis nestled amidst the turmoil of laundry. I lifted it with both hands by the scabbard, pushing the blade out an inch with my thumb on the crosspiece. In theory, it was perfectly safe to handle the grip. In theory. Despite the visual buzzing of the metal, it made no sound.

I lay on my twin bed with Thanatopsis at my side, staring at the ceiling until I heard my father stirring. I waited for the creak of his floorboard before getting up.

"*Hola, papi*" (Hello, dad).

"*Imbécil. ¿Quieres darme un infarto?*" (Idiot. Do you want to give me a heart attack?)

I gave him a hug and a kiss on the cheek. "*Te quiero enseñar algo*" (I want to show you something).

"*Vaya. Tengo que irme.*" (Get out of here. I have to go).

"*Dame dos minutos*" (Give me two minutes).

"*Voy hacer el café*" (I'm going to make the coffee).

I brought Thanatopsis to the kitchen table and had to wait for the smell of Bustelo before my father would turn around.

"*¿Quieres?*" (Do you want?)

"*Por favor*" (Please).

He laid a double shot of espresso in front of me but did not sit. Only then did he allow his eyes to fall on my creation. "*¿Que coño es eso?*" (What the hell is that?)

"*Mi proyecto*" (My project).

"*Una arma.*" (A weapon.)

"*Es más. Es una herramienta. Lo construí. Cada parte. Hasta forjé el metal*" (It is more than that. It is a tool. I built it. Every part. I even forged the metal).

He picked up the scabbard, poring over the craftsmanship. The wood of the sheath and leather of the grip reflected the light of the lamp overhead. But the metal of the handguard buzzed visibly. "*Ni siquiera puedo mirarlo. Me molesta los ojos*" (I can't even look at it. It hurts my eyes).

He gulped another shot of coffee, rinsed the cup, and left.

I was in my seventh floor office, grading final lab reports for NEC 4001, when someone knocked on my door. The only things hanging on my wall were my diplomas, Thanatopsis, and a photo of my parents and me at Tropical Park. Beyond the frosted glass, the light in the hallway focused Georgina's silhouette.

"Hello, hello," I said. "Come in."

She opened the door and leaned on the frame. "*Still* grading?"

I leaned back in my chair. "What's up?"

"Nothing. Just wanted to see how you're doing." She picked at the door frame.

"Come on," I said. "You know how much I have left to do. Out with it."

She took a deep breath. "I'm taking a sabbatical."

"Oh? Very nice!" I leaned in. "Cooking up something new? Desmond's Oubliette is a mainstay now."

"I'm taking on a bit of private work." She smiled with one corner of her mouth. "I think you should come with me."

"Next semester I'm handling PRC 1101, NEC 4301, and overseeing a few master's projects."

"I've seen the schedule, Pablo."

"Then why even ask?"

"I received a very generous offer, and when they asked if anyone else was available, I floated your name. Here. In case you're interested." She walked over to my desk and laid a business card in front of me. She folded her arms across her chest.

"The Whiteshore Group. Why do I know that name?" I knew the answer, but I wanted her to say it.

"They're a security firm."

"Mercenaries."

"Private military contractors. With a fat government contract, very little oversight, and open minds."

"Working in Iraq and Afghanistan. Are you going into an active warzone?"

"No. They've set up shop in the Redlands."

"Just for you." I folded my hands on the desk in front of me.

"For *us*. And we'd still be teaching."

"It's one thing to teach these kids how to protect themselves, Georgina. Arming a bunch of mercs is something else entirely."

"Everyone—Nick, Rhea, Giorgio, Melody, *Carmen*—has something else going on."

"This is my career. I love this school. I love what I do."

"I'm not saying quit, Pablo. There are opportunities out there. You don't want to be turning in reagents to the damn Bursar for the next twenty years."

"Those are essential for the labs."

"Once upon a time, Pablo Diaz, you were *it*. Everyone thought that, if he ever stepped down, you were the anointed. But you haven't published anything in over a year. You take job after job to make ends meet, so you get passed over for tenure. You just keep looking for the quick fix. This floor is as high as you go. You'll be under him forever, Pablo." She pointed at the ceiling. The only thing above us was Emérico's office.

"I need to finish these grades."

She scoffed. "Do that. I have a meeting with my department to go over the division of labor for next semester."

I nodded without speaking.

I only ever saw her again in passing or at faculty meetings. We never criticized each other or exchanged barbs. There were occasional glances. Cordial. Distant. She seemed to have everything she wanted. I hoped it made her happy. I hoped she felt complete. I hoped that one day we might come together as friends.

Those hopes gnaw at me still.

25
Behind the Curtain

DRIVING THIS FAR west on Tamiami Trail is like emerging from a tunnel: the urban sprawl of residential complexes cedes its dominion to the Everglades. Tamiami Canal runs parallel with the road, thirty feet wide and seething in the wind and rain. Beyond the canal, the sea of sawgrass stretches to the horizon.

Fifteen minutes from the last vestiges of the city, two rusted metal posts jut from the ground. The sign tasked to them has fallen; the constant wind, rain, and humidity oxidized the screws and bolts meant to hold the placard in place. Some generous soul must have propped up the sign between the posts. White, block letters pop against the bureaucratic brown: Flight 592 Memorial Parking.

The memorial stones form a giant arrow that points to the crash site of ValuJet Flight 592, some two miles away in the homogenous River of Grass. Dirty, concrete pillars stand tallest at the center and shorten as they reach the edges of the formation. The central pillars are about five feet tall, while the ones comprising the perimeter are short enough to trip over.

A marble memorial, three feet wide and six feet long, serves as the tip of the arrow. The names of the 110 victims of Flight 592 are engraved on the stone in three columns. A few cheap beers and half a bottle of Dewar's White stand sentinel around the communal headstone. A miniature American flag, planted at a corner where marble meets concrete, has faded in the sun. Toys for children—the kind from a fast food kid's meal—litter the ground, along with dozens of coins, glass beads, sea shells, dead flowers, and a dollar store rosary. Rusted outlines of Christmas ornaments obscure a few names. A Honduran fifty dollar bill flutters beneath a river stone. A plastic cake topper reads "Happy Mother's Day."

When the plane crashed, it was in a near vertical attitude; witnesses say she barreled straight into the earth. Recovery crews struggled for weeks, contending against the violence of the impact and the hungry swamp. In the end, only 68 victims were identified, some by as little evidence as a patch of flesh, a jawbone, and—in one instance—a single tooth.

24 years prior to the 1996 disaster, Eastern Airlines Flight 401 had crashed in nearly the exact same place, but she landed on her belly. Flight 401 never received a memorial, despite 101 souls lost. The 75 survivors tried their best—twice, very publicly—to have a monument erected, but to no avail. A bit of capitalistic ghoulishness kept this tragedy alive in the public eye: recovered parts were installed onto new planes, and more than once, passengers on board the retrofitted vessels claimed to see the deceased flight crew.

The crash sites' locations defy salvage and warding alike. This is the perfect place for a conduit, to tap into the various energies—magical, ghostly, primordial—that mingle and clash between the two spots.

A hazy orange glow marks the city to the east.

A black Range Rover sits in the gravel lot. Despite the Chancellor's meticulous preparations, I still hoped that this location might be unguarded. I park next to the SUV and position my headlights so that they shine past the memorial.

In a dirt clearing, a humanoid statue of visually-buzzing cold iron clutches an orb of wraithglass to its chest. The burning ectoplasm inside the orb roils and seethes like a miniature ocean, tinting the swamp in rippling, blue light.

I ease myself out of the borrowed Crown Victoria. Drops of rain flash to life in the wash of my headlights and disappear into darkness. Gravel crunches under my feet as I approach.

Georgina Desmond sits in the lotus position on a quilt. The bands of the quilt are primarily black, but the stripes stitched throughout are the raucous pinks, turquoise, yellows, and whites favored by the Miccosukee Tribe. Their casino is the first thing you see when Tamiami Trail meets the Everglades. Their village is ten minutes west of the ValuJet Memorial. No member of the tribe has ever attempted to join the College, and when magi come asking about their medicine, we are told to enjoy our stay at their village and are closely monitored thereafter.

There is a small black box next to Georgina and a wicker basket at the edge of the blanket nearest to me.

"Archmagus Diaz." Her braided hair is tied into a bun on top of her head.

"Good evening, Archmagus Desmond," I say.

"It must be close to morning by now."

"I can't really tell," I say and point at the light pollution rising from the city.

She looks me up and down. "No sword. No bag. Should I be insulted?"

I clench my jaw. "Emérico took Thanatopsis."

"Smart of him." She smirks. "You look haggard, Archmagus."

"I haven't slept." My eyes burn. I am aware of the weight of my clothing.

"It seems as if you have been to every corner of the city." She pats the quilt next to her. "Come. Have a sit."

The quilt looks thick enough to smother pebbles, soften the harshness of packed earth. My knees shake at the idea of any kind of rest. I clench my fist to silence my sinking heart. "I need to keep moving. This isn't my last stop."

"If you're too scared to share, there's another in the basket," she says and points. She watches me without blinking, barely breathing.

"Georgina, I don't have time for this."

"Make a little. For an old friend," she says. "Might be I can keep you out of trouble."

"You're under Emérico's enchantment."

"So is every archmagus, excepting you. It won't hurt you to listen."

I inch closer to the blanket. When she doesn't make a move, I close the distance between us and put my hand on the basket lid. I envision a cobra striking my hand, chains wrapping around me, a gun firing a slug between my eyes. I rip the lid off. A white quilt, folded, embroidered with green and blue squares.

"Nothing to worry about," she says with a smile. The darkness does nothing to hide the sunken, bruised circles around her eyes.

I spread the blanket and ease myself to the ground, my hip and shoulder loudly reminding me of the ordeals of the past 48 hours.

"You got too many problems, Pablo. Made an enemy of the Chancellor. I can make that go away for you, if you like."

"You're on his side, Georgina." Now I realize the danger of the blanket. It feels like the pillow top on my mattress. The urge to lie down thickens my knees and elbows.

"And you should be, too. You always been. When's the man led you astray?"

"You know what he's planning."

"I do," she says.

"And you agree with it?"

"I do." She twitches her head when she says it. "How else are we going to wake up all these people, Pablo? The College has been open for three decades, and they still think we're a joke. You work too hard to not be taken seriously."

"I work hard because it's my job."

"And you love your job. You want to keep it?"

"Of course."

"Even though your father thinks you're a witch?"

I wince. "Low blow, Archmagus."

"Just the sting of truth. If your own blood don't consider your profession noble—a *calling*—then who will?"

I see my father at the kitchen table, eating cornflakes, calling me *brujo*, before the image of him vomiting on the floor obliterates both memories. "What's that got to do with anything?"

"Symptoms of the same disease, Pablo. Your father thinks you are some conjurer of cheap tricks. The city sees you as no better than a stage magician. All your work, bottled, memed, or fodder for reaction videos. Just a disrespect."

"We can't force magic on people, Georgina. That is going to get them killed."

"Ain't a cause in this world wasn't bought with blood. And you'll pay, too. Carmen told me so. She said if I tried to stop you, you would drown me in knee-high swamp water. You want your crusade? You'll have to kill me for it."

"I would never," I say. But if Carmen truly saw it, it is now guaranteed. I need to run from this place.

"You will. But we can stop it," she says.

"How?" I am hopeful of her answer, but I clamber to my feet, ready to get away from her, from this place, from Carmen's meddling divination. Maybe I can get to another Conduit before dawn.

She opens the black metal box next to her and pulls out a tattoo gun. "Let me ward you. I'll keep you from magic until we pull the ink out of you. By then, the city will have woken up, and Emérico won't have to come after you anymore."

"Even if I couldn't cast a spell, I would still try to stop him."

"You'd be without the means, Pablo. And the Chancellor wouldn't see you as a threat."

"But Carmen already saw—"

"I have never been one for prognostication." Georgina rises to her feet like a marionette. She takes up the corners of her blanket and snatches it up from the earth, revealing a casting circle made of cold iron attached to the Conduit. "I am much more partial to preparation."

I hold up a hand. "Don't!"

"You are too late to stop me." She steps into the casting circle, crouches down to lay one hand on the ground, and points at me with her other hand.

I dash forward and run face first into a wall of blue light. I crumple. I feel every stone digging into my back. I am a specimen, trapped under a lambent bell jar. "Desmond's Oubliette," I say as I sit up. Nick and I cast the same spell at the Plaza of the Tropics to keep the teeth and claws of the mermen at bay.

"*My* Oubliette, yes," she says. She stands, keeping her hand outstretched toward me, touching each fingertip individually to her thumb in sequence, then reversing the sequence. She's channeling to keep the spell up and active. That is why the mermen made it through my own casting; the spell needs to be maintained.

I get to my feet and push against the Oubliette. It is as hard as a wall. Whereas Giorgio's box was glass, this has no feel except resistance. "This isn't the first time I've been caged in the last twenty-four hours."

"No? But I think it will be the last."

"We can agree on that," I say. I pace around the bell jar, testing its limits, drawing a circle in the dirt at the edges of my prison. Five feet. She's given me five feet in which to breathe, to walk, to work.

I pull Officer Hernandez's knife from my pocket and unsheathe it. I get on my knees and begin digging a hole.

Georgina laughs. "Are you planning on digging your way out?"

I grimace at her and keep throwing aside the earth, past the rocks, until I find moist sand and gravel. I make sure the pit is square, a cubit's length this way and that. Even without my reagents, even though I have no milk and honey nor sweet wine nor barley to offer libations, the old ways will work. I line the hole with rocks.

"It doesn't have to be this way, Georgina," I say.

"Pathetic," she says, still channeling her spell. She clenches her fist and the shining barrier closes in on me. It stops before touching me. A gust tugs at my clothes and hair. The sound of my digging becomes muffled. I try to breathe, but the air in the Oubliette is too thin. She's going to choke me out.

When there's nothing else left to me, there's always my blood. She knows it, I know it, and the orcs that overran Little Haiti knew it all too well. I cut my palm and squeeze over the rocks, drawing a crude image with the droplets: a bident with a glob between the spokes, the symbol for Pluto.

White spots form in my vision. I rip off my shirt sleeve and wrap it around my hand as tightly as I can manage. "Drop the spell. I don't want to hurt you."

"What could you possibly accomplish, necromancer?" She squeezes again, forcing the air out of my lungs.

I try to swallow one last breath. I hiss as I exhale for a count of ten. I feel my heart slow. When I speak the spell, it comes from the diaphragm, and the wisp of sound that escapes me shakes the pebbles outside of the Oubliette.

Georgina takes a step forward. When the Oubliette's shape wavers, she stops herself. She has to stay in the casting circle or her channeling will fail. "Pablo, stop!"

The bushes and sawgrass around us sough and snap. Georgina's blanket rises in a gust, snaps in her face, and disappears into the darkness.

Wraiths rush out of the sawgrass, translucent blue in the light of the orb. They've answered the clarion call of my bloody sigil. Leading the deathly mob is Kiki Famoso, the foreman from the Downtown Necropolis. Free of flesh, he and his cohorts can move through Nox with preternatural speed. They're honoring our agreement.

"*¿Su órdenes?*" (Your orders?)

"Get her," I say.

The wraiths surround her. One of them, what could be a man, tries to dig his hands into her chest. A blast of light from within her obliterates him.

Georgina yells at me. "Did you think I would not prepare for such gambits?"

I hear *him* in her voice. But he can't be here. He's at the College, siphoning all the ambient magic in the city into himself, pouring it back into every living soul, that they might awaken to an iota of power, use it, and want more.

I struggle to get to my feet. My head swims. "Push her out," I say, pointing at the circle. "Find a body! Anything!"

A few wraiths disappear into the sawgrass.

"Can you be so myopic?" Georgina says. "Can you be so *selfish?* We are giving the world a gift! Instant enlightenment!"

"They'll hunt us!" I sip air, fighting to keep from blacking out.

"Our new followers will defend our cause."

"People will die!"

"Peasant," she says. "Empires are mortared with blood."

To the north, the sawgrass bends and branches snap, accompanied by moans and snorts. Figures burst through from the thicket and climb out of the canal. In the blue light, they glisten with algal mud, their crude bodies fortified with serrated stalks, alligator hide, python meat—whatever the wraiths could find close to hand.

The mass of wraiths lift Georgina off her feet and carry her away from the Conduit, toward the water. She screams. They stuff her mouth with their malformed hands, crush her fingers. They toss her onto the ground.

The Oubliette falls.

Doubled over, I cough until I taste blood. I take greedy gulps of fetid air.

I turn to the mass of wraiths and cobbled monstrosities. The ghosts part as I approach.

They have her pinned to the ground, her mouth crusted with grass and mud, her hands grappled to keep her from casting. Fresh cuts zigzag across her face and arms. Georgina's eyes reflect the burning ectoplasm. She mumbles something and chokes.

I unwrap my cut hand, squeeze, and daub her face with my own blood, trying to draw a ward on her struggling forehead. I speak words of exorcism, expulsion, and restoration into the ward. Perhaps one or all of them together can drive out Emérico's enchantment. The ward flares.

Her eyes blaze blue. I see wisps rise from her irises. "She is mine!" Emérico's voice rattles around my skull. Their face is pure hatred.

I will expel him. I will save her. Even if it means I kill her.

I grab them by the neck and push their head into the canal. The ward sizzles under the water, bubbles rising to the surface. I hold them under until my muscles burn, until my elbows feel like they are going to snap, until I have to remind myself to breathe.

Only then does she stop struggling.

The ward's light stutters and fails.

Georgina's face floats just below the surface. Her eyes stare at nothing. Bruises ring her neck. A single bubble escapes her mouth, a remnant of an action her body is incapable of repeating.

I have to pry my wrists from her clenched fingers. Desperation latches onto my innards. I turn away from her and vomit. "Get her out!" I say.

The amalgams of flesh and vegetation rush into the water and help me lift the body of Georgina Desmond onto the muddy embankment.

I try to wipe the water from her face, the purple blotches from her throat. My hands shake, but I cannot feel the tremors. A thin line of water sluices from the corner of her mouth.

There are no traces of Emérico in her face, her eyes. Just my old friend, my colleague, my victim.

"Please, no." I wrap my mouth around hers and try forcing air into her lungs. I taste scum and decay and algae. I cannot fill my lungs deeply enough. I can't make a seal around her mouth.

I point at the nearest wraith. "Get inside her! Expel the water!"

The ghost dives into her chest. Georgina's body crawls to hands and knees and coughs up the lifeblood of the Everglades.

"Lie down! Breathe for her!"

The ghost controlling her body sucks down ragged breaths. More water and filth spew forth. I feel more than hear the words. "Her heart is beating," the ghost says through her mouth.

"Keep doing it until she tells you to get out!" I say. I pace around her, gnawing at my fingernails, squeezing my hand until blood drips from it. If she doesn't make it, what will all this have been for? One life or a million, the cost is the same.

"Pablo," Georgina says. She's staring up at me, water glistening on her face.

I kneel beside her, take her hand. "Are you okay?"

"You drowned me," she says, her voice croaking.

"I know. I'm sorry. He didn't give me any choice."

"Let go of me." She pulls her hand from my own, staggers to her feet, and backs away from me, toward her remaining blanket. "You think breaking that spell was doing me a favor? You think letting these"—she waves at the wraiths—"jump into me was okay? It isn't enough to know your nightmares, Pablo Diaz? I have to live with them, too?"

"Georgina, please! I'm sorry!"

Georgina picks up the white blanket and wraps it around herself. "Are you going to drown the whole damn city, Pablo?"

"Georgina!" Rocks dig into the flesh of my knees.

She walks to her Range Rover and slams the door. It takes her an eternity to start the engine. She churns up the gravel as she speeds away.

I sit back on my ankles, hold my head in my hands. I try to concentrate on my breathing, but all I see is Georgina's face in the canal. All my work, all my blood and sweat, has any of it ever gone toward something productive? Aiding criminals. Loosing witches. Giving my father a stroke. Murder. Have I ever produced anything that wasn't pain?

Little wonder I couldn't summon my mother's spirit as a child; she couldn't wait to find the beyond.

I should stay here until famine and the mosquitoes eat me up. That could be my one good thing, the damning coda to a ruinous existence. Emérico could have his new world, his new followers, and I could be forgotten. A nothing. Oblivion could have its perks.

Anything but this constant and crippling failure.

"*Jefe. Jefe, mire la hora*" (Boss. Boss, look at the time). Kiki stands over me, tapping his empty wrist in a mockery of life.

"I don't have a watch."

"*Ni yo. Ya sube el sol*" (Nor I. The sun is rising).

The ground around me, once black with the shadows of the memorial, leans toward the blue of pre-dawn. "What does it matter? I'm no hero."

"*¿Luchabas para ser héroe?*" (Were you fighting to be a hero?)

"I don't know what I was fighting for."

"*¿Eres profesor, cierto?*" (You're a professor, correct?)

"Yes."

"*¿Cómo vas a enseñar sin alumnos?*" (How will you teach without students?) Thus sayeth Kiki Famoso, as simple and direct as a sledgehammer.

"Help me up," I say.

"*Sabes que no puedo*" (You know I can't).

I sigh and push myself to my feet. My ankles, knees, and elbows crack. My shirt sticks to my skin. The mosquitoes have eaten me alive. Every raised welt pulses in time with my heart.

"Go. All of you," I say to Kiki.

Kiki the foreman whistles. The ghosts rush back to Nox to take their places.

I limp over to the Conduit and stand in the iron circle attached to it. The bubble of ectoplasm roils and shakes as if it is aware of my presence and intent.

I close my eyes and raise a hand to the human figure. I visualize its outline solidifying. Static builds up in my hair, making it stand on my neck and arms. I can taste and smell and press against an eddy of multicolored light. I begin tugging at it, pulling as much of it into me as I can, until I become the focus of the Conduit.

I cast my senses away from myself. I fly over the city. I find every cemetery and chip away every ward. I touch every gravestone, every plaque, every mortuary slab, feel every wraith in the city. I tap them, push them back into bodies, make them crawl through the earth or push out of mausoleums and kick open freezer doors.

The wraithglass orb above me cracks. Ectoplasm sizzles away as it meets the morning air.

I trudge back to the commandeered Crown Victoria. The door closes like a coffin lid. I wrench the key. The engine struggles to turn over but coughs its way to life. I pull away from the memorial, onto Tamiami Trail, and gun the engine toward my fate.

26
Blue Hour

THE DRIVE EAST takes me through utter darkness. I've done the unforgivable. Words don't exist that could close this rift between Georgina and me. To my left, the Tamiami Canal rages in a way I never thought possible. Gusts of wind raise white caps that froth against the far bank. Ahead of me, the sky ahead shifts from black to gray.

The ubiquitous housing complexes and strip malls return and the familiar names reappear: *El Palacio de los Jugos, La Carreta, El Rinconcito Latino*. All the store fronts are shuttered. The early risers waiting for their styrofoam cups are nowhere to be found, but they are out there, and it won't take much prompting for them to use the magic Emérico has given them to disastrous ends.

I floor the gas as I turn into my neighborhood. My back tires spin for a second before they gain enough traction to shoot me forward. Giant green garbage cans line the entire block, waiting for pickup, as if Waste Management would somehow be immune from the apocalypse.

I park the borrowed Crown Victoria behind my Civic. I leave the police cruiser to survey the damage the last two days have wrought upon my poor four-cylinder: roof caved in, front passenger door crumpled, side view mirror nowhere to be seen. Will I ever drive this car again?

Most of the lights on our side of the house remain on. I check my pockets. When I don't find my keys there, I check the floor of the squad car, to no avail. They must have found their way to the bottom of the Everglades. My phone and wallet, miraculously, are accounted for.

I walk up to the front door and whisper a password. The deadbolt clicks open. I enchanted the door years ago. My father had complained about scratches on the paint after a seedy night.

Beer, stale vomit, and standing water join forces in an olfactory assault. The gurney left black tracks on the tiles where my father collapsed. The

EMTs must have torn the leather of his recliner when they lifted him. If he ever sees that, it might give him another heart attack.

The light pours in through the broken back door and reflects off a puddle of rain in the hallway.

Dad can't come home to this. I grab a towel and mop up what I can.

Outside, I see my shed's door in the grass. The light is still on in there, but the floor is splintered beyond saving, littered with pieces of visually buzzing metal: the remnants of my lantern.

My father's domino box sits on the patio table, filled to the brim with water. Scattered dominoes stand in the porch light or glow in the shadows. I dump the box and scour the backyard until I gather the full set of 55. I bundle them in a large dishrag and stuff the box with paper towels.

I try to force the back door shut. I shove it back into the frame, but the lock won't budge.

As I move toward my room, past the darkened bathroom, a dead man appears in the mirror, filthy and crooked. I start, and so does my reflection. Every part of me is damp or itchy. A shower would be magical. Scald the filth away. But there's no time. At least I'll fit in when I reach campus.

The closet in my room is open, full of clean shirts. Without a shower, they won't do me any good.

My doctor's bag sits at the foot of my twin-sized bed. I grab it.

I enter my father's room. The picture at his bedside arrests my attention. My parents on their wedding day. My father looks off into the distance, chest puffed. My mother's chin is down, but her eyes are up. She's smiling straight into the camera. Her eyes follow me as I approach. That smile could win the gods. I pocket the small frame.

I whisper my deadbolt to lock, possibly for the last time.

The fastest route to Santa Inés Hall begins at FIU's west entrance. A red light stops me from crossing the intersections, but even if it were green, I would not be able to progress.

Hundreds of people throng the sidewalk. Somebody has rolled out a portable basketball hoop and stood it on the right corner of the entrance; an American flag hangs limply from its pitiful height. A few other flags—Cuba, Colombia, Venezuela, Brazil—adorn the shoulders of the mob.

A sandwich board stands proudly on the opposite corner. One like it stood on Eighth Street for most of my life. The original showed Fidel Castro in a coffin. My likeness has replaced Castro's in this new iteration. Below my graven image, blue swirling script lists all my faults: *cobarde, inútil, traidor, mentiroso, asesino* (coward, useless, traitor, liar, murderer).

Some in the crowd carry crude signs of cardboard and sharpie, with slogans meant to cut: "*Díaz destruye. Emérico salva*" (Diaz destroys. Emérico saves); *Pablo el zángano* (Pablo the Idiot); *Nuestro Emérico* (Our Emérico). A man in a guayabera and Panama hat holds a megaphone as high as he can and rails into the handpiece. And everywhere, everywhere, wooden cooking spoons clang against pots and pans.

I know this mob.

I have been a part of them: when the Marlins won the World Series in 2003; every time the Heat won the Finals; when Castro died in 2016. We danced through the streets to the discordant beat of cookware.

I have known them well enough to avoid them, too: when Border Patrol raided the family home of Elián González, when a Cuban MiG shot down a Brothers to the Rescue Cessna for dropping leaflets over the island. During such times, the mob reels about, drunk on rage, thirsty for teargas.

And now, they're here to stop me.

I turn on the Crown Victoria's strobes and inch my way across the intersection. My bowels turn to water as all the heads turn in my direction. Every eye squints with malice as I flick the switch for the siren twice.

They begin to part, reluctantly, turning to each other.

I drop the sun visor, hoping to avoid their collective gaze. The police cruiser crawls forward. I *whoop-whoop* again.

The megaphone blares, "*¡Es el!*" (It's him!)

They swarm the Crown Vic. I slam the brakes, lest I kill somebody.

The cruiser begins to rock, a foot at first, but momentum is with the mob, and soon it feels like the whole car is bouncing side-to-side. They brandish their signs at me, rattle the door handles, rip off the side view mirrors.

I touch the gas every so slightly and begin to advance again. Their shrieking rises to a fever pitch, as if I had run someone over, although they still pace the car. They rail against the audacity of my forward progress.

Someone throws a milkshake against the windshield. Pink suds cover every inch of glass. I hit the brakes. The windshield wipers barely return my vision.

The window to my left cracks. The face behind the punch is all hate. "*¡Maricón! ¿Vas a reanimar a mi madre? ¡Hijo de puta!*" (Faggot! Are you going to reanimate my mother? Son of a bitch!)

Like the orcs of Little Haiti, they thirst for blood. My blood. I have been stabbed, beaten, and wheezed through Nox for them. I abandoned my father for them.

I throw the car into park and grab the jar of salt from my doctor's bag. I throw a pinch of salt into my mouth and slap my hands on the dashboard to the rhythm of the rocking. I recite:

They groaned, they stirred, they all uprose,
Nor spake, nor moved their eyes;
It had been strange, even in a dream,
To have seen those dead men rise.

A wind whips through the hair of the crowd, and for just a moment, the pounding abates. Part of my army is close. I can feel them. All of them.

I alternate the slaps, faster, sending the entire horde into a jog.

The basketball hoop falls on my windshield and spiderwebs form at the point of impact. A massive wad of spit oozes down the glass on my left.

I keep slapping the dash until the real screaming starts. Rage disappears, replaced with the screeching of unadulterated terror. From the direction of the largest cemetery in the city comes a crusty, dingy, disheveled horde that fills the entire street. The living faces flee. All that remains are grimy bodies, surrounding me on all sides except ahead. The silence is absolute.

I try to spit out salt, but there is nothing left in my mouth, save for bitterness.

I dig in my doctor's bag for a KN95. Even after securing it, I inhale through my mouth and exhale through my nose: morgue breathing.

I put the car into gear and drive forward.

※

The bodies around me stand still, an army in varying states of decay. Almost all wear their funeral best, lending them an officious rigidity. Mud cakes most of the suits and dresses, but a few corpses gleam in the wan light of morning, stained only by having rubbed shoulders with their previously-interred neighbors.

They part in unison as I drive forward. They fill the street behind me. No other movement stirs them once they take their places. It feels like I'm driving through a terracotta army.

17th Street snakes its way through the southside of campus, passing only three buildings, each separated by a parking lot: Wertheim Performing Arts Center, Santa Inés Hall, and FIU Stadium. I cannot see beyond the stinking mass.

I pull into the first lot, where Elisa, the police, and the Russians are waiting for me. The paddy wagons and squad cars line up cop-style, driver's window to driver's window.

I pull myself out of the Crown Vic.

Hernandez is the first to emerge. He's tied a bandana around his mouth. "Thought you might have gotten cold feet," he says.

The police and Russians converge on me. The cops lock eyes with me while most of the Russians immediately light cigarettes.

"Your party, your plan," Sandobal says. She has Orlov handcuffed to her left wrist, leaving her firing hand free.

"Don't be heroes," I say. "You'll know the corpses you have to protect. They will approach you. Get them as close to the College as you can and then fall back so more can find you. Don't approach the doors or the figurehead. Don't even try to engage the defenses. Bullets won't work, and if you put up any resistance, they'll come at you."

"What will?" Hernandez says.

"Everything. Even the damn stones." I squat down and dig in my bag until I find my boxing wraps. I weave the fabric around my wrist, around the knuckles, between each finger. I finish the other hand and pound my fists together. The runes blaze to life, blinding me.

I've only activated the wraps. There's no reason for them to have overloaded the way they did. I can feel each rune vibrate like a phantom phone call.

I hear people swarm around me. When my vision returns, I find Orlov standing in front of me and his retinue huddled around me; Elisa, by dint of the handcuffs, has been allowed into the circle. The other cops look on from afar, trigger fingers hovering.

"Are you all right, *koldun*?" Bogdan asks at Orlov's shoulder. He pinches a cigarette between his thumb and forefinger, crushing the filter, taking small, furtive puffs.

Orlov offered these men up, knowing they might die. They are hardened gangsters, but today a timorous tightness stretches every lip, pinches the corner of every eye. They need reassurance or they'll never manage to cast a spell.

I raise my hand, flex my fingers, so they can see the glowing runes on the wraps. "I used these against Baba Yaga, but they didn't glow like this. Campus is supercharged. Great for you all. You should have no trouble with your shields," I say. "Be far from others when you cast. Remember what Abram did to the squad car?"

A ripple of laughter. The horror of what they're about to face is immense. But an ember of hope can fire the forge of magic.

"What about us?" Orlov says and hoists his cuffed wrist in the air.

Sandobal, pulled forward, catches herself before she stumbles. "Easy!" she says.

I address the Russians and the cops. "Take out your foci. All of you!"

They pull out rosaries, photographs, a piece of ceramic plating.

I look at them, one-by-one. No one will meet my eye. "You want to make it to noon? Remember this: your foci are the batteries, but you are the engines. Shape your shields around yourselves; you don't want to push away what you're trying to protect. And when you do cast, get as many bodies as close to you as possible. Got it?"

They nod and murmur agreement.

"Follow me, then." I lead them out of the parking lot into a Hell of my own making.

The corpses stand silent in the street, on the sidewalk, on the lawn. I crouch down and maneuver between them. The smell of moist earth and rotting flesh mingle. Someone puts a hand on my shoulder. I look back and find Hernandez. Behind him, a Russian clings to his tac-vest. I hear choked coughs and gagging farther down the line. I turn back and shoulder my way through the orchard of decaying flesh.

Something flashes to my right. North of us stand several dormitories. Ghostly faces stare from the darkened windows: the undergrads have taken to their phones, hoping to record a video worthy of some iota of fame.

They don't know they're lending Emérico power, serving his ends, transmitting his plan to every nook in the city, the same way the onlookers on South Beach empowered Baba Yaga.

The dead have created a perimeter halfway around Santa Inés Hall, but leave a No Man's Land of about thirty yards before them.

I turn to Hernandez and point him west. He pounds my shoulder and the conga line of cops and criminals move past me into the sea of corpses. Each of them touches me in some way—a pat on the shoulder, a fist bump, a hand shake—before disappearing amongst the standing dead. Am I sending them to their deaths or are they saying goodbye before my own?

The crowd gets too thick to keep track of my allies beyond ten feet. The only indicator that they're still moving is the scraping of feet.

Four days ago, I might have believed Emérico incapable of attacking police. There's no morality left in him. Only the naked desire for power and the willingness to eliminate anyone that gets in his way.

I idolized him. I made him my savior. I thought he, amongst all people, might have the means to make a better world. But he never wanted a school. He wanted a throne. God damn me, I would have built it for him.

A hand grabs my shoulder. A corpse. "Kiki?"

The corpse nods. "*¿Qué estamos esperando?*" (What are we waiting for?)

"*Los de más*" (The rest).

More bodies crowd around me, each a magical bomb to throw at Emérico.

By now he is so deep into his ritual that he won't have any attention to spare for my assault. But he knows I'm coming. He's had days to prepare and Carmen at his side.

The blue light of pre-dawn fades, but the brilliance of a new day is nowhere to be found. Instead, the storm from last night lingers, a thick gray blanket ready to shed tropical rain thick enough to drown the very air I breathe.

I check my phone. 7:19.

To the south, a rumble. In the distance, in the adjoining Tamiami Park, a trickle of corpses appear, followed by a tidal wave of rot. They climb the chain link fence that divides FIU from the park until there are so many bodies pushing against the fence that the supporting posts topple. They complete the perimeter. We have Santa Inés Hall surrounded.

I stand and whisper a command: "Now." Hundreds of thousands of corpses hiss or roar, filling the air with a mist of atomized death.

I summon a shield of translucent blue around the nearest corpses and myself and attack the only place I've ever truly belonged.

27
An Ecstasy of Fumbling

THIRTY YARDS OF St. Augustine grass stands between the College and me. A path made of red pavers in a herringbone design leads right up to the doors. In the weak light of dawn, the doors' carved patterns blend into muddy shadows.

I've walked that path thousands of times, always with noble intent. Those doors have opened for me, awaited my hand. I won't let Emérico take this place from me.

I run toward the College, clutching my doctor's bag to my chest. A thought shoulders its way into my mind: *class doesn't start for another hour*.

Then the dead overtake me. Their crusty bodies scrape by, coating me in dirt and worse. The smell—earthy, cloying, rotten—forces its way into my stomach. In my dash for the doors, I've forgotten to breathe through my mouth.

I keel over and vomit. My nostrils burn. I try to blink away tears, not daring to touch my eyes with my filthy hands.

A red bolt of lightning arcs from the clouds, striking the bodies ahead of me. The boom forces my hands to my ears and rattles my rib cage. The blast atomizes a dozen corpses. A gust carries away the smoke and ash.

Even though the bile has stuffed my nostrils, I can taste cigar smoke and newsprint and the first scoop of espresso grounds from a foil package. These smells (not really smells at all, but the faintest impression of personality) reveal the source of the magical assault: somewhere in the city, someone's *abuelo* woke up and turned on the TV, and what he saw—the attack on the College—was an attack on everything *he* believed in. That indignant old man tapped into the power bestowed on him by Emérico and sent a lightning bolt right at my army.

A bony hand reaches under my arm and lifts me to my feet. One of the corpses. It wears a suit and its tightened lips can no longer close over its teeth. It tries to move its jaw, but I can't hear anything. An ectoplasmic hand—translucent and blue—extends from the corpse's arm and passes into my own.

"*Ponte las pilas*" (Put in your batteries), Kiki says and withdraws from my mind. It is something my father would say. I take my parents' picture out of my pocket. I thumb the frame, try to hold my mother's joy and father's pride in my mind's eye. Light ripples through the runes of my boxing wraps. My father holds himself up with such dignity, such pride. At his arm, my mother beams, bashful and mischievous. A golden dome of light springs forth from me, surrounding the corpses I must ferry to the doors.

No sooner is my shield up when another lightning bolt crashes into it. This one is purple and trailing it is the scent of Royal Violets, the baby cologne found in the house of every Cuban grandmother in the city. *Abuela* is awake now, too.

The doors of Santa Inés Hall loom ahead of me, the panels bouncing with each stride. The Hanged Man bearing my face dangles by his foot from a blooming branch.

From beneath my feet, a scraping noise like nails on chalkboard. The bricks begin to grate against each other. I throw myself onto the grass to my left. Corpse-Kiki follows me.

The entire pathway roils like a breaker at the shore, tossing the dead off of itself. Loose of the earth, the herringbone rears up like a cobra, bricks breaking away from it to float freely in midair. The "head" of the pathway strikes down, crushing the assaulting cadavers and launching a hail of masonry at my forces. Each thud cracks a skull, snaps a knee backward, explodes a chest. The golden glow of my shield catches half a dozen bricks, suspending them mid-assault.

I heave myself to my feet and take in the field around me. In both directions, domes of colored light approach the College. The first few corpses lay their hands on the doors. In response, the doors piston open. The merciless violence of the action sends the nearest corpses flying back into the oncoming force, broken and flailing. The doors clang shut and my ears ring.

For a moment, I glimpsed the foyer. Dark. No Dolores. For years, I have entered and exited this building under the brim of her glasses. The late nights when the custodians would find me in my office, shaming me back home, even *then*, some intern would be managing the front desk.

Never empty. Never. And never forbidden to me, not even on my first day. But the chaos of the last two days—Baba Yaga, the mermen, the orcs—have driven her away from her post.

Above me and to my right, on the tiered balconies, panes of glass shatter. I scan floor-by-floor, trying to spot whatever hellish servants Emérico has unleashed.

More glass shatters. Abram Orlov laughs.

I find his red bubble to my right. Above the din of scraping brick and pounding feet, each of Orlov's barks is answered by a crash of glass or a metallic clang. He punches the air with his free arm. Each punch sends bricks flying at Santa Inés Hall.

He laughs like a man unhinged.

I warned him against attacking the College. He could have been safe and sound in a hospital bed or a jail cell, but he chose to be here, chose this moment to let loose. I almost keep my mouth shut.

Then I see her. Elisa doesn't have her shield up because Abram's covers the two of them completely. Even so, she is trying to drag him back from the front lines. She digs her fingers into his gunshot wound, pushing her nails and his bandages into the leg.

Abram bellows. The red shield disappears.

The herringbone pathway rushes across the lawn, roaring like a rollercoaster, aimed at the golden bubble Elisa produces.

I throw the strongest uppercut I can. The runes of my boxing wraps glow. They multiply the force of my attack, which bats the brick serpent against the walls of the College.

The pathway is up again immediately. It is stone, not flesh and blood. It doesn't tire or feel pain. The tail end lashes out, makes contact with Elisa's shield, and the golden bubble gets flung thirty feet backward. Elisa and Abram fall into the crowd.

Somewhere inside of that stonework, a demon or spirit is following Emérico's orders. If I can exorcize it, my army will only have to contend with the doors.

I fall to my knees and root around my doctor's bag for the jar of salt. Finding it, I pour a pile in front of me. I flatten the salt into a summoning circle and draw a sigil of binding into the salt. I lay a nearby brick atop the pile. I dig my fingers into the crystals, careful not to disturb the symbol, and start chanting. The words are of creation, of art, of conjuration, but they are words of power, of subjugation of form: "*And what shoulder? & what art, / Could twist the sinews of thy heart?*"

A shadow passes over me. I keep chanting.

Above me, the snake path rears up, ready to crush me.

I can't stop chanting. If I stop, I'll be crushed. "Art twists your sinews!"

There is a pop in front of me, the same sound as a paper grocery bag being whipped open. A figure about a foot high, almost human, made of ill-fitting stones cobbled together, stands atop the summoning circle: an earth elemental, bound by Emérico into the bricks. "I release you from service," I say, and drag my hand through the circle of salt.

The earth elemental salutes and dives into the grass.

The shadow over me wavers. With no force to animate it, the bricks of the herringbone bone path start to fall from the body of the stone snake.

I grab my bag. Try to scramble away. Falling masonry thuds around me. A chunk hits my right leg. There is a snap, so much louder than a body should produce, like slapping a yardstick against a desk. The pain is immediate and unmistakable and blinding. It sucks the wind from me.

I crane my neck to watch my demise. Above me, what remains of the colossal brick snake rushes at me. I don't even have time to scream. Feebly, I cover my head with my arms.

Jostling shakes my shattered bones, waking me. Abram stumbles as he drags me away from the College. Arms, legs, back; they all shriek.

I taste blood, feel around my mouth with my tongue, and realize I have mangled my bottom lip. Something warm covers my right leg. "Pissed myself?"

"No. You're bleeding out," Abram says, lowering me to the ground. "It's over, koldun."

Floaters form in my vision. Blood pressure's low.

"Don't move," he says and puts a hand on my chest. An empty handcuff hits my sternum, its counterpart still clamped to Orlov's wrist.

"What happened?" I say. "Where's Elisa?"

I crane my neck to look at Santa Inés Hall. The corpses still hiss and mass against the walls.

"You played your part perfectly, *koldun*. I just had to talk to them and they popped right open," he says, staring at the handcuffs. The sun hits the back of his head, rendering his face a black void punctuated by two glacial eyes.

"Where is she, Abram?" He may have slipped his cuffs, but if I know Elisa, she'll be on him in seconds.

"She won't be bothering either of us anymore." Abram produces a service semiautomatic from his belt.

I try to yell, but my crushed chest is barely capable of breathing. "What did you do?"

"Try not to think about it. I had hoped, when all this was over, to learn from you. And now I doubt you'll make the hour. Before you go, recommend a tutor."

I try to prop myself up, but the stabbing pain lets me know exactly where my left arm is broken. "I should have shot you in the heart."

"Such an ugly thing to say before we part. In these final moments, try to show a little dignity. There is nothing—"

Abram chokes. His hand spasms and he drops the gun to the grass. He lurches in my direction, falls to his knees, and jerks forward, inching toward me. I try to crawl away but I feel myself about to swoon. His face keeps getting redder, his eyes bulging.

A ghostly, feminine hand emerges from his chest, grabs my wrist.

I hear Elisa in my head. "I can't hold him much longer."

"There's nothing"—I choke on blood—"I can do for you."

"I know that, idiot. Help yourself so you can finish this!"

I reach out to the nearest corpses with the lingering magics in my fingertips. Six of them come running and dogpile Orlov.

Abram wrests enough control away from Elisa to speak. "No, Pablo! *Koldun*, please!" I clench my jaw, and they tighten hands over his mouth.

I need my bag. I feel the ghost of Elisa Sandobal depart my flesh. Seconds later, a corpse comes running up with my doctor's bag.

"Charcoal," I wheeze.

The corpse pushes the black stick into my hand.

"Bring him… close." It takes everything in me to lift my right arm to Abram's chest. I hear him gag on fingers of the dead. I try to draw a circle on his shirt. It's shaky work, but I slash through the circle three times.

I draw three concentric circles on my own shirt. "Salt," I say. The corpse gives me my jar, already opened. I take a handful of salt and pour it into the pocket of Abram's shirt. "*Sana, sana, culito de rana. Si no sana hoy, sanará mañana.*" I chant the old cure.

When transferring damage from one body to another, the participant need not be willing, as Abram Orlov finds out. I scream as my bones knit together, as my fleshy lip seals itself. Orlov responds in kind as his femur breaks, tearing through his femoral artery. The corpses drop him into a quivering heap. He passes out from shrieking.

Curled up on the grass, blood pooling beneath him, Abram's pallid face twitches. He gasps for breath.

I stand up, slowly, but there's no need for such caution. I have made myself whole. I spin around, trying to identify the last corpse Elisa hijacked. "Are you still here, detective?" I say.

A corpse shambles up to me. Elisa's hand reaches into me again. "Don't fuck this up," she says. "And make sure my family is taken care of."

"What are you going to do?"

I hear the familiar chime of the Aperture, then she's gone.

I take a deep breath, flexing my arms, chest, and back. I do a set of air squats. All the pain is gone. All of it. I feel remade. Hungry. *New.*

I pick up my doctor's bag and head back toward the College.

Without the pathway to stymie them, the corpses have reached the entrance, and the doors are happy to respond, sending some bodies flying back, chewing and pulping the scattered few that dodge their outward swinging.

The exterior marble tiles swing away from the building like shutters in a gale, pulverizing the nearest corpses before slamming back into place.

"The doors! Concentrate on the doors!" I say.

The corpses surge forward. I feel the stampede in my molars. Against such a press, the doors can only rumble.

"Shame on you, Pablo Diaz! Shame!" a young female voice booms above me. I look up and see the figurehead of Santa Inés point down at me with her free hand. Beneath her other arm, she is holding a bleating lamb. "You? *You?* Of all people! This place has been your refuge for seventeen years." Wood cracks as the figurehead detaches itself from the bowsprit. Shivers as long as two-by-fours and as sharp as swords fly toward me. I don't flinch; I remember my parents. A gold bubble appears around me, arresting the missiles mid-flight.

Santa Inés drops down, crushing a pair of my soldiers beneath her wooden feet. "We have comforted you at your lowest, hidden you without question! Is this how you show your gratitude?" She's as tall as the doors. She releases the lamb beneath her right arm. It's the size of a great dane. Santa Inés tosses the dead aside like ragdolls while her companion kicks corpses in half.

With no other options and a colossal wooden teenager bearing down on me, I begin yelling. "Bombs! Bombs! Bombs!" Some of the corpses on the frontlines explode into peonies of blue light. The ghosts fly out, spectral and glowing. Santa Inés claps a phantom in her giant hands, spraying everything around her with ectoplasm.

A fat ghost in an ill-fitting suit floats up to the wall, drives his hand into one of the marble panels, and pulls a struggling red imp out by the neck. The demon tries to take flight but the ghost flings him to the corpses below. He is swallowed up with a shriek. The ghosts continue their search, disappearing and reemerging from the masonry, grappling with the demons that Emérico has pressed into service. The walls, at least, stop attacking.

"This is obscene!" Santa Inés says. "End this now and Emérico will forgive you! He will welcome you back into the fold." Even as she begs, palms upturned, she kicks away any corpses that get near her, pops any ghost within reach like a water balloon. She has the face of a freshman taking PRC 1101, but her every move menaces my army.

She's irreplaceable. Centuries old. I don't want to hurt her, but she won't keep me from the tower. An ingenious torture device.

I ball my fist. The runes of my boxing wrap sizzle white. I throw a single punch. The space between us crackles and sparks and she explodes into sawdust.

The creature left standing in her place is small, no bigger than a toddler, with furry limbs, red skin, a tail that comes to a spearhead, and yellow pupil-less eyes. It trembles as I walk up to it.

"Disarm the rest of the traps," I say.

The imp licks its scaly lips with a bifurcated tongue. "He'll—he'll end me," it says, in the same girlish voice of Santa Inés.

"I'm standing right in front of you, *imp*."

The imp flies into the building.

"Back up!" I say. The corpses nearest the doors shuffle away from the building.

I place my hand on my upside-down likeness. "I'll make things right."

The doors whine, long and low, as they open for me. I cross the threshold.

Something buzzes. There is a flavor in the air—*bacalao* (smoked cod), musty paper, and incense. Did Emérico just cast a spell?

Inside the foyer of Santa Inés Hall, chunks of decayed flesh and sawdust coat the floor. Floating particulate hazes the weak light. Somewhere behind the desk, a phone rings.

Despite the open doors, my army crowds the threshold, unable to push past an invisible barrier. The sky outside looms a steely gray above them. Staring through the open portal, I can discern the pattern of the illusion Emérico has set up: to those outside, it must seem as if the doors just reappeared. A simple illusion and a wall of force has cut me off from the rest of the world.

No matter. I am precisely where I need to be. I push open the door separating the reception area from the atrium with my shoulder.

Pale light filters into the atrium from the high windows. To my immediate right, the coffee bar stands empty and sad.

Booths run along the curving walls in both directions. Dozens of circular tables dominate this side of the atrium. Every shadow could hide an imp. The tiles could come to life at any moment and seek my throat.

Every step I take rebounds off the roof. I walk heel-to-toe but each exhalation echoes back at me. My ears thrum from the absence of sound. My heart pounds against my ribcage. I stink of death. My head swims from taking shallow breaths through my mouth.

Ding.

One last slap in the face: In the center of the atrium, the elevator doors ensconced in the central tower open. Through the empty space of the elevator car, I can see the skull that adorns the double doors leading into my lecture hall. Emérico knows I won't step into a steel box for him.

He has sent the elevator down as a mockery.

"I'm coming for you!" I yell into the elevator.

I steel myself for the long climb up to the Aerie.

28
The Funhouse

THE FIRST STEP up the winding staircase doesn't kill me, nor does the second or the third. I travel up and to the right, in the same direction as medieval spiral staircases. Even if I had Thanatopsis, I would be at a disadvantage, since I'm right handed. Attackers from above could skewer me easily.

I reach a wall sconce on the eighth step, where I am bathed in flickering orange light. The metal brazier on the wall is real enough, but the light it casts comes not from coals and fire, but an LED.

A showman will always be a showman, even in the face of building codes.

By the time I reach the tenth step, I begin to marvel at my luck. Where are the buzzsaws in the floors, the spears from the ceiling, the poisoned darts from the walls? Where is my inescapable boulder? Does Emérico think so little of me? Did he not expect me to make it past the doors?

I purse my lips at the insult, all the way to the second floor landing. My heavy breathing echoes around me, until I find the entrance to the library. I glimpse the shadowy stacks, the empty tables, the forlorn hanging overhead lamps. This place should be brimming with potential practitioners but all I can see is the same emptiness that greeted me at the front desk.

He *must* have thought I'd be dead by now. How else could he allow me to ascend to his office? All that planning for this moment, knowing I'd oppose him to my death. Surely he didn't think a few imps would deter me?

I start taking the stairs two at a time. I barely register the entrance to the third floor, the upper library. The effort makes my feet bark, but that is nothing compared to the slap in the face of being underestimated.

I arrive at the fourth floor, home to the Conjuration and Transmutation departments. Always buzzing with the activity of TAs and adjuncts, rarely visited by their department heads. Rhea and Giorgio would rather be at home or the shop, respectively, than under Emérico's gaze. That was a weight I could shoulder when those cowards couldn't.

By the time I reach the next floor, the pains of a sedentary lifestyle begin to groan in tune. I can feel every bone in my feet. If I had chosen carpentry over necromancy, would my body be better equipped for this ascension?

Fifth floor: Abjuration and Evocation. Derelict. Two departments run effortlessly by a pair of self-aggrandizing truants. How I have envied their wealth, their accomplishments. I could have been just like them and walked into Emérico's trap.

I am forced to use the handrails now, pulling my lagging body upward. If I keep this up, by the time I reach Emérico, I won't have anything left in the tank for him. There's no Orlov upon which to foist my debility.

The sixth floor houses the offices of the Illusion and Divination departments. I don't stop at the landing, just try to move past Carmen's foresight and Melody's vilification of me on every local channel. If I make it to the top of the stairs, succeed in what I've begun, will there be anything left for me to recover?

Seventh floor. My floor. Necromancy. As high as I could ascend without being summoned further. My refuge, my prison, my domain.

Did I ever love this place? I was proud of it, certainly. I reveled in the authority it gave me—the name, the title.

But did I love it?

I came here so often. I came to escape my life, my father, the person I was outside of this building. It is so easy to get lost in my work instead of facing what I knew I should face.

Was that my mistake?

I don't stay on the landing any longer. Halfway up the last flight, the orange light of the electric braziers cannot compete with the blue light coming from Emérico's office. Half a turn more and I'll be there, to face my mentor and my savior, to stop him from juicing up the city and bringing all we've built all tumbling down.

Only ten short stairs between us.

Gravity shifts. The stones of the stairwell grate against each other and crash into place. My feet find no more purchase. The floor rushes at me, but even before my head makes contact, my legs are falling down the slide.

I don't feel all seven turning, tumbling stories. I pass out before reaching the bottom.

"Pablo," Emérico says.

Warmth and light push at my eyelids. I peek, and the first sight that greets me is his lambent skull. I jump up and almost swoon again from the headrush. I have to squat down to steady myself. My right hand lands on my doctor's bag.

I'm in his office. The morning's steel gray sky has given way to a brilliant blue day. The sun is nowhere to be seen, meaning it must be close to noon.

I have failed. Completely and utterly.

"It is over, Archmagus Diaz. You can relax." He sits behind his desk. His polished teeth gleam, betraying neither smirk nor frown. A toothy expanse of indifference.

I cup my head in my hands, fall to my knees. All the pain, for nothing. My reputation ruined, for nothing. Sandobal and Orlov dead and every corpse in the city out of its grave, just so he could sit his throne and stare at me.

"Relax. Have a seat." He extends a hand in front of him, motioning toward an armchair that I've never seen before in this office.

I stand. I consider the armchair. I pick up my doctor's bag and shuffle to the nearest window. The city is laid bare before me, rolling out its green canopied urbanity. I look down the side of the tower. No corpses. The brick pathway is back in place. The figurehead of Santa Inés has been restored to her usual perch.

"How long was I out?" I try to keep the incredulity out of my voice. I'm at his mercy now, and shouldn't question his power, but even he couldn't clean up the mess I made in a few hours. It would take at least a day.

"Does it matter? Sit," he says.

I turn to look at him. In all my years of service, there has never been a chair opposite Emérico's. That would put him on equal footing with whoever sat across from him, something he would never allow. I bore it because everyone else had to, and because I thought he deserved such a lofty perch. So why, after so many years, after his grand plan is complete would he find humility?

Next to his desk sits another object I've never seen: a wooden umbrella holder, brimming with handles in various shapes and materials. I see a parrot's head painted ludicrously blue, a hissing silver snake with emeralds for eyes, a gnarled golden fist. They're all too familiar, but I've never seen any of them outside of a movie screen. There are two handles I have seen, however. One is the hilt of Thanatopsis. The other, a white plastic "J" last held by Carmen Espinoza.

"I won't sit. Even you couldn't have fixed all this in—what? Three hours? Four?"

Emérico slams his bony fists on his desk. The thud is flat, like dropping a bag of flour. "You dare question what I can and can't do?"

"Can't?" I say. I approach his desk, unafraid.

"Cannot?" The blue fire in his eyes dims.

Even the air is wrong. So perfect. So still. Stacks of books squat lifelessly behind us. Not a mote of dust stirs the air.

"I've never known you to care about the weather," I say. I reach into the umbrella stand, not for Thanatopsis, which surely is a fake. Emérico would never put that sword within arm's reach of me.

"One can never be too prepared," he says, holding onto the edge of his desk.

I pull the umbrella with the white handle free. Sheets of clear plastic bunch up between the white spokes. "You didn't put this here."

"Preposterous! I alone decide on my decor!"

I lower the tip of the umbrella to the floor, find the latch with my other hand, and open Carmen's umbrella with a whooshing pop.

"You fool! That's bad luck!"

"That is," I say, once more correcting his contraction.

Below the canopy of the umbrella, the floor turns from marble to vinyl. I can tell the tiles are normally white, but an unseen light casts them in red. I push down the confusion and instead look up through the panels of the umbrella. The vaulted ceilings of Emérico's office are gone, replaced by the economical drop ceilings of the Dungeon.

I point the umbrella in front of me and find the source of the redness: a glowing exit sign in a darkened laboratory, just above an emergency door.

"I'll see you soon," I say to the half-assed illusion of Emérico. I jog over to my doctor's bag and grab the handles, still mercifully attached.

"Just take a seat, Pablo! It's over!"

I push open the metal crossbar and enter a hallway, also bathed in red light. The emergency lights have activated.

I walk to the next laboratory, but the pane of glass inset in the door reveals only a darkened room.

The pain in my forehead returns. I begin to remember. I was either concussed or else I swooned when the staircase turned into a funhouse slide, dumping me eight stories below Emérico.

No watch on my wrist. I tuck the umbrella under my arm and fish my cell phone from my pocket. Quarter past eight! How much of the city wakes up before nine if there's a hurricane? In a state of emergency they'd just sleep in, right?

I walk down the hallway, looking for a dividing corridor, but never find one. When I pass a fifth door, I know something is wrong. No hallway in the dungeon has more than four labs on a side.

I hang Carmen's umbrella from the door handle and start walking away. When I reach the next laboratory, it is hanging from what should be the new handle. Melody loves the M.C. Escher feel of non-Euclidean illusions. But I still shouldn't be able to walk forward indefinitely.

I open the umbrella and raise it in front of me. I walk forward, but the door next to me doesn't move. I keep walking, trying to watch the floor. I have to squint, but I'm able to pinpoint the lines between the tiles, moving ever so softly, soundlessly, in the opposite direction of my steps.

Giorgio Hellas has turned this place into a giant treadmill.

I lean my head on the glass panel of the nearest lab door. Inside, the darkness bursts with light, so that I have to shield my eyes. I find myself looking at… myself. I am sitting on Abram Orlov's couch, the one in his office at the Eight Ball. In front of me, Yuri's corpse cavorts and recites "The Tsar and the Thief."

I raise the umbrella to cover half of the window and peer through the darkened, illusion-free lab. Across the room, I spy another exit sign.

It's possible that the floors could continue moving as I walk through the laboratories. They might not be attached to the walls. Hell, the rooms might be switching positions as I walk through them; the cubes of Giorgio's pyramid did so when suspended above the Bird Road Art District. I won't know unless I enter.

I pull open the door, smell rot and whiskey and sea salt and cigars. I cross the room slowly, walk right through the illusory Yuri, glimpse Orlov's tears, but what I'm really watching is the dark floor through the umbrella's revelatory lens. I reach the exit on the other side of the room as Baba Yaga jumps out of my pocket. "Pablo, son of Tristan! You should know better than to bring a cell phone into the well!" I open the door and find another of the Dungeon's hallways.

I point the umbrella back from whence I came. Baba Yaga disappears. Painted on the door where I originally entered this illusion is a simple line drawing of an umbrella. Just a capital J topped with a semicircle.

Carmen might as well have drawn herself blowing a kiss. If she allowed herself to be enchanted by Emérico, it's because she already glimpsed the future. She knew full well that I would make it here. She's left me all the bread crumbs I can swallow.

I run back through Orlov's office, burst into the first hallway, and stop. I can't move up and down the hallways, so my only option is across, to a different lab.

Inside, the periphery shows night, lit by a porch fluorescent. Tetch and his clan slam dominoes on my patio table while my father grins at Tetch's shoulder. Tristan's joy stabs at my heart.

My illusory father turns to me. "*Hola, m'jio*" (Hello, my son), he says. "Why don't you sit down for a game?"

I raise the umbrella, in spite of my tears, and find an exit sign where the door of my shed should be, decorated with Carmen's sigil. I don't allow myself a last glimpse.

I cross another hallway, into my distilled nightmare. I'm in my childhood bedroom, the cutout silhouette of my mother on the floor. Emérico exorcizes the trio of haunts. "You would never have survived without me, Pablo. I made you!" I scan the room with the umbrella. Where the rend into Nox should be, I find the marked exit door.

In this new hallway, I peer through the plastic of the umbrella. More red outside of its edges, more hallway, more doors. But through the revelatory membrane, I see my deliverance: the staircase that hides the Well.

I retrieve my cell phone again, ready to power it down. As I hold the brick of tech, I realize I need it on.

One can't expect to cheat the Devil without collateral.

I tap the bricks at the back of the stairwell. A lambent blue line draws itself from floor to ceiling. The wall separates and cool air blows back my hair.

The white void and brass sign reading "Bursar" appear. With them, some new additions: a long wooden desk to serve as a counter, and two free-standing brass grates acting as teller windows. The Bursar, bloated and grinning, stands behind the left operating queue, while the other remains empty.

"You could add some flooring next," I say.

"Even on the brink of annihilation, you cannot help yourself, can you?"

"There's something about you that just brings it out of me, I guess."

"Ready to save the city?"

"Yes, and apparently you're a part of it," I say. Carmen's umbrellas, littered throughout the illusions of my greatest failures, led me to the door of the Well. If she divined the future before being enchanted, then there must be something in here that I need to beat Emérico.

"Who do you think clued Archmagus Espinoza into this little game?" Impossibly, his smile widens, revealing more glistening shark's teeth. "You *could* have been invincible when you faced the Chancellor, but your dull simian wits could not handle the most basic of instructions." He reaches under the desk and starts laying items on the counter. A handful of orc tusks rattle on the wood like dominoes. The dragon scale clinks down. He drops the massive kraken's beak with a thud. "Look well and tell me what is missing."

My stomach turns. The answer to his question is simple: the items I refused to collect. But I would never have violated the sanctity of that unicorn; I summoned it and it served me dutifully. Taking its blood would have been tantamount to treason. And I certainly wasn't going to steal Tetch's son's head just to provide this monster with a scalp. I may be damned, but I'm no villain.

"I came here for a way into the Aerie, Bursar." Emérico's office earned that nickname the first time he flew out of the building. Since then, it's been his roost, but only ever in whispers, and never to his face.

"True, true." He steeples his fingers in front of him. "And had you set your insipid morals aside and chosen instead to follow my exceedingly simple directions, I could have provided you with a way in. Allow my new assistant to explain."

From beneath his desk, he retrieves a golden bird cage. Inside, the shrunken chicken hut broods over a bed of newspaper. Baba Yaga sits in a tiny rocking chair on the hut's porch, wearing the same clear green visor that the Bursar sports. "Pablo! Son of Tristan! How your failures compound!" She cackles. "You *are* an Archmagus, yes? And yet you cannot glean what all these glittering prizes might have afforded you."

I almost scream. I could slam my hands on the counter, smash what little I can see in this pocket realm to bits.

But the Bursar is rubbing his thumbs against his forefingers. He's trying to feed, as he did when he acted as my cut man.

I take a few deep breaths until I can no longer feel my pulse. "I have a job to do, and if you were truly trying to help me, then you'd realize there isn't much time left."

The corners of the Bursar's mouth droop into a scowl. "Typical Pablo. Always in a hurry. Never any time to socialize."

Baba Yaga cackles. "The boy is busy, Bursar. Allow him some respite."

"Silence, hag!" The Bursar reaches for her cage.

The Iron Tooth Witch snaps and the bars of her cage briefly flash white.

When the Bursar's glistening hands contact the metal, he makes no sound, but I can hear his flesh sizzle. "You bawdy, miniscule cannibal."

"I spawn devils like you into existence." Baba Yaga spits on her porch. "I've allowed you to handle me in this manner so that I, too, could have a last chat."

I need them focused on me, not on each other. "Then enlighten me, Baba," I say. "What are the reagents for?"

She cocks an eye at me. The simple invocation of respect—grandmother—works its own special magic on her. "Dragon scale, durable as fired steel and supple as leather. Troll scalp, to lend regeneration. A kraken's beak, hard as diamond. Orc tusks, those pure expressions of rage, can act as a binding agent, especially when ground into a powder. And unicorn blood, slick like quicksilver, courses with magic."

The Bursar here interjects, side-eyeing the hag. "When simmered over a low fire kindled by a precious heirloom, the process renders a potion of invulnerability."

I close my eyes and bring my fist to my mouth. I might have lived.

The Bursar moans and smacks his lips. "Always so free with your emotions, Archmagus. I could bottle you, given time."

"Time is exactly what we don't have." I retrieve the cell phone from my pocket and lay it on the table. "Here's my offer. If you want out of this jail, you'll get me into the Aerie. And you'll give me something strong enough to break Emérico's soul cage."

Baba Yaga jumps to her feet and begins stamping her porch. "You force me into a jar, but would loose this filth to walk the Earth?"

The Bursar rummages beneath his desk and surfaces holding a sledgehammer. "This should do." He slides it under the teller grate.

White marks scuff the head of the sledge. Most of the shaft is yellow but wood grain shows where the paint has chipped away. "Is this one of Giorgio's?"

The Bursar grins. "Not at all."

I look from him to Baba Yaga.

"Don't look to me for answers," she says. "You're the one bargaining with a devil."

I grab the hammer below the head. "How do I get to the Aerie?"

"You walk me out in your pocket and I take us there." He touches the phone. His body stretches and is sucked into it, as if it contained a tiny black hole.

"You had better not fail," Baba Yaga says. "Smash his sarcophagus to pieces, the same way you savaged my poor babe." She caresses the banister of the porch.

"What will you do?"

She eases back in her chair with a grunt and begins rocking. "What else? Await your return, of course."

I stuff the phone in my pocket and turn away from the counter. I take three steps and the portalout of the Well and into the Dungeon slides open. I do not miss a step as I leave the realm.

The walls to the Well seal themselves behind me. The air settles around me. Redness still bathes the stairwell, from the emergency lights, and in front of me spread the hallways of Emérico's accursed Dungeon.

There's no tearing of my pocket this time, no diminutive villain emerging from my phone. I blink, and the Bursar stands before me, looking every bit the devil cast in red.

The slits in his face dilate as he inhales, his neck ballooning to twice the size of his head. He looks down at my hands, holding my doctor's bag on one side, gripping the sledgehammer beneath the head on the other.

"It seems you have everything you need," the Bursar says.

"Then get me to Emérico."

The Bursar sucks his teeth. "Are you so eager to meet your doom?" He looks me over and sighs. "I will miss you, Archmagus."

"Don't worry. As soon as I'm done with the Chancellor, I'll find you."

He shows me all of his teeth. "Don't be so sure."

"If there's one thing I can count on, it's your gluttony."

The Bursar grimaces. "Adorable." He raises his hand, his padded fingers suspended in a snap. "Open your mouth."

I lower my brow and speak through tightened lips. "Why?"

"Otherwise, the change in pressure will blow out your eardrums."

"How thoughtful of you," I say. I turn my head from him and slacken my jaw.

He waits until I turn my stupid, slack-jawed face back toward him.

"There he is. My favorite ape." He grins at me and snaps.

29
Mayhem Managed

ONE MOMENT I am in the Dungeon and the next, I am in the Aerie. A cannon booms with the change of scenery. The air I have displaced rattles the windows in their sills, frees the ribbed vault ceiling of its dust, sends loose paper fluttering in the stacks of books and scrolls that flank the passage to Emérico's desk.

The Bursar teleported me right in front of the elevator doors. Beyond the stacks, in the open space in front of his desk, Emérico's eyes flash. He kneels on the floor, hands steepled in front of him.

Strike or die.

I drop my doctor's bag, take up the sledgehammer with both hands, and run straight for the Chancellor.

He doesn't flinch. The only movement from my skeletal mentor is the flickering of the blue flames in his eyes.

I raise the hammer. I am ready to strike him down.

He keeps his reverential pose in the middle of a casting circle made of salt. Arrayed around him, six black candles sizzle and sputter, aligned to the conduits spread out around the city. The candle flames buzz like vibrating sparklers. Is he somehow using cold iron as a wick?

I skid to a halt.

The skeleton is in front of me, but the consciousness is missing. Where is he, if not right here, in front of me?

I lean forward. He couldn't have made it this easy. No one plans the last few days out, as Emérico has, just to let a breeze blow out some candles and ruin their master plan. Over the sizzle of the candles, I hear something sharp, high-pitched, grinding.

I grab the sledge below the head with both hands and nudge at the salt with the tip of the handle. At least, I try to do that. The salt doesn't move. I bring the handle to my face and examine the part that I tried to use to disturb the circle.

A slice of wood is missing. No sound, no smell, no flash. Just disintegration.

Had I dived head first into him, I would have puffed out of existence.

I skirt the circle to the right, holding my breath, sucking in my stomach, sidling around my errant mentor. His soul cage—the sarcophagus into which he has bound his essence—is right behind him. I check the floor and see no salt or paint or blood, no reagent that could be used to raise a barrier.

Emérico has shielded his body with the most powerful piece of abjuration I have ever seen. But his body is just a skeleton that he animates. The tether that binds his soul to this world is in the stone body of his sarcophagus. How could he leave it unguarded?

A monstrous slab of oak is fixed atop the stone lid and serves as a desktop. Emérico's original desktop, salvaged from the *Santa Inés*, was donated to the HistoryMiami Museum decades ago. That one acquisition revitalized the institution and has kept it afloat for the past twenty years. It is embarrassing to think I used to waste a couple of Saturdays every year making pilgrimages downtown, just to pay homage to the coffin of a lich.

Now I'm standing over his soul cage, ready to end him.

I try lifting the desktop with one hand. I put down the sledgehammer and try with both hands. The lid slides less than an inch before getting caught on the stone lip for the sarcophagus. I have to squat beneath the corner and dig my shoulder into the wood just to slide it a couple of inches. I'm panting, but I can see into the sarcophagus.

I wedge the sledgehammer between the lid and inner wall, using the shaft as a lever, pushing the rest of the lid off. It crashes down on Emérico's throne, shattering the onyx into a thousand skittering shards.

Bent over, sucking down air, I find Emérico's last trap: Thanatopsis.

I lay the sledge on the edge of the tomb and climb into the stone coffin to pick up my doctoral thesis, my sword, my greatest work. This has to be a message. My grandest feat next to his greatest undertaking. Did he think leaving it here would somehow deter me? If I made it this far, then he has to know there's no stopping me.

No. He hid it here. To be forgotten. He thought me a failure, and Thanatopsis a trophy. I stare at the back of his lambent skull far too long.

I ease my sword to the floor with the strap of the baldric. I take up the sledgehammer for the last time.

I raise it above my head and twist my body into my first swing.

Somehow, I am looking at my frozen form. It stands inside Emérico's sarcophagus, sledgehammer raised, ready to arc through the air and end this torment. My face: red, hateful, driven. A rainbow cloud swirls around me.

"I thought we might parlay," Emérico says.

I am but a few steps removed from where I was. My awareness has been shunted out of my body. I spin to face the kneeling Chancellor. The skeleton is there, but standing over him is a rail-thin man wearing a cassock and a mozzetta, the red half-cape of a bishop. He stands in the casting circle, hands tucked into his crossed sleeves. His face is gaunt, his hair white and severely receded. Liver spots dot his creased forehead. His eyebrows bush like a cactus.

"We've nothing left to say to each other," I say, but I move toward him.

Dozens of ghostly copies of this old man swarm around him, either detaching themselves from his body and running away, or racing into the Aerie from the city at large to merge with him. The ones returning pin thin strings of light to the mozzetta of Emérico's robe and then fade out of existence.

Iridescent ropes, much thicker than the web of threads leading out into the city, shimmer from five of the six candles and loop around Emérico's right arm, disappearing into his sleeve.

"What is happening?" I say.

"I am as a fountain. I pour myself into the city, so that those who did not know their own thirst may recognize their want."

"Those strings connect you to the people?"

"It is how I share the magic with them."

A few of the thin strings connected to his robe burst like fireworks. The embers peter out before they reach the floor. "You're killing them," I say.

"Very few. The flock that lives shall come seeking answers, and you and

I, together, can gather the faithful. All you have to do is stop swinging that hammer."

"Nothing you can say will convince me to stop."

Emérico pinches the air and tugs gently, as if testing a fishing line. A glowing green wire appears, attached to his chest. The wire leads to his sarcophagus, and from the sarcophagus, I lose sight of it to the east, in the direction of Jackson Memorial Hospital. "If you kill me, Pablo, your father dies."

"You're a god damn villain." This is the answer to Emérico's final riddle, the reason his soul cage is unguarded: he has bound my father to it. If Emérico dies, Tristan goes with him.

"I am the master of this house, your mentor," Emérico says. "I am prepared to leave you bereft of everything you hold dear. I advise you not to interfere any further."

"I trusted you!"

"And for that trust, I gave you everything. Excepting direction, I suppose. I should have pushed you out of the roost, as it were, but you were complacent here. My greatest failing is that I was too soft to force you to make something better of yourself."

"Better than what?"

"Than my peon. My lackey. My poor imitation. No other department head toils as you do. You are a slave to this building. Meanwhile, your peers have consistently shown themselves your superiors by doing great things. Are you so scared of the world at large?"

"I believed in you. Believed in your mission. In the College's mission. I found power through study and wanted to give that to others."

"Keep telling yourself that lie. Everyone else sees the truth. You are a coward and a hermit, incapable of success in a world brimming with abundance. You remain the same little boy I saved all those years ago. And here I am, having to save you once again, from yourself. Make the right choice, Pablo."

"I chose this place. I chose this life. I won't let you take it from me."

Emérico sighs. His skeletal shrug twitches my father's fragile filament. "His thread. Your decision."

I am back in my body. I still grip the hammer, immovable, above my head. When normal time resumes, I could throw it away.

I can still see the lifeline suspended to the east. It is the same blue-green as the readout of a cardiac monitor.

Dad, or the city?

Life. A little more life. With him.

The T.V. told him I wasn't a hero. That's when I touched his chest. That's when I caused his stroke.

What sort of life am I leading him back to?

The motion above me begins. Ever so slowly. I don't know if I'm guiding the hammer or just holding on.

Dad or the city?

Failure and family?

Misery and success?

I came here on a mission. I am not going to let Emérico stop me now. I am not going to let him lead me anymore. I am no longer the passenger. I'm the engine, driving this sledgehammer through the air, arcing it down.

Padre, perdóname.

When the head of the hammer touches the stone, the entire sarcophagus crumbles as if it were made of tempered glass. One moment, there is stone. The next, there are but pebbles.

The rubble clicks and soughs to the floor.

The windows of the Aerie shatter.

I am thrown upwards, into the ceiling. I fall twelve feet onto my back.

The first breath I take is a shuddering gasp. I fill my lungs so deeply that I feel my ribs expand.

Pain. For a moment, that is all I know.

I try to turn onto my side. Bad idea.

I wheeze. Try to ball up. Can't.

Silence. Sips of breath.

Then the cracks start: long black lines of empty space race across the vaulted ceiling, raining down dust.

I cover my face, try to inhale clean air. I lurch to my left. My hand touches something familiar: Thanatopsis. I use it as a cane, first lifting my head and torso, then clambering to my feet.

A crack runs down a nearby column. The floor begins to split, spider-webbing into strands of emptiness. Emérico's circle is gone. Emérico is gone. All that's left of him is a robe and mozzetta and an inert skeleton.

The cracks race across the floor, but slow to a stop as they reach Emérico's mozzetta. His death has triggered a curse. In his vanity, Emérico bound the existence of the college to his own life. He hasn't just killed my father. His death will destroy the College, as well.

I hobble toward the elevator, Thanatopsis my crutch, stumbling on each new crack. I pass the creaking stacks of books and scrolls, their shelves now leaning like drunks or sinking into the floor or toppling against each other. I grab my doctor's bag.

Next to the broken sarcophagus, the floor is mostly clear. I retrieve my mother's jar from my doctor's bag, along with my witch hazel and chalk. Emérico's candles have gone out but are otherwise unmoved by the chaos. I chalk a circle around them and me. I snap. Fire leaps from my fingertips. The candles spark to life.

I sit, Thanatopsis across my lap. I hold up my mother's jar in my right hand. I snort witch hazel from my left hand until my vision shifts, until I'm back in that multicolored cloud.

Emérico's candles do indeed have cold iron wicks. That was his sympathetic connection to each of the conduits. The candles are burning again, but without someone to operate them, the conduits aren't siphoning off the magic in the air. Miami will suffer the fate of Lisbon in 1755. I reach into the sparking flames. My fingertips burn. My flesh crisps. I do not care. I keep going until I feel a resistance. I grab at it and pull, taking hold of the strand of power from the candle, wrapping it around my arm like a rope.

The smell of my own flesh is sickeningly sweet. Is this the last memory I'll have of breathing? I can see the curse pouring out of Emérico's robe. He won't allow the College to exist without him. He will destroy Santa Inés Hall just to spite me.

By the time I have grabbed the third rope of magic connecting to the conduits, no physical muscle in my left arm is uncooked. I have to push magic into the bone to animate the arm.

The magic is everywhere. I can feel everywhere. See everywhere. The waves crashing on the Beach. Freedom Tower downtown. The marinas of Coconut Grove. The murals across B.R.A.D. and Wynwood. The farms of the Redlands. The urban sprawl of Kendall. FIU, sitting atop Sweetwater. Every nook of the city hides some of the magic.

I breathe it in as I gather the last ropes from the conduits, pull as much of it as I can into me, and use it to fix Emérico's curse. The magic fills me, so that my hairs stand on end, until it burns them away.

I have nowhere to put it all.

The floor cracks in front of me, just beyond the chalk line.

I push the magic into the cracks. Into the mortar. Into the foundation. I fix the doors, the shattered figurehead. Glass floats up eight stories and melts into solid panes. I seal the Aerie.

With the College whole, I send the bodies of the dead to their final rests, follow them from the College down the Turnpike or up 107th Avenue, until they resume their graves and I repair the peace I have broken.

Still there is more magic. A whole city's worth.

I sigh.

Before I do what I know to be necessary to save the populace of Miami-Dade County, I take up Thanatopsis with my right hand and cut a horizontal slit into Nox.

The slice hangs open, a blackness in midair. "*Papá, ¿estás ahí?*" (Dad, are you there?)

From the darkness, a glowing figure appears. He strides up and kneels down in front of me. But it isn't my father.

"*Ya se fue*" (He already left), Kiki Famoso says. "*Lo reconocí. De vez en cuando trabajábamos juntos. Tremendo cabrón. Tremendo carpintero. Mi más sincero pésame*" (I recognized him. From time to time we worked together. Tremendous bastard. Tremendous carpenter. My deepest condolences).

"*Gracias*" (Thank you).

"*A la orden*" (At your service).

Nox seals itself.

It takes all the magic in Miami to rip my soul from my body and cage it in my mother's earthenware jar. Just as I did with Baba Yaga on the beach, I turn myself into a magical spigot, channeling all the magic through me. This time, the process rips away molecules of flesh and muscle and organ and blood, until all that's left of me is my will, my bones, and the magic stored in them.

I don't need to huff anything to see magic. I raise my skeletal hands to my head. There is a clicking, not unlike wooden wind chimes scraping each other. I sigh, and a cloud of oxygen fills my vision, the puff tinted blue and gold.

Thus does the College of Practical Arts still stand, here in the Magic City.

Epilogue

From the desk of Pablo Diaz, Chancellor,
College of Practical Arts,
Florida International University
Friday, September 6

My fellow citizens,

As we head into the weekend following these harrowing few days, I and the faculty at the College of Practical Arts extend our deepest sympathies to those who have suffered through the mayhem initiated by Emérico de Menezes.

Like all of you, we were deceived into believing Mr. de Menezes to be an altruistic and upstanding member of our community. We thought of him as someone who upheld the mission and standards of the College of the Practical Arts and who operated with the most noble of intentions. We labored, as we thought he did, to improve the lives of our neighbors through education.

For those that recently experienced the practical arts firsthand, and for the first time: we are keenly aware that your experiences run the gamut from exciting to traumatic. Those seeking to come to terms with their exposures can contact us through our website, call our toll free number listed below, or visit us in person during normal operating hours.

We remain steadfast in our dedication to our most unique of cities, we endeavor to continue teaching our most unique of disciplines, and we reaffirm the words of our motto: *Prosperitas ministerio* (Prosperity through service).

Classes resume Monday.
Yours in service,
Dr. Pablo Diaz, PhD, AM

To: COPA Leadership (carmen.espinoza@copa.fiu.edu, georginadesmond@copa.fiu.edu, ghellas@copa.fiu.edu, mcintyre@copa.fiu.edu, melodycoghlan@copa.fiu.edu, TheGOATWizard@copa.fiu.edu)

CC: doloresgarcia@copa.fiu.edu
From: pdiaz@copa.fiu.edu
Subject: Transition to Traditional Model

Staff,

In light of recent events, this e-mail should suffice in place of a face-to-face meeting.

All classes will resume Monday, in person and on campus. Those who were previously holding their classes off campus will transition back to the College proper. Students have already been made aware (and I have yet to receive a single complaint).

Our primary responsibility is to our student body. Plan your extracurriculars accordingly. Alternatively, I am accepting resignation letters in person or through e-mail. As of recently, I am available 24/7.

In addition, please introduce yourself to the new Bursar at the earliest opportunity. She is champing at the bit (with iron teeth, no less) to meet all of you. For your convenience and the safety of the body politic, I have had lockers installed in the foyer of the Well.
See Dolores for keys.

Yours in service,
Chancellor Diaz